Praise for *The Freedom Clause*

"*The Freedom Clause* is a delicious novel featuring rich, complex characters exploring deep questions: How can we love fully and remain true to ourselves? What happens when lovers bound by marriage try one night of freedom per year? I couldn't put the book down and cheered at the perfect conclusion. Nora Ephron fans will delight in this debut."

　　　　—Amanda Eyre Ward, *New York Times* bestselling author
of *The Jetsetters*

"*The Freedom Clause* is a bold, honest examination of a young marriage that hooked me from its first page. Creative in concept, rich in self-discovery, and written with warmth and nuance, Sloane's is a saucy and smart debut you won't want to miss."

　　　　—Carola Lovering, author of *Tell Me Lies* and *Can't Look Away*

"You'll want second helpings of this delectable, sexy debut about a woman learning how to prioritize her pleasure. I ate it right up."

　　　　—Courtney Maum, author of *The Year of the Horses*

"As surprising as the proposal itself, *The Freedom Clause* is a beautifully written, deep dive into marriage and the critical importance of finding one's own voice. This novel is an emotional journey that reads like a thriller. . . . I couldn't put it down."

　　　　—Annabel Monaghan, author of *Nora Goes Off Script*

"An honest, empowering, and sexy tale of a young woman finding her voice, finding her strength, and finding great orgasms along the way."

—Taylor Hahn, author of *The Lifestyle*

"A raw and propulsive portrait of a marriage on the brink, Sloane's novel is fun, surprising, and nuanced. *The Freedom Clause* will expand your perspective on what true fulfillment can look like with an exciting, unique bonus: delicious recipes!"

—Caitlin Barasch, author of *A Novel Obsession*

THE
FREEDOM
CLAUSE

THE FREEDOM CLAUSE

A Novel

HANNAH SLOANE

THE DIAL PRESS

NEW YORK

A Dial Press Trade Paperback Original

Published in the United States by The Dial Press, an imprint of Random House, a division of Penguin Random House LLC, New York.

THE DIAL PRESS is a registered trademark and the colophon is a trademark of Penguin Random House LLC.

LIBRARY OF CONGRESS CATALOGING-IN-PUBLICATION DATA
Names: Sloane, Hannah, author.
Title: The freedom clause : a novel / Hannah Sloane.
Description: New York : The Dial Press, [2023] | A Dial Press
Trade Paperback Original.
Identifiers: LCCN 2022039675 (print) | LCCN 2022039676 (ebook) |
ISBN 9780593447321 (trade paperback) | ISBN 9780593447338 (ebook)
Subjects: LCGFT: Novels.
Classification: LCC PS3619.L63 F74 2023 (print) | LCC PS3619.L63 (ebook) |
DDC 813/.6—dc23
LC record available at https://lccn.loc.gov/2022039675
LC ebook record available at https://lccn.loc.gov/2022039676

Printed in the United States of America on acid-free paper

randomhousebooks.com

2 4 6 8 9 7 5 3 1

Book design by Diane Hobbing

For Natasha Zuccolo Rawdon-Rego

"It had not occurred to him that she might not consider herself to be the *minor character* and him the major character. In this sense, she had unsettled a boundary, collapsed a social hierarchy, broken with the usual rituals."

—DEBORAH LEVY

"Beware; for I am fearless, and therefore powerful."

—MARY WOLLSTONECRAFT SHELLEY

THE
FREEDOM
CLAUSE

Prologue

Dominic isn't expecting to meet the best thing to ever happen to him during his first week of university. He sees her in his first lecture. On Chaucer. Female characters defy the patriarchal order, the lecturer explains, they hold all the sexual power. A hand flies up. A woman in the front row, a meticulous note taker, questions this theory: "What about Griselda who serves her husband in preparation for his wedding to a new bride?"

Her voice is calm and quiet, appealing. Dominic's eyes drift to her hair. Ruby red, unapologetic and defiant. Her features are soft and willowy, enchanting.

Smiling, the lecturer says: "At least one of you took my summer reading list seriously."

The theater erupts. The girl is embarrassed, clearly, her ears turning a deep shade of red that matches her hair. Dominic doesn't expect her to speak again.

"As seriously," she says in a calm tone, "as one can take a reading list that's one hundred percent white male authors."

The laughter stops, the auditorium grows uncomfortably quiet.

Did she really just go there? Dominic's mouth drops a fraction. He thinks about her for the rest of the day.

THE next evening, he sees her in a crowded student bar. He's thought about her so often, he does a double take. It feels serendipitous, a minor celebrity spotting, and he stares until the girl has no choice but to glance his way, acknowledge him. He freezes, wondering what to say. *I've been thinking about you. Is that your real hair color?* Seven mortifying seconds pass before he finds his tongue.

"I thought it was brave the way you took on our lecturer yesterday."

"Ah." She smiles to herself. "Making an enemy of him, not my smartest move."

Her eyes are a lovely shade of green, misty and perplexing.

"I'm sure you can win him over."

Worried, he stops himself. Did that sound creepy? It definitely sounded creepy. She peers beyond him, no doubt searching for an escape.

"Did you get through the entire reading list this summer?" he blurts out.

Her gaze returns to him, more interested now.

She nods. "And some. What about you?"

"What did I do?" he asks dumbly.

He spent the summer feeling like an intruder, the way he always does. His dad, Sadie and the twins are a self-contained unit. He felt like an outsider the minute he came to live with them, aged fourteen. Four years on and he feels the same way. Boarding school helped, but the holidays always dragged on, those long summer days that revolved around the twins: swimming, tennis, rollerblading, picnics in the park. Sadie invited him along but it was easier to decline and keep to himself. Even though he hates spending time alone, always has, he preferred his own company to the gaping envy he felt. Sadie's a great mother—dedicated, kind, *present*—and he can't help but compare it to his own experience.

What did he do this summer? He spent a lot of time in his room in the basement, reading. He watched porn too, plenty of it, wondering when he might have the chance to experience this in real life. But he can't tell this girl all that! She's watching him, waiting.

"I read a lot." He swallows, certain his discomfort is on display. "Kicked around the house, kept to myself."

"Kept to yourself," she repeats, eyes flitting past him, searching the depths of the bar. "Difficult family situation?"

His head flies up in surprise. He's probably offering her a perfect view of his nostrils.

"How did you know?"

She's not even looking at him as she responds.

"Just a hunch . . . I can relate."

Spellbound, he murmurs, "Really?"

"Oh sure. I've been desperate to leave my family. I swear if they disappeared tomorrow, all I'd feel is relief."

Her eyes meet his again. This time, he notices small gold flecks deep in the greens of her eyes. He has a strange sensation that this woman could be his family, or that she will be, or that he wants her to be. He thinks of their first lecture and he wants to ask: is she always this direct in her conversations, this fearless? But a hand thrusts between them. A girl asks if they could please leave, right now?

"My friend isn't feeling well," the girl explains in a casual tone. "See you around."

And she vanishes, before he has a chance to ask her name.

DAPHNE. Two syllables. The minute he learns her name, he says it all the time. In Greek mythology, she tells him, she's the daughter of a river god, her name associated with fountains, wells, and springs. If Daphne is water then he dives in, no intention of surfacing. He belongs with her. He loses himself completely. She features in all of his university experiences. When he asks Daphne to marry him, they are twenty-one. Finals are fast approaching. The marriage proposal is reckless, foolish. He knows this, but he doesn't care.

"Don't you want a few more relationships with other people?" she asks in disbelief.

"Never," he responds confidently.

That's the thing about all those summers spent reading. It's made him an impossible romantic. Why would he look elsewhere? Daphne, his best friend. She makes him happy and relaxed. She makes him laugh and orgasm. She offers no judgment, a safe space he can burrow into, a refuge from the past.

"Only you," he says, certain of it.

THE
AGREEMENT

NEW YEAR'S DAY. DOMINIC WAKES up and his hangover greets him immediately. His back sticks to the sheets, coated in a sheen of sweat. His breaths are soft and shallow. With closed eyes, his hand skims blindly along the bedside table, landing on a familiar shape. But there are no texts, no interesting emails to read. He opens and closes Twitter, followed by Instagram and, in a fleeting fit of boredom, LinkedIn. It's noon, and he feels a familiar twinge of guilt. Daphne has been up for hours. He hears the spin of a laundry cycle nearing completion. Dirty plates scrubbed clean. The kettle's high and angry whistle. His wife's productivity puts his own to shame. He should help, Dominic thinks, swinging his legs off the bed. He reaches for a discarded sweatshirt, navy and hooded, and pulls it over his head. Opening the door, the scent of lunch wafts toward him. His stomach rumbles happily.

"Daph-ne," he calls out, aiming for singsongy, but his voice is a low croak.

He finds her leaning over the kitchen counter in a faded white top, denim jeans that hug her curves. She doesn't see him. Humming along to Spotify, clutching a pen delicately in her right hand, she's absorbed in her notepad. Dog-eared and tattered, it contains recipes she's crafted over the years, annotated with painstaking precision. Her damp hair hangs in loose curls. Small beads of water drip down her back. She looks fresh and energetic, the opposite of him. The kitchen surfaces gleam and sparkle, the heavy scent of synthetic lemon and lavender hangs in the air. He feels clammy and parched and gross but he can't help himself; he hugs her from behind, pecking her neck with small kisses and breathing in her scent, a mix of honeysuckle and citrus. His hands glide over her hips, and lower, toward her thighs. He nuzzles his nose and lips into the back of her neck in what he hopes is a seductive manner.

"Morning, sunshine!" He attempts a sexy drawl, but it's a hoarse bellow.

"God, you scared me!" she shrieks, swatting him away.

"You look great," he murmurs into her ear, softer this time, and he tries again, his hand hovering lightly against her hip.

She elbows him in the ribs. "I'm busy here, get off!"

So much for trying to start the new year on a spicy note, he thinks, shoulders sagging in defeat. Embarrassed by his pathetic seduction attempt, he switches topic.

"Grilled cheese?" he asks, snaking a hand past her.

She slaps his wrist affectionately. "Not yet. Here, take some of this."

She places something in his hand. A bottle of Nurofen. "You're the best," he sighs. "And you made coffee."

"With frothy milk!" She beams proudly.

"Wow," he says, leaning back against the kitchen counter, arms folded over his chest. "You used a present from The Parents already!"

The Parents: Nigel and Plumb, neither of whom treat their daughter well, and his dad and Sadie. Dominic's mum passed away a few years ago and the less said about that, he thinks, reaching past Daphne for a mug, the better.

"Is the milk frother our favorite Christmas gift this year?" he asks.

"Let's think about this," Daphne responds, tilting her head to one side. "My parents got their least favorite child a teeny-tiny cashmere sweater, which *could* be a genuine mistake . . . or a vague insinuation to lose weight?"

Daphne couldn't get the sweater over her head, it was *that* tiny. It was a ridiculous move from her parents, especially given her body is amazing, she just doesn't believe it. He once told her she looked like she belonged in a different century. It was meant to be a compliment, he pictured Vermeer painting her portrait, immortalizing her features. Her response: *back when women were allowed to be bigger.* Why did her mind go there? He wasn't talking about the proportions of her hips and calves (all perfect); but his wife sees herself as *unattractive.* And maybe he's to blame? Maybe he hasn't done enough to make up for the years she was torn down, her confidence shredded? They laughed about the sweater on Christmas Day but he noticed the hurt in her eyes. He catches it again now as she laughs it off.

"I think it's kitchen gadgets for the win," Daphne adds, flashing him a smile.

She's talking about his dad and Sadie, the practical gifts they send, arriving promptly in the third week of December each year, without fail.

"Right," he snorts, "because nothing says sorry-I-abandoned-you-for-six-years-before-taking-a-detached-interest-in-you-again like: the instant pot!"

"Or the compost caddy!" she chimes in, referring to a few years ago.

"Or the water filtration pitcher!"

Daphne tilts her head back and laughs. She has a lovely laugh, honeyed and layered and playful. His life's goal is to make her laugh often.

"At least those gifts don't come with a mean subliminal message," Daphne points out.

True, there's no hidden agenda with his dad. Occasionally an email floats in linking to something obscure: *Thought this might interest you.* Most recently, it was an article about the decline of trout in the North Sea. Dominic was mystified. It's still contact, he told himself, it's still a sign he cares. Whereas Daphne's parents are a special case of brutal.

"There's nothing subliminal about that doll-sized sweater, crumb cake. That was plain vicious," he says, pouring himself coffee, adding frothy milk and popping two Nurofen. It occurs to him that he hasn't lifted a finger. "Can I . . . help?" he asks feebly.

"Brush your teeth," she responds immediately. "Your breath smells like rotting weasels."

"How many of these weasels?" he asks, burying his face in her neck, exhaling heavily.

She laughs softly and twists away. Leaning over her notebook, she scribbles more notes in the margins, no doubt brainstorming another recipe. He places his chin on her shoulder, looking at what she's working on.

"Stop distracting me," she murmurs in a monotone.

"My head feels extremely heavy right now. I need a place to rest it," he admits. "So, last night was fun."

She stops scribbling.

"Do you even remember getting home?"

He hears the smile in her voice. Having drunk too much, he can't answer this.

"We got a cab?" he begins hopefully.

"No cabs." She turns, fixing her gaze on him. Her eyes are bright green, playful. "We ran home but you worried it looked like you were chasing me so you yelled 'We're happily married, I promise' to anyone we passed."

This sounds vaguely familiar, and *exactly* the kind of thing he'd do.

"Ah." He grimaces. "Glad my neuroses rarely surface when I drink."

"It was cute," she murmurs. "And an absolute miracle you didn't trip and fall flat on this adorable nose of yours."

She stands on her tiptoes and kisses it.

"This crooked thing?" he asks quietly.

But she doesn't answer. She's back in turbo mode, pulling a small covered saucepan from the oven, lifting lids, stirring the soup, flipping a slice of bread with a spatula. He loves watching her, the way she has it all under control, but finally Daphne offers him a withering look.

"You're like a dog waiting for its walk. Go on, I'll bring these out when they're done."

He laughs, holds his hands up in mock surrender, and retreats to the living room. His laptop sits across the room, staring at him in open judgment. He should use the free day to make progress on writing but he doesn't have the energy. Instead, he turns on the TV. The first channel he lands on is a nature documentary. *The lion is the king of the jungle, he is the king of beasts, he is the king of copulation.* The narrator's deep voice booms around the small living room. *The lions mate every fifteen to thirty minutes. Up to 100 times a day while the lioness is in heat.*

What must that be like, Dominic wonders, recalling his unsuccessful attempt to turn Daphne on in the kitchen. She barely even noticed. When was the last time his touch made her want to drop everything and rip his clothes off? Remembering her comment about his breath, his face puckers in disappointment. There is *nothing* sexual about a weasel. He hears Daphne's phone going in the distance. Someone is trying to FaceTime her. Their flat is tiny, the kitchen and living room separated by a doorless archway that makes it almost impossible to have a private conversation. Daphne picks up.

"Par! Happy New Year, love! Wait . . . what's wrong?"

Dominic lowers the volume. He makes out Daphne's close friend, Aparna, crying through the phone's speaker, and Daphne trying to soothe her. Dominic stands up, wanting to help. But as he enters the kitchen he sees the back of Daphne disappearing into the bedroom and closing the door. Disappointed, he returns to the living room. He stands uncertainly on one foot, gazing around the room like a lost flamingo, wondering how to occupy himself.

—

DAPHNE leans against the bedroom door and peers at her phone. Aparna is always calm and in control but today she looks broken.

"Take your time, Par," Daphne says reassuringly. "I'm not going anywhere."

But Aparna can't even speak and Daphne wishes she could dive into the phone and hug her. She knows Aparna well, they go back as far as her earliest days with Dominic, and she's rarely seen her this upset. Usually, Daphne is emotional and Aparna is handing her Kleenex. It's been this way for seven years. The girls in her secondary school were bitchy, unnecessarily cruel but the moment she cast her eyes on Aparna during her first week of university, unpacking in the dorm room across the hall, and inviting her in for a cup of tea, Daphne felt safe. In fact, she kind of has Aparna to thank for meeting Dominic. After they finished their tea, Aparna suggested checking out the student bar that evening and Daphne agreed. She hadn't expected much to come from it. She didn't think of herself as the type of woman who attracted admirers. She was ordinary. She definitely wasn't lusted after, ever, but in the pub, she noticed a shape out of the corner of her eye, tall and broad, and she was pretty sure the shape was watching her. The details came a few seconds later. Dark hair. Blue eyes. Mischievous grin. That nose, slightly crooked. He looked confident and self-assured. Why was he looking at her? A tampon must have fallen out of her handbag or something equally embarrassing, she decided, bracing herself. But he surprised her, explaining that they were in the same English class. She and Dominic spoke for three minutes, the entire conversation a magnificent blur, until Aparna tugged on her sweater and asked if could they please leave, like right now? Daphne did what any good friend would do. She told the man whose name she didn't know that she'd see him around while her heart sank. She took Aparna to their residence hall and held her hair back all night. And the whole time, Daphne replayed that stunning yet brief interaction. She permitted herself the luxury of imagining what the night might have looked like if Aparna *hadn't* eaten a reduced-price shrimp cocktail sandwich for dinner. She thought about him early the next morning too as she dabbed concealer beneath her tired eyes. She thought about him as she set off early to lectures, hoping she might see him. That's all she expected: a sighting. But he arrived early too. She recognized him immediately, the tilt of his shoulders, his jerky movements, enthusiastic and clumsy. Her eyes darted away, not wanting to appear eager. She focused on her Biro, the doodles on her pad, until he slid into the seat beside her. She could have clapped with joy. Instead, she greeted him casually. It sounded like the most non-Daphne thing she'd ever said:

"Oh, hey, you."

"So," he began, grinning as he wriggled out of his coat. "Was your friend really ill last night or is that a code you two use to escape undesirable men?"

She digested this remark. He thought men hit on her. He thought enough men hit on her to warrant dreaming up an escape code with a friend. This made her smile. An enormous smile that informed him exactly how much she enjoyed his company. So much for playing it cool.

"What if I said it *was* a code?"

He groaned dramatically. "Then I'd drop out of this class immediately."

She liked the way he spoke, with emphasis and enthusiasm. She liked his expressive face, the bulge of his blue eyes, the way his lips moved quickly. His fast intelligent thoughts.

"And do what?"

"Horticultural studies," he said, waving at friends entering the room. She followed his gaze: two boys, similar builds, dark floppy hair. Clocking her, the boys discreetly selected a different row. "I've always wanted to become a . . ." He paused, shrugged, struggling to find the word that would complete the joke.

"Garden gnome?" she offered.

"Exactly," he said, lips curving. "That's your future wedding present, FYI."

"And who," she asked, pausing for effect, "am I marrying?"

"No!" His eyes widened in dismay. "Am I *that* bad a flirt?"

She laughed openly at this.

"I don't plan on meeting my husband until closer to thirty I'm afraid."

"Stop! Why?"

She wanted her twenties to be a period that liberated and defined her. God, she sounded pretentious, she *knew* she did, but she plunged ahead with the reckless confidence of an eighteen-year-old who has adulthood all figured out. She'd live in a gorgeous flat in London, filled with character: hanging plants, a big pile of books, an enormous kitchen that she'd throw raucous dinner parties in. She'd have glamorous flings, impetuous one-night stands, a succession of relationships, each one better than the previous, culminating in meeting the man who was indisputably perfect for her as she turned an appropriately old age.

"And that's thirty," she informed him in an authoritative tone.

By then, she'd have accrued enough experience from a decade of dates, failed relationships, and sexual encounters to be certain of her identity. She would know her sexual preferences and how to voice them. She would be confident in her decision to settle down, so confident in fact that she would not use the words "settle down." She stopped talking, pleased with herself, pleased she'd conveyed the message: try harder if you want to charm me. ("Harder than already saying he wanted to marry you?" Aparna would point out later.)

Dominic watched her the entire time with an expression of complete absorption.

"You don't sound like a planner at all."

She smiled. He had her all figured out.

"Capricorn," she confessed. "It's in my nature."

"Hmm," he paused, seeming to weigh something up in his mind. "I understand this one isn't in your ten-year plan, but do you want to grab a drink after this lecture?"

She hadn't dared hope for this. She glanced at her watch, as though seeing it was two in the afternoon might help her conjure a better response. She looked up, smiled nervously.

"Sounds fun."

What an understatement! During this time, other students filed in and filled the seats around them. The lecture hall was full, loud with chatter. The door swung open. A short man in glasses and a charcoal suit appeared, shouting: "Professor Green is stuck in Bath. You can all go." There were whoops. Students leapt out of seats. Daphne felt a flutter of nerves. She took her time. She packed her bag slowly. She saw him waving to his friends on the other side of the hall. They were mouthing to one another. Oh no, she thought, her heart sinking. She misunderstood. He meant *group* drinks. Nothing romantic. Or maybe, even worse, he'd withdraw his invitation completely, in favor of hanging out with his friends.

"What's your name?" he asked, turning to her.

"Daphne."

Her smile faded. She understood what was coming: *Sorry Daphne, I made other plans.*

"I can't," he shouted to his friends across the theater. He pointed at her. "Got a first date with Daphne over here."

Bright red, that's the color she went. People turned and stared.

She wanted to confess that she had never, not once in her life, been this girl, the recipient of so much attention.

"You ready, Capricorn?" Dominic asked in a mischievous tone, his blue eyes sparkling.

She felt seen, admired. It was a beautiful feeling. She clung to it all week. She needn't have. Dominic remained demonstrative. An audience never fazed him. He was loud, uninhibited, happy to tell strangers how lucky he was, how much better than him Daphne was. He said as much in his speech on their wedding day. An entire marquee of guests laughed at him, at young love. Daphne laughed too, but she never took it for granted, the feeling of being adored. Not once, not ever.

She shakes off the memory. She turns her attention back to Aparna, sobbing gently into her crumpled tissue. Aparna looks just about ready to begin talking.

"Joe dumped me," Aparna reveals between sobs.

"Oh no!" Daphne's face softens. "Oh love."

Joe isn't worth it, she thinks indignantly. Aparna deserves someone who makes her feel special. Aparna seems to read her mind.

"I just want to meet my Dominic," she sniffles. "You know?"

"Oh, honey. I know."

———

DOMINIC collapses on the sofa and turns the volume up. He notices a hole in his sock, the left one. His big toe is poking through, examining its surroundings with brazen curiosity. Dominic stares at his toe, willing it to disappear. The hole in his sock seems to represent his futility today and on all days. His inability to help Daphne. Or Aparna. His inability to focus on the book he's been thinking about for years. Or connect with his father in a significant way. God, now he's thinking in metaphors. He really is in pathetic shape. The deep voice continues its slow narration. *During this period, the two lions are inseparable. They will not hunt nor eat. They remain this way for two or three consecutive days. The alpha male will mate with other lionesses too.* Dominic watches the alpha lion mounting the lioness. His roar is full of sexual confidence. Oh god, he thinks slowly, the hole in his sock represents his total lack of sexual prowess. *And only when he grows tired are lesser males given the opportunity to mate with the females in the pride.* It's childish and self-loathing. It's insecure. It's everything Dominic is in his weakest moments but he goes there. He inserts himself in the documentary. And he would *not* be the alpha. He would be that weedy looking lion on the periphery. The one that definitely isn't getting any action. His best friend Mark would be the alpha. Tall, blond, and muscular, Mark is a charmer. He has his pick of single women whereas Dominic relies on humor to charm people (and even that only works half the time). Yes, that lion on the fringes, gazing enviously at the copulating couple, is Dominic. The lion who is absolutely not living his best life. And that's no reflection on Daphne, he thinks. She's the best thing to happen to him. It's solely a reflection on him, and his sock drawer.

Eventually, Daphne's voice grows louder. She's in the kitchen. Closer yet. She appears in the living room. Their eyes meet. She looks angry.

"Let's get Dom's opinion," she says, motioning for him to make room.

She hands him her phone. Dominic peers at Aparna's tear-streaked face and swallows. He doesn't like it when women cry. It makes him anxious.

"What's going on?" he asks softly.

Aparna wipes her eyes. She takes a deep staggered breath.

"Joe dumped me."

"Oh." Dominic exhales in surprise. "I'm sorry, Par," he says gently, channeling Daphne's energy. "That's awful. You're too good for him though. You know that, right?"

He only met Joe a handful of times. Not a keeper, he and Daphne agreed after the first meeting. Dominic listed reasons why. Joe had a habit of misusing the word "literally." Joe smelled strongly of the cheap cleaning products used in public urinals. You mean bleach, Daphne responded at the time with a raised eyebrow. Yes bleach, he nodded, his wife's grasp of vocabulary far better than his own. Slightly concerning given *he's* the one with aspirations to be a writer. And for a moment, Dominic's mind turns again to his novel-in-progress, all twenty pages saved on his laptop, thought about often, assiduously avoided at all costs. His writing is like a strict form of worship. He respects it, and is deeply afraid of it too.

Seeing how upset Aparna is, he wants to say something funny. That's his role after all. Throw Dominic into a tense situation and he'll undo it with a ridiculous remark. But Daphne jumps in first.

"And guess what?" Daphne says, outraged. She's tying her hair up in a high messy ponytail. It hangs to one side and bounces each time she shakes her head angrily. "He dumped her because they weren't having enough sex. How ridiculous is that?"

"Oh," he says, buying time with a head scratch. "It's not that ridiculous, is it?"

Daphne opens her mouth in shock.

"So, Aparna should've given him more blow jobs and then Joe wouldn't have broken up with her? Is that right?"

"I didn't say that!" he responds indignantly. "You asked for my opinion!"

"Go on," Aparna implores, as though he's the oracle of breakups.

He holds the phone out until both he and Daphne show in the frame.

"Well . . . how many times a week were you having sex?" Dominic asks carefully, knowing he is dipping into dangerous waters.

"About twice a week," Aparna answers.

He winces and Daphne pounces.

"What?" Daphne says archly.

He swallows. "Twice a week isn't *that* much at the beginning of the relationship."

"Yes it is! It's a lot."

Aparna cuts her off. "Let him talk, Daph. This is helpful."

"Well, as a guy . . ." He pauses, scrunching his face up. There is no way he can come out of this looking chivalrous. "You know that number is going to trail off over time. So, really, you want to be having it every day, or at least every other day, at the start."

"They weren't even seeing each other every day."

Daphne's tone is curt. Anyone would think they were discussing *her* sex life.

"I was definitely too tired sometimes," Aparna admits despondently.

"Right!" He leaps on this point. "Whereas men are never too tired. We'll always prioritize sex. Over anything."

"Is that right?" Daphne asks testily.

"To a point," he clarifies, sinking deeper into the sofa. "We'll prioritize sex up to a point."

"Maybe you're right . . ." Aparna nods slowly. "It just seems like it came out of nowhere."

Silence. Dominic rushes to fill it.

"Or maybe the chemistry was off? Or maybe there was someone else?"

Aparna's small pixelated face crumples. "Someone else?"

"Not helpful!" Daphne hisses, swatting his arm before switching to therapist mode. "Aparna, you *will* get over him. I know it. And you get to go on dates! Honestly, I'm jealous."

"Honey!" Dominic's head snaps up. "If there's something you want to tell me . . ." he adds, trying to strike a joking tone, although his ego is bruised.

Daphne laughs, and his bungled advice is forgotten.

"No! I just mean—" Daphne laughs again and touches his arm. "Aparna's going to be doing what our twenties are *actually* for. The first-date excitement. Fancy cocktail bars. Kissing gorgeous men. All I do is hang around at home trying out recipes."

He passes the phone back to Daphne and folds his arms over his chest. "Is that right?"

"You'll forget all about Joe," Daphne says into the phone. "I don't see you with him anyway. You need someone emotionally intelligent. Someone considerate and funny."

"Right, I need someone like Dominic," Aparna says, her eyes soft, her voice whimsical.

Dominic's face twists in disbelief. "I have the emotional intelligence of a wombat."

Aparna's hurt falls away, and a small smile emerges.

"An adorable wombat," Daphne says with a quick wink, cocking her head back toward the bedroom and signaling she's going to start her goodbyes.

—

DAPHNE clicks the bedroom door shut. She leans against it.

"Par, how are you feeling now? I hope you don't let anything Dom said get to you. He means well, but he doesn't always have the best way of . . . expressing it."

Aparna nods. "I'm okay. And it was helpful." She pauses, looking embarrassed. "You're lucky Daph, you know that, right?"

"What do you mean?"

"Dominic makes you feel safe and loved. And that's so rare."

She nods in agreement. Dominic jokes his spirit animal is a Golden Retriever. His needs are simple: avoid being alone at all costs. He clings to Daphne, he adores her.

"Thanks so much for the pep talk," Aparna says, blowing her a kiss.

"Of course, love. Call me anytime."

As they hang up, Daphne plugs her phone in to charge and returns to Dominic. He is clearly hungover, touching the sofa with a fondness most reserve for babies, pets, and cashmere. She follows his gaze to the TV. Two lions are mating with furious abandon. The voiceover alone is ridiculous. Dominic shifts his position, making room for her.

"Look!" He points. "I have a hole in my sock."

"Why don't you just throw it away?"

"I . . ." he stares at her in disbelief. "Don't know?"

Sometimes she offers the simplest, most obvious advice and he looks at her like she's a genius. Daphne is the practical one. She likes lists. Moreover, she enjoys checking items off her lists. Dominic enjoys being loud and silly. Making people laugh, even if it's at his own expense.

Locking eyes, he asks softly: "How are *you* doing?"

She sighs. "I hate that Aparna's upset."

He nods. "She'll move on. He wasn't anything special."

"I wish she saw it."

"She will with time." Dominic smiles, reaches for her hand. "You'll help her."

She nods, jerks her head toward the TV.

"Can you turn that down a bit?"

"Sure," Dominic lifts the remote, turns the television off. "Nothing has the power to undo the male ego like the mating habits of lions."

It's a joke but his laugh is hollow. She watches him. She wants to check in about what he said earlier but he beats her to it.

"Did you mean all of that?" He begins in a curious voice. "Being envious of her dates?"

"Oh, that . . ."

Her voice trails off. Did she? She senses it's wrong. To be this young, this comfortable. She can't shake the sensation she missed out, that your twenties are meant to be about dates and relationships and heartbreak. She'll never experience the highs and lows of dating. She'll never hurt the way Aparna is hurting. It's bratty to complain that Dominic was her first everything but occasionally she wonders: what if she'd met Dominic ten years later?

"Sometimes I wish we'd met later in life."

Watching his face fall, she feels awful.

"I didn't realize that," he admits quietly.

"Not all the time," she adds, eager to smooth it over. "Sometimes I wish I had a few more life experiences under my belt. It's no reflection on you. Or on us. It's just this idea I had about how my life would turn out. You know, everything I thought I wanted right before we met. But I'm still glad I'm married to *you*." She taps his knee gently with her index finger. "What about you, did you mean all of that?"

"All what?"

"About men," she says in a halting voice. "Prioritizing sex over everything."

—

He was a virgin when they met, they both were. At eighteen, they felt a little ashamed it had taken them this long to do it. The first time was awkward, clumsy and fumbling, but he felt invincible afterwards. He'd lost his virginity, flinging it out of the window without a backward glance! They had sex all the time after that; there was so much time for it. Those mornings when they woke up cold (it was always cold) and huddled for hours beneath the sheets. Or between lectures. Or quickly in a dark anonymous bedroom at the endless trail of student parties. But nobody warns a young couple getting married upon graduation that soon they'll experience a profound lack of sex. Even Dominic doesn't initiate as often as he used to. Now, they both have jobs, him in advertising, Daphne at the law journal. Jobs that cause stress and anxiety. It's easy to rely on excuses. You're too tired. You'll do it another night. You'll make time for it at the weekend. Until the lack of sex becomes its own source of stress and anxiety. Until the lack of sex becomes a big hovering albatross over your relationship, something you're aware of but afraid to address. Until you wake up and it's New Year's Day and you can't even remember the last time the two of you had sex. Was it three months ago, or five? And now she's asking him if sex is a priority? Yes! Sex has always been important. And the lack of sex? That's important too. If he's honest with himself, it's been weighing him down for a while, making him feel unattractive. His wife is young and pretty and she never *wants* him. But now she's talking about how she wishes she could go on dates with other men? That revelation was a gut punch. But as he turns the revelation over in his mind, he begins to wonder: maybe they don't feel so differently after all?

—

He takes a while to respond and she watches him nervously.

"Oh that." He studies his hands. "Well . . ."

"Go on," she implores.

"Yes?" He glances up to assess impact. "I mean, it's important to men."

"Okay," she says unsteadily.

"I know you didn't want me saying it to Aparna, but it's true," he admits, smiling sadly. "If the sex isn't good, or it's not often enough, it's a reason to break things off, for sure."

"We had a lot of sex at the start."

"We were like rabbits."

"But now, hardly ever. Does that worry you?"

A troubled look crosses his face.

"Yeah, it bothers me," he mumbles.

"A lot?"

He bows his head. It drops down so far she grows concerned he might be about to cry. "Well . . . yes. If we're being honest."

It pains her, hearing the way his voice cracks.

"I can make more of an effort," she blurts out, eager to make amends. "I think I just have a low libido . . . or something."

He pulls a face. "It's not all on you. We can both make more of an effort. I guess we've talked about it before though. Last year, remember? We were a bit drunk, after that party in Chelsea, and it got better for about a month and then trailed off again."

She blushes. It's true, they rarely have sex. She has wondered, in bleaker moments, whether this part of her life is over. Like a hobby she did as a child, tap dancing or horse riding, once seemingly important and now irrelevant. The truth? Sex never left her speechless. The first time was dreadful. The climax was distinctly anti-climactic. Only later did it occur to her that she hadn't climaxed at all. They had a lot of sex at university but sheer volume didn't help. She simply didn't orgasm much. She assumed there was something wrong with her. The tilt of her pelvis maybe. Or her inability to let go and be present.

It's not that she didn't enjoy sex, however. She enjoyed it in moderation, the intensity of their bodies wrapped together. All that touching and kissing, leading somewhere, a distant goal never quite reached. The few times she did orgasm, she couldn't articulate what made it happen. It was frustrating. The lack of control over this seemingly important thing everyone raves about. She decided not to think about it at all . . . until now.

"You could . . ." She pauses. "Watch porn?"

Dominic turns a deep shade of red. He avoids her eyes.

"You mean . . . ?" she begins.

His head is bowed down, but she sees him nodding.

She frowns. "When?"

"Whenever you go to bed first. Or when you're reading in the bath."

"And that isn't enough?"

Dominic takes a deep breath. "It fills a need, but it's not the same as the real thing."

She nods to herself. She glances at her nails.

"What do we do?" she asks, genuinely unsure.

They could see a sex therapist, she thinks. Maybe he's thinking that too?

"I honestly don't know," he stammers. "How would you feel about a . . . three-way?"

Her mouth drops. This was *not* the direction she expected him to go in. She doesn't see how adding another person to their bed would solve anything? If anything, it would just make her jealous and miserable and . . .

"Seriously?"

"I don't know . . ."

She feels prudish admitting it. "I wouldn't want to watch you having sex with someone else."

His eyes meet hers. He shakes his head emphatically.

"Right, right. I wouldn't want that either. Honestly, forget I said it."

Easier said than done, she thinks, as her mind whirs with possibilities. The problem is it all feels quite . . . seedy. She tries to stay open-minded.

"Are you thinking about . . . maybe . . . an escort?"

His eyes meet hers. He looks surprised, and amused.

"No! Definitely not!"

She exhales with relief. "Okay. Good."

He reaches for her hand and squeezes it.

"We could . . . see other people though?"

"Like dating?" she asks in horror.

"Sort of. Isn't that what you said to Aparna, that you feel like you missed out?"

"God no! I was trying to make her feel better! I don't *actually* want to go on dates. It would be . . . just no, and I hate the idea of you with anyone else."

"Right," he nods, looking relieved. "I do too, but I think we can both admit our situation isn't . . . ideal."

"I know," she agrees, and she feels a lump growing in her throat.

She thought they were happy together. Aren't they? Her eyes meet his slowly. He says exactly what she needs to hear.

"Come here," he says, opening his arms. "I love you so much. You know that, right?"

She nestles into him, deep in the crooks. It's not just a mental connection, she tells herself. She loves his physical presence too, his masculine scent, the outline of his shoulders and back, how their bodies fit together, the familiarity of him. So why doesn't she want to rip his clothes off? Her mind turns to earlier when he touched her in the kitchen. She felt no desire for it. The problem is he's *too* familiar, the sex feels routine.

They lie together, staring at the ceiling. As he strokes her hair, she thinks about her best friend in tears, wanting to find someone like Dominic, someone who makes her feel safe and loved. I am lucky, she reminds herself.

"I don't think I could do the open thing, Dom," she whispers slowly. "But I want you to be happy. I wish there was a middle way."

It's a concession. One she makes because she thinks the conversation is over. It feels safe admitting this. She'll make more of an effort to have sex. Tomorrow, or next week. That's how they'll fix this.

"Maybe there is," he murmurs as he strokes her hair.

—

HE says it before he's fully worked it out in his mind. But once it's out there, it's stunningly clear. He respects her for not wanting an open relationship and he agrees, he'd feel weird about Daphne being able to have sex with other people whenever she liked. But what if it was just one night? What if one night this year they could both . . . it sounds strange in his mind, even stranger out loud. But isn't this it? The middle way Daphne just mentioned? His voice sounds distorted, unusually high as he repeats it.

"What if we both had one night off this year?"

She raises her pale face to his. Her moss-green eyes are wide and troubled.

"What do you mean?"

Forget her family. Forget the tiny sweater. Now *he's* the one shredding her confidence. He wants to take the words back, swallow them whole, but he does the opposite.

"What if we both had one night off this year?" he repeats. "To have sex with whoever we want?"

—

A prickling sensation on her arms. The fair hairs, hundreds of them, rising up in protest. What is he even saying? She shakes her head, willing him to stop. But he goes on:

"Once a year. With a total stranger. Clean and detached. No messiness."

She hates that the flip side of loving Dominic so intensely is his ability to inflict hurt. Pain unravels across her chest and stomach. It takes a minute to realize it's not pain. It's panic and it's everywhere! Mainly, it's in her breath. She can't inhale. She imagines turning to stone before his eyes, and this fantasy brings her a short sharp burst of pleasure—he'd deserve it.

"Is that really what you want?"

He looks young and boyish, scared by the magnitude of what he's asked for. But his tone is composed as he admits: "I honestly worry what the next sixty years of marriage looks like without it."

She begins to cry. Candidly, she's surprised it took her this long. Crying comes naturally, high in her list of skills. Top three, for sure. The flow of tears continues, her vision misting before blurring over completely.

"Don't cry," he begs, leaping up for tissues.

"Are you trying to get out of this?" she asks, wiping her eyes.

He looks confused. "Of what?"

"Our marriage."

He shakes his head. "Not even close. I think it could *help* our marriage."

Her laugh is one of disbelief, forced and throaty.

"By sleeping with other people?"

"We'd both have one night off to do whatever we like. But at the same time, we're totally committed to each other, we're devoted to our marriage," he murmurs softly. "Just think about it for a second, Daph. It could be this fun sexy secret between us."

Except nothing about this sounds fun or sexy. She listens to panic racing around her body, shrieking like kids on a rollercoaster. Why is he acting so calm, she thinks, as he leans in and smiles against her lips. His hand lingers on her waist, on that bare patch of skin between her top and jeans, and she feels herself recoil.

"Why are you suggesting this?" she responds stiffly. "Open marriages are unrealistic. They hurt people. This would hurt me."

He shakes his head. Taking her hand, he strokes the fleshy part of her palm.

"I don't want an open marriage either," he says gently. "That wouldn't suit either of us. Like you said: a middle way. One night a year."

A middle way! She wishes she'd stayed quiet.

"I'm not really sure that was in our vows," she jokes hollowly.

"True." He shrugs his shoulders. "But we could think of it as an added clause to our marriage. Like a . . . freedom clause or something."

She presses her lips together, raises her eyebrows. She has nothing to contribute.

"I'm thinking out loud here," he admits, "but let's just say you're out at a bar and you meet a stranger you find interesting. Under this freedom clause you could . . . take it further. But only once a year. Just for that one night."

She tries to follow him. "We'd both take the same night off?"

"No." He scratches his forehead with his thumb. "It could probably be more organic than that."

"I'm not saying we're doing this," she clarifies, dabbing her eyes with a tissue, "but enlighten me here: if we don't choose the same night, how would we not spend countless other nights consumed by jealousy, worrying it's happening at that precise moment?"

He looks worried. She knows this look. He gets it whenever she's talking about her family. His expression turns from worried to earnest.

"I couldn't have predicted the first night I met you," he says simply, smiling at the memory. "Just as neither of us can predict the night we might meet someone who intrigues us. This way, we leap on the opportunity whenever it arises. A one-night-only offer. No room for jealousy."

She almost laughs—there is *absolutely* room for jealousy! She imagines sniffing his shirts, rifling through his pockets for crumpled receipts. She doesn't want to be *that* wife. Her hands shake. This time, her crying is melancholy, a distinct weep. She always does this when she's angry. It infuriates her, it feels so *weak*. He hands her more tissues. She blows on her nose and regards him warily.

"How do you *know* I wouldn't get jealous?"

"Because it's just sex," he says, shrugging. "Bodies doing what they were placed on earth to do. Something we can compartmental-ize. It's got nothing to do with our love."

He's wrong, she thinks. It's impossible to compartmentalize sex. It has everything to do with their love. She watches Dominic as he picks up her discarded tissues, scattered on the sofa and on her lap, the floor too, depositing them in the kitchen bin.

"If you're so keen on sleeping with other women," she pauses, reaches for a fresh tissue and blowing loudly, "then why only once a year?"

"I don't want an open relationship," he says softly. "Whereas one night out of 365? That's as tiny as that god-awful sweater your mum gave you."

"What about affairs?" she asks bleakly. "What about catching feelings for the person you sleep with? There's so much room for it all to go wrong."

He studies her carefully. "But I trust you. Implicitly."

Trust, she likes the sound of that. She also likes goals, boundaries, feeling in control. But this? It's messy and chaotic, it'll be the ruin of her.

"I swear I'm not trying to be selfish here. Honestly, I'd only want to do this if we both enjoyed it. Our marriage stays closed, but with a little room for fun."

Silence.

"Come on, Daph," he says softly, "hear me out."

"I have been hearing you out," she hisses.

He leans his head forward, pressing his fingers to temples.

"I'm being open and honest about what's lacking in our marriage. I don't think that makes me a terrible person, does it?"

Really, he's annoyed with me? she thinks incredulously.

"I'm all for openness, honesty, but that doesn't make me a fan of you sleeping with other women."

"And I'm not interested in a lifetime of celibacy."

She bristles. "Have you ever thought that maybe the reason I have a low libido has something to do with your skills in bed?"

He flinches. Immediately, she wishes she could retract it.

"Okay, that hurt," he says slowly. "But there's probably some truth to it. Maybe some more experience could help me get better."

Masterful, she thinks angrily, *the way he turned that insult around.*

"We're not celibate, that's a stretch," she says, standing up and beelining for the kitchen. "I can't have this conversation right now. I need to finish lunch."

But as she stirs the soup, she tries to recall when they last had sex. Was it three months ago or four? Either way, they're only having it five or six times a year, and that's on a good year. Sex just isn't as important to her and if her libido doesn't match his . . . then is his proposition really so bad? She carries the soup and sandwiches into the living room. She sits cross-legged on the floor, leaning over the coffee table, and he does the same. She wonders if he's going to bring it up again, but he's quiet, murmuring occasional compliments about how this meal hits the spot. The silence is almost worse. She knows they're both thinking it. Finally, she places her spoon down and takes a deep breath.

"If we were to do this," she begins slowly, "we'd need boundaries. Ways to hold each other accountable."

"Are you . . . serious?" His mouth drops open.

She nods her head firmly. "If it's this important to you then the least I can do is . . ." She shrugs. "Try it."

His eyes shine with warmth.

"We can put it in writing," he says, leaping up, rummaging through the coffee table. He brings out a yellow-lined pad, the one that contains all their Scrabble scores over the years, and turns to a clean page.

The Freedom Clause:

1. We only do this one night a year for the rest of our marriage.
2. With just one person for that one night.

"Your turn," he says, handing her the pen. "What do you want to add?"

A big part of her can't believe she even raised it, let alone that she's actually agreeing to this. She stares at the page and focuses on what she *doesn't* want. She doesn't want it to mean anything. She doesn't want him to have an affair. She doesn't want to catch an STI. She doesn't want to know about the incredible sex he has with other women. Her lower lip begins to tremble as she takes the pad and writes:

3. We only sleep with people our partner doesn't know. Not with friends/family members (obviously!)
4. A different person each year (to avoid affairs).
5. We practice safe sex (condoms).
6. No questions asked (we don't discuss what happens with each other, and we can't seek out the details around each other's sexual encounters).

"These are all great," he says, squeezing her shoulder.

She wants an enormous hug, the type she gives friends when they're upset. She wants his reassurance she isn't losing him. He should understand, she thinks irritably, that a shoulder squeeze isn't good enough right now. It feels patronizing, the type of touch she expects from a distant uncle. Helplessness sets in. A wave of anxiety crashes over her.

"One more!" he says in an excited tone, taking the pen and paper from her.

7. This is between us. We don't tell our mutual friends about the Freedom Clause.

She shakes her head angrily.

"I tell my friends everything. You *know* that."

"I just think they'd judge us. A lot, actually."

How can she *not* lean on Aparna and the girls for support? But she pictures telling them about this agreement. She imagines their worried faces, the delicately worded questions loaded with concern. In another world, she'd find it funny. But he's right. There *would* be a lot of judgment. A lot of speculation about what was going wrong in her marriage, and that would be humiliating.

"What if I hate it?" she asks, picturing herself, alone and miserable, no friends to confide in, nobody to lean on.

It's a terrible thought. She's on the brink of tears again.

"Oh, Daph." He pulls her in, smothering her forehead with tiny kisses. "What about this? We only commit to five years . . . until we're thirty, then we reassess?"

"Five years?" she repeats faintly.

Even that feels like an awfully long time. Five years of not telling Aparna she's having sex with other people. Or that Dominic is! That's the more likely scenario, she reminds herself.

"That's only sex with five people!" he exclaims, his voice high and animated, enthused. His hangover seems to have vanished. "One each year! Doesn't sound so bad, right?"

Daphne sinks into the sofa. Her body is shattered, even her eyelids feel heavy. She doesn't answer immediately. She rests her head on a cushion and closes her eyes. Slowly, she musters a response.

"It sounds a little . . . better."

"And by then, we might even want to start a family!"

Not this again. She's never felt that interested in motherhood.

They've discussed it. Dominic seems to think once she hits a new decade, her maternal instincts will magically kick in.

"Let's not get ahead of ourselves."

She opens her eyes, drawn to the window. Late afternoon. The winter sun is low and weak. It filters casually through the window like a passing friend who doesn't plan to stay long. Her gaze turns to her husband, she watches him writing again.

1. We only do this one night a year for the ~~rest of our marriage~~ next five years.

"What if I say no?" she yelps.

"Let's just try it, please?" he asks, offering her a reassuring smile.

He sinks next to her. Gripping her shoulder, he massages the muscles gently.

"We'll try it," she says despondently.

"Good!" he beams. He swoops in close, his eyes level with hers, blue and optimistic. "And it's only one measly night a year. Really, what's the worst that can happen?"

In the years that follow, this remark will ring in her ears. How naïve they were, she will think to herself. One night a year isn't measly. Not at all; it's seismic.

YEAR
ONE

IT'S NOON, AND DAPHNE BOLTS out the door. She doesn't know where she's hurrying exactly, only that she needs to escape the office, the confines of her small cubicle, even if it is bitterly cold outside. The National Portrait Gallery is almost empty. It feels rebellious, turning off her phone, tucking it into her handbag. But the pure pleasure of it, being alone, drifting from portrait to portrait, dependent on no one, blissfully out of reach. She peers into each oil painting, she studies the creamy skin and pinched lips, tired eyes and deep wrinkles. She recognizes herself in certain portraits. That young girl is Daphne: the one with the forced smile, golden hair pinned to the crown of her head, elbows pinned tightly to her sides. That older woman too, grimacing as though in pain, with gray hair and a heavy emerald dress. She pictures their inner dialogues: what worries them, what keeps them awake at night, when did they last feel fulfilled?

Her footsteps echo through the hollow rooms. It's just her, the bored security guards, and the women who hang in gold frames. *I should do this more often,* Daphne tells herself, and by this she means solitary activities. When she is in their flat, Dominic is never far away. He brings his laptop home and sits at the kitchen table, hunched over it. He is hard to ignore, even when he is trying to be quiet. Dominic types loudly, often murmuring the words he is tapping out, he yawns noisily, and Daphne swears that nobody on this earth chews an apple as boisterously as her husband. As he works, he takes up space. He stands up and stretches, he nuzzles into her neck and asks how *this* sounds. She loves it when he runs work ideas past her (like she has a clue what works in the world of advertising, but Dominic takes her feedback seriously). There are nights when Dominic isn't working, when he plays football or video games with his friends Mark and Simon, and she might get some time alone. But the last time that happened, Poppy and Abby popped over with wine and they watched reality TV. What she really needs, she tells herself now, her eyes large and sorrowful, is time *alone*. Time to ponder. Time to self-recriminate. Time to chew over their conversation three days ago.

In truth, she's thought of little else. She's imagined all the different ways she *could* have responded to Dominic's proposal. Given a second chance, she'd unleash every unhappy thought about their marriage. Like the fact she does the cooking and cleaning, and she picks up the dry cleaning, and she fixes the flush on the loo whenever it breaks (often), and she buys Christmas and birthday presents for their friends, and she hunts for the best deals on flights, and she puts together vacation schedules that contain the perfect ratio of adventure and relaxing-by-the-beach time. She does this out of love and loyalty and kindness but also because she's better than him. Better at multitasking. Better at prioritizing. Better at life. Oh, but the male ego! She couldn't possibly say that. And now, on top of everything she does already, he wants sex! Okay, let's talk about that, she'd say, because she thought he'd been feeling indifferent too. She can't remember the last time Dominic initiated. Or was he expecting her to do that too, on top of the aforementioned list? She'd point out how infuriating it is to hear his suggestion. What a slap in the face! As though she has endless hours in the day to dress sexily and lure him into bed. But it's not that he wants more sex with *her*. He wants to have sex with strangers—beautiful women with tiny waists, enormous chests—and she should accept this, and continue cooking and cleaning and fixing the flush on the loo while he sows his wild oats, should she? But, of course, it's too late now, she's already agreed.

Classic Daphne. Never prepared with the right response at the right time.

She keeps moving from portrait to portrait. The women are beautiful and rich. Poor and troubled. Cold and haughty. Earnest and hard working. Their necks drip with jewels. Their fingers are calloused. She thinks about the Freedom Clause. She pictures Dominic kissing another woman. She imagines him removing her clothes, placing his lips on her cleavage, panting and thrusting. Her handbag drops to the ground. The thudding noise startles her.

"Sorry!" she whispers to the security guard, bending to pick it up.

She smooths down her skirt. She hears someone enter the room. Turning, she sees his sandy hair. Navy coat with gold buttons. Weathered boots that squeak against the polished floors. She pictures walking up to this man and suggesting drinks. A suggestive wink that leads to casual sex, her legs wrapped around his waist. An unhappy laugh escapes her lips and the security guard's suspicious eyes are on her again. The Freedom Clause is never going to work. At least, not for her.

—

"Dominic, can I see you in my office?" Gerry calls out.

Dominic leaps up. Gerry is his boss, and one of the best managing directors in the agency. He's well respected and levelheaded (unlike the so-called "screamers," who lose their temper regularly). His office is on the tenth floor, overlooking the endless trail of pedestrians scuttling beneath them, opening umbrellas in the rain, hailing cabs. As he enters, Gerry motions for him to close the door.

Dominic takes a seat and glances at Gerry in earnest.

"Everything okay?"

Gerry smiles and brings his hands together.

"I want you to take the lead in the Denzer pitch next week."

Denzer is a boutique hotel group with a line of high-end spas.

They've a presence in London, New York, Paris, and Madrid with plans to expand into Asia. Usually, a senior pitch team would go in, Gerry and his peers. Dominic clears his throat nervously.

"You want *me* to lead the pitch? Are you sure?"

Gerry nods. "My goal, as your manager, is to help you reach this position one day." He gestures to his desk, his office. "Which means putting you forward for opportunities."

It should be music to Dominic's ears. The big office. The managing director title. The salary. It's just . . . he's not sure he wants it. The job comes with a large element of corporate bullshit. There is a certain way to behave to get ahead. The posturing. The email etiquette. The echo chamber of buzzwords. It all seems so *fake*. Plus, there are months when his workload is so overwhelming, he barely sleeps. He has zero control over his schedule. Late nights working on pitch decks. Weekends catching up on client deliverables.

"Leading the pitch will get you on the path to vice president," Gerry continues in a voice that suggests he thinks he is being very generous right now.

Dominic's smile is thin, his words filled with guilt.

"That's really . . . great of you, thanks."

—

DURING the second week of January, Daphne hits her stride. She *loves* this month, she reminds herself, even if most people don't. For Daphne it's the one month of the year, she points out to anyone who will listen, when the world adopts her habits of productivity. Bloated from Christmas, everyone is ready to hit the refresh button, buzzing with New Year's resolutions. Daphne gets a strange thrill from that communal energy, that hardwired focus to be a better person. Also, it happens to be her birthday month. She doesn't need anything extravagant. Low-key is fine: coffee in bed, a day in the office, shared tapas with Dominic and a few close friends that evening.

She wakes to her alarm. Sitting upright, she checks her phone just as Dominic walks in. He's whistling the birthday tune, taking great pains not to spill a tray containing a slim vase holding a solitary pink-red tulip, a French press, two mugs, and a plain white envelope.

"From your parents," he explains, setting the tray down and handing her the card.

"Thanks, love."

She sighs happily. She takes a long sip of coffee. Ripping the envelope open, she examines the card. The front contains an illustration of a mouse eating a block of cheese. Inside: *Happy birthday, Daphne. Enjoy the day and enjoy this card. Love, M&D x*

"Enjoy the day and enjoy this card?" Dominic repeats, peering over her shoulder. "Who writes that?"

"People," she responds humorlessly, "who spent all of three seconds on this card."

"This is why we hate cards."

She pulls him in for a kiss.

"We do, don't we? Presents are *much* better."

"Exactly, and you'll get yours later. But first"—he breaks off, pausing dramatically and grinning at her—"enjoy the day!"

In the office, her colleagues, eight in total, sing an off-key verse of "Happy Birthday." The rest of the day passes slowly. She interviews a lawyer over the phone for a "40 under 40" feature set to run next month. She receives happy-birthday texts, messages on Facebook and Instagram. At five P.M., she slips on her black knee-length coat and tugs her scarf over her head.

There is plenty of time before their dinner reservation. Instead of taking the tube, she walks down the refined streets of Bloomsbury. She threads past crowds and pigeons in Trafalgar Square. She passes Temple, quiet and sedate, St. Paul's Cathedral looming up ahead. It's cold and bracing, the high wind hitting her hard as she walks over the

Millennium bridge. The sky is a heavy liquid black, and the Thames ripples beneath her.

An arm flashes out, startling her.

"Could you take a photo of us? We just got engaged."

"Of course," she responds.

She takes several photos. Portrait. Landscape. Let's see the ring. Let's try one of you two kissing. She doesn't begrudge their happiness. She remembers when she got engaged. They were students. Bristol, finals looming, a terrifically sunny afternoon in early May. Sitting with Dominic, cross-legged on Brandon Hill, staring at revision cards in their laps, at the park too and, beyond that, the city's expanse of sloping houses, tiled rooftops.

"I'm going to miss this," Daphne remembers saying, "this city, this park, this hill. Everyone I care about within walking distance. I love this feeling of being high up, above it all."

Dominic pressed his lips against hers. His mouth opened and the words popped out.

"Marry me?"

She didn't say yes immediately They were so young, after all, so inexperienced. But he assured her he didn't need other relationships: "Oh, I'm so happy." And she was! It didn't matter that in the past she'd assumed her twenties would be a defining period of dates and freedom. This was better, she'd found her person! Getting engaged young was fun. They leaned into how reckless it was. They threw a wedding in the autumn that was fringy and bohemian, a wedding that said a loud and emphatic "fuck you" to tradition. No church. No white dress. No champagne. The ceremony was brief, perfunctory. The party lasted all night in a barn in Somerset. The air was cool, crisp. The trees a distinct shade of auburn. Live music. Dancing. Beer and cider. A large pig, skewered, rotating on a stick. A meal their guests spoke about for years.

It's close to seven as she reaches London Bridge. She finds the restaurant easily. It's dimly lit, buzzing and vibrant, filled with chatter; the thick warm air stinks of garlic and cheeses, herbs and olive oil. She's led to a table at the back and there they are: Dominic and Aparna, Abby and Poppy, shrieking and hugging her. They've ordered Cava, they explain, as she takes a seat. The waitress floats by and wishes her a happy birthday. Presents: satin green gloves, a cookbook, a succulent in a hand-painted yellow pot. She saves Dominic's present until last. A book, she thinks, staring at the small rectangular package wrapped in gold paper.

"Be careful opening it," he whispers.

She unwraps it slowly, turning it over in her hands. A faded copy of *The Canterbury Tales*. Small and old, the pages are delicate and creased, musty.

She raises it to her nose, inhales softly.

"It's an early edition," he explains.

"It's beautiful," she coos. "I can't believe you did this!"

"It's how we met," he responds with a smile. "Chaucer's our Tinder."

That makes everyone laugh. The rest of the evening is a blur of wine and tapas, speeches from her friends. It's just the way a birthday should be, even in the most hated month of the year.

———

"SEEN the new graduate?"

Jason is leaning against his cubicle, his peanut-butter breath lingering in the air. Jason is universally disliked for being lazy, gossipy, unhygienic, and there are a number of theories circling in the office as to just how much peanut butter he inhales each day. Eyes glued to monitor, Dominic types speedily, conveying in a passive-aggressive tone that he is busy. And he *is* busy. Ever since they won the Denzer account he hasn't stopped.

"Nope," Dominic responds sharply, fingers flying over the keys.

"Roxie Clemson. Total fox."

Dominic notices her a few days later. Blond hair, cropped short. Bright red lipstick. Charcoal pencil skirt. He's struck by her confident posture, her loud voice that dares him not to notice her. Jason's right, he admits reluctantly, she *is* a fox. He's pretty certain every male in the office has fantasized about unzipping those knee-high boots.

Like all graduates, Roxie rotates through teams. She joins his in June. Five long months have stretched since the Freedom Clause discussion. January and February were tough, the energy in the flat shifted perceptibly. Daphne was flat, withdrawn. Even her interest in food—her primary passion in life—dwindled. She ate slowly, ponderously. Sometimes he caught her studying him; perhaps she was trying to figure out if he'd done anything yet. I haven't, he wanted to tell her, to set her mind at ease, but that would have violated rule six: *No questions asked (we don't discuss what happens with each other, and we can't seek out the details around each other's sexual encounters).* He assumes, by equal measure, this means they can't discuss what *hasn't* happened.

And a lot hasn't happened. So much hasn't happened that he's beginning to wonder if he overestimated his ability to have sex with anyone in the world besides his wife. He knows there are ways to have sex if a man is desperate enough. But *paying* for it feels gross and underhanded and plain wrong. And wait, didn't he flat-out tell Daphne he *wouldn't* do that when they were discussing potential options on New Year's Day? Ruling *that* out, he begins to wonder if he is left with no sex. Because that's how it's seeming. Did he think the world was swimming in single women waiting for a night of fun? Worries creep in that he's unattractive. Sure, he's got a broad enough chest and good enough shoulders but he's not exactly ripped, is he? He does push-ups and press-ups and weights. He keeps up with cardio. He plays football every Tuesday night. But maybe that's not enough? Because if he was attractive, then why would it be this hard?

There was that assignment in Leeds in April. The work trip coincided with his birthday, which was annoying and unavoidable, although Daphne made it up to him that weekend by throwing a huge surprise party. So yes, he was alone on his birthday, sitting at a bar, sipping on a beer when a pretty brunette wearing a low-cut floral dress glanced in his direction. He smiled and asked what she was drinking, an innocuous enough question, except he hadn't known she had a boyfriend returning from the bathroom, a stocky man who stared threateningly until Dominic paid up and left. Then there was the woman standing in front of him at the bar last week as he waited for Mark to join him for drinks. She was *very* cute. Short with curly hair, large hazel eyes, a dimpled smile. She apologized her order was taking so long and he told her not to worry. He learned her name was Katy. She smiled at everything he said. She seemed annoyed when her friends drifted over, in case his attention might shift. But Dominic's focus was completely on Katy, he was almost fanatical in his focus, until Mark arrived and did what Mark does best. He took Katy's number and thanked Dominic for being a great wingman. Anytime, Dominic had sputtered in response.

Dominic wonders if he miscalculated his powers of seduction. Meaning: he has none. Meanwhile, Daphne seemed happier the past few weeks. She's enjoying spring, she tells him, but what if it's *not* about spring? What if it's about the Freedom Clause? Maybe men are hitting on her all the time? He's spiraling, and he needs to stop. Except men *should* be hitting on his wife, he reminds himself, she's super attractive and feeling jealous over this makes him the world's biggest hypocrite.

Just as he's reflecting on all of this, Gerry appears. Roxie follows him.

"Roxie, this is Dominic. He's our star talent. Dominic, this is our new graduate."

Dominic stands up, pretends to look surprised by the introduction. It's not like he's been counting down the days.

"Dominic," he says affably, shaking her hand.

"Roxie."

She's wearing a fitted dress, orange-red, the color of tangerines and already the atmosphere in the office shifts. Everything feels brighter, lively.

She smiles at him, revealing pearly white teeth.

"I've heard great things about you."

He raises an eyebrow, turns to Gerry.

"Is that right?"

"Teach her the ropes, will you?" Gerry says in a distracted tone, striding away.

"That was abrupt," Roxie remarks, staring at his back.

Dominic shakes his head. He's used to Gerry's shortness this time of day.

"All good. He's just hungry."

It's noon. Everyone on his team has scattered, the cubicles empty. They're left to stare at each other. She's beautiful, he thinks, staring into her gemstone blue eyes.

"Ready for some rope learning?" he asks pleasantly.

Roxie nods. He walks to a filing cabinet, taps it twice.

"This cupboard is where we keep paper copies of all our contracts. Don't ask me why when we live in a digital age. We just do."

"Got it," she laughs softly.

"And this," he says, taking three steps over and tapping on a cubicle, "is where you'll sit. Next to the printer *and* the scanner. Lucky you!"

"Does that mean . . . ?" She pulls a face.

He nods. "Gerry . . . me . . . the entire world hovering behind you all day. Afraid so."

He wheels a chair to his desk, gestures her over. They sit close, their knees almost touching. She smells of jasmine, citrus. A notepad rests in her lap.

"I'm giving you access to this drive," he explains, double clicking on a folder. "Try to contain your excitement."

Shielding her eyes with her hand, she peers closely.

"What's this?"

"Our shared drive," he says with a heavy sigh, "also known as my life for the past four years. Every piece of work we've ever engaged in."

She covers her nose and sneezes twice, delicately. "I'm seeing a lot of PowerPoint."

"Bless you. And yes, they call me the Microsoft whisperer."

That gets a proper laugh.

"Fascinating. I might have to cancel my date tonight."

His head snaps up, unable to hide his curiosity.

"Anyone fun?"

She shrugs. "A hedge fund manager."

She must be what . . . twenty-one?

"He sounds . . ." he pauses, frowns. "Kind of old for you."

She flicks her hair. "Kind of my type."

An Outlook calendar reminder for his next call pops up on his screen: All Team call regarding Quarterly budget review. He groans softly.

"What's that?" she asks innocently.

"Get ready," he responds, his voice loaded with sarcasm, "for the most exciting call of your life."

FROM: *Roxie Clemson*
TO: *Dominic Symington*
SUBJECT: *Ultimatum*

Would you rather be a) trapped on this conference call for seven years or b) cover your naked body (every

inch) in peanut butter and be Jason's personal snack bar
for the next month?

FROM: *Dominic Symington*
TO: *Roxie Clemson*
SUBJECT: *RE: Ultimatum*

It gives me great displeasure to admit this but . . . personal snack bar.
P.S. Who's the heavy breather on the line?

FROM: *Roxie Clemson*
TO: *Dominic Symington*
SUBJECT: *Heavy breather*

I assumed it was you.

FROM: *Dominic Symington*
TO: *Roxie Clemson*
SUBJECT: *Wrong*

How strange, I'm known for my featherlight breathing.
Can someone please set off the fire alarm so we can cut short this
miserable call?

FROM: *Roxie Clemson*
TO: *Dominic Symington*
SUBJECT: *Fires are no laughing matter, young man*

It's almost like you don't care about up-tiering client revenue.

———

THEY'RE in the office, working late. Version 18 of a client deliverable. Gerry left hours ago, something about his daughter's music recital. Exhausted, Dominic sees double each time he looks at his screen. When the food arrives, they take a break. Roxie drops into a chair across from him, kicking her feet onto the table. She has very long legs, he thinks, frowning as he averts his gaze. Sitting back, her eyes are glued to her phone.

"You don't seem very happy," Roxie blurts out suddenly.

He glances up, surprised.

"I am happy," he says in a monotone.

"You should be! On track for vice president. Gerry loves you. You're the golden boy . . . your parents must be proud of you."

"My dad is," he concedes.

"What about your mum?"

He doesn't want to get into it. His mother died the summer he graduated from university. Liver failure. At least that's what the hospital informed him, and it made sense. She treated her liver like a dumping ground. They weren't close by then, and a small part of him was uncomfortably relieved—knowing that if she came to the wedding, she'd make a scene—but it was painful all the same: the woman who had brought him into the world no longer existed.

Dominic busies himself. He opens the delivery bag and removes plastic containers, he peels back lids to reveal steamed dumplings, sticky noodles, sesame garlic shrimp. But it floats back to him, guilt for making so little effort in the years before she passed. It was hard to keep track of her. She moved often. She didn't respond to calls or messages. She lost her phone. Or the line got disconnected. She'd call him on a number he didn't recognize, and their conversations made little sense, her remarks slurred, difficult to decipher. Generally, ten minutes in, she'd progress to being openly hostile, shouty. And then they lost touch completely. The last he heard she was living in a homeless shelter connected to a church. His reaction was cynical: she's there for the Communion wine.

"Want the truth?" he asks in a pleasant tone.

"I want this dumpling," she admits, licking her lips, "but the truth would be nice."

"I don't care about this job. I don't want vice president if it means . . . this."

He gestures around the empty kitchen as though to emphasize how pointless it is.

"What do you want?" she asks softly.

He raises an eyebrow.

"Promise not to laugh?"

She nods.

"I want to write a novel."

Her look is one of total astonishment. "Really?"

He nods gravely.

She grins. Her advice is comically simple: "Then do it!"

"I need *time* to do it. Difficult when you work 14-hour days."

"Sleeping is for wimps," she responds with a smirk. "But seriously, make it happen."

"Make it happen?" he teases softly. "That's your advice for me?"

Roxie cocks her head to one side. "Something tells me you have a lot of fascinating thoughts swirling around in that handsome head of yours and the world needs to hear them."

It's a double compliment: he's fascinating *and* handsome. It makes him smile all the way home. You, he thinks, are very dangerous.

—

"Wow, vice president," Daphne says, raising her champagne glass. "VP also means Very im-Portant, you know."

Dominic grins, straightens his tie. He looks good in a suit: handsome, successful. Truthfully, he'd look just as good in sweatpants. There's an unsubtlety to his looks that surprises her. She just never pictured herself with the classically good-looking guy. She wonders if people study them and wonder why they're together. People other than her family, that is.

To celebrate his promotion, they're eating at a swish restaurant. She got properly dressed up. Cream silk shirt. Navy pleated skirt. The highest heels she owns.

"Gerry said mid-year promotions are unusual," Dominic informs her in a happy tone, "but I deserved it."

"That's great."

Daphne hopes she sounds enthusiastic, even though she doesn't feel that way. She raises the menu to eye level, hiding behind it. It's an expensive sushi restaurant. The prices make her uneasy, but they can afford this now, she reminds herself. Dominic's salary is about to leap by thirty percent. Then there's his bonus. But is he happy? She lowers the menu. She catches Dominic sipping his champagne, beaming at something on his work phone. Probably a congratulatory email. He *does* seem happier.

When the waiter returns, Dominic orders too much: miso soup, soy glazed edamame, pickled cucumbers, yellowtail tartare, snow crab nigiri, toro and red snapper and tuna and albacore sashimi, soft shell crab roll, wagyu beef. She's tempted to protest softly, but it's his night, after all, and it's fine to overdo it.

As the waiter leaves, she smooths down her skirt, chooses her words carefully.

"Does this change how you feel about the job then?"

His eyes crease in confusion. "What do you mean?"

Is he serious, she thinks? She considers when he accepted the job, right before graduation. She was with him when he got the call. He was excited, he wanted to be financially independent. When she asked what he'd be doing, he shrugged uncertainly, but she didn't judge him for it. None of them knew what their jobs would entail. They were babies back then, eager to start their careers. But as each year passes, he's grown less passionate, more worn down. She doesn't want him to stay in a job he hates out of some outdated notion men must provide.

"I mean, up until a month or so ago, you complained about the hours, the fact you didn't have time to sleep or write." She scrunches her face up. "But lately it seems like you've been able to enjoy the job more."

Dominic fiddles with his chopsticks. He places one atop the other, a careful balancing act. She wonders if he's doing this to avoid looking at her.

"I guess I do like it more now. I can't even explain why. It just seems . . . better."

"Do you think it's because you knew the promotion was coming?"

"Sure, that's part of it, I guess," he responds, holding her gaze and nodding. "Things just seem a bit easier in the office, more of an all-hands-on-deck team mentality."

It makes no sense to her. If anything, his workload has increased. He comes home later than ever, he's always on his work phone. She's noticed the increased space the job occupies in his head.

"Even Jason?" she persists.

His nose wrinkles in distaste.

"No, he's awful," he says, and this makes her laugh. "But we have interns and graduates rotating through. They help a lot."

"You're still working all the time though."

He searches her face. "But I'm here now."

"Yes, but you've looked at your phone five times in the last two minutes! If Gerry needs you this much . . ." she breaks off, not sure where she's going with this. She feels like she's ruining his celebration. She decides to back off. "He just seems so overbearing."

Dominic nods, and puts his phone away at least. Their appetizers arrive. The waiter slowly places each item on the stiff tablecloth. She tries the yellowtail tartare to begin. She eats slowly, small mouthfuls. It melts on her tongue. She watches Dominic eat. He's clumsy with the chopsticks. His movements are fast, impatient.

"Delicious," she murmurs, which is true, but she feels this reaction is expected of her.

"So good," he agrees.

As he inhales his miso soup, she tries again.

"Have you ever thought about looking for a job that you might really love?"

Wiping his mouth on his napkin, he responds in a defensive tone.

"I can't leave Gerry in the lurch like that. Not after he's just promoted me too."

The tables on either side of them are quiet, serene. Pairs of diners who have little to say to each other but don't appear concerned by this. Watching Dominic, Daphne worries she's about to cause a scene, but she can't help herself.

"I think you might be lying to yourself. You want out but you're too scared."

"What?" he sputters. He stops eating and stares at her, his blue eyes widening in amazement. "Why would I be scared?"

And now she feels scared. Frightened to tell him the truth. But she can't sit by and watch him do this. He is more than the paycheck he receives each month.

"Because your Dad makes a lot of money and you've been conditioned to aspire to that."

"What?" he says again in a quiet voice.

She feels her cheeks growing red. She lowers her voice, not wanting the other tables to hear.

"I think some of this is your deep-seated need for parental approval."

"Could we not?" he asks with a small sigh. "I really don't want to discuss our respective daddy issues tonight."

"It's the money too. Money motivates you, even if it leaves you feeling overworked."

She waits for him to fight back. He could point out she's enjoying this very expensive meal. Surely she likes money too? But he doesn't go there. He's much too nice to stoop to that level. He studies his plate quietly. It makes her sad that he has no retort. Even a hurtful one would be better than complacency.

Softly, she asks: "When are you going to have time to focus on your novel, my love?"

Silence. His novel is a touchy topic. He refers to it in vague terms quite often, but rarely wants to discuss it in detail. She watches him pick apart the softshell crab roll, as though inspecting it for lice. He plucks at the edamame next.

"Good question," he says at last, tearing at the edamame with his teeth. "I don't know."

She folds her napkin into small pieces in her lap. "How's it been . . . going?"

"It's one big mess is what it is," he admits with a sigh of discontent, eyes darting around the restaurant. "It's nowhere close to resembling a finished novel or . . . a screenplay or *anything* really. I don't know what I'm doing. I'm probably doing the world a huge favor if I never touch the damn thing again."

Surprised, her eyes widen. This is the most he has admitted to her about writing in months.

"Maybe take a break for a while then, my love, and wait for inspiration," she offers as she prods at the sashimi.

She takes a slice of tuna, dips it in soy sauce, and stares uncomprehendingly. Even soaked in soy sauce, it's fleshy, raw. She places her chopsticks down, and sits back.

Glancing up, she sees he's watching her, his eyes sad and soulful.

"I don't know what I'm doing," he admits with a gloomy shrug.

Her heart swells. She reaches across the table for his hand.

"That's okay," she says with a slow smile. "None of us do."

—

THERE'S excitement in the office. They're being sent on a corporate retreat. The final weekend in September. It's on a posh estate, the type period dramas are filmed on, Jason informs him. Set on four thousand acres, home to peacocks, an orangery, mazes and lakes, a walled garden and ancient bluebell woods. Dominic used to dread these events. Not *another* weekend dedicated to work, but Roxie will be there. She's continued her rotation into another group but they keep up their email banter, teasing one another, and she makes fun of her new team, and how incompetent they are.

The partners and managing directors are placed in rooms in the main building, a stately home, while the rest of the employees are in converted barns dotted around the estate. They gather in the Grand Hall and Roxie sidles over to him, standing so close her arm grazes his. Dominic tries to focus on what they are being told, but all he can think about is her arm, resting against his, familiar, casual. They learn about activities: archery and falconry, clay pigeon shooting and wild food foraging, cooking classes, yoga and meditation. Dominic is excited for the day ahead, until he realizes he and Roxie are in separate groups.

"That's no fun," Roxie protests, rolling her eyes at him.

Dominic tours the orangery. He joins a cooking class. They cook with fresh vegetables grown on the estate. The phrase "farm to table" is used frequently. Daphne would love this, he thinks with a pang.

She's on a girls' trip to Norfolk this weekend. He sends her a text ("Look! I made a wild mushroom risotto!") and hops in the shower before the evening begins. Soaping his body, he thinks about Daphne. It's safer to do this, thinking about Roxie scares him. *Come on, now,* he thinks impatiently. He wants a chance to do the Freedom Clause this weekend, doesn't he? Then why is he hit with nerves, intense butterflies in his stomach?

Turning the shower off, he wraps himself in a towel and glances at his phone. Daphne wants to know which herbs he used in the risotto and will he make it for her when they're back home? She sends a photo: Daphne, Aparna, Poppy, and Abby huddled on the windy beach, their hair blowing wildly in opposite directions. He almost hears her laughter. Whatever happens tonight, he thinks, staring at the photo, is sealed with her approval.

ASSIGNED seating for dinner. Dominic's table is a snoozefest. Graham, the head of Healthcare, sits to his left. A notorious bore, Graham talks about revenue targets. Even Roshni in Human Resources, sitting across from him, looks bored senseless, and she usually maintains a strict poker face. Wendy in Accounts Payable sits to his right. She asks about each of his clients, hoping to figure out which invoices she personally processed. Dominic's consumption of alcohol is enthusiastic. As dessert is cleared, he leaps to his feet.

He finds Roxie leaning against the bar, absorbed in her phone, a chocolate brown clutch tucked delicately beneath her arm. She's wearing a sleeveless fur vest, tight black jeans, kitten heels. The lock of blond hair prone to falling into her face is held back with a small gold clip.

Glancing up, she breaks into a smile.

"Did you shoot this today?" he teases, pointing at her fur vest.

"God no! That would require some coordination." She laughs.

"It's fake," she adds, grabbing his hand and pressing it to her waist. "See?"

His heartbeat quickens at her touch. Her skin is warm, soft and supple.

"Are you fake too?" he whispers, almost surprised by how effortlessly he nails a flirtatious tone.

"Oh, I'm real baby," she whispers, eyes glinting mischievously.

Glancing away, he locks eyes with the square-faced bartender. He glowers at Dominic impatiently, bored by whatever's playing out between him and Roxie. He's seen it a hundred times before. Dominic orders drinks and they take their seats by the fireplace. Enormous armchairs, thick velvet, mustard yellow. Roxie is telling him about clay pigeon shooting. She slips a foot out of her kitten heel, tucking it beneath her. The movement is oddly intimate, familiar.

"Has Roxie told you her news?" Gerry interrupts them, grabbing a seat.

Dominic looks at her expectantly. "You have news?"

"I've asked to join your team once my rotation is done," she admits in a coy tone.

He'll see her every day! Pleasure pulses through him.

"That's incredible," he sputters, smiling. "Amazing for our team."

He notices her body relax, a long exhalation, as though she was nervous about how he'd respond. Why would she be?

Gerry is grinning. "I'm thinking she shadows you. You need the extra support, right?"

"I do," he hears himself say.

"And now," Gerry says, clapping his hands together, "we drink."

Watching Gerry stride toward the bar, he knows what's coming.

"Shots," he explains to Roxie. "Tequila is his poison."

"Good," she fires back without hesitation. "Let's get drunk and make bad decisions."

She's bold, bolder than he'd dared hope.

"Dominic! Over here!" his boss calls, gesturing toward the bar.

Twelve shots are lined up. Dominic groans softly. Gerry is a devoted family man. He leaves work early to do the school pickup, but this weekend he's off duty. Dominic holds back a little, sticking to beer. He's thinking about later.

Happily, he blurts out to Roxie: "Which building are you sleeping in?"

"The Old Porter's House," she responds loudly over the din of the bar.

"Nice?" he asks.

She ignores this question. Maybe she misheard him?

"Room seven, it's my *lucky* number."

He pauses, wanting to strike the right tone. Moreover, he doesn't want to presume anything.

"Lucky number for lots of folks," he responds carefully.

She shrugs. "I'm feeling lucky."

She lifts a hand to her collarbone. A soft smile plays on her lips. He's about to ask *why* but her name is being called and she floats toward the other graduates in her intake.

I'll be back, she mouths.

He watches as she's swept away. Gerry hands him another beer.

"Maybe we should slow down a little," Dominic suggests kindly. "Hangovers aren't as easy as they used to be."

"Just you wait." Gerry smiles affably. "Try adding two screaming monsters into the mix."

"How are the twins?"

"Sleeping through the night at last. Those first few months almost killed us."

Gerry looked wretched after the twins were born. He took two weeks paternity leave. Returning, his face was etched in tiredness. He looks better these days. Sure, there are graying temples, wrinkles around his eyes, but he's got his energy back.

"Are you and Daphne thinking of starting a family?"

"Daphne's not sold on kids," Dominic admits with a small sigh. "But I think she'll change her mind eventually. Once you hit your thirties your priorities change, right?"

"It all changes." Gerry groans dramatically. "My twenties feel like a lifetime ago. So do my thirties for that matter."

Roxie floats back, grabs her clutch from the bar. Raising a hand, she waves at him.

"Turning in," she admits with a small yawn.

"Really?" Dominic yelps.

What happened to all that talk of feeling lucky?

She pulls a face. "I should. Bad headache."

"Can I walk you back?"

He hears it in his voice: alarm mixed with desperation.

She shakes her head. "Don't think that's a good idea."

She gestures to the swell of colleagues nearby. Is she telling him to be subtle?

A little mystified he says: "I hope your headache goes away."

"Oh, it will," she says in a loaded tone, her eyes holding his. "I'll sleep with my window open . . . you know, for the headache."

"Right," he says, winking, "for the headache."

THE moon is crescent shaped. He follows the signs to Old Porter's House and his shoes pound against the gravel. His footsteps are fast, impatient. He stops for a moment. Breathless, he listens to the stillness of the night, suddenly fearful. He runs through their conversation: her room number, seven being her lucky number, the window she would leave open. Her words were an invitation. He'd be a fool not to. Finally, Old Porter's House comes into sight, a gray stone building. He circles it twice before approaching the only open window on the ground floor.

He peers in. White bedsheets gleam in the darkness. He slides in clumsily, lands unsteadily. There's a rustling from the bed.

"You took your time." Roxie laughs. "Strip off and get in here."

He removes his coat, letting it drop to the floor. His sweater, shirt, jeans. He strips until he's naked. He hesitates. What if . . .

"Get over here, stallion."

How presumptuous! He runs to her. He scoops her up and kisses her eager mouth. She bites his lower lip. Her skin is soft and warm, welcoming. She grabs his back.

"Roxie," he murmurs, "you have no idea how g—"

She lets out a scream. It's high and shrill and he swears he will carry that sound to his grave.

"What the fuck?" he asks, springing away.

"Dominic?" she asks, in a voice of genuine confusion.

She's flailing, grabbing at the sheets and pillows to cover herself. There's a scraping noise. Turning, a familiar profile fills the window. The blood drains from his face.

"What's this, Rox?" Gerry asks slowly, sounding surprised. He laughs, adding: "Ménage à trois?"

In a flash, Dominic reevaluates it all. The room number. Feeling lucky. The window left open. Intentional comments. Sadly, they were intended for someone else.

"But you're married," Dominic stammers, reaching for his clothes.

"So," Gerry responds pointedly, "are you."

A knock at the door. A gentle voice of concern. The door opens too quickly and there's Roshni, in the hallway, in a rose-patterned nightgown. Roshni looks tired, confused. She says something about hearing a scream, her words trailing off as she takes in Dominic's state of undress. She glances at Gerry, hovering in the window.

"I was walking past. I heard a scream too," Gerry says hurriedly.

Roshni nods slowly. Her eyes move to Roxie, wrapped in a bedsheet. Roxie looks afraid, embarrassed. She runs into the bathroom. They hear the slide of a bolt, heavy sobs. Dominic swallows. It looks terrible . . . and the Head of HR walking in? Even worse. At least he's no longer naked, he thinks as he slips on his loafers.

"Dominic," Roshni says in a calm voice. "Please return to your room. We'll discuss this in my office on Monday."

Oh god, he thinks in terror. What on earth will he tell Daphne?

—

SLOE gin. Dry vermouth. Manzanilla sherry. Thyme infused gin. She shouldn't be here, Daphne thinks, closing the leatherbound menu. A moment later, she's taking another peek. She can't afford a single cocktail. She's never been a big spender but with Dominic's decision to hand in his notice, she's being extra scrupulous. It surprised her when he admitted he needed a change, but she was pleased for him too. He'd finally come to his senses!

She begged for details. What was Gerry's reaction? Did he try and convince him to stay? But Dominic looked a little wretched about the whole thing. Maybe he felt bad about letting Gerry down? Or scared? She gets that, it's a big scary step into the unknown. But he can look for other jobs, and focus on his writing. Quitting his job was the right thing to do. Even if she has to rein in her spending. Which is why she shouldn't be here tonight. But her younger sister, Mimi, texted her the other night (*hey sis, how about a drink?*) and Daphne didn't have the heart to say no. So here she is, staring at an expensive list of cocktails, waiting for Mimi, who is very late. The habit of a lifetime.

She should've known her extravagant sister, always wanting a scene, would suggest somewhere this expensive. A glitzy hotel bar that just opened in King's Cross. Mimi travels so often that she doesn't even rent a place in London anymore. She's constantly in far flung, impossibly glamorous locations, every expense taken care of, and yet

Mimi isn't filled with gratitude for her luxurious lifestyle, nor is she generous. She's an exact replica of their mother: blond hair, blue eyes, high cheekbones, the longest legs. Daphne hates being envious of Mimi. She knows comparing herself to others is a one-way ticket to unhappiness.

"For you," a voice says, breaking her reverie.

She glances up, surprised, and sees a wide expanse of muscle: chest and shoulders. This bartender is beautiful. His skin is smooth and brown, glimmering in the dusky lighting.

"For you," he repeats in a deep voice.

She glances at the martini in alarm.

"I didn't order this."

"The man behind did," he explains. "Sends his compliments."

She's embarrassed and delighted, confused too. This never happens!

"Which man? Where?" she asks a little too eagerly.

The bartender steps to one side. Dark tailored suit. Thick gold watch. He's attractive. Italian or Spanish. He looks . . . angry? He's shaking his head, muttering. The bartender notices too. His hand snakes toward her. The drink is retrieved.

"Sorry," he mumbles. "One minute."

Immediately she understands. Daphne can't help herself. She swivels in her stool. She finds the martini's intended recipient. This woman is stylish. She is in her forties. Elegant hair, curled and smooth, pinned back with a silk magenta headscarf. The woman looks vaguely famous. Perhaps all women in their forties with hair that blond and figures that slender resemble news anchors. Daphne doesn't know where to look. Mortified, she studies her phone. She sends Dominic a text: *Mimi is late. OF COURSE!* He replies immediately: *No surprises there. Have fun with the brat.*

"Whatever you want. On the house."

She glances up. He looks sheepish. She reads the name badge: *Ash.*

"You mean a free drink?" she asks in astonishment.

"Of course. Sorry again."

He has a lovely voice. She wants to put him at ease.

"That confirmed my suspicions I should never leave my sofa on a Monday night."

He gives her a slow appreciative smile.

"Thanks for not being a dick about it."

"Since you're offering . . . I'll take a Rhubarb Gimlet."

"Good choice. Hot date?"

"Nope, seeing my little sister," she begins just as her phone beeps. It's Mimi: *Not going to make it. At a PR event and it's so boring. Sorry!!!* Daphne's eyebrows shoot up. "Oh . . . not anymore. She just canceled."

"Typical?"

"Sadly. My whole family is a bit . . ." She pauses, struggling to find a word that accurately depicts them. "Unreliable."

She sees his interest pique. He's leaning forward, elbows on the counter, peering into her soul.

"Tell me," he begins quietly, "when did they first devastate you?"

NOBODY worried about her weight when she was four. Daphne's thighs were chubby, and chubby thighs were acceptable at that age, moreover they were adorable. That was around the time her dad first asked Daphne what she wanted to be when she grew up. Daphne's gaze went straight to her mother and the answer popped out: "I want to be just like Mummy." Plumb, her mother, tittered appreciatively. Her father leaned forward and patted Daphne on the head. Daphne felt like a well-behaved family pet. It wasn't the worst feeling.

Daphne was asked the same question when she was twelve. They were eating breakfast. Scrambled eggs, soft and runny. English muffins, lightly toasted, smothered in butter. Her dad wheeled the video camera out. An enormous device, it sat awkwardly on his shoulder like a big boulder. He asked Henry first, and then Mimi. Finally, he turned to her:

"What do you want to be when you grow up, Daph?"

A memory floated toward her of just how pleased they had been the last time.

"I want to be just like Mummy."

"Daphne's too chubby to be Mummy," Henry piped up.

Cutlery dropped to the floor, a rare moment of clumsiness from Plumb. Daphne swallowed. She didn't know where to look. The kitchen felt very small, much too warm.

"Henry, we've discussed this. Don't use that word with your sister."

"Daphne's too *ugly* to be Mummy."

"What did we say, Henry?" her dad responded sharply, hitting pause on the video camera. "No C and U words around Daphne."

She hated Henry already. He was nasty and competitive, mean. Whenever she burst into tears over his "pranks," her parents scolded *her* for being a crybaby and told her to stop being emotional. Daphne was tone-deaf but Henry played the oboe perfectly, and he was the best tenor in the choir. Daphne was bad at sport, whereas Henry was top of his class in tennis, track, and javelin. And he loved physics! Daphne didn't know any other students who liked that subject. She hated science! Henry was going places. Her parents said this often. Daphne hoped they were right. She wanted Henry to step on a high-speed train and never return.

Then there was her younger sister. Mimi wasn't talented at anything, but she was attractive. Petite with ocean blue eyes. Shimmering blond hair and long limbs and a charming smile. Everyone agreed. With looks like those, she would go far. Daphne's siblings had destinations: great genius and great beauty. But where would Daphne go? She overheard her parents talking about her. *Daphne's a bookworm.*

She cries a lot, doesn't she? I wish she were better with her siblings. Strange how she's best when she's left alone. What happened to the compliments she received as a toddler? *Daphne's adorable! Look at those cute thighs!* Somewhere along the way, her approval rating had dropped.

THEY were dragged to a wedding. It was rare for Henry, Daphne, and Mimi to be united by a common cause: they *really* didn't want to go. They didn't want to wear formal clothes. They didn't want to be on best behavior for eight hours straight. At least the ceremony was short. The buffet stretched on for days. Spinach dip and pasta salad. Tender beef and garlic shrimp. Barbeque chicken and sticky rice that stuck to her teeth. Doughy pita and potatoes au gratin. Meringues and jelly and brownies and . . . Daphne sensed her mother watching as she loaded up her plate. When Daphne returned for seconds, Plumb swooped in, too close for Daphne to see her face, only her lips, thick and voluptuous, the color of wild roses, moving quickly: *Girls don't eat those portion sizes.*

In the years that followed, Plumb fed her vegetables, steamed fish, snacks that tasted of cardboard. On Sundays, Daphne was nudged onto the scales. Plumb peered at her weight, scowling as she wrote down a number denoting her daughter's imperfection. Plumb tried various tactics to make her lose weight. She would buy glossy fashion magazines and tell Daphne: *this is what your life could be like if you just put your mind to it.* Daphne would stare in miserable defeat at the frivolous images: beautiful men in black tie lusting after glamorous women in designer dresses. The women had slender necklines and high cheekbones and voluminous hair and voluptuous lips. The women wore fabulous jewels, they enjoyed champagne and dates at the opera and vacations on the Côte d'Azur and yachts, so many yachts. It was a fantasy. Daphne understood this, even at that tender age. She understood her mother's logic was faulty. These images would never happen to Daphne, not even if she spent the next two decades starving herself. Regardless, she understood the message being conveyed: her eating habits, her weight, were a disappointment.

The best way to win Plumb's affections was to ask about her childhood fame. Plumb would smile and tell the story Daphne knew by heart. The auditions Plumb went to when she was five. Long lines of hopeful girls. Plumb selected out of thousands of hopefuls for the laundry detergent commercial. She signed with a modeling agency when she was fifteen. One time, Plumb was mistaken for Twiggy. Daphne found this story strange, how proud her mother was to be mistaken for someone else. Plumb kept photos from her modeling days in a box beneath her bed. A young Plumb in gold-sequined hot pants and tight miniskirts. Thick eyebrows darkened with pencil. High cheekbones that shimmered in bronzer. Poring over those photos, Daphne felt in the presence of greatness. Daphne was the opposite. Insignificant. Inconsequential. Inadequate. She would never be skinny, she would never be a model, she would never measure up.

Eventually, Daphne stopped. Stopped trying to starve herself. Stopped trying to be the doting dutiful daughter. She talked back. She rolled her eyes. She unleashed her emotions, her anger and sadness, her irreverence, her opinions. She gave up on being pretty and thin, quiet and graceful, but her parents doubled down on their criticism. She was too emotional, too direct, too unruly, too opinionated, too sarcastic. Daphne began to wonder who she was. The person her parents wanted her to be didn't feel like her, but their constant criticisms felt even harder to bear. It was easier to stay quiet, tucked inside a good book.

How freeing it was to arrive at university. She made a new family in Aparna and Dominic, Poppy and Abby. She remembers the first meal she ever cooked for them. Roast chicken with carrots, mashed potatoes, gravy. In a tiny kitchen the students shared. The smoke alarm went off. The gravy was lumpy. The carrots were under-cooked. But her friends thought she was a genius. Her new boyfriend said with utter conviction: *You're the most talented person I know*. Dominic began to list off her talents, Aparna jumped in too, followed by Poppy and Abby. Daphne glowed, and she began to understand what love was meant to feel like. It wasn't conditional, it wasn't an occasional sliver of sun between clouds of criticism. It was about gratitude and acceptance. It was seeing someone exactly as they are and celebrating it. It was the freedom to cry in the student kitchen with the smell of gravy hanging in the air, and for everyone around her to smile. She wasn't too emotional; she was Daphne, and they adored her for it.

As she tells Ash about her family, she watches him wipe down surfaces, replace bottles of liquor, move dirty glasses into the kitchen, and bring out clean glassware. She pauses now. She glances around the bar, and sees how dark and empty it is.

"Sorry," Daphne blurts out. "I don't usually monologue. Are you trying to close up?"

"Absolutely not!" Ash exclaims. "You just tore your heart out and shook its contents at me. I'm in awe, love."

Embarrassed, she deflects. She points at her empty glass.

"These go down pretty quickly."

"Made you another." He slides it her way. "Deserve it."

She sips it greedily.

"Your turn. On family, I mean."

"In a nutshell: stereotypically pushy Indian parents. They wanted me to be a doctor or a lawyer, and give them grandchildren, and instead . . . how unfortunate. They got the gay actor!"

She wonders how often he's made this joke. The words come out too easily. But if she asked him enough questions, in enough ways, she suspects his hurt would surface.

"Ah, we're both disappointments. Must have been hard on you, growing up."

He looks away, his features pinching together.

"I can explain why. In very specific ways. But not tonight."

"I like your name," she says, pointing to his name badge.

"Ashwin. Sanskrit. Means of great wealth. Really backfired on my parents." He laughs, and pushes a paper napkin toward her. "We need to hang again."

She stares at the digits written in black marker pen. "You want to hang out? With me? Why?"

His eyes move over her as he considers his response. "A bunch of reasons, I guess. There isn't a scrap of ego in you for one. You don't expect anything from anyone. You were shocked when I handed you a drink from that man. Shocked when I gave you a drink on the house. I guess it makes sense. People disappointed you."

She winces. "I've never been very good at . . . confidence."

He shakes his head. "There's confidence alright, I saw it as you told me about not trying to be what your parents wanted you to be, doing it your own way." He pauses, assessing her. "I'd say you're quietly confident, that's your style. There's an independent streak."

She smiles to herself. It's a luxury, hearing a stranger list out compliments.

"And I don't know," he continues. "I just like you. There's no bullshit. The minute I asked that question, the onion's all there to peel away. It takes guts to be that exposed and vulnerable. Just handing it to me on a plate. Do you know how refreshing that is? How much I'd give to access my feelings the way you just did? Shit, I'd nail my auditions every time."

"Ash," she says, her eyes filling with tears.

He grins. "Okay, weepy."

She wipes her tears away. "That's the nicest thing anyone's ever said."

He points at the smudged napkin. "Girl, you just lost my digits."

Asн tells her his dreams of acting and singing. After each shift, he stays up late working on screenplays, tales of revenge and redemption, heists going wrong. Everyone ends up dead or in prison, except for the guy they underestimated because he's brown and gay, and he outwits them all. He keeps the diamonds and gets the girl . . . except in Ash's version: the boy.

"A story told a million times," he says in a semi-indifferent tone, though she knows he cares deeply. "But it could be told in better ways."

He tells her about Ibrahim, a man ten years his senior. Ibrahim has broken up with him so many times that Ash has lost count. Whenever Ibrahim swoops in—and it's always Ibrahim's choice—he wreaks havoc on Ash's life. But it's hard.

"The saying no part," Ash clarifies. "I love him, even if he puts me through the wringer."

"Saying no though . . ." She hesitates, not wanting to appear patronizing. "It might be healthier?"

He pulls a face. "Healthy is a bit boring, isn't it?"

"I'd prefer boring over devastated."

He shakes his head. "But I hate loneliness. It always wins."

He is close to tears. She can almost taste his loneliness.

"Can I hug you?" she asks softly.

When they hug, it's like embracing reinforced steel. He sighs into her and she feels she's known him much longer than an evening. An evening without food, her stomach reminds her, growling unapologetically. Laughing, Ash peels himself away. He brings her fried squid, piled high in a deep bowl, topped with fresh sea salt. All this talk of Ibrahim is getting him down, he admits.

"Distract me," he implores.

Her mind goes to the Freedom Clause. She's not allowed to share their agreement with mutual friends, but Ash? He has nothing to do with Dominic. She probably *can* tell him without breaking the rules, right? She's desperate to confide in someone. She takes another piece of squid, chews thoughtfully.

"How?" she asks cautiously.

"What's your passion?"

She points to the bowl.

"Squid is your passion?"

She laughs heartily. The squid *is* delicious. She licks the salt from her fingers. From her lips too.

"Food. Obsessed with it. It's always given me joy even if my family made me feel bad about how much I ate. Want to hear something super geeky?"

"Naturally."

She scans the empty bar, suddenly nervous.

"I have this little notebook at home where I make tweaks to my recipes. I'll practice the same recipe over and over just to get it perfect."

Ash pulls a face. "I don't think that's stupid. It's kind of cool. What would you do with your passion for food, if you could do anything?"

She smiles, her shoulders relax. This question is easy.

"I'd be a food writer."

He leans forward. He's watching her closely now.

"Where?"

Even talking about it makes her heart race a little. She wants it so badly.

"A food magazine. But those jobs crop up like once every five years."

"But you can write?"

She nods. "I work for a law journal. I write for them."

"You're a writer," he grins, "just like me."

She frowns to herself. "Yes and no. The content I write is so dry and dull, I don't even consider it writing. I'm not one of those people with big ambitions, you know, the next big novel everyone reads. My husband has those aspirations, he's the writer in our house."

"Don't fall for it!" Ash grabs his forehead in mock horror. "Everyone I *know* has big plans to do something. You're actually doing it every day at work. I'd consider *you* the writer."

Everyone I know has big plans to do something. Her thoughts turn to Dominic. Outside of fantasizing about his novel's eventual success, she wonders: did he ever get much pleasure from writing? No, he didn't. She catches herself thinking in the past tense, and feels a flash of guilt. She's not being supportive. But truthfully? Why is he avoiding it? *Now* would be the perfect time to work on his novel or screenplay or whatever it is. He's unemployed, he has endless hours in the day to focus on writing . . . is it awful to admit this? She wishes he would cut his losses, walk away from it.

Ash is watching her, his expression critical.

"Why are you waiting for this dream job? Why not just start it now?"

She sucks in her breath. "How exactly?"

He looks at her as though it's obvious.

"Start writing outside of your notebook. Start your own Substack."

"Those are blogs, right?"

"Daphne!" he winces. "The term blog is *so* 1998."

She laughs and shrugs. "I wouldn't even know where to start."

He beckons with his hand. "Pass me your phone."

She unlocks it, slides it over, and watches him download the Substack app. He talks her through how it works. He asks her what she wants to call her account, but she isn't sure. She'd probably want to keep it anonymous. He sets it up, fingers moving quickly. No details. A blank canvas. She pictures leaving the app untouched for years. Ash must be a mind reader.

"You've got to write a post this week," he says, holding her gaze. "Promise?"

She can't let him down. "Promise."

DAPHNE doesn't tell him about the Freedom Clause. Her third Rhubarb Gimlet does. She comes clean, and acknowledges the terrible anxiety she feels whenever Dominic stays out late. Her mind wreaks havoc, picturing all the ways her husband might be enjoying the Freedom Clause. There is a recurring scenario, she admits in a despondent tone. She pictures him hooking up with a beautiful woman with long feathered hair and a sultry foreign accent, hitching her skirt up and . . . she breaks off.

"Is this normal?" she asks incoherently. "It doesn't *feel* normal."

"Back up!" Ash looks angry. "Did he force you into this?"

"No!" she leaps to his defense. "It's a fix for the fact we don't have sex."

"A fix for both of you, or for him?"

She exhales slowly. She feels torn because honestly? She doesn't see herself making use of this agreement but, seeing Ash's expression, she feels compelled to defend Dominic.

"He was definitely thinking about both of us."

Ash's eyes narrow. He doesn't look convinced.

"He sounds . . . persuasive. What've you done with it?"

"The Freedom Clause? Absolutely nothing," she admits in a deflated tone.

Ash nods slowly, unsurprised.

"Why not, Daphne?"

She squirms a little in her bar stool, unsure of what to say, or even where to look. She glances at her nails, bitten down, the cuticles ragged.

"I have no idea how to hit on men. What am I meant to do?"

"There's no formula," Ash says with an easy smile.

She rolls her eyes. Clearly, Ash has a high success rate. She can just *tell*. But for Daphne, the mere thought of hitting on someone fills her with panic. Daphne knows her brand: she's friendly, approachable, at *best* she's the girl next door type. She pictures trying to seduce a man. One moment she's casually chatting to him and the next, she's placing a hand on his arm and suggesting they go somewhere quiet. She sees the man's expression changing, and *not* in a good way, she hears him stuttering apologies as he explains he doesn't think of her that way. Sighing, Daphne scoops the last of the squid from the bowl and licks her lips.

"Daphne," Ash says, studying her thoughtfully, "all you need to know about men, gay or straight, is we're never offended by a woman hitting on us."

This draws a small smile. "I should just hit on men indiscriminately, should I? I couldn't handle that."

He looks confused. "Handle what?"

Isn't that part obvious? she thinks impatiently.

"The rejection."

His face changes, and she sees that he's reassessing her.

"You know I deal with rejection all the time? I *have* to as an actor. I have to pick myself up constantly and just get on with it. And so do you. Who cares if a guy doesn't like you back? That's *his* loss . . . but with your attitude?" he says, gesturing toward her, "of course you'll get rejected."

But it's not about attitude. There are certain people who will get rejected more often, and that's just the way the cookie crumbles. Daphne is one of those people. She is talented in plenty of areas but not in the art of seduction.

"The thing is," she begins, her voice floundering, "men don't really go for women who look like me."

She doesn't expect this reaction. He throws his head back and laughs loudly.

"Honey, I've worked in bars since I was fifteen. I've seen every type of man hit on every type of woman. There are a lot of people who'd take you home."

She blushes. "It's just so . . . out of my comfort zone."

He shakes his head at her like she's daft.

"Isn't that the whole point?"

She begins to say something, but changes her mind.

"Go on," he urges.

"In truth," Daphne begins hesitantly. Her voice is soft and quiet. She sees him leaning in to catch her words. "I just don't think I'm a sexual person."

His face creases in concern. "Oh no."

She feels an intense heat spreading across her face.

"It's true," she insists quietly.

"Those are just the words," he says softly, "of a woman who hasn't had a great orgasm yet." His eyes flit past her. "Can I help you?"

"Glenfiddich. Neat."

She hears a deep voice. A northern accent. Daphne swivels again, a little unsteadily this time. His clothes are strange and mismatched: a tweed jacket, a red bow tie. He looks like a magician performing at a children's birthday party. His hair is unruly, strawberry blonde. Okay, she thinks. He's not gorgeous, but he's not . . . *unattractive*. She considers what Ash just told her. Rejection is part of the process. Why not give it a try?

"Hello," she says with a dazzling confidence that she attributes to her fourth cocktail of the evening. "I'm Daphne."

Stuart is staying here, she learns. In the hotel attached to the bar. They chat for a little while, and when she asks to see his room, he nods calmly and asks for the bill. How surreal, she thinks semi-lucidly, as time slows, it almost stills. She watches the scene with hyper-attuned awareness. There is her friend Ash passing the bill toward Stuart. And there is Stuart reaching for the pen. And there is Ash again, offering her a sly wink. As she and Stuart walk toward the elevator she feels his hand moving squarely over her buttocks. Ash will be watching. She wants to glance back and grin at him and whisper thanks for the pep talk, but now they're in the elevator and Stuart is leaning in, pressing into her. He tastes of whisky, truffle fries. Daphne smiles into his mouth, elated by her success.

"What's your job again?" she asks, breaking away.

He's from Manchester, a research scientist. In London for a two-day conference. He's on a panel tomorrow. She asks about the panel, but doesn't listen to his answer.

"Lost you, haven't I?" he says in an amused tone.

She smiles sheepishly. "Little bit."

They look like a couple, she thinks, glancing in the elevator mirror. She's seen herself beside Dominic plenty of times, but it's strange to see this Daphne leaning into *this* chest. Her face is relaxed, seemingly unfocused. His hand rests on her shoulder. His other hand reaches for her hair, smoothing down a curl. It's a surprisingly tender gesture. A high-pitched ping. The elevator doors open. She follows him. The hallway is long and dark, lined with thick red carpet. She feels jittery, as though she's entering Narnia. She's about to sleep with a man who is not her husband. She's about to *double* the number of men she's slept with in her life. He reaches into his pocket, withdraws a key card. This part should be easy, but the white plastic refuses to cooperate. The small circle on the door's keypad flashes red twice. He mutters under his breath in exasperation and Daphne suppresses a small smile. He might be feeling nervous too, she reminds herself. He tries again. One more time and the circle flashes green. They sigh in unison.

Striding in, he flips the lights on. His room is small and chilly. There's a large wrinkle in his bed. Beside it, a well-thumbed copy of *The Economist*. Stuart follows her gaze.

"Let's just say, my evening plans improved greatly."

She smiles, accepting the compliment. Sitting on the low bed, he pulls her in. His eyes roam her face, his expression alert and focused. The bar lighting was soft, casting him in a pleasant glow, but now she sees deep wrinkles, crinkles by his eyes. How old is he? Forty something? He isn't married, she knows this much. He told her, downstairs in the bar, that he has a sixteen-year-old daughter he sees twice a year. His hair is thick and she touches it, stepping closer. Stuart removes her clothes, beginning with her coat. It drops dramatically to the floor. He tackles her winter boots next. Thick and leather, the untying of all those laces, the lowering of the zips, requires familiarity and patience. Stuart fumbles, and she pitches in to help. He tugs on her tights in a determined fashion, revealing pasty white legs that haven't been shaved in two weeks. He lifts her dress up, over her head.

She stands in front of him, in just her underwear. She wishes she was wearing something nicer, something that *matched*. Her yellow cotton knickers have a conspicuous rip near the hip from that time they snagged in the dryer. Her navy bra, size 34B, is in chronic condition, sagging everywhere. She's had this bra for *years* and it doesn't really hold up her chest so much as exist, in noncommittal form, the fabric nestling ineffectually against the outline of her breasts. Daphne's concerns move on to wishing the room were darker. She's worried he'll notice her misshapen breasts, the right one perceptibly larger than the left. She sucks in her stomach that is nowhere close to flat. Subconsciously, her hands creep forward. Stuart doesn't notice. He's spending a lot of time on her breasts, kissing and nuzzling them, as he works the clasp behind her back, the material giving way finally. She feels curiously removed. This moment is between Stuart and her breasts, and she is an impartial third-party witness. Maybe Stuart picks up on detachment because he's pulling her in, kissing her on the lips.

She reminds herself that this is what the Freedom Clause was designed for. An evening just like this, and she'd better make use of it. This thought galvanizes her into action. She strips his clothes off with matronly precision. Naked, he looks small. His body is narrow, condensed, hairless save for a few strawberry blond hairs sprouting up patchily around his chest. She is reminded of Dominic's body, the dark hairs all over his chest and stomach. There's nothing wrong with Stuart, she reminds herself, he's simply different. And maybe Stuart is comparing her to former lovers right now? This thought startles her. Daphne is a novice in the swimming pool of sexual experience. She needs inflatable arm bands. She needs to stay in the shallow end, treading water. She wonders if Stuart can sense this. She kisses his shoulders and nipples, his hairless stomach, his groin. She takes great pleasure in watching his cock begin to harden and she takes him in, using a combination of hand and mouth, alternating in pace and pressure, just as Poppy has described. Poppy likes talking about blow jobs, she's definitely the most experienced of all her friends.

"What do you want me to do?" he murmurs.

She doesn't answer. She's utterly engrossed in the task of pleasing him, and it *is* a task, one she wants to see through to completion. When his hand moves to her thighs, she flits it away. She doesn't understand, logistically, how he can reciprocate simultaneously without repositioning a lot of body parts, testing out new angles, and that seems like a bad idea when they are already here, in a perfectly acceptable rhythm. She keeps going, wanting to make him orgasm, and he makes a strange sound, one of disbelief. When he pulls away and maneuvers her, she offers no resistance and now she finds herself lying on her back, staring up at him.

"What do you want me to do?" he repeats, more insistently this time.

She shrugs her shoulders. "Whatever you want."

He moves between her legs and begins to rub her with his thumb. His skin is rough and calloused, his pace much too fast. It's almost like she told him there's a mosquito bite down there, and asked him to really go for it. She tries to relax into it, this rubbing-itching hybrid. She tries a series of positive reinforcements in her head—you like his thumb there, don't you?—but without conviction. Besides, it's hard to relax when the overhead lighting is this harsh. The ceiling lights glare down at her. They are distracting, blinding, the type of lighting used in theaters. An acceptable form of lighting only if she were stepping onstage, an audience awaiting her opening line. Glancing down, she notices him watching her and it dawns on her that she *does* have an audience. She panics upon realizing this. She won't be able to orgasm! She can't! Not when he's staring at her this expectantly. And what, exactly, does he think will happen as a result of this rubbing motion that's close to, but not quite *on,* her clitoris?

The problem is, his expectation that she'll orgasm does the opposite: it guarantees she absolutely will not. She rolls her hips toward him, gesturing for him to enter her, and mercifully, he agrees to this. He retreats momentarily. He's hunting for a condom, she gathers, watching him rifle through his wallet, muttering to himself until he plucks one out at last. As he tries to enter her, it becomes abundantly clear that she's dry. Bone dry. It takes a lot of posturing, a lot of saliva before he slips in, although the word "slip" is too generous. It's a solid, persistent push. She feels like a stiff old door, resistant to being thrust open until Stuart commits to throwing his entire weight behind the action.

And this moment, right here, is what she meant when she told Ash she's not a sexual person. She's lying on her back as he thrusts in and out of her. She's feeling a lot of things right now and, of note, none of them are pleasurable. Dryness. Pain. Boredom. She wills him to orgasm soon. She considers the expression "even bad sex is good" and presses her lips firmly together, thinking how wrong that expression is. Clearly a man uttered those words because bad sex is not good. Bad sex has never been good. Bad sex is up there with dental work and having the middle seat on a long-haul red eye. Hold that thought, position change! He's grabbing her hips and flipping her over. Why do people go crazy for this, she asks herself. What she finds strange—stranger perhaps than the pain and the boredom—is the fact that she is here, in this hotel room with another person, but she's never felt more alone. There is a gripping loneliness in being on all fours, staring at the headboard, and hearing a man's grunts from over her shoulder as he slams against her from behind. It is the most alone she has ever felt. And she is certain too that she is the only person in the world who does not enjoy this. She is abnormal, for other women would be orgasming right now. He groans, a long low noise that reminds her of the stick-shift car they once rented in France, the one that felt on the cusp of dying each time they turned on the engine or attempted a steep hill. When he flips her over again, she feels a lot like an inanimate object. And when he asks where she'd like him to come, she leans hard into this idea of being an inanimate object.

"Anywhere," she responds with a small shrug.

He looks at her incredulously.

"Where's that girl in the bar who wanted this so badly?"

She hears it now, the small flecks of anger in his voice. The hairs on her back stand up.

"I'm still here," she says timidly.

His eyes harden. "Anywhere, really?"

His tone is combative. His anger irrefutable. She nods slowly, wishing she could retreat. He pulls out of her. He flings the condom over his shoulder and it lands on her left foot, sticking to her skin stubbornly like gum beneath a table. And now he's crouching over her, balancing his feet on the soft mattress, jerking off angrily, viciously, right above her. She feels it again. His fury.

"Coming!" he yells.

His semen. Sticky and hot, spurting into her hair and scalp. She clamps her eyes shut. She feels it trickling down her forehead. At least it is over now, she thinks with relief.

"Did you even enjoy that at all?" he asks, collapsing next to her, out of breath.

"Yes," she says in a clipped tone. "Why do you ask?"

"It all just felt a bit business-like," he remarks.

She closes her eyes. She wants him to disappear.

"Here's some money for a cab home," he says.

Her eyes fly open. He's reaching for his wallet.

"You don't have to," she says weakly.

"I'd like to. Please."

She accepts his money. Leaning forward, she peels the condom from her left foot. They turn away from each other, pulling on their discarded clothes. She begins to say goodbye, but he signals he'll see her to the door. This is awkward, she thinks, as he follows her out, trailing behind her, into the elevator, down six flights, through the lobby and outside into the cold.

He helps her do up her coat. Lowering his voice, he says:

"So, I still get the impression you didn't have the greatest time tonight, it's a tad surprising given you were pretty forward in the bar." He places a hand on her chin, tilts her face up. His eyes search hers. "Think about what you like having done to you ahead of the next time, yeah? It should always be good for you too."

She nods. Out of the corner of her eye, she sees a cab approaching.

"I'll get this," Daphne murmurs. "Enjoy the panel tomorrow."

Stuart leans in, pecks her lips. He strokes her hair, smooths it down. Daphne feels better. This tenderness, this compassion de-cheapens the evening. He smiles at her.

"Every future conference is going to pale in comparison to this one."

"I'm sure it w—"

The remark dies in her throat. That person, emerging from the cab is . . . an important detail surfaces. Mimi suggested this bar. This one, because she's staying here.

"Daphne, you waited!" Mimi says in glee. Her eyes land on Stu-art. She absorbs them both in a flash. His crumpled clothes. Her guilty expression. "Who are you? And what," Mimi asks, her voice lowering a fraction, "are you doing with my *married* sister?"

DAPHNE takes a long bath, shampoos thoroughly and places her wet hair in a towel. She slips on a dressing gown and pads into the kitchen. Opening the fridge, she's ravenous. The squid, it's all she's eaten! Mindlessly, she pulls ingredients from the fridge. She moves quietly, as she retrieves onions and heats oil in the pan and makes the dress-ing, not wanting to wake him. She's sitting down to eat when he appears in the doorway, sleepy and tousled.

"Did you shower?"

She freezes, wondering how guilty she must look in this moment.

"Bath." She pauses. "Thought it'd warm me up. It's cold outside."

"How's Mimi?"

She pulls a face. "Super late."

"How late?"

"Hours." Somehow, miraculously, her face is neutral. "I became BFFs with the bartender. He gave me free drinks."

Dominic takes a seat beside her. His hand rests on her knee, his fingers make small circular motions against her skin. She's nervous he'll *know,* that somehow he'll pick up another man's scent on her. Or maybe not, she thinks, watching him peer into her bowl.

"Oh," he exclaims cheerily, "it's The Daphne Salad. Can I have some?"

She made this salad when they were students at Bristol. They woke up at noon and Daphne had a specific craving: hot sausage, baby kale, mozzarella, caramelized onions and blood oranges. Sounds strange, Dominic said in response, but Daphne returned an hour later, groceries in hand, and they devoured it. It became a once-a-week ritual.

She nods, slides it over.

"Mmmm," he responds, mouth full of kale. "Hits the spot every time."

Shifting focus onto him, she asks, "How was your night?"

"I worked on some job applications," he says.

He stabs forcefully at the salad. His aggression makes her wonder if unemployment is taking its toll. It's been two months since he quit and he's not getting far with applications.

"What kind of jobs?"

"One is for a think tank, a reach for sure. The other is for an ad agency."

"Is that what you want? Another ad agency?"

"Nope," he admits in a frustrated tone. "But I have the experience they need. And I hate causing stress over my situation, especially right before Christmas."

She pulls the towel from her head, letting her hair fall to her shoulders, loose and damp.

"Honestly, it's fine," she responds, fiddling with strands of hair. "We have a little money we can dip into."

He taps his fingers on the kitchen table like he's playing the piano. It's a nervous reflex.

"I'll find a job soon."

His hand moves from the table to her knee, drifting slowly up her thigh. Her body tenses. Oh god, she thinks, I can't handle this tonight.

Fixing his eyes on her, Dominic sighs.

"Tell me about this bartender, then. Was he sexy?"

"The sexiest."

"Daphne!" He breaks into a pout. "Really?"

"Oh yes, but I'm not his type, sadly. Lovely gay man."

He grins. "Almost got jealous there."

She raises an eyebrow. "The ethical nonmonogamist gets jealous, does he?"

He pulls her in for a kiss. Can he sense it, she wonders again?

"Sure, I do," he murmurs. His hand drops to her back. "Coming to bed?"

"Be right there."

Left alone, she stacks the dishwasher. She wipes down surfaces. She runs a dirty cloth beneath the tap, wringing it out. She cleans when she's stressed, but what she really needs right now is obvious. She stares longingly at her phone. She imagines telling Aparna or Poppy what went down tonight. But it's one of the rules: no mutual friends are allowed to know (and all her friends know Dominic). Even if she were to break that rule, she's a little bit scared of what they would say.

It's past midnight but her mind is whirring. She pulls out her phone. Her finger hovers over the app Ash downloaded for her. She opens it, surprised to see a notification. Clicking on it, she smiles. Ash is her first subscriber. She stares at the blank page for a long time before she begins to type. You can always delete it in the morning, she tells herself. She writes to nobody in particular. But importantly, she writes.

Confessions of a Highly Emotional Cook:

I-Can't-Believe-He-Came-In-My-Hair Salad

The Highly Emotional Cook, that's me. I've always been called an emotional person, and I often use cooking as a way to process my emotions. I might go into preparing a meal feeling sad or stressed or angry, and by the time it's ready, I feel closer to normal (whatever normal is). To-night? It feels like a good time to start since it might just be the most ridiculous evening of my life. I wish this could be a liberating story, the way having sex on my own terms as a woman should be, but I'll let you in on a secret. It wasn't. I had sex with a stranger, a man who is not my husband, and he came in my hair. And I don't even think that's the most humiliating part of the entire evening (oh really? you might be thinking). Because in-stead of enjoying sex, the way it's meant to be enjoyed, I let my insecurities take over. I thought about what my body looked like (with a keenly critical eye) and I didn't assert the things I like doing or, more importantly, what I wanted done to me (confession: I'm not sure I even know what I like). When he asked where he should come, I said anywhere. And, to be clear, we're not talking a small amount, ladies. No, a LOT of ejaculate, plenty for my hair and my scalp. My face too.

I should clarify that the man who came in my hair was not a monster. He was not an absolute dick. He's just a lot better at asserting what he wants in life than I am. I won-der if this is a distinctly male trait? Not to say all women are unassertive, far from it. But I know that I struggle in this area. I am a dreadful people pleaser to anyone who is remotely nice to me, which means most of my sexual encounters (fine, all of them) are spent helping my partner chase his orgasms. But where does that leave mine? Honestly, I think all my orgasms are hanging out together, getting their hair treated or chatting in a hot tub or knocking back cocktails with no intention of stepping out to find me. It's on *me* to find *them*.

Later, in the back of a cab, this man's semen hardening in my hair, I felt a familiar sensation: shame. It's a long-term companion. We go way back. I've always felt shameful about my body, ever since I was young. I've always felt larger than my mum and my sister (although they are both models so there's that). I definitely have the waist of a woman who can never say no to a cupcake. I don't think I should feel bad about that, but often I do. I am a regular-sized woman with curves, soft parts. My husband LOVES the way I look so why do I put pressure on myself?

So now you're getting a sense of who I am. The Highly Emotional Cook. I find it healing to cook. I find it's in the kitchen that I'm most able to contemplate my pain, my insecurities, and my anxieties. And tonight was no different. The salad helped. The shame sloped off.

I love this salad. The first time I made it, I was a student and horribly hungover. This salad is about indulgence. It's about being kind to yourself when you are feeling low and off-kilter and you need compassion from the world. This isn't a low-calorie salad. It's a salad for women who drink too much and make mistakes. It's a salad for women who know what bad sex feels like. It's a salad for women who aren't perfect, and never will be. It's a decadent salad. It's a flawed salad. Ladies, it's our salad.

I-CAN'T-BELIEVE-HE-CAME-IN-MY-HAIR SALAD

Feeds: one (because tonight is all about YOU, baby)

Ingredients:
- Half a bag of baby kale
- One sausage link
- Red chili pepper flakes (for the sausage)
- One whole fresh mozzarella ball
- Half an avocado, chopped into inch-sized cubes
- A handful of walnuts
- Sunflower seeds
- Half of a large orange (preferably a blood orange, if it's available), sliced into segments with the whites removed
- One red onion, chopped into long thin slices
- A generous squeeze of honey (for the walnuts)
- A box of tissues (if you're emotional, like me)

Dressing:
- Olive oil—four tablespoons
- Balsamic vinegar—one tablespoon
- Juice of one lemon
- Half of one shallot—finely diced
- Mustard—one tablespoon
- Honey—half a teaspoon
- A pinch of salt and pepper

Method:
1. Wash the baby kale leaves thoroughly, as though those leaves are your hair and you want every last scrap of that man off you. Place in a large salad bowl.
2. Caramelizing red onions takes a while, but it's well worth the effort and patience. I happen to have some in my fridge to-

night but for those of you who don't spend most of the
weekend cooking here goes: chop the red onion in half
and then cut into long slices. Pour some olive oil in a frying
pan and drop the onion in. Leave on a low heat for about
30 minutes. Stir occasionally. Add a little water if the onion
makes a crackling noise in the pan. Keep stirring. Add a little
salt and sugar. Once cooked, drop into the baby kale salad
bowl.

3. Chop the avocado, blood orange (whites removed please), and
   the mozzarella into large chunks. Marvel at how easy that was.
   If only orgasming with a stranger could be like this. Drop the
   avocado, blood orange, and mozzarella into the baby kale salad
   bowl.

4. Pour a little butter into a frying pan. Add the walnuts. Stir for
   2–3 minutes over a very low heat, coating the walnuts thoroughly in the butter. Remove from the heat and drizzle with
   honey. It should smell great by now, so great that your tender
   nostrils might forget the stale scents from earlier in the evening. Add the honeyed walnuts to the salad bowl.

5. Study the sausage and be thankful it's lifeless, it doesn't expect
   attention or admiration from you. Cut it into chunks, leaving
   the casing on.

6. Using the same frying pan you used before, add red pepper
   chili flakes, followed by the sausage chunks. Add more olive
   oil if you need it, you probably won't.

7. Cook for approximately 6 minutes over a medium heat until
   sausage is crispy on the outside and cooked through, stirring
   frequently. Once cooked, add to the salad bowl.

8. In the meantime, prepare the dressing. Mix the olive oil and
   balsamic vinegar together in a glass. Add the diced shallot, the
   juice of one lemon, the honey and mustard, and salt and pepper. I've put recommendations on measurements above, but

please taste and adjust to your liking. Be assertive about what you like in a dressing. Try to recall this assertiveness the next time you leap into bed with a stranger.

9. Add the dressing and sprinkle some sunflower seeds over everything. Sink into your sofa and eat slowly, savoring each bite. Sure, you may not have made many great choices today, but this salad is one you can be proud of.

Thanks for reading my first entry! I'm hoping this can be a place to share my recipes and maybe more. I will write again soon.

Yours,
The Highly Emotional Cook

—

NEW Year's Eve. The theme: eighties glamor. Leg warmers. Shoulder pads. Blue eye shadow. Big hair. The venue: their Putney home, the size of a postage stamp. Tonight, their flat is noisy, crowded, and oh so hot. Friends congregate in the kitchen and living room, spilling into the bedroom and tiny balcony. There are whoops as the song "Take On Me" floats on.

Dominic is in the kitchen, playing beer pong. He's on the winning team. If there is one skill he has mastered, above all others, it's the ability to throw a Ping-Pong ball into a plastic cup. *I will go far in life,* he thinks self-mockingly. He hears Daphne's laughter as she floats through the rooms, replenishing glasses. Her punch is blood red, wickedly strong.

Daphne calls his name. Her hand is on his shoulder. She's Madonna in "Material Girl." Strapless taffeta pink dress. Long-sleeved gloves. Diamanté choker. Blond wig. Her outfit makes him smile. Typical Daphne, putting great effort into everything she does. She assembled the outfit carefully, over a series of weekends, plucking each item from the depths of thrift shops.

"Dom, I want you to meet a new friend," she says giddily. "This is Ash."

Daphne has a tight knit group of fun girlfriends. They watch reality TV and go for pedicures and meet for happy hour wine. They are serious too: about their careers and culture. Serious about attending the latest Rembrandt exhibition and meeting up at the British Film Institute and seeing that Noël Coward play before its run ends.

Ash is *nothing* like her other friends. His face is, Dominic pauses, searching for the right word . . . iconic. High cheekbones and sculpted lips, manicured eyebrows. He's ripped, Dominic thinks vowing to hit the gym more often. He's wearing a black leather jacket. Underneath, a white tank top with WHAM emblazoned on the front. A small cross hangs from one ear. Daphne told him about Ash but she omitted to mention his movie star looks. Why does this bother him? It's not like he's *threatened*. Or is he? The intensity of their friendship is pretty unusual given they only met a month ago. She seems to text him all the time.

"Great to meet you," Dominic says, forcing out a friendly tone.

"Same!" Ash responds amiably, shaking his hand.

Ash has a steel grip; it's like shaking hands with The Rock. Okay, he is *absolutely* threatened by this guy.

"Great outfit. You're . . . Prince?"

Dominic glances down at his white ruffled shirt.

"Yeah, Daphne wins though."

Daphne responds with a happy twirl.

"Ash is a writer too," she explains, gesturing toward him.

"Nice," Dominic says, his smile thinning.

He knows it's weird to be this protective and secretive over his writing, but he worries talking about it might *muddy* it somehow. Truth is, he's pretty good about muddying it up by himself. At this point, it's a collection of random scenes, with multiple points of view, and time lapses, and dream sequences, and he has no idea how or what to shape it all into. The manuscript requires significant fine-tuning. He can admit it: he's overwhelmed. Even though he has so much time now, he makes endless excuses to avoid it. The scenes gaze at him, hungry for attention. Even Daphne, usually so patient, has been hinting he get on with it.

"How fun!" Ash says enthusiastically, sharing details of his latest project. It's a screenplay, one he's actually *completed*. A heist movie set in London. It sounds pretty good, Dominic thinks, draining the last of his drink. Ash smiles at him, asking: "What about you?"

"Mine is . . ." Dominic pauses, his mind whirring in panic. There is nothing to reveal! There has been no progress! Daphne looks intensely uncomfortable. She looks nervous *for* him. He clears his throat, starts over. "It's a contemporary piece, looking at a group of male friends living in London. How they struggle against . . . their privilege."

He closes his mouth and considers what he just blurted out. If that's *actually* what he's writing about, it's news to him. Ash looks confused, Daphne too.

"What is it?" Ash is asking.

Dominic blushes furiously, wanting this conversation to end.

"It's a fluid structure currently."

"Right." Ash glances away. "I might run to the bathroom."

Relieved their conversation is over, Dominic tugs on Daphne's hand, pulling her onto the makeshift dance floor. Queen blasts on. "Don't Stop Me Now" and Aparna shouts: "Dance-off!" Their friends gather closer, a loose circle forming around Prince and Madonna. Dominic's dance moves are flashy and over the top, ridiculous leg kicks, clumsy floor spins. Daphne dances slowly, twisting her hips sexily, staring moodily. She secures the crowd's approval and they chant her name in unison. As the song ends, Dominic bows graciously and Daphne accepts her victory. It's almost midnight, someone shouts. Five minutes.

Daphne's face is flushed. She wraps her arms around his waist.

"We're out of punch. Party fail."

He kisses the top of her head.

"That means everyone loved it!"

He knows Daphne well, and he knows she's making a mental note, ahead of the next party, to make more next time. Maybe she'll write it in her recipe notebook. Come to think of it, he hasn't seen her writing in it in a while.

"Ready for a new year?" she asks, tugging affectionately on a shirt ruffle.

"It'll be our best year yet," he says.

He's aiming for optimistic, but the words tumble out clumsily. How *can* it be a great year when he isn't even employed? She won't admit it, but he knows she's cut down on spending. He knows she's worried how long they can survive on her salary alone, a meager one at that.

"I'm proud of you," Daphne whispers, her voice lilting and alcohol-fueled. She's an adorable drunk. "For walking away from that job."

His face stiffens. He doesn't deserve praise. He lost the job and he lied to Daphne. Please stop, he thinks, feeling sick to the stomach.

"For prioritizing your happiness over that big salary," she continues.

He feels an intense urge to come clean. Even in her state of intoxication, she senses something is up.

"What is it?" she asks, her gaze sharpening.

But he can't come clean, not about his job anyway.

"I didn't do it this year," he blurts out, surprising himself.

"Do what?" she asks slowly.

"The Freedom Clause," he admits in a miserable tone.

"Oh, that." Her voice is cold, perturbed. She raises a hand to her forehead. She presses delicately, as though blotting red wine from a cream rug. "I thought we agreed not to share details with each other."

"I just wanted to reassure you."

Her tone sharpens. "Reassure me?"

"We don't have to keep doing this. If you don't want to."

He presents it as though he's doing *her* the favor, but canceling the whole thing would be an enormous relief. The failures of the last year flash to mind. The woman in Leeds with the scary boyfriend. Katy, who lost interest in him as soon as Mark waltzed in. Roxie, who wanted Gerry, not him. He'd still have his dignity, and his job, if it weren't for the Freedom Clause.

The countdown begins. Thirteen. Twelve. Eleven.

"Let's drop the whole thing," he shouts over the din, reaching for her hand.

Ten! Nine! Eight!

"Why though?" she shouts back.

She looks flummoxed.

Seven! Six! Five!

"Because you're not enjoying it! Let's just forget it."

Four! Three! Two!

"What makes you think I'm not enjoying it?"

One! Happy! New! Year!

The familiar faces of their friends, everywhere, surrounding them, laughing and drinking, hugging each other, dancing. Everyone crammed into the small living room is beyond happy, elated. Except for Madonna and Prince. Dominic stares at her in astonishment, his body rigid, gripped in fear. Daphne stares back, her chin raised stubbornly.

Oh shit, he thinks. *She's enjoying it.*

YEAR
TWO

Aɴᴏᴛʜᴇʀ Jᴀɴᴜᴀʀʏ. Iᴛ'ѕ ʜᴇʀ ʙɪʀᴛʜᴅᴀʏ again. Dominic wakes her up with coffee and kisses. She hums in the shower. She blow dries her hair. The tube is crowded and she doesn't get a seat. At the office, she receives a signed card and a wobbly round of "Happy Birthday," just the same as last year, and the year before that. She slips out early for brunch with Ash. They meet in a popular Israeli place. He's sitting at a small square table in the middle, easy to spot. Mustard-yellow cotton cable-knit cardigan. Racing-green ankle-length trench coat. Silver backpack. Chuck Taylor's. Seeing her, he leaps up and launches into "Happy Birthday"—the Stevie Wonder version—dancing slowly, clicking his fingers, not caring who watches. Daphne laughs, and allows herself to be spun around for a few seconds. They take their seats.

"Since I'll be working later," Ash says, pulling a gift from his backpack.

The packaging is long, cylindrical. She tears at the wrapping paper, her mouth dropping open as she realizes what he bought.

"I did my research," he continues proudly. "I asked a lot of people, actually, and the verdict is: silicone-based is best for women."

She feels herself blushing. "You bought me lube?" she whispers, glancing around the restaurant.

Ash nods, looks at her strangely. "Sounds like you need it! Based on that painful experience in the hotel room?"

Mortified, she stuffs it up her sweater. The lid pokes up near her bra. "This is huge, I'd need a decade to get through it!"

He grins. "Largest size I could get. I'm optimistic," he explains, "even if you aren't . . . yet."

"I don't need this."

He looks confused. "But I thought you said it wasn't good for you?"

"Only because I was feeling self-conscious."

Ash takes his glass of water, sips from it as he considers this. "Why though, you shouldn't."

She glances at the people one table over. A mother and her teenage son. The tables couldn't be pressed more closely together, she thinks, leaning forward to whisper.

"I'm not very comfortable being naked with a stranger. I feel a bit . . . yuck."

"Well," Ash responds lightly, "what's your exercise routine?"

Her eyebrows shoot up. He's hit a nerve. "Are you saying I—"

"I find my workouts make me feel better," he explains calmly with a small shrug of the shoulders. "I feel off if I miss a day. Do you have a routine?"

She hates this question. There's been an implosion of options lately, it's like learning a new language. Poppy used to do Bikram yoga but now she swears by high-intensity interval training. Overnight, Aparna became addicted to an early morning boot camp class near her office. There's a SoulCycle instructor whose classes Abby never misses. Everyone's identity seems to be tied to an exercise routine. Where does she even begin? It's intimidating, not to mention each class costs a small fortune.

"I'm not good at that," she says firmly. "You should have seen me at school. The netball coach actively went out of her way to discourage me from trying out for the team."

Ash isn't fazed. "Nobody is at first. We could work out together."

"You want me to lose weight?"

He rolls his eyes at her.

"I'm not your mum, and it's not about the scales. They're going to move up and down from salt intake and water retention and all sorts of factors you can't really control. It's about empowerment. Pushing your body in new ways, hitting goals, toning up. You'd love it!"

"It's expensive though, and with Dominic being out of work right now, I can't really . . ."

"Running is free."

"That's what we'd do?" she asks hesitantly.

"Sure, and squats, burpees, crunches . . . that kind of thing."

He looks committed to doing this, and she half worries he'll turn up on her doorstep tomorrow with exercise bands and a stopwatch. Her inclination is to laugh it off.

"I don't know," she says reluctantly. "I have, like, zero coordination."

"I think you'll love it once you get into it."

"You sound pretty confident for someone who's only known me two months." She lifts her mug, takes a small sip of coffee. "When would we have time? Between my office job and your auditions."

"Please," he continues, undeterred. "I've had like four auditions in the last year."

The waiter returns and Daphne scans the menu. She waits for the waiter to walk away with their orders before pulling his gift out from beneath her sweater.

"You should take this back," she urges. "You'll use it more anyway."

Ash's hands fly up. He shakes his head emphatically.

"No way, it's for *you*! And let's get some smaller samples to keep in your wallet."

She hesitates, before slipping it into the tote perched on the back of her chair.

"But aren't women supposed to, you know, produce their own?"

"Well," he asks earnestly, "is that what happened to you?"

"I shouldn't need it," she responds in a miserable voice of defeat.

"Yes, you should," he says curtly. "There's this *ridiculous* misconception that women are naturally wet but *clearly* not every man is going to be super talented in making that happen. Most probably aren't. There's no shame in needing a little help so there's less . . . chafing and pain, right?"

Chafing and pain, that sounds familiar.

"Okay, maybe it would help," she admits, pulling her tote onto her lap and peering more closely at the bottle.

"And your sex life isn't a Hollywood movie, okay?"

She gives him a look. "I'm *well* aware of that."

"Meaning, you might actually have to put some work into getting an orgasm. You don't just lie back and wait for fireworks."

"Ash," she says abruptly. "Are you accusing me of being a lazy lover?"

"I wouldn't dare." He smiles slowly. "I just think you might need to commit some time to figuring out what really gets you going."

He's only trying to help her with this gift, she reminds herself. The mother and son glance over with interest. Ash smiles brightly, unbothered.

"Thanks for the . . . silicone thing," she mumbles before trying again. "Thanks for the lube, Ash. Sorry I reacted that way."

"That's the spirit," he says cheerily. "And we're running this weekend, right? Dust off your spandex!"

Confessions of a Highly Emotional Cook:

Green goddess smoothie (even if you don't run like a goddess)

I'm lying on the floor of my friend's kitchen, in great pain, typing this out with one finger and the angle is . . . awkward. We went for a run this morning. Why would you do that to yourself, you may be asking? Especially in JAN-UARY. Valid question. My body feels similarly. It's doing the human equivalent of when your laptop freezes and you see that spinning multicolored circle of despair. You tap your keyboard helplessly and you get nothing back.

My friend isn't worried. He's chucking fruit and vegetables into his blender, reassuring me this is just my body throwing a tantrum and we'll kick it into shape. As you may have gathered by now, I am NOT a runner. Our friendship will suffer from this.

GREEN GODDESS SMOOTHIE
(EVEN IF YOU DON'T RUN LIKE A GODDESS)

Feeds: two (one of whom may be in better physical shape)

Ingredients:
- 3 bananas
- 1 avocado
- 2 generous handfuls of spinach leaves
- Some low-fat plain yoghurt (no idea how much, my friend is unhelpfully telling me to "eyeball" it)
- A lingering pour of almond milk
- 6 ice cubes

Method:
1. Place all the ingredients in a blender. Slowly is fine. Everything hurts. Slowly is understandable.
2. Hit the blend button. Okay, that noise is loud and terrifying, but not as bad as the sound of your breathing during miles

three and four. Was it even breathing? No, it was the wheeze of someone in bad shape, in desperate need of a ventilator.

3. Watch the ingredients as they're pulped into mush. Yes, this is exactly how your body feels. It's going to feel like this for days.

4. Pour into two glasses. Glare at your running mate as you drink it, especially as he suggests doing this again next weekend.

Yours (wearily),
    The Highly Emotional Cook

—

DOMINIC sits on a park bench in the freezing cold, studying his gloved hands. He's thinking about the enormous bottle of lube that appeared on her bedside table. Where did *that* come from, he asked? Daphne laughed and suggested they try it out. He didn't hesitate. He can't remember the last time she initiated. Keen bean, she teased him. She seemed to enjoy it more with lube, which meant he enjoyed it more too. It makes him wonder if they should look into other stuff. Maybe there's some toys that . . . a football flies into his lap, breaking his reverie.

Two boys are staring at him, waving their arms in the air. Their mother stands behind. Thick dark hair, windswept. Sunglasses and a long brown wool coat, running shoes and sweatpants. Hands thrust deep in her pockets. She looks cold, eager to be home, unfriendly.

"You've got quite an aim there," Dominic says, standing up, kicking the ball to them.

The ball rolls with perfect precision toward the taller boy.

"What are you doing out here?" the boy asks, stepping closer.

Thinking about a humongous bottle of lube my wife brought home? Dominic hesitates, and almost begins to laugh. The boys wait.

Their mother does too. He has the sense this family will stare him down until he answers. Why is he wavering? He has nothing to prove.

"I have no idea what I'm doing with my life," he admits, lacing his fingers together.

"Miserable when that happens, isn't it?" the mother says.

She flashes him a brief smile and her unfriendly demeanor vanishes. He opens his mouth, but before he can answer another question flies in.

"Do you want to play with us?" the younger boy asks earnestly.

Surprised, Dominic locks eyes with their mother.

She snorts derisively. "We don't bite. Promise."

He shrugs. "Shouldn't you be teaching them *not* to be so nice to strangers?"

She doesn't blink. "You look innocent enough."

That makes him smile. He falls into step with her.

"Lucinda, by the way."

"Dominic."

He extends a hand, but she tut-tuts about formalities. They walk across Wimbledon Common. The boys kick the ball to him, or at least they try to, the younger one's aim especially wobbly, and Dominic returns it. Eventually, the boys lose interest and sprint ahead. Occasionally, their mother yells at them (their names are Oscar and Cody) to slow down.

"What's got you down, then?" she asks, removing her sunglasses and staring.

Her eyes are black-brown, hard to read. She raises an eyebrow, waits impatiently.

"I messed up badly," he admits in a low and steady tone.

"How exactly?" she asks, one eye on the boys.

She radiates an innate confidence even as she is silent, waiting for him to answer. He wavers, not sure he wants to tell her the entire humiliating tale, but he'll never see this woman again. Why not? Besides, it's a relief to talk, to share what went down—or more accurately, what didn't—with Roxie. He chose the right audience.

"These things happen," she says in an offhand way.

Lucinda is sharp, intelligent, sparing with her words. She's unlike anyone he knows. Maybe that's why he keeps talking to her, not questioning where they're going until they reach a Victorian home with a large gray door. Definitely wealthy, he thinks, staring at the tall gabled home. Lucinda is fishing around in her handbag for keys.

"Faster!" Oscar wails, hopping from foot to foot.

"Hold it in," she implores.

Dominic laughs as the door flies open and Oscar darts in.

"I hope he makes it in time," Dominic says, taking a step back. "Lovely to meet you."

"Don't be daft," Lucinda snaps, beckoning him in. "Warm up for a second."

THE minute they are inside, Lucinda realizes she needs to jump on a work call. Foreign rights issue, she adds, as though this explains it. Cody bursts into tears.

"They're just hungry," Lucinda calls over her shoulder. "Crackers in the pantry. Cheese in the fridge."

Cody tugs on his hand and leads him into the pantry. Daphne would go mad for all this space, Dominic thinks, staring at the neat rows of spices and teas, dried pasta and rice. Cody admits he doesn't want cheese and crackers. Can they have boiled eggs? Dominic smiles, sure they can. He finds a saucepan, fills it with water. He boils the eggs and sets a timer. Oscar might want cheese and crackers, he thinks, opening the fridge door. He makes a mess, the cheese crumbles easily. He toasts bread. He spreads the margarine on thick, the way the boys like. He tells them it's better with jam, that's what he liked at their age.

"Do you like English muffins?" Cody asks, watching him move around the kitchen.

"Can I let you in on a secret?" Dominic responds in a serious tone.

The boys nod, their expressions grave. They lean in closer.

"I prefer crumpets," Dominic whispers.

Oscar frowns. "We don't eat crumpets in this household."

Household? He smiles at this and wonders if Oscar mimics his parents often. When lunch is ready, the boys dig in enthusiastically. They love boiled eggs, especially *these* boiled eggs, they tell him, and Dominic feels a swell of pride.

"What does your mum do?"

"She's a literary agent," Oscar says proudly.

"Maybe she can give me some tips," Dominic responds. "I'm working on a book."

Their eyes go wide. Their comments swoop in fast.

"Mummy can help you with it!"

"Mummy's the best."

Lucinda is back. She kisses the boys on their foreheads and asks if they like their new chef. Immediately, the boys inform her their new chef is actually a writer.

"Is that so?" Lucinda says, clicking the kettle on and asking if he wants tea.

He nods, presses the tips of his fingers into the dark grooves of the walnut table. He feels nervous. He's in the home of a literary agent, and now he's beginning to wonder if she *might* represent him. It's not too much of a stretch, is it?

"That's a new one," Lucinda says, a smile on her lips. "Writers using my kids to win me over."

His hands fly up in alarm. He's anxious to set the record straight.

"Not at all!" he sputters in earnest.

She laughs. "Kidding."

She takes her time making tea, and then she takes a seat across from him. She bites into a cracker. She picks at the cheese. She opens a packet of chocolate digestives, offers him one. He watches her movements, elegant and precise. She reminds him of a bird, all sinew and strength. She doesn't eat much. He wonders where her energy comes from.

The fact he's a guest kicks in and Dominic leaps up, clears the plates.

"We should keep him," Oscar informs his mother.

"Where? In a cage?" Dominic jokes as he stacks the dishwasher, pretending to look worried.

Oscar giggles in response.

"Can we watch cartoons?" Cody asks, pulling on her sleeve.

"Just one."

The boys whoop in triumph. They scuttle away like beetles.

Lucinda offers Dominic an amused look.

"Were you like that at their age?"

He scratches an imaginary itch by his left shoulder. Staring at her, he wonders how on earth to answer.

THROUGHOUT his childhood Dominic felt adrift, certain of one fact: he did not belong. Not with his father who left without warning. *He'll come crawling back,* his mother shouted at the door. He returned two evenings later, with several soft leather suitcases. He packed with painstaking precision, rolling shirts, socks, and boxers into neat bundles. As he marched toward the Volvo, Dominic's mum ran behind, hurling insults across the lawn. *Does that whore give good blow jobs?* Curtains twitched. Faces appeared in windows as the car sped away.

The house grew still and quiet. Silence crept like thickening mist. It was a silence that defined his mother. She withdrew into it, rarely leaving home. She was sedate, day and night spent on the sofa. Empty bottles lined the kitchen. The television was almost always on. She had no interest in Dominic, his schoolwork. He had always been closer to his dad, but now they only spoke twice a year: his birthday and Christmas. He looked forward to it, but inevitably, the conversation was overwhelming. For one, they *didn't* connect. His mind went blank in a fit of nerves and excitement. The conversation felt stilted, belabored. Later, he picked their conversation apart, reliving the awkward pauses and heavy sighs, the noises in the background: a kettle boiling, the high-pitched screams of a newborn.

A postcard arrived from Florida. Blue skies. Palm trees. Scrawled on the back, a message so short it was insulting. *Dominic, having a great time and sending you love, from Dad.* Dominic burst into tears. His father never took *them* on holidays. His mother snatched the postcard and tore it into tiny pieces. Later, when she was asleep, he pieced it back together using tape and hid it, a token of his father he must keep.

Although he was young, Dominic understood they were running out of money. His uniform didn't fit. The house was falling apart. He avoided the mice gathered in the basement. He leapt over the caved in part of the staircase. In a slurred voice, she blamed his father. *He left me this death trap.* The universe was against her, she said another time. But was it the universe's fault when he found her lying on the landing in a pool of vomit? Dominic shook her frantically until one filmy eye popped open, rolling idly, unwilling to focus. Terrified, he screamed. When she responded, her voice was a deep croak. *Leave me alone, you fucker.*

She surprised him when she lost forty pounds and befriended a musician. Fabrizio was Italian. Dark eyes, thick moustache. He invited his friends over, and Dominic was a useful accessory. *Open this, will you? Run and get Mummy ice.* Dominic stayed up late, listening to the pitch and swell of their laughter. Strangers filled the home, sleep-

ing on armchairs and sofas. Fabrizio rose at noon to make coffee. He
drank it thick like syrup, dark as the night. He smoked like a chimney
and sang like an angel but his real talent was the cello. He played in an
orchestra that traveled across Europe and America. Dominic closed
his eyes and smiled as Fabrizio described San Francisco. Cable cars
running down perilously steep hills. An orange-red bridge that glim-
mered in the sun. Why didn't Fabrizio travel with the orchestra anymore? It was an innocent question, but Fabrizio snapped in response.

Dominic envied his passion and talents. When he played, his body
grew charged with purpose, his fingers moving in precise ways, eliciting exquisite sounds. His dark eyes turned somber, his face light
and wondrous, ethereally beautiful. Fabrizio played as though the
cello were an extension of his body. The music was sorrowful and
lonely, reminding Dominic of his darkest, most melancholy moments. It stirred in him emotions that were heavy, complicated. Fabrizio should play all the time. The drinking and dancing, the women
were a distraction. The music mattered most. It was otherworldly, a
reprieve from ordinary life. Dominic wished he had a purpose too.
He asked if Fabrizio might teach him. Fabrizio clapped his hands,
delighted by the prospect of a protégé.

The lessons were a disaster, short-lived and tearful. Dominic had
no understanding of the Italian words flung at him, but he understood Fabrizio's temper was steadily worsening. His bruises were
slate-colored. They gave up on music lessons, but Fabrizio's anger
was an open valve, impossible to seal. Dominic was getting changed
for swimming class when a teacher pulled him aside. Can you explain this, the teacher said, tapping his right shoulder lightly. His
skin was a tapestry of browns and purples. He didn't remember much
about the rest of that day, except his dad picking him up from school.
He looked nothing like the man he remembered. His beard had vanished. Dark suit, paisley tie, gold-rimmed glasses, polished leather
loafers.

"What happened to the Volvo?" Dominic asked in the car park.

His father let out a short, sharp laugh.

"Sold it for the price of a ham sandwich."

Dominic ran his fingers over the soft leather. He was used to the school bus, the assault of farts from his schoolmates. The silence unnerved him.

"Do you still go to Florida?" he asked finally.

"Florida?" his father asked in a confused tone.

"That postcard you sent."

He knew exactly which drawer it still sat in, taped together.

"I got burnt to a crisp and never went back," his dad responded with a hearty chuckle.

His father's laughter stopped as they pulled into the driveway. Dominic saw it all through his eyes. The uncut grass. The unopened mail. The peeling wallpaper and stained walls. The damp patches on the ceiling. The sink overflowing with dirty dishes. Dominic felt ashamed, an accomplice to this filth. His father let out a low whistle.

"Pack some things. We'll come back for more."

Nervous, he blurted out: "Where is she?"

His father's expression softened.

"The school called some people they know who are chatting to her."

"Nice people?"

His dad paused. "People who can help."

He packed in silence while his father stood on the landing. He was nudging the carpet with his polished shoe, peering at the spot where Dominic found her in a pool of vomit.

"I didn't realize it got like this, Dom."

Dominic enjoyed seeing his unease. He had been miserable for years. At last, his misery could attach itself to someone else. When they stopped for roadside burgers and fries, his dad tried to explain himself.

"I left her the house with most of the mortgage paid off. She had a good job back then."

Dominic watched his dad wipe his mouth with a napkin. Staring at the smear of grease, Dominic felt his stomach flip. Was *he* meant to have helped her keep up the mortgage payments?

"I considered custody," his father continued, "but I'd already hurt her. If I took you too, I'd push her over the edge. But she went there anyway. What a mess. What a big old mess."

It was late by the time they pulled up outside wrought iron gates that required a pin code. Peering through the darkness, he saw a circular driveway, a red brick house, navy door, gold knocker.

"I know what you're thinking," his father said, rolling the car forward as the gates opened. "Sadie, as the crude expression goes, comes from money. She bought this place and it's one of the reasons we haven't got married. Her money would officially become my money and, knowing your mum, she'd fight for it to become *her* money."

Dominic wasn't sure where this was headed, but he'd never heard the word money so many times in one breath. His dad looked nervous and he wasn't sure why.

"Don't worry," his dad continued. "I don't live *off* Sadie. I'm doing well for myself. As men, we need to work hard and be high earners, you know?"

Dominic appreciated the collective "we." They were a unit, buddies.

"I get it," he lied.

"Good! So, you'll also get that we need to see how this goes. Sadie and the girls . . . well, they don't really know you. We have to see how they adjust. But if you keep to yourself . . . then everything should be fine."

Dominic nodded numbly, wanting to ask why, exactly, they didn't know him. He unclicked his seatbelt and followed his dad inside. The house was quiet, it smelt of potpourris. Sadie was in the kitchen, unloading the dishwasher. Her dark hair was hidden behind a headscarf. She turned and their eyes locked. She paused a beat too long before smiling. Dominic read into her hesitation. He did not belong here either.

—

"I got a job!" Dominic tells Daphne as she arrives home.

She stops in her tracks, drops her tote to the ground. It lands on its side, and a solitary orange rolls out.

"Really?" she says, stunned. "What kind of job?"

He grins. "Dropping these two kids off at school and doing the end of day pickup. Kicking a football around with them, that kind of thing."

"Oh!" she says in a surprised tone. "So this isn't one of the jobs you applied for online?"

She unbuttons her coat and hangs it up in the hallway on a peg.

"No. Totally new thing! It just happened an hour ago!"

"I'm not following exactly," she grins. "Tell me everything."

She carries her tote into the kitchen. Dominic tells her about his afternoon in the park while she unpacks. She forgot the onions, she realizes and briefly, she considers sending Dominic to the supermarket. He has a lot of energy he could do with burning off. But she's not completely sure she follows this new job.

"So it's . . . looking after two children?"

"Amazing kids," he says, nodding his head eagerly. "Super cute, you'd love them."

Daphne had a bad day in the office, her laptop crashed mid-article. Their temperaments are mismatched. His energy is off the charts.

"And their mother is . . . ?" she asks a little tersely.

"A literary agent!" he says with childlike enthusiasm.

She stills, beginning to understand his excitement. "That's pretty cool. Do you think you'll show her your work?"

Dominic nods his head. "That's the plan. I mean . . . she hasn't offered yet, but I think I could ask her to review it in time, once we've built a working relationship. Right?"

She retrieves a Granny Smith from her tote and throws it. He raises an arm, catches. "So that's the goal here? Help out with the kids and show her your work?"

"Sort of." He takes an enormous bite, grinning. "She wants me to read her manuscripts too! The slush pile, you know?"

"Oh?" she says, feeling in the dark again. "It's a childcare role and also a . . . literary assistant?"

"Bit of both." He shrugs nonchalantly. "Just to tide me over. Some extra cash. And I'll be out of the flat! I'll be doing something!"

She scratches her forehead. She doesn't have the mental capacity to figure out *why* this job sounds strange. She feels a mood brewing. It's probably over forgetting onions or her super frustrating day. She needs a second to decompress. But he has a point, getting out of the flat and being productive will do him good.

"I'm happy for you, honey."

She's starting on dinner when she calls out to him.

"Is this woman married?"

Dominic pops his head around the doorway, looking nonplussed. "I don't know. I didn't ask."

She nods slowly. Of course he didn't.

—

DOMINIC walks Oscar and Cody to school, holding their hands. They marvel at the snow, and the sky, bright blue and still. Reunited each afternoon, they cling to him at the school gates. They tell him about their days, the highs and lows, the boring parts too. He wants to know who received best-student-of-the-week (not Sophie again!) and whose birthday it was and who got a minus for talking in class and which books they chose during Reading Hour and who called in sick. He spent five years in an office. What a waste, he could have been doing this.

—

ASH wants to know how the lube is going. He says this on the phone. On her *work* line. Which he has a habit of calling as he makes his first coffee of the day. His morning begins approximately three hours after hers.

Daphne stands up. She glances around the sleepy office before responding.

"It's a giant leap forward," she whispers down the phone.

"Does that mean it made you . . . ?"

"No."

"No?"

"But it was . . . easier."

"Easier to what?"

She smiles. Under her breath, she responds: "Lie back and think of England."

He laughs.

"I don't think you should settle for easier, love."

"It was *better*."

Distinctly better. It felt sexy too. The lube made everything feel different, even her curves. They rubbed some of it onto her chest and she swears, she looked like a porn star. It's the first time she's felt *that* way. But something else happened. She leans back in her chair, checking the row behind her cubicle.

"It led to some conversations," she whispers, "about what *else* we could be doing."

"You mean like him making you come for a change?"

She rolls her eyes even though he can't see.

"We did some online shopping."

His voice grows interested.

"Find anything good?"

"It vibrates."

"That's a great start," he's saying.

"And it goes around him."

"Do we like it?"

It made her orgasm in less than three minutes.

She pauses, smiling. "It might just be the best thing ever."

Ash laughs so loudly down the line that she swears she could place the handset in her desk drawer and still hear his cackles.

SATURDAY, late afternoon. Hours have passed. She hears rain on the window, its relentless patter. The hum of traffic. The curtains are drawn. Their bedroom is a dark cocoon. Sweat cools on her back. Dominic's hand is between her thighs. His soft breaths flutter against her skin.

"A doctor fantasy, huh? Should I invest in a white coat?"

She smiles. "Sure, that could be fun . . . anything I can get for you?"

"Not yet," he admits, holding her gaze, "but I'll have a think, and let you know."

A sleepy silence fills the room, one they are both comfortable with.

"What's she like?" Daphne asks finally, turning onto her stomach.

"Who?"

"Lucinda."

He smiles.

"Cold. Intelligent. Fierce. Not one for small talk." His hand grazes her lower back. He kisses her shoulder, whispers against her skin. "Intimidating as hell."

Dominic has told her snippets. She's married, but he's often overseas on business.

"Do you think they still have sex?"

"Who knows," he says, kissing her nose. His hand creeps around her thigh. "Definitely not as much as us."

"Well, that's a recent development for us."

"A very good one."

"Today's been a marathon," she admits with a self-satisfied sigh.

"We might need more batteries."

Good point. She stares at the vibrating cock ring. It's a ghastly shade of bright pink. Is it greedy, she thinks slowly, to want to orgasm naturally, without the help of this battery-operated device? If she wants Dominic to make her orgasm, then she needs to know what makes her orgasm. She is so inexperienced in this field; there must be books. She rolls onto her back. Immediately, his hand is on her breast. He circles her nipple lightly. His skin glistens, she supposes hers does too. They stink of sex. It hangs in the room, distinctive, pungent.

"I want to meet her."

"You will, crumb cake."

She smiles to herself; that's an old nickname. She's always found it cute. "If I'm a crumb cake, what's she?"

Without missing a beat, he responds.

"Iceberg lettuce."

—

NATURE walks and trumpet practice and parent/teacher conferences and concerts and birthday parties. Dominic doesn't need to attend it all, but he does. It surprises him, how thrilling they are, these two little people who rely on him completely. He talks to the other parents and teachers. Within weeks he's part of their tight-knit community. When the football coach goes down with mono, he doesn't hesitate. It's a no-brainer.

—

"EVERY Saturday?" Daphne repeats, stunned. "You're coaching football *every* Saturday?"

"No," he corrects her. "Coaching is on Tuesdays, matches are on Saturdays. I can't miss either, obviously."

Daphne feels herself pout.

"For how long?"

"Only until the school year ends."

"But it's only February!" she yelps.

"It's *almost* March."

She frowns. "Aren't those jobs meant for other teachers? Or a parent?"

Silence. Daphne gets the sense he volunteered before anyone else could.

"I'm practically one of the parents at this point."

Does he not see how strange that is?

"I just . . . I worry this job's taking over your life a bit."

He sighs. "It's fine."

"It worries me," she admits, taking his hand, pulling him onto the sofa. "What about boundaries? You're more of a father to those boys than their real dad."

He pulls an annoyed face. "It's not my fault Zach's always gone."

"No," she concedes, "but when I factor in the estranged relationship with your dad it makes me think . . ."

"What?"

She winces. "That maybe you're trying to give these boys . . . the childhood you wish you'd had?"

"No!" he insists.

"I thought the whole point of this job was that it's temporary," Daphne continues carefully. "Low stakes, a little money coming in, get her thoughts on your novel. But from where I'm sitting, this temporary job is taking over your life, and you haven't even shown her your writing yet."

He shakes his head. "I'm trying not to overthink it. Right now . . . I don't know, I'm fulfilled and finally doing a job that means something. And I'll show her my writing when the timing feels right."

"I didn't realize . . . that's great," she says, her eyes softening. "I mean it, honey. I'm happy for you."

—

Dominic arrives early. He locks his bike, wipes his hands against his jacket. Approaching the front door, he hears Oscar's incessant chatter and smiles.

"They're all yours," Lucinda says.

She's speaking on a panel. She's wearing deep red lipstick, navy trousers, a white shirt. She's eating toast and he can't help himself.

"I thought it was a breakfast event?"

"I'm there to talk about the world of literary agents," she says, shrugging on her navy jacket, throwing him an exasperated look. "Not for the poached egg scene."

A black car draws up, beeps twice. Dominic flattens himself against the wall as she sweeps past. He watches her long strides. It's taken time to establish a rapport. Longer to get used to her cutting remarks. To not take them personally, or at least not *too* personally.

He turns around and almost steps on Cody.

"How's Mr. Cody?"

Cody giggles at the formal prefix. He runs to the sofa, buries his face between the cushions, and squeals in delight. Cody might be charmed by him, but Oscar makes Dominic work harder for his attention. He's watching cartoons, the volume turned up high.

"Daddy's coming home tomorrow," Cody says, smiling up at him.

"Great," Dominic lies.

That explains Lucinda's mood. Whenever Zach returns, they bicker and Lucinda's voice goes high and scratchy. She could probably use a hug, but he suspects she'd punch him if he so much as tried.

It's a good day. After taking the boys to school, he finishes a promising manuscript. He writes a two-page summary and takes the stairs, two at a time. Her office is perched at the top of the house. It's a sacred space, free from children, meticulously tidy. He leaves the manuscript and notes on her desk. He takes a seat in her chair and tries to picture the world through her eyes. All that unbridled confidence. The world hers to take. He looks at his watch; time to pick the boys up. The walk to school is frigid, and he half considers bundling them into an Uber to get home. Cody tugs on his hand.

"Can we draw later?" he asks, gazing up intently.

Dominic smiles. "Sure."

At home, he pulls out crayons and paper and they draw each other. Dominic points out his nose looks larger on paper than in reality. Oscar retorts that this is his artistic impression. Cody ignores the task and draws a picture of his family, stickmen style.

"That's great, Cody!" Dominic remarks, peering over his shoulder.

There's Lucinda, in green, wearing a triangular-shaped dress. Cody and Oscar are in black, the same height, wishful thinking on Cody's part. And there's Zach, in red. He looks like a hunchback.

Cody offers it to Dominic. "Take it home."

Dominic smiles. "But it's your family. We can pin it to your fridge."

"Cody's drawn you. Look," Oscar says, pointing, "that's your backpack."

He looks more closely. The hunchback squiggle is actually his red backpack.

"That's very sweet of you," he says, taking the drawing. He'll show it to Daphne later. "And if I bought a green backpack, would you draw me as a green stickman?"

"No. You're red because we love you," Cody explains matter-of-factly.

Dominic stares, at a loss for words. He wonders if it can be true. He's only known them a couple of months. The boys reach for more paper, they fight over the special silver pen. He considers what Daphne said: *Are you trying to give these boys the childhood you wish you'd had?* He denied it vehemently but he sees it now. That's exactly what he's doing.

"Maybe you should draw some pictures of Daddy," he says carefully.

—

For his birthday this year, they invite Mark and Simon—Dominic's closest friends from boarding school—over for dinner. Daphne stands in the kitchen making his favorite: fish pie. Salmon and haddock, scallops and shrimp, shallots and leeks. It's a mash-up of a few recipes. Gordon Ramsay. Jamie Oliver. Instead of potatoes, she uses filo pastry. It's a rich and creamy dish. She pairs it with a rocket salad: radishes, balsamic vinegar, cracked black pepper.

The boys are huddled on the narrow balcony off their bedroom, drinking beer. She joins them with a glass of Viognier, standing in the doorway, one foot resting on the other. Dominic is telling them about his free personal training session at the gym.

"So much for building up my strength," he says with a wince. "Can barely move today."

The boys poke fun at him. Dominic encourages them. Smiling, Daphne wonders if every only child does this? Welcomes attention in all its forms, including constant ribbing? Mark tells them about a property he's interested in buying. He works in investment banking, and his idea of affordable is vastly different from her own. A two-bedroom duplex in Chelsea with a roof terrace.

"The asking is 3.85 million," Mark shares casually. "Which

sounds like a lot, but that location is only going up in value. It's a solid investment."

Daphne can't bring herself to respond. Mark is in a button-down white shirt. Dark navy suit trousers. A fleece vest stamped with his company's logo. She finds it strange that he can afford any clothes he wants, but he chooses the company uniform. Even at the weekends, he brings out that silly fleece vest. She doesn't *mind* Mark, he's not a terrible person, he's just lacking in self-awareness at times. Simon is dressed more casually. Gray denim jeans. White t-shirt. Simon is a programmer. He designs video games in his spare time. Simon tells them about his recent conversation with a recruiter. There's a startup he might join. The stock options alone would make him a fortune if the IPO happens.

"Nobody wants to go to Google or Apple anymore," Simon tells them. "You've got to get in early. First hundred employees. To make the equity they put on the table worth it."

Daphne suggests they move inside. She's decorated the living room with balloons and streamers. Dominic laughs appreciatively and pulls her in for a kiss.

"Are you two thinking of buying soon?" Mark asks as they take their seats.

Daphne smiles humorlessly as she pulls wine from the fridge and fills their glasses. She makes a meager salary at the law journal and their shared income has dipped drastically since Dominic changed jobs. It's unlikely they'll be able to afford to renew their lease, let alone buy. Not that she minds. Dominic pushed for Putney: close to his friends. She'd happily move to a different part of London like Islington, or Tufnell Park.

"I don't think so," she says. "The deposit alone on most places is a fortune."

Mark chews thoughtfully. "Fair enough."

She locks eyes with Dominic. He looks tense. Probably because his new job doesn't come with a big salary or the promise of an IPO.

"Dominic actually got a new job recently."

"What?" Mark places his cutlery down, slaps Dominic on the back. "Damn, we should grab some champagne! What kind of job? Where?"

"In Wimbledon."

Mark looks confused. "Which ad agencies are down there?"

"No, it's with a family."

"Like a family-run business?"

Dominic wipes his mouth with his napkin. "No, it's childcare. I'm taking care of these two boys . . . Oscar and Cody. And reading manuscripts for their mum, a literary agent."

She's come around on the job, but it's gratifying to see that at first blush, she's not the only one who finds the details confusing. She sits back in her seat, takes another sip of wine.

"I know it's a huge change from the agency," Dominic admits, glancing around, assessing their reactions, "but it feels right."

"He's even signed up to coach the school football team," Daphne chimes in.

Mark looks perturbed. Notably, there's no more suggestion of champagne. Gradually, their conversation moves on to Daphne's job and mutual friends. Later, Mark returns to Dominic's new job as they discuss a trip to Cornwall this summer.

"Will Mary Poppins be allowed the time off?"

Mark's tone is more careless than snide, but Dominic sputters.

"You can't even be nice to me on my birthday?" he jokes affably.

"I was kidding."

She doubts it and jumps in. "That 'joke' says a lot more about you than about Dom finding a job he loves."

Silence. Nobody knows where to look.

"I didn't mean anything by it," Mark says, his voice flat and indignant.

Simon attempts to diffuse the tension by waxing lyrical about her cooking. Daphne nods and starts to clear the plates. Dominic jumps up and helps. She feels his hand squeezing hers as they reach the sink. They lock eyes, and Dominic blows her a kiss.

—

LUCINDA is home when Dominic and the boys return from school. She's standing on the staircase, removing a pair of tights. He gapes at her bare legs. Smooth and toned. It's not about her legs, he reminds himself, it's that she's never home early. She has a headache, she admits in a dispirited tone, pointing to the top of the house. He watches her dainty ascent and glances at his watch. He needs to be out of here in two hours for a date with Daphne. Close to the time he's meant to leave, he texts Lucinda asking how she's feeling. When Lucinda doesn't reply, he calls Daphne.

"Oh," Daphne says, sounding deflated. "We could go to a later showing?"

"I've no idea when she's coming down," he whispers.

"That's not okay for her to do that to you," Daphne responds firmly.

"I know," he admits, unsure of what to do. "How about we try for tomorrow night instead?"

Daphne agrees, but he hears the frown in her voice. Dominic makes the boys chicken nuggets with sweetcorn. He switches on the radio and as a classical tune—"The Blue Danube"—floats on, he gathers Cody in his arms, waltzing him around the kitchen island. Cody giggles uncontrollably.

"Are you ready for haute cuisine?" Dominic asks, pulling nuggets from the oven.

The boys' faces are blank. Dominic explains what he meant.

"What else is ort?" Cody asks.

"Haute," he repeats slowly.

"Haute."

"Ask your mum for Lobster Thermidor."

"Lobster?" Oscar pulls a face. "That's like eating Sebastian."

"Sebastian?"

"From *The Little Mermaid,*" the boys say in unison.

They watched that film last week. And only about fifty times before that.

"Hmm," Dominic responds, "I thought Sebastian was a crab?"

There is a lengthy debate about the different forms of crustaceans, ultimately resolved by Google. He takes them upstairs for a bath, and bedtime stories.

"Having fun?" Lucinda observes from the doorway.

She's showered, her hair is wet. Barefoot, she's wearing dark denim jeans, a cream sweater rolled to the elbows. Her eyes are more intense, mascara darkening her heavy lashes. Kissing the boys goodnight, she floats downstairs. Daphne's comment rings in his ears. *That's not okay.* If Lucinda is feeling better, shouldn't *she* take over the bedtime routine? He lets the thought go. Cody is debating the merits of an under-the-ocean theme for his next birthday party, a mere seven months away, as Dominic tucks them into their twin beds. Oscar's side of the room is neat whereas Cody's is a war zone. It's a point of contention, but Dominic envies the boys these arguments; he always wanted a brother.

He finds Lucinda downstairs, reading his two-page summary of a manuscript, glass of wine in hand. She nods, pleased by his observations. Their partnership is working. She's taught Dominic her tastes, the books she wants to represent and why. Dominic might love a manuscript. Still, he'll understand unequivocally why it's not right for Lucinda.

"I like the way you've put this together."

"Good."

He's learned brevity is best.

"Hungry?" she asks.

Dominic glances at his watch. It's eight o'clock.

"Sure."

Often, she's racing to work or returning home in a fiendishly bad mood. She rarely slows down, and he's curious to see this side of her.

"How's the headache?"

No answer. She's in the kitchen, opening cupboards impatiently. It sounds like a demolition project in there; he shouts this out and she chuckles in response. She returns with a bottle of wine. Red, unopened. A blend, she tells him, predominantly Mourvèdre. She forgets he's in his twenties, he informs her, any wine will do. This gets a smile. He helps her with the cheeseboard. Manchego. Stilton. Camembert. Olives. Cornichons.

She opens the wine, slipping it between her narrow thighs. A firm tug, a pleasant pop. It's a generous pour. This doesn't surprise him in the least. He sees how much she drinks whenever he glances in the recycling bin. He feels like a spy clocking these details, adding them to the sketch in his mind of a household he doesn't inhabit. The wine relaxes her. Her movements are slower, deliberate. The contours of her face soften. She touches the nape of her neck. She lifts her thick hair, holding it up and releasing it, holding it up again.

"I got a call from Jenny tonight," Lucinda begins.

Jenny has a son in Oscar's class. Dominic chats to her at the school gates.

"Jenny asked me," Lucinda continues with a smile, "where can I get a Dominic?"

He isn't immune to her compliments. He smiles slowly. He takes an olive, bites down hard. Bitter and wet, juicy. Suddenly ravenous, he takes another.

"And it's not lost on me how much you do for us, and the school.

Looking after the boys, reading manuscripts, staying late, coaching football, matches on Saturdays. It's a substantial time commitment, a bigger job than the one I offered you. I hope Daphne doesn't mind."

Of course she minds, but Daphne would mind even *more* if he revealed that.

"It's fine," he reassures her. "But a little warning whenever you need me to stay late would be a good thing."

There, he thinks proudly. He said it, he set up boundaries! Daphne will be pleased.

"The boys are happy," Lucinda reflects, her voice a low murmur. She barely seems to have registered his words. "They adore you."

"I adore them too," he admits.

She's close enough that he sees the individual strands of her hair. Subtle traces of gray by the roots. By the weekend, it will have vanished. Lovely hair, he is thinking when she sobs softly, unexpectedly. It's alarming! She's not one for displays of vulnerability. She twists away, embarrassed. His mind races. Was her headache an excuse? Is something terrible happening to her at work or with Zach? Where *is* he anyway?

"Are you all right?" he asks in a desperate tone.

She dabs her eyes. She's dainty in everything she does, even crying.

"We all need you so much," she admits hoarsely. "It scares me."

Her face is blotchy. She's crying over *him*, he thinks incredulously? He moves to comfort her. He strokes her back. Touching her, he feels how frail she is, there is barely any flesh to her.

"Don't worry," he says in a soothing tone. "I'm not going anywhere."

She doesn't respond right away. When she does, it's a whisper he barely makes out.

"I need you."

And then, her mouth is on his. He makes a muffled noise, a low

moan. She's more experienced, he can taste it. Just as he can taste
how inevitable this moment was. Her hands pounce playfully, like a
kitten with string. Except the string is his chest, thighs, shoulders.
Their clothes scatter and she is taking him by the hand, leading him
up the stairs, past where the boys sleep. He never steps into her bedroom. He stares up at the large bay windows, the enormous mirror
above the fireplace, the bed. He catches a glimpse of their silhouettes.

"I've thought about this since the first day we met," she admits,
climbing onto the bed.

He is surprised by this. He feels a jolt of pride. *See,* he tells himself, *you* are *attractive.*

"In the park?"

"Telling me about your childhood. I wanted to kiss you."

"Really?" he says unsteadily, not sure what to make of that.

Lucinda lies against the sheets. Reminded of Roxie, he hesitates.
He braces for rejection, but her hand curls around him possessively.
She arches her back. He knows her body, but not like this. Somewhere in his brain, he acknowledges this is a bad idea—she is his boss,
after all—but curiosity wins. Daphne has been his only experience
up until this point. Daphne, a fast-fading memory as he nestles between Lucinda's thighs. She tastes of salt and cream, a spice he cannot
define. He wants to linger here, in the most intimate part of her.
Lucinda orgasms easily. Maybe he can kid himself he's a decent lover.
The truth is, he followed her incredibly detailed, precise instructions. Where to touch her and how much pressure to apply and when
to switch from tongue to finger and back again. Her tone, surprisingly calm, reveals countless lovers before him, offered identical orders. Lucinda knows how to pleasure him too. She understands the
best angles to deploy, especially as she sits astride him, clenching her
pelvic muscles in masterful ways. Sure, sex has always been good.
Never *this* good, he thinks. Sprawled on her bed, he is suddenly ex-

hausted. He notices the wind rattling against the panes. The bay windows are closed, the blinds raised. His eyelids are heavy, deliciously indolent. He's almost asleep when he feels Lucinda's hand on his waist.

"I'm thinking of taking the boys to Corsica. Once work calms down. Renting a villa. If not this year, then next. Anyway, you should come."

"Mmm, I'd love that," he murmurs.

"Good," she says, "we can fuck like rabbits."

Daphne. His eyes spring open.

"I can't," he says tersely.

"Why not?"

He feels her glaring in the dark.

"Daphne and I have an agreement."

Turning to face her, he outlines the rules of the Freedom Clause. He emphasizes that it is just one night a year, that to sleep with her again would be a clear violation.

"I see," she says slowly. "Do you and Daphne still have sex?"

He hears it in her voice, the competitive edge. She wants to be a defining moment in his sexual journey. He swallows, unsure of how to respond. He doesn't like discussing Daphne while they are in bed together. It feels wrong, disrespectful to his wife. But he answers honestly.

"Yes, quite a bit lately."

It's been the best surprise, their sexual reawakening. He props himself up on one elbow and stares out of the window. He pictures his bike ride home, locking up, walking into their flat. Will Daphne know? She's intuitive . . . perhaps he should shower here?

"One night off a year?" he hears Lucinda asking.

He nods his head. Lucinda is bold and opinionated. He waits for her to criticize their marriage, their agreement, to inform him of all the ways it makes no sense. Her face is close, her smile enormous, it eclipses her face. Her fingers dance down his arm, over his elbow.

"Then we should make the most of tonight."

—

Confessions of a Highly Emotional Cook:

A seasonally inappropriate Warm and Wintry Lamb Stew
that gets better with age (just like us)

I'm drinking red wine from a mug (it was closer in reach than the glasses), and feeling a bit low and sorry for myself tonight (I did warn you I'm an *emotional* cook). A few reasons, I think. I always feel strange on those last few days of my cycle, right before my period. And it doesn't help that it's gone cold again. I'm making a wintry classic: lamb stew. This isn't what I thought I'd be doing tonight, but my husband has to work late so the film we planned to see can wait. I'll admit I was excited to have a date night, but there's also something comforting about hunkering down in the cold and making a meal out of items plucked from the far reaches of your cupboards and your freezer. And what I enjoy about a stew is that the flavors intensify and taste even better on day two (here's hoping my date night plans for tomorrow turn out better too). And who doesn't love leftovers? Is now the time to debate whether cold pizza the next morning is better? Let me know your thoughts. Speaking of you, the reader, I've been keeping an eye on you. I now have a whopping 32 subscribers. Thank you whoever you are. I don't know how you found me, but I'm so glad you did.

A SEASONALLY INAPPROPRIATE
WARM AND WINTRY LAMB STEW
THAT GETS BETTER WITH AGE (JUST LIKE US)

Feeds: eight (or: two people for four nights)

Ingredients:
- 1 kilo boneless lamb shoulder, trimmed and cut into 1 ½-inch cubes (and if cutting it feels intimidating, ask your butcher or supermarket for help)
- 3 tablespoons extra virgin olive oil
- 2 tablespoons red wine vinegar
- 1 cup red wine
- 3 ½ cups beef broth
- 1 large cabbage cored and shredded—use about 4 cups
- 1 medium onion, diced
- 1 leek, cut into ¼-inch rounds
- 5 garlic cloves, minced
- ¼ cup chopped fresh parsley or coriander
- 3 medium carrots, peeled and cut into ¼-inch rounds
- 2 potatoes, peeled and cut into 2-inch chunks
- 1 large can of chopped tomatoes
- 2 ½ teaspoons smoked paprika
- ¼ teaspoon freshly ground pepper
- 2 bay leaves
- 1 teaspoon oregano
- 1 teaspoon thyme
- ½ teaspoon red pepper flakes
- 2 teaspoons salt

Method:

1. Choose a large pot or Dutch oven (if you don't have one, and you can afford to splash out, please consider treating yourself. My Dutch oven was a generous present from a friend and it makes me ridiculously happy) and heat oil in it over a medium-high heat. Reflect on the word *choose*. Is it a choice your husband is making to work late? Because he used to do this an awful lot in his old job too.

2. In a large bowl, season the lamb with salt and pepper and then cook in batches in the Dutch Oven until the lamb is brown all over. Compare the brownness of the lamb to your pale, sun-starved arms. Picture the summer. I know it doesn't feel like it's coming, but it will. One day. Transfer the lamb back to the bowl.

3. Drop the cabbage into the Dutch oven (as quickly as he dropped your movie night plans) and season it with ½ tea-spoons each of paprika, salt, and pepper. Cook for just a few minutes to infuse the seasoning and remove to a bowl.

4. Add onions, leek, garlic, carrots and potatoes, along with salt and pepper. Cook for about 5 minutes. Glance at the clock. Realize right now you should be inhaling popcorn and watch-ing trailers.

5. Add paprika, red pepper flakes, oregano, and thyme and stir for a minute. Okay, the movie would be starting right NOW. And the reviews are so good. And . . . girl, you have got to get better about rolling with the punches. Plans change. People move on. Focus on this delicious stew. Change into sweat-pants. See the night in as an indulgence.

6. Stir in tomatoes. Add wine, stock, vinegar, and bay leaves and bring to a boil. And now there's an open bottle of red wine, barely any of which has been used. You know what to do.

7. Add lamb to the Dutch Oven and reduce heat to a simmer. Cover pot and cook for about an hour. The next hour must be spent wisely. Tonight, for me at least, that means running a bath and reading the Ann Patchett I just picked up. But on other nights, I head straight to reality TV. Just as the housewives do, occasionally stir drama . . . I mean stew.

8. Add the cabbage and cook for another hour until the lamb is very tender. Repeat step 7 in terms of how you spend that hour. Yes, I did get back in the bath tub.

9. Discard bay leaves. Stir in beans and cook another 10 minutes to heat them through. Stir in parsley and adjust the seasoning, if necessary. Yes that was a LOT of steps and effort. Which is why you need to make enough for eight people and enjoy leftovers for four-ish days. By then, you will be SO sick of this stew you won't want to see it until it's actually winter again. That's a personal guarantee.

Yours,
    The Highly Emotional Cook

—

Asн was right, exercise gets easier with time. She experiments with barre and hot yoga, pilates and high intensity training. After each workout, she strips down. Catching sight of her pale skin in the mirror, she fights her negative thoughts. She is not ready to call herself a toned goddess, but she challenges herself to say something neutral: *this is what you look like and there's nothing to be ashamed of.*

—

"Do I look okay?"

What a question! She's wearing a little black dress, short enough,

at least when she's sitting, for him to admire her thighs, how toned
they are from running. Her face is sun kissed, her lashes heavy with
brown mascara, her lips the color of strawberry jam.

"You look *hot*."

She smiles at this. She stares out of the window as they pull out of
Paddington station. He's been dreading this party ever since the em-
bossed invitation arrived two months ago but he tries to look on the
bright side.

"It's nice to get out of London."

"Into the deep commuter belt of Berkshire," Daphne teases.

He pokes her ribs. It's not the home Dominic moved into when he
was fourteen. His dad and Sadie sold that place and relocated to another town. For the schools, his father explained at the time. That
must have been five years ago, the twins are seventeen now.

The train journey isn't long. They arrive at the station, hop in a
taxi and, ten minutes later, pull up outside a Tudor mansion. Tall and
wide, ornate. Linking arms, they walk toward the front door, gazing
appreciatively at the decorative half timbering, steeply pitched gable
roofs. The heavy walnut door opens and Sadie appears. She's in a
dark green dress, ankle length with a halter neckline. She looks fabulous: glossy dark hair, glowing complexion. A thick diamanté necklace rests against her collarbones. She ushers them in, hugs them
tightly. She compliments Daphne's dress, and tells Dominic just how
well he looks.

He thinks of Sadie as "the stepmother" but truthfully, outside of
their first introduction, she's always been effusively warm. She was
probably nervous as well, that first time they met, but he was too
young and self-involved to acknowledge it. He grew worse with
each passing year. Coming home from boarding school, Sadie would
tell him he was growing so tall and handsome and he would turn
away in embarrassment. He hated the attention. He remembers visi-

bly squirming, glaring at the woman who stole his dad away, but was Sadie *really* to blame?

"Party's in full swing," Sadie explains as she leads them through the parlor.

"Where do we put presents?"

"That's so kind!" She beams. "Over there's good."

She points to the long dining table. He adds their present to a growing pile.

The garden is enormous, sprawling. Magnificent trees. Trellises with creeping vines and blooming flowers. A large white tent at the far end, on the lower lawn.

"That's for later," Sadie explains, the sit-down dinner for fifty.

"Sounds fun," he responds.

Sadie smooths her hair back. She looks nervous.

"Everything okay?" Daphne asks.

"I really want today to go perfectly for him, you know?"

"It'll be great."

Sadie smiles gratefully. Most of the guests are older, fifties and sixties. Apart from Dominic and Daphne, and the twins. Emily and Pippa wave frantically, darting across the lawn. They're so tall! He barely recognizes them. They want to give him a tour of the house.

"In a minute," Dominic grins, glancing around for a drink. "Be right back."

He returns with two champagne flutes, offering one to Daphne. She's asking the twins which universities they're applying to.

Turning to Sadie, he asks: "How've you been?"

Sadie tips her head to one side thoughtfully.

"Good. You know, Em and Pip have been talking about seeing you all day."

"Really?" he asks, unable to hide his surprise. He glances over at the twins. Tall as beanpoles, their shoulders hunched forward. They look awkward. He suspects they hate their dresses, too formal, too much satin. He remembers that age, the feeling of deep discomfort. All he wanted was to fade into the background. "Can't imagine why," he adds with a small shrug.

"They've always looked up to you, the big brother in London."

"That's sweet," he responds instinctively.

Sadie looks a little crestfallen and he worries, did he say the wrong thing? Her hand flutters up to her neck, stroking the necklace. Her eyes dart toward him and he's struck again by the notion she's worried. Not just about the party.

"We've put you next to them for dinner."

"Great."

"Like I said, they're excited," she volunteers, looking at him strangely. "They're teenagers, you know. Never want to tell me anything. But you . . . I'm sure they'd love to talk to you about their lives . . . if you were interested, of course."

It feels loaded. The way she says this.

"Sure. I'd love to hear about it."

"That means a lot. To them . . . and to me."

Something clicks.

"Since when do the twins . . . you know, want to talk to me?"

Sadie raises an eyebrow comically.

"Since forever. They were always a little obsessed with you."

"Really?" he says, almost in disbelief.

"Oh my god!" She tips her head back and laughs. "They'd get so excited when you came home from school for the holidays."

He squints, casting his mind back.

"But you were always taking them out places when I was around."

"We had to drag them out to give you some peace and quiet. All you wanted at that age was to be left alone."

Huh, she picked up on that, and respected it. The funny thing is, he wanted to be left alone because it made him sad to see this perfect family unit that didn't include him. He was young, unsure of himself. He did a lot of skulking. It's a shame he hadn't seen it from another angle: two young girls who felt shunned by their older brother. A mother who didn't know what to do about the moody teenager she'd inherited. Was he really that oblivious?

"I'm sorry," he says in a low voice. "I was very . . . focused on myself back then." Hearing himself, he laughs. "That's code for *selfish,* by the way."

"It's okay." Sadie's hand rests on his arm. "You were just a kid. You went through a lot before you came to live with us."

They never discuss his mother. Maybe Sadie felt it wasn't her place, or a line she shouldn't cross. But acknowledging he went through a lot is monumental. His eyes fill with tears and he's grateful Sadie doesn't see it, she's walking away. Daphne does though. Turning, she raises an eyebrow at him. Dominic flashes her a quick smile of reassurance.

He notices his dad across the lawn. They look alike, he sees it now: the same tall, broad build. Blue eyes and wavy hair, although thankfully his hair isn't gray and thinning (yet). He hasn't told his dad about his new job. Dominic doesn't know why he's worried. It's not like his dad hasn't disappointed him repeatedly over the years. His father gives him a thunderous slap on the back. His friends are wearing navy jackets, khaki trousers. Dominic is introduced. Lots of handshakes, gruff hellos. After some small talk, he and his dad step out of the circle.

"Good to see you!"

"Wouldn't miss it for the world," Dominic responds chirpily.

That's not true, he and Daphne had lengthy conversations about whether to attend.

"All good with you?" his dad asks, nodding his head in a way that makes it difficult to respond with anything except an identical head nod.

"Great, yeah," Dominic finds himself saying. "You?"

His dad smiles breezily. "We're wonderful. We don't see you enough. Anything new?"

"Yes, actually," Dominic says uncertainly. "I left the ad job."

His dad slaps him on the back again.

"Ah, did another agency poach you? A step-up, I expect!"

Dominic shakes his head. "More of a step . . . in a different direction."

"Good, it's important to take risks in your career. I want to hear more . . ." he glances around the garden, "another time. There's a lot of people I should talk to. I'm sure you get it."

Dominic tries to swallow his disappointment. His dad's response is *technically* supportive, but it feels like the bare minimum of interest. More guests arrive. He watches his dad stride away. Notably, he looks more relaxed in the company of others.

Shaking his head, Dominic returns to Daphne and the twins. They're giggling over an Instagram account he's never heard of. The twins admit to being desperate to move to London.

"Can we visit? Please?"

"Sure. That would be great."

"It would," Daphne agrees, threading her fingers through his and smiling.

They sit down for dinner. They're finishing the main course when a microphone lets out a short, high-pitched sound. Groans. There's his dad, glass of champagne in hand. On a small raised platform. He begins by telling friends how much this moment means to him. To be turning sixty and surrounded by everyone he cares about. He lists out the groups: golf friends, church friends (this surprises Dominic, he doesn't remember his dad being religious), his colleagues from various jobs, and his family. Please don't, Dominic thinks, as his dad points at him.

"My son, Dominic, is here with his beautiful wife, Daphne. Dominic's been a Vice President at a leading ad agency in London but, like me, he's an ambitious one. He's starting an exciting new opportunity. I'm sure he'll be CEO any day now."

His dad claps, forcing others to follow his cue. Barely anyone in the audience knows Dominic. The claps sound resoundingly unenthusiastic. His dad moves on to talking about Emily: a master in Biology and a competitive presence on the lacrosse field! As for Pippa, she's the linguist, fluent in French and Spanish. Glancing at the twins, Dominic whispers:

"My new job is . . . looking after two kids. A glorified babysitter. I'm pretty sure CEO opportunities are limited."

Laughing, his sisters commiserate.

"Biology is the only subject I didn't get a C in. Master feels a stretch."

"And I dropped Spanish last year. I've no idea why he said that."

"You mean . . ." Dominic's eyes bulge. "This isn't just . . . with me?"

Emily and Pippa look at him like he's stupid.

"Come *on*," Emily says impatiently. "He *loves* to embellish."

"Dad has no idea." Pippa is grinning now. "He's not exactly hands on, is he?"

"Understatement of the century," Emily chimes in. "But he means well."

"Right," Pippa nods, still smiling. "His EA is good at picking out gifts."

"Seriously?" he shakes his head, smiling. "His assistant sends us all those kitchen gadgets we get for Christmas?"

The twins nod in response. Dominic glances at Daphne. Her eyes are dancing with amusement. Emily's voice echoes in his head the rest of the night, making him smile. Come *on*.

—

DAPHNE finds a note stuck to her front door. She peels it off slowly, examines it:

> Hi Daphne, can you pop up when you have a moment? Thanks!
> Sally (apartment above).

Daphne can't think of a time they've spoken beyond polite hellos in the hallway. She contemplates showering first. She just ran four miles. Her hair is knotted, greasy. She doesn't need a mirror to know she's taking sweaty to a whole new level, but she takes the stairs two at a time.

Sally's feet: bare, each toenail painted a different color. She's wearing high-waisted denim shorts, bottle blue, frayed at the hem. A turquoise crop top. She smiles and beckons Daphne in. The layout of her flat mirrors Daphne's. The scent of cat food hangs perceptibly in the air. As if on cue, a shorthaired cat with gray-blue fur and orange eyes jumps down from a window ledge. It strolls toward Daphne and brushes against her calf, purring loudly.

Sally has large caramel eyes and hair that women tend to envy: luxurious and dark, soft and feathered. She wears tassel earrings and stacking rings and headscarves. Single until recently, her new boyfriend has a heavy step. Dominic calls him Thunder Foot.

"This is awkward," Sally begins, clasping her hands together. "I got a package and opened it without paying attention to the name on the front . . ."

Daphne shrinks back. The books, four of them! She wishes the floor would open up, swallow her whole.

"Thank you," she stammers, closing her fingers around the package. Why did she order so many books about orgasms?

"Don't be embarrassed," Sally responds in a sincere tone.

Easy for you, Daphne thinks. She presses the package firmly to her stomach, willing it to vanish. Sally watches Daphne with a strange expression. Her smile is slow, private.

"You know . . . Dyson and I like to experiment."

Daphne stares back uncomprehendingly. Thunder Foot's real name is Dyson?

"If you ever want to join us," Sally continues in a light tone, "we'd be . . . down to play."

Down to *play*. Did Sally really just say that?

"With me?" Daphne asks.

Daphne's entire body is coated in sweat. Her hair is stuck to her scalp and her neck. These are not circumstances under which she imagined a proposition.

"Sure," Sally responds. Each time she nods, her soft bangs bounce. "Why not?"

"I'll think about it," Daphne promises.

She does. She thinks about it all the time.

"Have you ever thought about experimenting with women?" Ash asks her.

They're in a subterranean bar that only plays music from the nineties. As Sinéad O'Connor floats on, Daphne wonders bleakly if nothing compares to Dominic because she has nothing much to compare him to?

She shakes her head. "It didn't ever seem like a thing that would happen to me, opportunity-wise."

"Opportunity-wise?" Ash repeats, cracking up. "We're not talking about a six-month placement in Paris. So . . . what do you make of it?"

"I don't know." She shrugs, takes a long sip of her martini. "I just never thought about it."

"Let's try again," Ash says, studying her. "How do you feel about it?"

Her face is hot. She tightens her grip on her glass.

"I just said . . . I don't know. Why?"

"Because you're saying a lot of words that don't tell me how you *feel*," Ash observes, adding quietly: "About being in bed. With a woman."

She sits taller and takes a hurried sip. "A bit nervous, if I'm honest."

"Why?"

"Fear of the unknown. Fear . . ." She cocks her head to one side. "I'd like it? And what does that say about me and the choices I've made if I do?"

"Sure, you might like it. Is that a reason to say no?"

She rakes a hand through her hair.

"No . . . but what about all the other things that could go wrong?"

He looks confused. "Like what?"

She's drained her drink, already! Ash signals for two more.

"They might laugh at me! Or get bored of me and just have sex with each other."

Ash makes a frowning expression.

"I really doubt laughing at you is what they have in mind."

She clears her throat, speaks hurriedly. "Plus, I can't."

"Why not?"

"Dom and I agreed to one person a year. This is two. It would break the rules."

Ash stares at her in thoughtful silence.

"But there's no rule around whether people can watch," he says at last with a soft smile. "You pick Sally or . . . what do you call him again?"

"Thunder Foot."

"The other can watch."

"That simple, is it?"

Their drinks arrive. Gin martinis, straight up, with a twist.

"You know what? It's as simple," he begins, clinking his coupe against hers, "as you choose to make it."

—

"WHATEVER you just did," Daphne sighs. "Do it again."

That's the best thing about his night with Lucinda. Everything she taught him. Daphne's reaction makes him feel like a decent lover. Or on the path to it. Daphne mentions she bought some books. She's reading each one in turn, she tells him.

"That's a very academic approach," he remarks with a smile.

—

SHE'S becoming a keen student in the literature of the female orgasm. She underlines sections, dogears pages. She masturbates often, paying close attention to each scenario playing out in her mind, sharing it with Dominic. In her fantasies, she's more confident, and she's working on that in real life too.

Sex is becoming vastly more enjoyable and she wants to understand *why*. Yes, it's the lube and the vibrating cock ring and what she's learning from her self appointed reading assignments, but in a lot of ways it's *separate* from that. It almost feels like she doesn't need to do all this extra work because Dominic has figured it out for her. It's only been a recent development, in the last few months or so, that he's become better in bed. He knows exactly how to touch her and where and for how long. Where did he suddenly learn this? Does it matter, she reminds herself, when it gives her such satisfaction? But part of her, the competitive part, the perfectionist part, wanted to figure it out on her own, hence the books.

Looking back, she is amazed that she settled for so long, that she didn't demand her own orgasms, that she placed her sexual needs last. She intends to make up for the lost years. With that in mind, she leaves her number on Sally's front door. They text back and forth. They arrange a mutually convenient time: a Saturday afternoon in the autumn when Dominic will be busy, overseeing football matches.

The day arrives. She walks up the stairs. She takes a deep breath and she knocks.

Confessions of a Highly Emotional Cook:

The Most Perfect Stone Fruit Tart

Please put down ALL HOT LIQUIDS before reading on. I'd hate for you to burn yourself on account of what I'm about to share. The couple living above me invited me into their bedroom because they like to *play*. I am, un-equivocally, not the type of person this happens to. Let's be clear on that from the outset. This experience came at an important time. I've been learning to love myself more, and it felt like a test: would I be able to remove my clothes and relax fully in the presence of others? Would I be present or would a spiral of self-sabotaging thoughts ('are they judging my thighs right now?') haunt me?

I was nervous as I walked in. I've found it hard to es-cape my anxious mind with just one sexual partner in the past, let alone with two. And I know what you're think-ing—a threesome??—so I should clarify that I accepted the couple's offer with one condition: I was only inter-ested in a solo experience with the woman, but her boy-friend could watch. That way, I wouldn't break the agreement I have with my husband, that each of us is allowed to have sex with one other person, once a year. I know this sounds incredibly strange and specific—we're not in an open relationship and not entirely monogamous either—and yes, it *is* strange and specific, but let's debate the strangeness and specificity another time please. Alternatively, just go for it in the comments.

Back to my neighbors: if the boyfriend was displeased, he hid it. I worried he'd be an unwanted distraction. Or a domineering energy we couldn't escape. I worried I'd feel self-conscious, but none of these things happened. He sat in an armchair, coral pink, in the corner of the bedroom, arms folded neatly across his chest and there was something quite earnest about his expression. I found it endearing. He was quiet and obedient, respectful. I almost forgot about him.

Sitting on the bed together, we kissed. I felt her fingertips on my waist, dancing on my thigh. Her fingers were soft and light, they fluttered like a bird. The extraordinary beauty of this experience lay in its speed, or lack thereof. It reminded me of lazy afternoons in the thick of summer, that feeling of having the whole day, the entire city to yourself, luxuriating in the fact you have nowhere to be.

"I don't know what I'm doing," I confessed.

She laughed and said she felt the same. It broke the tension. We peeled our clothes off. She had curves that went on for days. I traced and kissed them. Staring at me, the full naked length of me, she propped herself up on one elbow and said: "The female body is a work of art."

I stared back with a confidence I didn't know I had. I didn't recognize my voice when I asked her to touch me. She laughed softly and asked me to guide her where and

I did, with my hands, and my voice. She was slow and thorough until I needed her to not be those things. And then my body went slack, utterly dense. I closed my eyes and listened to my body humming.

She curled into me. I am not used to taking, but I allowed myself to. I wanted to bask in how utterly perfect life felt in that moment. And then my eyes flew open, eager to return the favor. Her skin was soft and warm, responsive. She guided me too. I watched, strangely proud of myself, as she tensed and cried out. We did not move after that. We lay together in the sheets, our bodies heavy, in need of replenishment. I heard a noise in the corner, a shifting, creaking.

"Can you get the leftover dessert?" she asked.

He left the room. When he returned, he was carrying two bowls. I felt like a child, sitting in bed, back propped against a pillow, eating greedily. Whatever was in the bowl was sweet and fruity, intensely bright, the colors of autumn.

"What is this?" I asked.

"I'll give you the recipe," she said.

And she did.

THE MOST PERFECT STONE FRUIT TART

Feeds: Four

Ingredients:
- 1 sheet of frozen puff pastry, let it thaw before use
- ¼ cup of all-purpose flour
- 1 tablespoon of butter

- 3 cups of chopped stone fruit (ours had apricots, plums, peaches, and cherries), stones removed
- A squeeze of honey
- A pinch of cinnamon and thyme (I know thyme sounds weird, but roll with it)
- 1 egg, lightly beaten
- Mascarpone cream
- Fresh basil

Method:

1. Heat the oven to 200 degrees Celsius/400 Fahrenheit. Consider how many recipes begin with this simple instruction. Laugh softly at this.
2. Sprinkle a little flour and spread butter on a 9-inch round tart or quiche pan (preferably non-stick). The flour and butter will prevent the puff pastry from attaching itself to the pan at serving time.
3. Line your work surface with parchment paper. Notice how delicate the parchment paper is. Have you ever noticed that before?
4. Using a rolling pin (or a bottle of red wine, as my neighbor confessed to using) roll the puff pastry out onto the parchment paper. Relax into the rolling motion, don't overthink it. Roll until the puff pastry is long and even.
5. Transfer the puff pastry to the tart pan, positioning it so that it covers the 9-inch base and up the sides. Do so lovingly and carefully.
6. Mix the fruit together in a bowl and add honey, cinnamon, and thyme before pouring it on top of the pastry. You might be humming as you do this. I can't explain why.
7. Brush the edges of the pastry with the beaten egg. Yes, just like that.

8. Bake until golden brown (about 25–30 minutes, depending on your oven). Enjoy the slow, pleasurable wait.

9. Add a dollop of mascarpone and some fresh basil onto each serving. Or two dollops, or three. Really, it's up to you. Isn't that the joy of life?

Enjoy! And, please remember, your body is a work of art.

Yours,

The Highly Emotional Cook

YEAR
THREE

"I WAS HOPING FOR A RAISE."

It's her year-end review. Gordon, her manager, has told her that her performance is excellent, she's a model employee, and they'd like to give her more responsibility. She goes in for the one thing she really wants. His response makes her feel like she asked for an all-expenses paid trip to Fiji.

"What . . . really?" He sputters. "But why?"

Because she hasn't been given a pay increase in three years. Because even then it was only moderate. Because he just said she was a model employee! Because her male coworker at her level, who doesn't work nearly as hard as her, is paid more (he told her what he made at the office party and she hasn't stopped thinking about it). Because of inflation. Because she deserves it. Because she has too much respect for herself not to ask. Plus, she's done her homework.

"Because the market rate is significantly more than what I make."

Gordon raises his bushy eyebrows.

"A pay raise is tough right now."

"I've been here for seven years, Gordon. You just told me I'm an exemplary employee. I also happen to know it'll cost you a lot more to replace me than it will to increase my pay by thirty percent."

"Thirty percent?" He sputters again. "Twenty is the best we can do and even that's only—"

As he pauses, she helps him out.

"For model employees?"

—

DOMINIC is proud. She asked for a raise and she got it! If only he could be that focused, that intentional with his novel. He's reminded of it each time he sifts through Lucinda's slush pile. He's envious of the good submissions. Surely he should use these to his advantage? They're a source of motivation, a reminder to stop procrastinating! Here goes: he fetches his laptop and spends ten minutes in Gmail. He reads a travel piece on Corsica. When he told Daphne about the trip Lucinda is planning, she looked peeved, mainly because *she'd* appreciate a free holiday. Right, he's supposed to be writing. He opens the Word document and reads it from start to finish. It doesn't take as long as he thought it would. It's not even a dozen pages. He could have sworn he had more. He scratches his head and tries to concentrate. Time to write the next chapter. He can do this. Staring at the blank page, he waits for inspiration. He waits so long that his laptop autolocks.

—

WITH the increase in pay, Daphne treats herself. She gets a makeup tutorial in a department store. She buys a cherry red lipstick that elicits a silly volume of compliments. She goes to a hair salon that specializes in curly hair. As he trims her hair, her hairdresser shares the best colors for redheads to wear. She spends a small fortune in hair products. She meets up with Poppy for drinks immediately after. *You. Look. Amazing.* Poppy wants Daphne to join her spin class. *Trust me, this instructor is the bomb.* The old Daphne would have said no, but why not?

The next day, Aparna points to an olive-green wrap dress in a shop window. *This would really suit you.* Daphne's reminded of the advice from her hairdresser. But it's absurdly expensive, she really shouldn't. Daphne finds spontaneity hard. Or at least she did before the Freedom Clause. But, she reminds herself, look what she's gained from impulsiveness. Leaving the store, she clutches the shopping bag proudly. Daphne doesn't understand why validation matters. Is it vain and superficial, she worries? It feels regressive and anti-feminist, somehow, to be spending so much effort on her appearance, to be *enjoying* the compliments, but she does enjoy them. She loves it.

—

DAPHNE's birthday is fast approaching. Dominic considers what to get her as he showers, as he cycles to work, as he waits for the boys at the school gate. There is *always* lingerie, fitting given the rejuvenated state of their sex life, but it feels too easy somehow, too clichéd. It's unbelievable, she actually wakes him up in the middle of the night! She whispers dirty things she wants him to do to her. He responds immediately. But if he tries to enter her quickly, the way he used to, she stops him. *You need to make me wet first.* She has strong opinions on the best positions, which ones allow her to grind her clitoris against him, and which are off limits. He's still thinking about lingerie when it flashes up on Instagram: upcoming tour dates for Florence and the Machine. Her favorite artist, that settles it. There must be a big smile on his face, because Lucinda asks what's going on. When he explains, she frowns. *God, you're really insufferable.* Lucinda's been grumpy ever since he made it clear their one night together was exactly that: one night only.

He sets his alarm early and makes Daphne coffee with scrambled eggs on toast. She likes her eggs on the runny side, goats' cheese sprinkled in. He walks in carefully, holding a tray.

"Happy birthday, crumb cake," he whispers, kissing her forehead gently.

She smiles sleepily. "Thanks, my love."

Lucinda's comment surfaces. Fair, they are totally insufferable.

—

It's been a lovely day, and it's only noon. Daphne's excited to treat herself to lunch at her favorite spot, right by the office. Leaving the building, she spots him immediately. His austere expression. His navy pinstripe suit and brown leather shoes. The briefcase in one hand and . . .

"Dad?"

He turns, blinking in the sun. The bouquet takes her breath away. Zinnias and foxgloves, roses the color of apricots. It's wrapped in pink tissue paper with a cream silk bow. Her parents have never surprised her with flowers before, even though she sends bouquets for Mothers' Day and Plumb's birthday, without fail. Her heart quickens a little.

"Are you . . . ?" she begins, thrown by his appearance.

"Daphne, hello!" he says rigidly.

"What are you . . ."

"Just had a board meeting nearby."

Semi-retired, her dad sits on the boards of a few FTSE-listed companies. He enjoys advisory roles, the routine of working a few days a quarter, keeping his mind just sharp enough.

"Thought I'd . . ." he pauses, gestures to the flowers, "pick these up."

Gazing at the bouquet, she hears herself gush.

"They're beautiful!"

She feels his shrewd gaze on her big hair, her gold hoop earrings.

"Oh, well . . . I saw the flower shop and thought it'd be nice to get these for Maggie."

"Maggie?" she repeats, confused.

"Across the street! She just had a baby."

Maggie, the neighbor. Don't let it sting, Daphne warns herself. Don't you *dare* let this hurt you. You weren't even thinking about him sixty seconds ago.

"Oh," she says with grim determination. "Maggie will *love* those. Want to . . . grab a quick bite together?"

She doesn't want to spend her lunch hour with him, but the words fly out too fast. Fortunately, he feels the same way. Glancing at his watch, he grimaces.

"I have a train to catch, and I don't want these to wilt."

"Right . . . of course," she responds quickly.

He points to her building. "This is where you work?"

She nods. "Seven years, if you can believe it."

He shrugs at her and, catching the movement, it makes her wonder: have they ever hugged? Not that she can recollect.

"Fleet Street . . . bit of an old boys club, isn't it?"

What's he getting at, she thinks suspiciously.

"Sure." She offers him a deliberately cute smile. "But the patriarchy's everywhere."

He nods dolefully. "I just . . ." He winces. "Unless you're going to win a Pulitzer, what's the point in a job that pays so little?"

"I'm actually very happy here," she responds in a prickly tone.

That's a lie. The pay raise made her feel good for approximately forty-eight hours, and then she remembered this job bores the hell out of her.

"Think you'll keep working here after you and Dominic . . . you know, start a family?"

He's presuming a *lot* right now. Daphne opens her mouth and stops herself, not today.

"Thanks for the birthday present, by the way."

He looks at her, really looks this time. A flicker of recognition crosses his face.

"Yes," he responds, straightening up. "Well, that was all your mother, you know. We hope you enjoy it."

The twenty-pound Waitrose voucher? She'll try not to spend it all at once. Although it'll be hard, she thinks sarcastically, given her salary is so clearly lacking.

"Yes, thanks. This has been *so* special. Now I have a salad to order and you"—she pauses deliberately—"have a train to catch."

Turning on her heels, she marches down the block.

"Bruno!" she bellows as she enters her favorite salad spot.

The owner grins at her. "Don't you look nice! Look at that dress!"

She smiles and admits it's her birthday today.

"Happy birthday! How about a coffee on the house?"

She'd like a lot of things today. Like a family that actually . . . she pauses, stops that thought. Free coffee? Sure, it's a start. On her way back to the office, she stops by a florist and treats herself. *No hard feelings, Maggie.* This bouquet is enormous, ridiculously over-the-top, and it makes her smile for the rest of the day.

—

HE's always found her attractive, but now she's *sexy,* and not just from running and working out. It's a *vibe.* He wonders if anyone else has noticed? She's got an interview at a food magazine today, the type of job she's been dreaming of for years. Daphne wakes up early. He watches her zip herself into a skirt, midnight blue, knee length and pleated. She's pulling on thick stockings, soft Italian wool. She reaches for a tight turtleneck that emphasizes her chest, ribbed and candy red. The color clashes against her hair. Even Dominic, who knows nothing of fashion, understands the clash is spectacular. The clash is deliberate. The clash screams confidence. She leans into the mirror to apply eyeliner. She runs cream through her hair.

"Good luck," he calls out, crossing his fingers and lifting them up. She grins nervously. "I want this job so badly."

"You've got this, crumb cake. I'd hire you on the spot!"

—

THEY don't hire her on the spot. Even though the interview went well. Even though she spoke with passion and eloquence. Even though she left glowing, certain she'd nailed it. That was twenty-two days ago. With each passing day, her confidence takes another hit. This feels exactly like dating: hope that turns to despair and, inevitably, self-recrimination. She's seen friends go through this, and she hasn't envied the emotional rollercoaster.

Finally, the HR person calls.

"I'm afraid the role went to an internal candidate."

Her eyes prickle with tears. Her body feels like a deflated balloon. She doesn't know what to say.

"Oh, I see."

She wants to wallow and cry. Can she hang up?

"But there is this *other* position we'd like to consider you for."

—

IT's April, his birthday. They meet at an upmarket restaurant bar with an industrial vibe. Steel and glass, exposed brick. Mark brings his latest girlfriend. Tabitha, another tiny brunette. Secretly, Dominic hopes it doesn't last. She seems precious, and his friends agree.

"Happy birthday!" Daphne calls out, walking toward him.

"You made it!" He stands up and waves.

Everyone else arrived a while ago, but Daphne's final meeting of the day ran on. He doesn't begrudge it. He expects as much. She's just started a new job and she's busy onboarding. She slides into the seat beside him. His eyes flicker over her appreciatively. Her black shift dress and metallic chandelier earrings. And then there's her hair—it's a statement—unruly and enormous. She looks like an eighties rock star.

Mark is talking about his job. Holding court, he pauses.

"Sorry, Daph," Mark murmurs in a soft, low drawl. "I just have to say, you're looking stunning. What've *you* been up to?"

Dominic inhales sharply. Is Mark flirting? He watches a smirk crossing Daphne's face and worries she might consider flirting back.

"Nothing much," she responds, her eyes light and playful.

Daphne reaches for an olive. She pops it between her lips, bee-stung, bright red.

Mark snorts. "Nothing much my foot. Tell us!"

Daphne shrugs out of her jacket. Her dress is simple with a square neckline, thin fabric. Mark watches her like she's the most exquisite creature on earth. Dominic sees it. Tabitha does too.

"Come on, Mark," Tabitha interjects, looking annoyed.

"I've just been exercising a lot," Daphne volunteers, easing the tension.

Daphne smiles at the table in a happy, relaxed way. She runs before work, she explains, and she does a fun weights class on Tuesdays and hot yoga on Fridays and occasionally an aerial silks and trapeze class on the weekends.

"And you got a new job," Dominic says, beaming at her like a proud parent.

"I did," she admits in a coy tone, tucking a stray strand of hair behind her ear.

Mark offers Daphne a strange smile. Close-mouthed and private, reserved just for them.

"Tell me more," Mark implores, his eyes circling her face.

Dominic frowns: tell *me*? Has Mark forgotten the rest of them exist?

"Well," Daphne begins, "at the start of the year, I applied for a junior editor position at a food magazine. I didn't get it," she admits with an adorable sigh of defeat. "The role went to someone internally, but I was offered a role in their sales team."

Daphne is hoping she can move into editorial when there's an opening. Listening, Dominic notices she's too discreet to mention her new job offers a significant pay raise over the law journal. She's officially the breadwinner. Proud of her, he's definitely uncomfortable about it too. He used to *provide*. What does he bring to the relationship now? Daphne is better in every way. What if one day she realizes this and just . . . walks out? The thought terrifies him.

"Okay, the birthday boy *definitely* needs a drink," Mark says, standing up and pointing at Dominic's face. "Who else wants one? Daphne?"

—

It's nothing like the law journal. Bright and modern, high ceilings, glass elevators. She works in a building called The Beehive, hexagon-shaped, honeycomb-colored. Hilary, her manager, is in her thirties, devastatingly hip. Boyfriend jeans. Oversized vintage jackets. Bright red librarian glasses. She ties her dirty-blond hair in a high bun. She's Scottish and direct.

"Ask me whatever the fuck you want," Hilary implores.

Daphne hasn't worked at a company that values culture before. An open-door policy for meetings. Lunchtime seminars. Buddy programs. Employees are encouraged to apply for funding toward a learning and development course of their choice.

"Anything?" Daphne repeats in disbelief.

Biting into a pink-yellow peach, Hilary nods.

"Last year, dickhead Steve did a sommelier course in France."

Daphne doesn't know who dickhead Steve is, but it gives her an idea.

—

Dominic finally asks Lucinda to review his novel-in-progress. She agrees, and he wonders why it took him this long. He spends all weekend polishing his pages, fifty in total. His excitement is off the charts. Daphne's is too. *This could be it! She could represent you!* On Monday, he prints the pages off for Lucinda. *Ah, the infamous work-in-progress? Leave it on my desk, will you?* He tries to stay busy, but his mind skips ahead. Could this be it, the seminal moment in his writing career? On Thursday evening, Lucinda asks him to stay late. They'll discuss his pages once the boys are asleep. He texts Daphne. She replies with sixteen fingers-crossed emojis.

Sitting across from Lucinda at the kitchen table, he opens his exercise book, pen poised. Lucinda suggests they do this over wine. He nods, happy to agree to anything.

"How do *you* feel about your writing?" she asks at last.

He blushes, unsure of how to answer.

"I don't know . . . Does it matter?"

Silence. This might just be the most excruciating ten seconds of his life.

"I think," she says, "you have fifty pages here, but I'm not sure what they are."

He writes NOT SURE in his notepad, followed by a question mark.

"What would you say the plot is?" she asks slowly, carefully.

"It's about . . . life."

"Life?" she repeats.

He nods. "It's about a man going about his . . ."

"Life?"

"Yes."

"And who are some of your inspirations?"

He straightens up and says confidently: "I'm going for Franzen meets Roth with the mainstream appeal of . . . Hornby."

"Right. But you're not those writers. You need to write in your own voice."

He writes: OWN VOICE in his notepad, directly beneath the

words: NOT SURE. Lucinda holds her hand up. He drops the pen. His fingers twitch. It's clear: she doesn't like his pages.

Feeling anxious, he admits: "You know, I don't think it's ready yet. I showed you too soon."

Lucinda raises her eyebrow. "How long ago did you start working on it?"

"About four years ago."

"Okay." She sighs. "I don't like to be this person. I hate this conversation as much as you do. I hope you understand that. But I need to be clear: these pages are no good."

"There are kinder ways to tell me I'm not talented."

She laughs. "Talent? You think *talent* gets you published? All my clients share one trait: they work hard. They write every day. Even on the days they're hungover or depressed or sick, they *work*. Talent has little to do with it. I work damn hard too. That's why people want me as their agent. And that's why I would never take you on as a client."

He sputters. "Are you saying I don't work hard?"

She blinks at him. Quietly, she says, "Not on this."

He strokes his neck, too wounded to speak. He sits back, arms folded across his chest.

"I don't see that burning desire in you," she continues. "I see your commitment with my kids, but not with this. But you know yourself better. The question you need to ask yourself is: are you committed to this or do you just like the *idea* of being a writer?"

Lucinda hasn't touched her glass yet, but she does now.

"You've given me . . . a lot to process," he concedes in a small voice.

Lucinda's face softens. "Just because you thought this was your path for a long time doesn't mean it has to be. It's fine to go in a different direction. Just think about what you want to do, what you're actually passionate about."

She sounds like Daphne. He can't bring himself to speak, even though the silence between them feels awkward.

"I'm only telling you because I care about you," she continues with a small smile. She stretches her hand out, and covers his. "A lot. Desperately in fact."

He could pull away, but after the battering his creative ambitions just took, he wants to be held. He feels conflicted, especially when he thinks of Daphne, waiting at home, eager to hear Lucinda's reaction. Then again, he wants to stay here a minute longer. He's worked hard to reach this point and he wants to bathe in it. *Danger, danger, danger* his mind screams. But he is doing nothing wrong, he tells himself. He is doing nothing at all, besides letting her hold his hand.

—

"WHAT does she know anyway?" Daphne scoffs when he gets home.

"It's okay," he says earnestly.

She smiles sadly. "But you've wanted this for so long."

"I know."

She pulls him down to the sofa and pecks his face all over with tiny kisses. He pulls back and looks into her eyes.

"I thought about it as I cycled back here and I think she was . . . right?"

"How?"

"I'm just not making the time for it. And when I so much as *think* about making the time for it, I'm filled with this . . . I don't know . . . existential dread?"

"Like it's something you ought to do rather than . . . ?"

"Exactly! I don't enjoy the process, but I love the idea of how it would feel at the end."

He's never admitted this before. Not to her anyway.

"So maybe this was a good thing?" she says tentatively.

"It hurts, a lot. But maybe it's what I needed to hear."

He fixes his eyes on her, as though reassuring her that he's okay, really.

"What would help? Hungry?"

"Starving, actually."

She moves to the kitchen, heats leftovers. He follows, hugging her from behind. They stand like this, listening to the steady monotone of the microwave.

"How's my crumb cake?" he asks tenderly.

She nods slowly. "Doing okay."

"How's the new job?"

As he eats, she tells him about the culinary course in Mexico City. It's for two weeks and costs a small fortune, but her company would fund most of it. She filled in the application for funding this afternoon. She's waiting for the company's approval. Dominic stops eating and gazes at her. She loves it when he looks at her this way, filled with admiration.

"You'll get it," he says, grinning. "When are you thinking of going?"

"Early summer might be nice."

He dabs his mouth on a paper towel. "Maybe it can overlap with when I'm away. End of June."

"As if I could forget," she responds in a dry tone. "How long is this Corsica trip?"

"Two weeks. She's paying overtime and everything. I think so she and Zach get quality time together."

"Sounds like they need it," Daphne murmurs, running her thumb absently over her lips.

"What about us?" he asks, looking concerned. "If you get into this course *we* might spend a month apart."

Dominic looks petrified by this. It's silly, but whenever she mentions a night out with colleagues or the girls, he tends to panic about what he'll do to occupy himself. She's thought about bringing it up, but now doesn't seem like the moment. He needs a little time to recover from the feedback on his writing.

She nods her head at his plate. "What do you think? Be honest."

It's chicken pot pie with a twist—she added curry paste, lemongrass, lime, red pepper flakes, and coconut milk—she wants to throw something unusual at her subscribers. She's up to seven hundred on her mailing list and it blows her mind.

"Delicious," he says enthusiastically. "One of your best!"

"Good! And," she adds, returning to his earlier point, "maybe a little time apart would be good for us. Absence and the heart, and all that."

"Fat chance," he says, shaking his head emphatically.

She smiles indulgently. "Sure, it'll be harder for you. Mr. Quality-Time-Together-Is-My-Love-Language."

"Don't forget about gift giving!" he says playfully. "A close second!"

She raises a cheeky eyebrow. "Luckily I can give acts of service to myself while you're in Corsica."

His eyes light up. "How about showing me what I'll be missing out on?"

The Sunday Times

Cultural Obsessions by Peggy Plintoff

For decades, women have discussed everything from the prominent hair emerging from their double chin to the latest despicable act their mother-in-law has performed. Why, then, am I delighting in a little known Substack account I was alerted to, and that I read well beyond the respectable hour to go to sleep? The Substack is called:

Confessions of a Highly Emotional Cook, and if you don't love it as much as I do, then let's go our separate ways, please.

The Highly Emotional Cook in question remains a mystery. A woman in her twenties, living in south London, married but in a somewhat open relationship. It is easy to dismiss her account as the work of yet another Internet amateur. Indeed, her recipes are not earth-shattering nor original. She doesn't have Nigella or Delia's skills, and while she's charmingly down to earth, she's no Jamie Oliver. She takes few risks, operating on safe ground. We all know how to make a lamb stew. We all know how to make lentil soup. But do we all know how to share the humiliations of a sexual encounter with a stranger and wrap the tale up neatly in a salad recipe that will be the best you taste this summer?

In her first post she describes what "might just be the most ridiculous evening of my life." What begins as an extramarital one-night stand culminates in the shame of a stranger ejaculating in her hair. Ultimately, it's an honest and vulnerable introspection on why men are better at expressing what they want.

I'm in my mid-fifties, I'm on my third marriage, and I'm not having sex with strangers these days. Regardless, her words chill me, because there is much in this confession that I recognize in myself, especially in my younger self. This angers me too. That another young generation of women is experiencing this. And by this, I mean sex that isn't particularly good. I mean that men remain selfish in the sack and women, raised to be people pleasers, enable this behavior. I didn't discuss the bad sex I was having when I was her age. I certainly didn't admit to it during my first marriage. Why? Pride, I think. Pride that others might intimate from this revelation that the fault lay with me. Loyalty too. How could I tell my closest friends that my much older, supposedly more experienced husband, a husband they all adored, didn't satiate me between the sheets?

Now, there are most certainly a lot of women climaxing every night of the week, assertive women who know what they want and demand it from their sexual partners, and good on them. But I'll hazard a guess that there are a lot of women in relationships where the sex is . . . just okay. And perhaps at times it's downright bad. And unless we discuss it, how on earth are we to change it? Women simply don't have as much good sex as their male counterparts.

Bravo then to the Highly Emotional Cook for sharing her tale of humiliating sex. And giving us a damn fine salad in the process. I urge you to read the Highly Emotional Cook's recipe and share in the comments below, or on Twitter, what your #HeCameInMyHairMoment is. Lastly, I can promise that you won't regret making this salad. I wish I could promise you great sex too. But sadly, I can't.

—

"She's very powerful, isn't she?" Cody whispers.

"I'll say."

Lucinda is working from home today. Her imperial voice travels down three flights of stairs. Dominic doesn't envy whoever Lucinda is speaking to, her tone dripping with contempt.

"Your knuckles are white," Oscar observes.

Dominic forces out a laugh, and loosens his grip on his tea. It scares him, how familiar this is. The drinking. The sporadic approach to parenting. The unnecessary drama. The need to tiptoe around whenever she has her moods.

"The moods never last long," Oscar says, watching Dominic thoughtfully.

Oscar is hopeful, Cody too. Dominic was like that at their age. It breaks his heart.

—

THEIR destination is a champagne bar. Gilded opulence, pure extravagance. Mosaic tiles. Streaks of red and gold dance up the walls. A man in a waistcoat leads them to their booth, offers menus.

"This place is ridiculous," she whispers as he walks away.

Ash beams. "Isn't it perfect?"

Daphne wants truffles and oysters and caviar, but first she wants to drink. She touches the PRESS FOR CHAMPAGNE button, breaking into a high happy laugh.

"You!" Ash reaches across the table, grabs her hand. "You asked for what you wanted and the universe DELIVERED. And now you've gone viral!"

They continue to order—champagne and cocktails, and champagne cocktails—heads spinning as they press the button giddily.

"I do feel bad for keeping it all from Dominic," she admits.

"Why?" Ash asks in a sharp voice.

"Because he knows absolutely nothing about my success."

"Nobody does." Ash shrugs. "Apart from me!"

"Right," she concedes. "But lots of people know about *The Highly Emotional Cook*. It makes me nervous. . . . It just feels a bit odd that he's so out of the loop."

"I think," Ash says sternly, "you stop giving yourself a hard time and just enjoy this."

The cave-aged Dorset Cheddar arrives. They inhale it.

Their eyes meet across the booth, and they begin to giggle.

"Do it," Ash teases. "Press that fucking button again."

—

"Seen my deodorant anywhere?" Dominic yells out.

He's reaching for toiletries, dropping them into his overnight bag. He wishes Daphne wasn't in the shower. It's always a squeeze when they're both in here. One tiny sink. The steady buildup of clutter. Daphne's hair products. His shaving gear. He feels frantic, even though his flight isn't until tomorrow.

"Maybe on the bureau in the bedroom?" she calls out over the heavy stream of water. "So anyway, Steve wants us to hit eighteen percent of annual sales targets next month alone!"

Daphne's been in her new job for about six weeks. She has targets that sound a bit aggressive but instead of being intimidated, Daphne seems up for the challenge. It surprises him. Even when they first met, she was talking about her big plans to be a journalist. He feels like she walked away from the law journal too easily. Or is this just his unease over her big raise talking?

"Do you miss writing?" he asks as she turns off the water and steps out of the shower.

He finds his deodorant, hiding behind a bottle of hairspray. He drops it into his toiletry bag and it lands with a loud clunk.

Daphne's eyebrows knit together. "Why do you ask?"

"I don't know, Daph. You always loved to write. I thought you'd miss it?"

Daphne gives him a strange look, pulling the towel more tightly around her chest. As she turns away, he scrutinizes himself. Is he still licking wounds over the demise of his own writing ambitions? Possibly. While it was a weight lifted in certain ways, it's still a scar. One that's only just beginning to heal over.

Their eyes meet briefly in the mirror.

"It's only until a role opens in editorial."

"Yeah, but that could take years! Don't you miss writing right *now*?"

She drops eye contact. "Honestly, I don't need it as much . . ."

Her voice sounds high and strange. Even her body language looks shifty. He feels his own anxiety rising. It's been building for days, ever since Zach dropped out of the holiday. Some sort of work emergency, Lucinda explained in an unconcerned tone as Dominic's panic went into free fall. Zach was meant to be the buffer between him and Lucinda. That's the only reason he said yes! He hears Daphne rattle a bottle of Ibuprofen, interrupting his thoughts. She raises her eyebrow: *want to pack this too?* He nods and she smiles, dropping it in his toiletry case.

"I feel bad for Zach," Daphne says as though reading his mind. She wraps the towel more tightly around herself. "Funny, Lucinda always struck me as the one with work emergencies."

She kisses him on the cheek and pads out of the bathroom. As the door closes, he forgets all about Zach. Wasn't she acting kind of strangely when he brought up her writing? It's almost like she *does* still write. He's sort of reaching here but what if she's *flirting* with a writer? Someone who commits himself to writing, that could be it. Maybe there's someone in the editorial team she likes? The thought unsettles him. It throws his day off balance.

It does more than that. It throws him straight into Lucinda's arms.

—

THE courtyard takes her breath away. Navy shutters. Terracotta roof tiles. Vines climbing up the walls. Blossoms and bougainvillea. She could stay here all day. Perhaps she will, she thinks with a hint of impatience. Her hosts are taking an awfully long time to photocopy her passport. Her phone flashes. Dominic . . . again! She's never known her husband to be *this* needy. He texts her every hour. He details each meal they eat. Every activity they do. He sends photos too!

Slow footsteps. Alicia reappears. This woman must be eighty but she's distinctly punk rock. Large sunglasses. Black leather dress with square gold buttons. Metallic sandals. Her hair is jet black, straight from a bottle, immovable thanks to the mighty power of hairspray.

"It's gorgeous here," Daphne gushes.

Her husband, Eduardo, appears. He's Glenn Miller Orchestra to Alicia's punk rock. Long-sleeved white shirt, chinos. He has a pockmarked face, a bushy mustache.

"Please. Follow us," Eduardo says, gesturing.

Eduardo and Alicia walk slowly, holding hands. They laugh gently. On the way to her room, they show her their private garden. Eduardo points out a hummingbird. Alicia teaches her the names of plants. Bromeliads. Dahlia. Agave.

Her phone buzzes again. Dominic. It's been four minutes.

—

THE villa sits atop a perilously steep hill. Below, a cove, a private sandy beach they visit each day. Clothing appears to be optional. Nude, blissfully carefree, Lucinda and the boys dip in and out of the water. Dominic feels prudish beside them. Occasionally, Lucinda throws on something skimpy. String bikinis, with not much string, or sheer tops that emphasize her dark nipples, her pert breasts. It's increasingly difficult to see her bare skin and *not* be reminded of what they did last year. In fact, he's beginning to wonder if that's *all* he thinks about. As he makes dark coffee each morning. As he stares at the Mediterranean sea, bright and sparkling and perfectly blue. As he snorkels and towels off. As he teaches the boys card games. As he makes lunch, salty sardines on crackers. The only time he doesn't think about it—the thing he shouldn't be thinking about—is when his mind is on Daphne. He texts and calls, but they're on different schedules. She wakes up six hours after him.

Five days into the trip. That's when his resolve goes, softening like butter in a hot pan. The day begins with croissants, dark coffee. A trip to the private cove. Lunch in a shaded square. They begin with a bottle of Sancerre. Straw sunhat shading her head, Lucinda peers out to sea.

"Blue, blue, so blue you could eat it . . . that's how Matisse described Corsica."

He nods slowly. The Sancerre has gone to his head.

"I'd rather bathe in it," he admits in a slow drawl.

It's not a particularly funny response, but Lucinda laughs loudly, reaches out, and squeezes his hand.

He tips his head toward the boys as though to remind her, they have company. Oscar and Cody don't look so good today. Cody didn't sleep well the night before. He had nightmares and woke up screaming. Oscar woke up too. And they are suffering now, in the thick and dense heat of the afternoon. Lunch arrives, and their heads fall forward into the big bowls of linguine.

"So," Lucinda whispers, eyes on the boys. "This Freedom Clause . . ."

"Yes," he says wearily, pushing grains around his plate.

"Why haven't we . . . again?"

"Us?" he repeats in shock.

"Yes," she snaps. "It's been a year, after all."

"No repeats," he explains. "One of the rules."

"Why?" she asks in total outrage.

He shrugs. "To avoid affairs."

She crosses her arms, she looks miffed.

"What if I put on a blond wig and call myself Suzie?"

He laughs but he senses she isn't joking. For one, her face is thunder. Lucinda pays and they return to the villa. The air is thick and humid. Their footsteps are slow and heavy. Cody falls asleep in Lucinda's arms. Oscar is whiny. At last, they reach the villa. The stone walls are deliciously cool. Lucinda pulls down the shutters. Oscar and Cody put up no resistance as she suggests afternoon naps.

Dominic takes his book outside, but it's too hot to read. He jumps in the pool and does thirty lengths. He comes in, wet footsteps leaving a trail across the floor. He's in the bathroom. Standing beneath the cold water, soaping his body. The shower door opens. Lucinda. She drops her towel. She is brown all over from the sun. Her body is petite and lithe. She takes a step closer and sinks to her knees. Her mouth is on his dick. He makes a noise that might be the word *no,* but it sounds more like a croak, low and unintelligible. Lucinda has no interest in his resistance. Not that he is trying hard. There is absolutely no way he can stop this.

It all happens very quickly.

Confessions of a Highly Emotional Cook:

Salsa Roja de Morita

Hello dear reader, I'm writing to you from Mexico. As you know (because I've not-so-casually referenced it in almost every post for the past eight weeks) I'm enrolled in a cooking course. Excited does not even BEGIN to cover it.

I love it here. The sun rises early, and it's hot and intense and beautiful. It's a ten-minute walk to the culinary school. The kitchen is sparse, each surface gleaming white. Our teacher is a tall woman with fabulous dark hair scraped into a high, severe-looking bun. She might be thirty or sixty. Honestly, it's impossible to tell. But she is humorless, strict. She tells me off for taking notes. We, as students, must commit her technique to memory!

I'll do anything this woman says because, trust me, her dishes burst with flavor. Light and spicy, delicate and crispy, smooth yet textured, a delight to taste, maddeningly difficult to re-create. Everything I have cooked until this point seems utterly boring and pointless. Moreover, it seems *pedestrian*.

I'm going to share a salsa we learned in class this morning. It's hot, sure to set your mouth on fire. The flavor is smoky, tart, and slightly sweet. It's complex and delicious. It's stunningly versatile, it can be added to tacos, grilled fish, chilaquiles, scrambled eggs, or just use it for your standard chips with salsa.

SALSA ROJA DE MORITA

Feeds: 2

Ingredients:

- 7 Morita chiles (the Morita chile is a stronger version of a smoked jalapeño and worth spending extra time to hunt down).
- 5 guajillo chiles, stems and seeds removed
- 5 cloves of garlic, unpeeled
- ½ pound of tomatillos
- ½ pound plum tomatoes
- 1 small onion, unpeeled and halved
- 2 tablespoons olive oil

- 1 teaspoon apple cider vinegar or white wine vinegar
- 1 teaspoon sugar
- ½ teaspoon salt

Method:
1. In a cast-iron skillet toast all the chiles over medium heat for around a minute—this adds to their smokiness—and remove.
2. Place the unpeeled garlic in the skillet next, toast for around 5 minutes. At this point, notice that everyone in the class is already on step 3 and PANIC.
3. Place a pot over medium heat. Add ¼ cup water, followed by the tomatillos, tomatoes, and onion for around 15 minutes—the tomatillos and tomatoes should start to pop and release their liquid.
4. Try not to look alarmed as the teacher claps her hands and shouts in Spanish. Focus on bringing two cups of water to a boil, turning off the heat, and adding the chiles. Realize she was shouting at Phil behind you. He dropped the tomatillos on the floor and she doesn't have extra. Send Phil a friendly smile. Let the chile-infused water mix soak for 30 minutes. Remove the chiles and reserve their soaking liquid.
5. Peel garlic and onion. Combine in a blender with tomatillos, chiles, tomatoes, onion, oil, vinegar, sugar, salt, and 1 tablespoon of the soaking liquid.
6. Pulse until you have achieved a relatively smooth salsa, with a little bit of texture remaining.
7. Adjust with more soaking liquid, if needed, and additional salt, to taste. Sit back and relax. Unless you're in a classroom and you're already onto the next recipe . . .

Enjoy!
The Highly Emotional Cook

—

It overwhelms him, the need to be inside her, and their mouths collide the moment the boys are asleep.

"Down," she urges softly, pushing him to her thighs.

Lucinda is childlike in these moments, easy to please. He likes the way she tastes, sweet and musky. He likes indulging her, hearing her low groans, feeling her shudders.

Afterwards, they lie naked together, tangled in drenched bedsheets.

"How's Zach?" he asks out of curiosity. "Everything okay with that work emergency?"

"Oh that?" Lucinda's eyes meet his unapologetically. "Actually, we had an enormous fight and I disinvited him."

He almost chokes. "What?!"

She sighs impatiently and shrugs.

His eyes go wide. "You lied to me?"

"Oh, are you *really* that upset," she implores, pulling his hand toward her, pressing his fingers to her hard nipple, "that he's not here?"

There is class each morning, but the afternoons are her own. The bright sun prickles against her skin. She speaks in halting Spanish as she buys a wide-brimmed sun hat. She buys bracelets, beaded and bright, that cling to her wrists. She visits parks and squares. She admires plants and trees. She sits in the shade of cafés reading and writing. She has never vacationed alone until now. Equally, she has never felt this unburdened, this carefree. Time is a luxury she relaxes into. A slower pace of life is not so bad. She imagines her future: a small cottage with a sloping garden, pines and cedars, poplars, a plum tree. Her days will be spent cooking, the radio playing softly in the background. Testing recipes, adding salt and stock, red wine, thyme and rosemary. Where is Dominic in this fantasy? Is he at work? Or is he at home too? She closes her eyes. She gives herself permission not to answer.

—

"I want to have Daphne over," Lucinda whispers, biting down onto his earlobe.

It's early, the boys will wake soon. Tomorrow they fly back to London. They will return to their former lives, their old routines. Whatever they have been doing here will end. They both know this. The sex they have reflects it. Frantic and urgent, the best kind.

"We can do that sometime," Dominic murmurs noncommittally.

Lucinda wraps her palm over the top of his hand. She rubs against his knuckles. Her movements are slow, sexual. Although everything with this woman, he thinks, is sexual.

"I want to meet her. Let's do it next month."

It's not a question. The power dynamic between them sharpens into focus. She is his employer. Daphne will come to dinner. Lucinda will get her way.

—

FINAL night. She slips on a black shift dress and strappy mules. Pink lipstick. She helps Eduardo light citronella candles, noting the table is set for four. Rafael, their grandson, arrives. As far as grandsons go, he's attractive. Long dark lashes. Expressive eyes. He's wearing a white linen shirt, cotton navy shorts, too much aftershave. He's young, a student at a nearby university. Alicia translates for him. Eduardo serves drinks. The tequila makes her head spin. It's a setup, they all know this, confirmed when Alicia and Eduardo feign tiredness after dinner.

It is a dense night, hot and still. Daphne dabs at her neck.

"In England, we call this weather a heatwave."

Rafael smiles. "This weather. It is April."

She nods, suspecting conversation will stall now their translators have retired. Rafael is sweet and nervous. He plays with his napkin. He gulps his drink. The garden is alive, humming with insects. Rafael takes her hand. They walk down the narrow, tiled path that leads to a large trellis, blooming with bougainvillea.

"You have beautiful chin."

She laughs a little. His face crumples.

"My English. Bad."

"It's fine," she says.

She leans in decisively. His lips taste of lime, salt. He is slow to respond, a little clumsy. *Am I the more experienced one?* she thinks in disbelief. She bites his lips, a brief teasing motion, and his hands respond, exploring the small of her back, between her thighs, peeling away her dress. Kneeling, he tugs on her underwear and she guides him, making it clear what she enjoys, moaning a little. *La boca,* she implores. An eager student, he follows her commands.

Noises float toward her, the chatter of friends, the slow strum of an acoustic guitar, the gentle trill of a woman's melancholy voice. She thinks of Dyson watching her last year, staring at her, and she feels a small fluttering thrill. Could a neighbor watch her now? Might they peer over the fence? Might they lock eyes? She's aware of her surroundings, but not like with Stuart, in the hotel room. She does so with an appreciative eye. How beautiful and inviting, how natural this moment feels. The bird over there on the fence, black with intensely luminous eyes. The sky, still and cloudless. It is star-studded and intensely dark. It hangs lower this evening, closer to her. She's gripped by a flash of intensity. There is shuddering and gasping. An urgent cry that might belong to her.

"Shhhhhh," Rafael says, sitting back, laughing gently.

But Daphne refuses to be quiet. She did that for too long.

She wants to be heard.

———

"LUCINDA wants you over for dinner."

He's terrified, almost choking on the invitation as he says it. He wonders, is it obvious? Just as it's obvious how incredible Daphne's trip to Mexico was? She's looking healthy, relaxed. Her hair is several shades lighter. She's swept it up high, off her face, fearful a strand will turn up in her cooking. Large freckles dance adorably across her nose and cheeks. Her sleeves are rolled up to her elbows. She's humming as she cooks, but she stops humming now and his heart lurches. She turns, surprised. Her smile is wide, she looks pleased.

"That'd be great. After hearing all your stories, I want to meet her."

Except Daphne hasn't heard *all* his stories, he reminds himself.

"Will Zach be there?" she asks, head bowed as she dices a hot pepper.

He leans into her from behind. He kisses her neck, and she laughs happily.

"Yeah," he murmurs softly against her skin, "I think so."

Zach being home makes what they are doing worse, bordering on the ridiculous. He watches her dicing shallots into tiny squares, her movements firm and practiced. Her fingers hover close to the blade, too close for his liking, and he springs back squeamishly.

"Can't wait to see if they're how I picture. By the way, when should we have that nice red she gave us?" Daphne is asking. "That was so generous."

Dominic stares at Daphne's back in open, stupid fear. What had Lucinda said? *All that working overtime. Something for you and your glorious wife to enjoy.* It made no sense, she paid him in cash for all his "overtime" already. The bottle sits above the fridge, glaring accusato-rily each time he enters the kitchen. The bottle: a daily reminder he is fucking his boss. Present tense. Because they did *not* stop after Cor-sica, even though they planned to and should have, even though Zach is home. Yesterday, they screwed in the downstairs bathroom while the boys watched cartoons. It is reckless behavior, and it must end.

"How about now?" he suggests, desperate to be rid of it.

"Now?" Daphne repeats, incredulous. "Thought she said it was special?"

It's a warm, rainy Tuesday evening. Dinner prep litters the kitchen. Shallots. Coconut milk. The juice of two limes. Fish sauce. Shrimp shells, pink and filmy.

"Why not?" he says with forced cheer.

Daphne reaches for the wine glasses on the top shelf. The good ones, a wedding present from his dad and Sadie. Shoot, he needs to text the twins. They head to university soon and he wants to wish them good luck. Emily, in particular, seemed nervous about it the last time he saw them. It was a weekend in May, he took them to an immersive cinema night for *The Sound of Music*. The girls acted like it was the most fun they had ever had. Admittedly, it was the most fun he'd had in a long time too. He grabs the bottle opener, opens it the way Lucinda taught him.

"When did you get so good at that?" Daphne asks, standing on her tip toes.

It seems like a cheap shot for sympathy, suggesting he acquired the skill from his alcoholic mother. Instead, he shrugs. Daphne rinses the glasses and he pours, generously. They clink glasses just as the doorbell goes. Their eyes meet and they exchange a smile of shared frustration.

"Typical!" Daphne huffs, walking away.

He stares at her tight denim shorts, white and frayed, the way they hug her thighs. She looks great, and she knows it. He swears there's a deeper sway in her hips. He hears her unlatching the front door. He sips the wine. It's despicably good.

"I had an audition right by here! Thought I'd drop in."

Ash has a distinctive voice, deep and honeyed.

"Come in!" Daphne says in delight. "Come in!"

"It smells delicious in here."

Their voices draw closer.

"Thai curry. Want to stay and have some?"

"Hey, Ash," Dominic pokes his head out, offering a friendly wave.

Ash gives him a quick distracted wave, his attention on Daphne.

"Pour Ash some of that red, will you?" Daphne calls out.

"The one we just opened?" he says in disbelief.

Meeting her eyes, he raises his eyebrows: *are you serious,* this *red?*

"Yes, that one," she responds in a clipped tone.

He retreats to the kitchen. Reluctantly, he pours Ash a glass. He presents it to him slowly and ceremoniously, like a newborn. He tops up Daphne's glass too.

"Thanks, princess," Ash says, winking at him. He takes a sip and makes a surprised expression. He leans in to study the label on the bottle. "Wow, top notch."

"A thank-you present from his boss," Daphne informs Ash. Her voice is high and proud. Dominic winces inwardly. "She has a wine cellar and everything. I get to finally see it soon. I'm going over there for dinner."

"I see," Ash says slowly. "What's she thanking you for, exactly?"

That orgasm. In the shower. Against the dresser. Beneath the stairs. Over the sink. He and Lucinda play a self-congratulatory game, ranking their encounters. Why, though? It's wrong, this whole sordid business. He takes a long sip and stares at Ash, not blinking.

"The kids told her to. They love me."

"Sure," Ash drawls, unconvinced. "The kids wanted you to have the Château Margaux."

———

DAPHNE's first thought upon meeting Lucinda is a simple one: you are trouble.

Matchstick thin. Her face is angular, her movements frenetic. She has intelligent eyes, dark and intense. What a horrible laugh, loud and jolting, like a chainsaw. Lucinda is too many things at once: impatient and cloying, complimentary and competitive. It's difficult to pinpoint where her authenticity ends, where the act begins. Daphne chooses to believe none of it.

She recalls a strange fact: her husband finds this woman intimidating. How silly, to fall for the stern voice, the didactic tone. It's armor. All Lucinda wants, all anyone wants when the layers are peeled back, is to be loved unconditionally.

———

LUCINDA is too loud, too eager. She springs on Daphne, fondling her earrings.

"Look at these delightful dangly things," she crows.

Daphne explains she bought them in Mexico but Lucinda isn't listening. She's frazzled, nervous. She's opening champagne, which makes no sense. They *just* made gin and tonics. He scans Daphne's face: what is she thinking?

"Smells delicious," Daphne remarks, walking over to the oven. "What are we having?"

"Beef short ribs and a salad."

"Mmm, beef," Daphne murmurs appreciatively.

"A tender, sexy meat," Lucinda is saying, "just falls off the bone, like a stripper."

What a strange thing to say, he thinks irritably. Lucinda's laugh is high and riotous. Daphne smiles politely. As she glances around, he sees the room through her eyes. The wildly overpriced flower arrangement that Lucinda insists on ordering once a week (*it cheers me up!*). The enormous kitchen island. Marble worktops. Bosch appliances. Bespoke cabinets that close silently. Handblown glass pendants, flown in from Italy. Waterford crystal glasses. Hand-painted dinnerware. The dark walnut table. The pink Persian rug.

Daphne is glancing outside. The south-facing doors lead to a garden. Zach occasionally invests time and energy in the garden. He sprouts strange-looking shrubs, misshapen tomatoes. The worst is the insect-nibbled strips of lettuce that Lucinda coos over, resulting in a lackluster salad unless she supplements it with Waitrose leafy greens.

Zach steps into view. His hair is wet, freshly combed, his receding hairline visible. The shampoo brands he uses promise stunning regrowth, boundless virility.

"Zach," Lucinda drawls. "Meet Dominic's outstanding wife."

All eyes fall on Daphne.

—

THE house is too clean, too quiet, too free of clutter. It's hard to believe they have children in a home this immaculate. The kitchen screams of decadence, money. And just how much are they drinking? Gin and tonics. Champagne. Red wine. They drink as though it's a race. To a finish line Daphne has no intention of reaching. Who are these people, she asks herself, Dominic included. Usually, he just wants to make people laugh. Tonight, however, he is watchful, guarded.

Lucinda asks Daphne dozens of questions and it makes her uncomfortable. The questions are unnecessary, loaded and competitive. But what are they competing over? Dominic looks unwell, his forehead shiny, his eyes desperately unhappy.

Daphne takes a slow sip of wine. She studies her husband closely.

—

His neck and back and armpits are uncomfortably hot. He feels un-well. Is it obvious? They sit down for salad. It's served in a large stone-ware bowl covered in hand-painted fish, bright shades of blue and yellow and green. Lucinda bought the bowl at a market in Corsica. Terrified it might break, she kept it on her lap the entire flight home.

Maybe this bowl represents their affair, he thinks dramatically, it shouldn't have returned to England. But now his attention is on what's *in* the bowl.

"That's strange," Dominic murmurs.

He stops chewing. It tastes strangely familiar. Slices of avocado, mozzarella, orange, sunflower seeds, caramelized onions, and the un-usual choice of sausage. He knows this salad!

"Good, isn't it?" Lucinda asserts.

"Delicious," Zach pipes up.

He's always thought of it as Daphne's salad. Salty and creamy, fatty and delicious. He's never seen it on a menu. It's too specific to Daphne.

"Daphne makes this salad. Don't you?" he blurts out.

Daphne's face shoots up. She moves her head from side to side, signaling: *please don't.*

"Not just Daphne," Lucinda shrieks. "Half the country's making it."

"What do you mean?" he asks politely.

Lucinda holds a slender hand up, gesturing to wait. She is a pain-fully slow eater. She seems to delight in beginning an anecdote just as she's about to eat, chewing thoughtfully, drawing out details. How strange. He used to find this endearing.

"It's from this Substack account that went viral," Lucinda explains at last, dabbing her mouth with a napkin. "The name of the salad's hilarious. I read about it in the *Sunday Times.*"

Utterly engrossed, he pushes his plate away. "Go on."

"It's called the . . ." Dramatic pause. "I-can't-believe-he-came-in-my-hair-salad."

Daphne shifts uncomfortably in her seat as Lucinda scrolls through her phone, giggling to herself. Her ears—Daphne's, that is—look brighter than the sun.

"Let me pull it up. Have you read it, Daphne?"

Daphne's eyes meet his apologetically.

"Umm, I think I heard about it."

"Who's behind the salad?" he asks not-so-innocently.

Daphne's face falls even farther.

"Half the fun! Nobody knows," Lucinda squeals in delight, holding her phone up. "Here it is: 'When he asked where he should come, I said anywhere. And, to be clear, we're not talking a small amount, ladies. No, a LOT of ejaculate.' Can you imagine?"

Unfortunately, he can. His imagination is running wild. His head might explode. *He* has never ejaculated in her hair before, which begs the question: who did? And did she enjoy it? And when?

He pushes the food around his plate in a leaden fashion. Of course, he's considered *how* Daphne might spend her one night of freedom each year but he didn't expect her to *write* about it, or for him to hear about it from his boss. Although, neither did Daphne based on her expression. He watches her pour more water into each of their glasses. She sips from her tumbler and studies her lap. She looks desperate to do anything except meet his insanely jealous gaze.

—

As Daphne watches Lucinda talking, her mind screams: *oh god, oh god, oh god*. It's mortifying, hearing the audiobook version of her recipe. Why can't they be eating *any* salad except this one? Although it's not Daphne's salad anymore, is it? The internet has claimed it.

Twitter named it the salad of the summer. This salad has reached celebrity status.

Daphne's still trying to adjust to the fact she has twenty-two thousand subscribers. Her gaze lands on Dominic. He's stabbing at the plate with a fork.

"How's the short rib?" Lucinda asks at last.

"Very sexy," she quips.

Lucinda's laugh is grating, loud like church bells. Daphne will happily take it over any more discussion of her salad.

—

"You're much more interesting than your husband."

Dominic glances skittishly from Lucinda to Daphne.

Daphne shrugs politely. "I'm not so sure about that."

Lucinda is gazing dreamily at Daphne. She's on the cusp of flirting with her.

"I've always found women more compelling than men," Lucinda stage whispers. "Give me Sappho over Homer any day of the week."

When Lucinda drinks heavily, she holds it together for a long time, but now she's approaching the cliff's edge. She looks destroyed, her teeth a demonic shade of red. He's reminded of his mother except she wasn't nearly as high functioning. Her falls were brutally fast, ugly. He glances at his watch and almost gasps. How is it only eight forty-five?

"Daphne," Lucinda begins giddily, "should join us in Corsica next year."

Not only is she falling, he thinks uneasily, she's taking him down too.

"And maybe," Zach interjects, "I'll get an invite too."

Daphne looks stunned. In this light, her eyes are spectral green.

"What do you mean?" she asks in a perturbed voice, her lips barely moving.

Dominic gulps down his wine.

"I was *uninvited*. Lucinda didn't need two men on that holiday, now, did she?"

Daphne's face goes still as she chews on the conversation. Glancing at Dominic, she assesses him slowly, incriminatingly.

"Strange, I thought Zach had a last-minute work trip. Why did I think that?"

Daphne's voice has hardened, stripped of its usual polish. Dominic swallows nervously. He didn't lie to Daphne, he reasons. He repeated a lie Lucinda told him, about a work emergency, and he neglected to inform Daphne when he learned the truth. He wonders if this was Lucinda's plan all along: invite Daphne for dinner, throw fuel over two marriages and light a match. He considers dropping to the ground, reaching blindly for Daphne's ankles, and begging for forgiveness.

Daphne excuses herself and walks away. His eyes rake over her white smocked dress, espadrilles. Her curled hair, styled half up, half down.

Lucinda smiles at him magnanimously.

"Your wife is divine."

—

He's allowed to sleep with one woman this year. Daphne just hates he did it with *her*. Sitting on the loo, she stares at her trembling fingers. She considers the facts. It's painfully obvious. She sees Corsica clearly. The supposed "work crisis." Dominic's hangdog expression. Lucinda's strangely competitive behavior. Two weeks on a foreign island? Daphne is certain of it: they're having an affair. There's no way this was a one-time thing. Is that why Lucinda wanted to meet her? She wants to get to know the wife of the man she's screwing?

Daphne leaves the bathroom and walks past the boys' bedroom.

The master is easy to find. Bay windows. Walls covered in old prints. A walk-in wardrobe, impeccably arranged. How does it feel to live in a house this large, and in this postcode? What must such privilege feel like? The bed catches her eye. Enormous. There's Lucinda's side, she doubts Zach reads Chris Kraus and Sheila Heti. Daphne spits on the pillows. How immature, how satisfying! She stomps downstairs and through the terrace doors. She wants to be alone, but Zach is there. Vaping, and desperate to be found. He nods at her, and then at his vape pen.

"Bad boy in me can't stop."

God you're a cliché, she thinks irritably. He was handsome in his youth, and therein lies the problem. He relied on his looks too long. Forgot to grow a personality. The thud in her temple is slow but persistent; it's been building steadily for hours. At this point, she feels categorically *terrible.*

"Do you have any aspirin inside?" she asks, fingers pressed to her temple.

"You know they're screwing, right?"

Earlier it was a *theory.* Earlier it could be *disproven.*

"Not until tonight," she admits. "How did you know?"

"She's nicer when she has a new person to fuck."

His mouth settles into a smile, if it can be called that. His smile terrifies her, derisive and sadistic, lonely too. It's a haunting smile, and she never wants to see it again.

"How long, do you think?"

"I'd say about a year."

She wants to vomit. She grips a patio chair and steadies herself. She hears Dominic calling out about an Uber and with forced cheeriness, she responds:

"Coming!"

—

In the Uber, all hell breaks loose.

"You're *sleeping* with her?"

"Someone came in your *hair*?"

"When did it start?"

"You've got a *following*?"

"Are you sleeping with her?" Daphne repeats.

Dominic feels the anger radiating out of her.

"Yes," he acknowledges in a heavy voice.

"How *could* you?" Daphne angles away from him, toward the window. "Do you love her?" she adds quietly.

"God no. It's just sex."

"And how is the sex?"

Animalistic. Addictive. Outrageously hot. Admitting this . . . He gazes at the fast blur of south London homes.

"I don't have much to compare it to," he says in a small voice.

"When did you two last . . ."

"Two days ago."

Her hand flies to the door handle.

"Stop the car! I'm going to be sick."

The car screeches to a halt. He follows her to beneath the honeyed glow of a lamppost. She leans forward, face inches from the ground. As she retches, he moves instinctively to rub her back.

"Don't touch me," she says coldly. "Since when?"

"Only once last year." He keeps going, eager to come clean. "That night we were meant to see a film . . . when she had a headache."

She straightens up. She wipes her mouth against the back of her hand.

"Did she really have a headache?"

"Yes." He pauses, takes a deep breath. "And then again this year. In Corsica."

She scrunches her eyes together tightly. "Which goes against—"

"The Freedom Clause," he stammers, hating himself.

"Did you consider that at all? Or were you just listening to your dick?"

He was definitely listening to his dick, but he knew it was bad.

"Both," he admits.

She looks at him like he's the most stupid person on earth. She turns on her heel and slides into the car, apologizing profusely to the driver.

"Ready?" the driver asks, addressing only Daphne.

"Yes, thank you."

"You okay, miss?"

Daphne sighs. "I honestly don't know."

"Just let me know," the driver says, giving Dominic a dirty look.

Oh, I'm getting a terrible *rating on top of everything else,* Dominic thinks.

"How could you do this to me?" she asks quietly, leaning forward, elbows on knees, covering her face with both hands.

Faced with her sadness, he wonders this too. What's wrong with him?

"It's awful, I get that. Totally unforgivable. I don't know, it just . . . happened."

"It just happened?"

Corsica. Skimpy outfits. The days she wore nothing at all. It felt as though every cell in his body was hardwired to notice, and respond.

"She's a woman. And I'm . . ."

"A man?"

"Yes," he says feebly. "It just . . ."

"Happened," she snaps. "I got that part."

"My self-control went to shit," he admits. "It was hard to say no."

"It was hard to say no," she repeats contemptuously. "I turned down a *threesome* out of respect for our agreement."

"A threesome?" He sputters. His mind snaps to the salad recipe. "Well . . . you broke the rules too!"

"How?" she says indignantly.

"We weren't meant to tell anyone about the Freedom Clause. But it sounds like you've been writing clickbait headlines about it."

"Don't be *ridiculous*." Daphne laughs angrily. "Nobody knows who I am, or that I'm writing about our marriage. I needed an outlet to process all of this, especially since we made sharing anything with our friends off limits. I *never* would've done it if I thought you'd read it."

"I can't *wait* to read it," he says sulkily.

Her voice drops an octave. "You wouldn't."

"Try stopping me."

"Dominic." Her voice is quivering with rage. "Don't you *dare*."

And something in her voice tells him he really mustn't. Although, sleeping with Lucinda might have wrecked his marriage for good anyway.

"Okay," he says in a quiet voice. "I won't."

Silence.

"You know what really kills me?" she says after a while, her voice suddenly tearful. "The Freedom Clause was meant to prevent this. The whole point of those rules was to *protect* us from this exact outcome."

He nods. It was his stupid idea after all, he was so confident in it.

"I'll do whatever you want. I'll resign." He swallows, hating what he's about to say. "I'll never see the boys again."

"I've lost my trust in you. I don't even know where we begin."

"What about therapy?"

"Therapy," she repeats angrily. "What, you want to pay someone to fix the problems *you* created? You don't just throw therapy out as an easy option, here."

"I mean . . . I'd pay for us to go! And I'd commit to the emotional work of . . ."

Daphne mimes butting her head against a window.

"Of making me forgive you?" she asks in disbelief. "This is why we made the rules!"

The damn rules. She isn't listening to his suggestions.

"We can stop the Freedom Clause!" he blurts out. "Or at least *I* can stop. How about I never do it again, and you can keep going until our five years are through?"

He hates this idea, but he's desperate.

"Don't you get it?" she murmurs, shaking her head. "You broke my trust. This goes way beyond the Freedom Clause."

"I know . . . but if I did stop, do you think you'd keep doing it?"

"Do you really think you have the right to ask that?" she responds with a small, pointed sigh. "Plus, isn't the whole point that it's spontaneous?"

"Okay . . . what if *you* had an affair?" he suggests in desperation.

"What?"

"To balance things out."

"Just shut up, for once in your life, would you?"

He feels himself spiraling. "I'll do anything. What can I do?"

She bites down on her lip in irritation. "I need you to promise you won't read my Substack," she says, meeting his gaze. "Can you do that?"

"I can do that," he responds quickly. "What else?"

She stares at him bleakly. "I have no idea."

Confessions of a Highly Emotional Cook:

Where-do-we-go-from-here lemon tart

I haven't written in a while and I apologize. Things between my husband and me aren't great right now. We are dealing with a rupture in our relationship and it's on me to decide whether I can forgive him, and what that for-giveness looks like, and how long that might take. And it feels like an awful lot of pressure on me right now, but all I feel at this point is exhausted.

I've detailed it in past entries, the fact we have a some-what open marriage. Once a year, we are permitted to sleep with someone else for one night only. It was a tough agreement for me to make, but I made it and I learned from it. And now I have learned that while he followed the whole "one person a year" part, he wasn't as respect-ful of the "one night only" piece. And what's awful (okay, it's ALL awful but what is ESPECIALLY awful) is that this is exactly what I worried about when we first agreed to the Freedom Clause. It took a lot of hard work and courage and faith on my part to leave that place of insecurity and embrace the freedom we both wanted for ourselves. I'm proud of myself. And yet now: look where I am. Right back at square one.

I am OBSESSIVELY reliving the days and weeks be-fore I learned he was having an affair, scouring for clues in my memory of how he spoke, how he appeared, pun-ishing myself for not having noticed sooner that some-thing was amiss. Why am I doing this to myself? I have no idea. Would figuring his affair out sooner have saved me from the pain I currently feel? Absolutely not. It is a pointless exercise designed to make me feel even more helpless, even more desperate, and low than I already feel.

I wish I could flatten this pain into something com-pact, like a package that can be thrown away. I feel dark and lonely, and depressed. I know you don't want me to wheel a terrible analogy out, but I'm going to wheel a terrible analogy out. My life feels like a horrible slow dance. One step forward. Two steps back. Turn to the left. Turn to the right. I suppose there are many options open to me. One of which is to walk away from this dance partner of mine. What would that look like, I keep asking myself. We were tadpoles when we met. How do we untangle our lives when everything we know of adult life has been experienced together?

I don't think he meant to hurt me this way. I think he's weaker than I am. I think he's lost, too easily swayed by the attention of others. Maybe I am being too kind, too forgiving. I am living in a world of maybes right now.

WHERE-DO-WE-GO-FROM-HERE LEMON TART

Feeds: two (when really you should only be feeding one)

Ingredients:
- Lemons (how bitter are you feeling?)
- Butter (as much as you need)
- Eggs (as many as you can throw at him)
- White sugar (however much you like)
- Vanilla extract (unnecessary)
- All-purpose flour (what is the purpose in any of this?)

Method:
1. Plan on making a lemon tart. An amazing tart, one that might last a lifetime.
2. Stare at the lemons in your hands. Ruminate on what went wrong.

YEAR
FOUR

S HE SEES HIS BETRAYAL WHENEVER her eyes land on his face. She hates what he has done. Just as she hates waking up each day, without fail, feeling low and lethargic. She has coping mechanisms—hot baths and cooking, reading and running, yoga, so much yoga—but there is a limit to their healing powers. Time is a commodity she will invest in. She needs time to heal, time to trust in her marriage again. She resists his attempts to touch her. There are days when she can't even look at him. How long will this continue? She doesn't know. She would like to not burst into tears in the work elevator. That would be a start.

—

HE misses her personality, the one she had *before* he screwed up her life, their marriage. Daphne is guarded, distant. She's on the other side of a moat, the drawbridge pulled up. Watching her, he wonders, will she ever let him back in? Will he ever be permitted to hold her hand or know what she is thinking? All of her is beyond his grasp. Just as all of this is his fault. And he hates that he has failed her again.

He hit a series of breweries that day—Mark and Simon were there—and when he crashed into bed that night, he tore through it like an addict. Daphne was away for the weekend. She and Aparna took the Eurostar to Paris to soak in the arts. To eat duck confit and mussels floating in white wine, garlic, and butter. Those were her exact words. Implicit too was the fact she wanted a weekend away from him. While she was doing that, he was going through her Sub-stack entries, right back to the infamous original post. Daphne was right to make him promise not to. But now he has read it, he can't *un-read* her sexual experiences, just as he can't unlearn how much pleasure she has received from people who are not him. And it weighs on him, but he won't screw up *again*. No more Substack. He promises himself this. He won't let her down.

—

SHE's leaving the office, on her way to Aparna's. They're having a night of vision boarding over wine and sushi when HOME flashes on her phone. She picks up on the second ring.

"Hi, Mum. How's things?"

Plumb is usually a modicum of calm, to the point of sounding medicated. She wants to offer the world her poised smile, her reassur-ance that everything is peachy. But today, her voice is wild, urgent.

"He what?" Daphne gasps.

A heart attack, as he was driving. He swerved into an approaching vehicle. The couple inside were killed instantly. By the time an am-bulance arrived it was too late.

"Too late?" Daphne repeats in horror. "Do you mean he's . . ."

Her mother is sobbing. Daphne stares at the ground, at her feet, in shock. She stopped moving at some point in the conversation, and pedestrians stream past her on both sides. A stupid thought presents itself: she is due at Aparna's in thirty minutes and she needs to cancel vision boarding because her dad is dead. More thoughts flood in. Like, she honestly thought at some point they'd move on from their awkwardness and have some semblance of a normal father-daughter relationship. But there's no more time for that now. And what about the couple in the approaching vehicle? Where were they driving? What were their dinner plans? What did they argue about? Did they have children or a wire-haired fox terrier that yapped and drove the neighbors insane?

Daphne makes gentle shushing noises. She'll catch a train home right now. Hanging up, for the first time in a long time, she feels the urge to call Dominic.

—

DOMINIC has a new job, working in the Corporate and Social Responsibility (CSR) team at a German bank. He selects charities to partner with, and donate to, although it feels like a half-hearted apology for the bank's cozy relationship with totalitarian regimes. He's not passionate about the job, not even close, but there's pleasure in the simplicity of the work. He finds it refreshing. The clearly defined responsibilities. The demarcated boundaries. No danger of sex-fueled vacations with coworkers. It feels like necessary penance. He sits on the forty-eighth floor and, on clear days, the sweeping panorama makes him feel like he owns London.

He feels genuine warmth toward Mary, his manager. In her fifties, kind and matronly. She never fails to laugh at his jokes, no matter how terrible, just as he never fails to compliment the baked goods she brings into the Canary Wharf office on Mondays. Dominic wants to ask why she spends her weekends baking for the colleagues she spends much of her week with. Instead, he smiles appreciatively, takes a tentative bite.

"This is . . . good?"

"I made it two weeks ago, remember?" Mary watches him closely. "Which is better?"

It reminds him of conversations with Daphne, back when she valued his opinion, and he feels a sharp pang.

"Hmm, let me see."

He takes another bite, chews thoughtfully. He feels like Paul Hollywood, without the credentials or the charisma. Honestly? This apricot tart tastes identical to the last.

"Definitely better."

Mary nods her head decisively.

"Salt," she explains. "A little extra does the trick."

The CSR team consists of two people. No opportunity for advancement unless Mary moves on. But this seems unlikely; Mary's worked here for twenty years and accrued forty-six vacation days a year. He wonders if he has lost all drive and ambition, or if it's simply on hiatus?

He's finished work for the day. He's on his way downstairs to the office gym when his phone vibrates in his pocket. He frowns. She never calls. He picks up immediately. The conversation is shocking, but brief. Daphne runs through everything she needs. A change of clothes. Something black. Help with funeral arrangements. Picking a casket, that type of thing.

"Whatever you need," he reassures her. "I'll handle it."

He knows it's wrong, but it feels wonderful. She needs him again.

—

PLUMB looks wretched, like a warning for shellfish allergies. Her face is puffy, eyelids pink and bloated. Daphne doesn't know what to say.

"You look thin."

The right choice. Her mother lights up like a Christmas tree.

—

A taxi drops him outside Daphne's parents' house. The front door is unlocked, and he lets himself in. The scent of perfume hangs in the air, pungent and overpowering. It's from the flowers, he realizes. Henry and Mimi are abroad on separate work trips, due back tomorrow. He hears Plumb running a bath upstairs. He finds Daphne making soup in the kitchen. He hasn't seen her in two days and she looks different. She's borrowed Plumb's clothes: white cashmere turtle-neck, black velour leggings, fluffy slippers. Her hair looks stiff and straight, voluminous. Turning, Daphne offers him a cynical look.

"I let her play around with it . . . and it cheered her up, okay?"

He nods slowly. "That's very *nice* of you."

"Thanks for taking the day off. You didn't have to."

He wanted to, and Mary insisted on it.

"No problem at all," he answers softly.

He drops his duffel bag on the floor. "I brought some stuff for you."

She nods, her eyes meeting his. She looks exhausted.

"Hungry?"

He ate a sandwich on the train, but he suspects she wants to feel useful and productive. Classic Daphne.

He grins. "Starving."

As he sets the table, they talk through funeral arrangements. It's all set for Tuesday.

"How does it feel being back?" he asks quietly.

Daphne shrugs. She ladles soup into two bowls and they take their seats. He stirs the green liquid slowly, wondering what it is.

"Broccoli and Stilton," she says, reading his mind.

"Delicious," he says brightly, hoping to cheer her up.

It doesn't work. She sighs heavily. Elbows on the table, she rests her head in her hands, offers him a gloomy look.

"I feel like a total monster saying this, but I'm not upset."

"That's okay. What do you feel?"

"Numbness. Or, if I'm really honest . . . *relief.* We just didn't get on and now . . . we don't have to pretend we do."

He moves his hand an inch closer. Her eyes follow. After what feels like a long time, but maybe it's only a few seconds, he places his hand over hers, lightly, hesitantly. Their fingers touch, but barely.

"I don't think that makes you a monster. Not even close."

—

THE morning of the funeral. Daphne wears thick wool tights, a long-sleeved black dress and ankle boots. She feels her mother's eyes roam over her.

"You look good. Black suits you," Plumb whispers in a surprised tone, pulling Daphne in for a hug. "Thanks for sorting it all out today. I'm proud of you."

Daphne's eyes fill with tears. She's never heard this from her before. "Thanks, Mum."

A pause. Plumb stares at her strangely.

"Are you on keto?"

—

THE Catholic church is modern and cold, unwelcoming. Daphne's brother walks up to the altar and takes a small bow. Today must be difficult for him. Dominic sees the grief on his face, but he can't pretend he ever warmed to him. Henry, the older brother. Full of his own self-importance. He never matured from the little boy telling Daphne he was going places.

Dominic can't stop thinking about the day when his own dad passes away. Dominic will be an orphan, and this realization makes him feel terribly scared, alone. He replays the conversation in Plumb's kitchen. He understands Daphne's feelings, but Dominic wouldn't feel relief. Dominic is already down to one parent and while his dad isn't perfect, he does care. He was delighted when Dominic emailed about his new job in CSR. He mustn't let their relationship slide, he tells himself, determined to call more often.

From the corner of his eye, he sees her shoulders begin to shake. Her cheeks are wet too. He takes a tissue from his coat pocket, offers it to her. Daphne whispers a hurried thanks, she blows her nose loudly. The noise reverberates down the line of pews. He feels helpless, awful.

All the pain he's caused, and now this. He's not even sure she'll let him, but he slips his hand into hers. After a few minutes, he raises his arm and, without missing a beat, she slides right in against his chest.

———

THE priest meditates on how difficult it can be to say goodbye to the ones we love, especially when it happens unexpectedly. We need to trust they are in a better place. Trust we'll see them again. Daphne frowns; she doesn't *want* to see him again. She's pretty certain her dad feels the same. At least Daphne understands why her mother always had a hard time loving her. Plumb wanted her to be slender, beautiful. But with her dad, it was opaque; she never got the sense he wanted to try. Although, she supposes, neither did she. Daphne was quiet and contemplative, in a family who weren't big readers. She retreated to her room, or curled up on the sofa with a book, while the rest of her family played rounders in the garden, or board games.

"Why don't you play with Mimi?" her dad asked her one day.

He was pointing to Mimi, lost in an imaginary world with her Barbies.

Daphne glanced up from her Point Horror book, shrugged.

"I'd rather read."

"Come on," he said impatiently. "Be a good girl, play with your sister."

Closing her book, Daphne threw him a suspicious look.

"Why can't Henry do it?"

Her dad snorted. "Barbies aren't for boys."

Daphne reopened her book.

"Well, then, maybe they're not for me either."

"I don't see why you have to be so difficult," he said with a tight-lipped frown. "The world can be a very unpleasant place for girls like you."

She tried to keep reading, but his comment stung. His remark contained claws and teeth that sunk deep into her skin, long after he left the room. Barbie was everywhere in their house. Mimi owned seventeen in total. Daphne hated those Barbie dolls in ways she couldn't articulate or understand. Each doll was impossibly thin, with a heaving great chest. Rollerblading Barbie lay near the sofa. She wore baby blue hot pants, a marshmallow pink crop top, white rollerblades. Daphne's fist tightened over her. It felt good, crunching down on the perfect plastic sheen. The snapping sound was definitive. Barbie's head rolled across the floor. Daphne felt a gush of euphoria, a pressure valve untightened somewhere in her mind.

Later, Mimi's wail filled the house.

"Why?" Plumb cried out in desperation. "Why would you do something so mean to your little sister?"

"I don't know," Daphne admitted, her eyes filling with tears.

Her dad scratched his head. "What are we even supposed to do with you?"

His eyes looked black, heartless. She pictured pushing him, watching his surprise register as he stumbled backwards and crashed through the glass window. How wonderful if this man was no longer in her life, she remembers thinking, and now he isn't. She got her wish. But what kind of daughter wishes *that*?

Her sniffles reverberate through the church. Even the priest sends her a sympathetic glance. Nobody would guess she's mourning the fact she never loved him, not the way the rest of her family did. Dominic's arm goes around her shoulder and she leans into his frame, weeping hard. She's missed this. Fitting snugly into Dominic's chest, his familiar scent. The way he lets her be, sitting with her, recognizing her pain. God, it feels good.

———

THERE is a small gathering afterwards. Dominic greets the caterers. He lays out food and wine. Guests pile in, they nibble on cocktail sausages and ham sandwiches, they gulp down their wine, they wipe their mouths against linen napkins. It's horrible, watching people eat this way.

"I see it in their eyes," Daphne murmurs. "They want more wine."

Dominic nods. "But they don't want to be *that* person at the funeral."

She laughs. He hasn't heard that sound in so long that he reacts to it, pulling her in, kissing her forehead. She takes an unsteady step backwards, retreating.

He flings his hands up apologetically. "Sorry, too soon." He glances around, trying to move past the awkwardness. "Nobody wants the prawn cocktail salad."

"Well, they're a health hazard at room temperature," she responds playfully.

"Different story with the cocktail sausages. Went by in a flash."

She smiles. "People will be talking about those for years."

"What do you think they'll serve at our funeral?"

She raises an eyebrow. "A joint funeral?"

He nods emphatically. "If you die first, I swear I won't last more than a week."

He's not even kidding. He's read about these couples: one dies, the other follows a week later. People find it romantic, when an elderly person dies from heartbreak, and it's definitely that, but he suspects it's fear of survival too. It's recognizing one's own innate helplessness without that other person. That'll be him, for sure, but Daphne doesn't think he's serious.

"Stop!" she laughs.

He grins. It's good to see that smile of hers again.

"Just awful, isn't it?" Henry says, popping up behind Daphne.

They freeze.

"Awful," they say in unison, shifting into frowns.

—

THEY are trapped. Henry is ranting about his latest scientific study. He works for a big pharma company and they're on the cusp of something huge, using laboratory rats. We don't care, Daphne thinks, squeezing Dominic's hand quickly in solidarity.

"Mimi, there you are," Henry calls out, beckoning her over.

Mimi arrived late, sitting in the back pew. Everyone noticed her. It was hard not to. Pistachio-green jump suit. Bright yellow silk shawl. Enormous shades even though it's raining. Mimi looks hungover. She also looks two margaritas away from being the life of the party.

"Hens! Daph!" Mimi clip-clops toward them in giant heels. "Dominic!"

"Why aren't you in black?" Henry asks with a small frown.

Mimi shrugs. "I haven't been to a funeral before."

"It's hardly a secret!" he responds indignantly.

Daphne smiles. She'd forgotten how effortlessly Mimi winds her brother up. Daphne slips her arm into Dominic's. She feels bad about earlier, her awkward rejection of his affection. She's certain she sees it now, his stunned surprise that she is touching him.

"Daph, you look *great*." Mimi's eyes flicker up and down her. "I guess you didn't need to wait for our inheritance for a new makeover. I just *love* your hair."

"Jesus," Henry hisses, "his body's still warm."

Mimi's eyes pop. "What's wrong with saying what we're all thinking?"

Are they all thinking it? It hadn't occurred to Daphne.

"I think it's gauche actually," Henry says in a pompous tone. He glances around, lowers his voice. "To discuss inheritance already."

Mimi rolls her eyes at Henry. "I'm sure he left it all to you anyway, the chauvinist pig."

Is Mimi drunk? Daphne wonders just as Dominic nudges her in the ribs. She can't look at her husband. He'll set her off. Mimi parts her lips, smiles, and a hiccup breezes out. Definitely still drunk. Daphne gives in, she explodes, so does Dominic, and Henry's glare only makes it worse.

—

"Mimi was kind of a riot, wasn't she?" Daphne says the next morning. "I can't tell if it was because she was drunk, or maybe I'm actually starting to like her more."

"Every funeral needs a Mimi," Dominic says sleepily.

"Maybe we should have her over for dinner sometime." Daphne pauses. "Maybe we're ready to . . . I don't know, actually have some sort of real relationship?"

"Away from the rest of your family?"

"Something like that."

"Sure, but we should keep an eye on your mum too."

"Actually," Daphne says, grinning at him, "she asked me out for lunch next weekend."

"To discuss the millions you'll be inheriting?" he asks in a deadpan voice.

"Please." Daphne swats at him. "He left me his *Readers Digest* collection, if I'm lucky."

—

The doorbell goes. It's Aparna. Daphne lets her in and they hug.

"I'm sorry I missed our vision-boarding session."

"Don't even." Aparna swats her arm gently. "How are you doing?"

Daphne shrugs. "Okay, you know . . ."

Aparna nods slowly. "Whatever you need, just say."

Daphne nods and leads her into the living room. They tear through magazines, pulling out the images they find appealing. Aparna is ambitious and her vision board reflects this: power suits, boardrooms, corporate jets. Aparna has a very specific goal: she wants to be head of HR at an organization by the age of thirty-two. Daphne's vision board is decidedly less corporate in tone, lots of food and books.

"Hey, Par!" Dominic calls out cheerily as he lets himself in.

He's in his football gear. Sweating intensely. He peers over her shoulder as Daphne applies the finishing touches. She leans back, pleased with the result: a bright tapestry of vineyards, mezze platters, books, travel locations.

"I like this," Dominic murmurs slowly.

His toe nudges the black-and-white image of a woman in lacy underwear.

Daphne glances up at him. "Shocking."

"Can I do one?" he asks, grinning.

"No!" she groans. "This is our activity."

"Fine! I need to shower anyway," he admits, kissing Daphne on the top of the head.

Aparna watches him stroll away.

"You seem happier," she says quietly.

Daphne stills. She hasn't breathed a word of Dominic's affair to friends, except for Ash. When she told him, she'd expected his judgment. She thought he'd tell her to leave that scumbag immediately. Instead, he asked her questions, pressing his fingers together in thoughtful silence as she answered, and then he asked more questions. And when she asked Ash why he wasn't telling her to leave Dominic, his response had been: *well, do you want to leave him?* And her answer was no. She wanted to stay in this place of uncertainty and pain, in which she still had him, even if what he had done nearly killed her. *Then I respect that.*

"I am," she admits. "We are," she adds.

Aparna nods. "You can lean on us, you know?"

"Us?"

"Me. Poppy. Abby. Somewhere along the way . . . it feels like you stopped."

Daphne's eyes prickle with tears. She's felt this way too. Her inability to tell her friends about the Freedom Clause has been hard. Clearly others have noticed the shift too. Aparna's deep brown eyes gaze into hers, waiting for a response.

"You're . . . you're right," she says, fumbling for an answer. "There's just been a lot going on and"—she shrugs a little, hating herself for being so vague—"sometimes it's easier not to share."

"It's fine," Aparna sighs. "So long as you're sharing it with someone."

About forty-thousand subscribers the last time she checked.

—

EMERGING from the shower, he overhears Daphne asking Aparna if she'd like more wine. He wraps a towel around his waist and treads softly into the bedroom, clicking the door shut. He unplugs his phone from the charger and commits to doing it.

"Dominic?" his dad shouts down the phone, sounding confused.

"Hey," he says brightly, pretending this is a regular occurrence. "Thought I'd check in."

He hears Sadie's muffled voice in the background, sending her love. And . . . barking?

"We're in the car, driving home!"

"Sorry, I can ring back some other time . . . is this a bad time for you?"

"Guess what?" his dad hollers. "We got a dog!"

Dominic bursts out laughing. "Is this to replace the twins leaving?"

"Pathetic, isn't it?" His dad chuckles. "How's the new job going?"

"Pretty good actually." He pauses. "And how are the twins?"

The conversation doesn't last long, maybe five minutes, but he feels good when he hangs up. And his dad follows through on his promise to send photos. Sprout is adorable, a chocolate-brown boxer mix. And Sprout is a lifeline, a reason to catch up.

—

DAPHNE watches her mother thumb through the menu. She's calculating the calorific content. Raw and grilled are the only acceptable forms of preparation. Big fan of seafood. Lobster. Shrimp. Oysters. Soup is a reliable option too. Or the trusty salad, but with the dressing on the side. Daphne has witnessed these orders over the years. She used to be impressed by Plumb's self-control, but these days it saddens her. When Plumb is on her death bed, will she really congratulate herself for resisting the cheeseburger time and time again?

"The cheeseburger," Daphne says decisively as their waiter returns.

"With salad or fries?"

"Sweet potato fries," she says with a smile.

She swears, she sees Plumb wince.

"And for you?" he asks, turning to Plumb.

"Butternut squash soup," Plumbs says with a tight smile, "and whatever you do, don't bring the bread basket."

Without consulting her mother, Daphne orders a bottle of wine. Plumb surprises her when she accepts a glass. She takes a small sip and nods her head in approval.

Holding her chin elegantly in her hand, Plumb says, "You must be wondering why I asked you to meet me."

Daphne leans her head to one side. Was it to bond? To make up for all those years when they didn't meet for lunch?

"You know my theory on women?" Plumb continues.

Daphne's eyebrows shoot up. "What's that, then?"

"We all want to be saved from something."

"Mum, that's a bit regressive now, isn't it?"

"I think I wanted to be saved from boredom. That's why I did it."

"Did what?"

"Cheated on your father."

This statement is so preposterous, so beyond anything Daphne pictured her saying that she almost laughs.

"You . . . what?" she stammers, incredulous.

Plumb taps her glass with her little finger. Daphne leans forward, tilts the bottle. She pours more for herself too. She loves a smooth red, the way it slips down easily.

"Being married," Plumb says with a small shrug, "felt like a totally different world."

Daphne doesn't follow. "From what?"

"Modeling. It ruins you, all that attention."

New York, Milan, Paris, Tokyo. Plumb loved fashion shows. The backstage drama. Last-minute adjustments. Screaming matches. Dramatic gasps when a model tumbled on the catwalk. All those people backstage working furiously, frantically, to pull it off. To inspire. To set the tone for an upcoming season. The shows made her feel special.

"I was never going to be famous. Not like Jean Shrimpton," Plumb says, staring morosely at the soup placed in front of her.

Daphne's burger is enormous. It stinks of oil and cheese and calories. She pops a sweet potato fry in her mouth, winks at the waiter.

The competition was fierce, Plumb explains, eyes dipping to Daphne's plate enviously. Her bookings dropped. The clients who *did* book her were smaller brands, their campaigns instantly forgettable. Her career dried up overnight. The jets, fashion shows, parties all vanished.

"And that's around the time you met Dad?" Daphne asks politely.

Plumb nods. Nigel offered her reassurance. She was the most beautiful woman he knew, he told her the first day they met. Nigel was indulgent, he smiled through her tantrums, her meltdowns. He offered her security.

"Can I?" Plumb asks, reaching toward her fries.

Daphne nods, pushes her plate eagerly in Plumb's direction.

"I thought Nigel's attention would be enough, but he got busy."

"With what . . . work?"

Plumb offers her a cynical look that indicates: *come on, what else?* Nigel's firm was acquired by a US company and there was talk of cuts. Nigel was stressed about his new boss, about being let go. They'd moved to the suburbs for his job and Plumb was lonely, miserable. She had no friends. She had a baby, Henry, who was a screamer, and a husband who rarely looked at her. Plumb thought fixing his work worries would help their marriage. She suggested they invite his new boss over.

"Nigel was not keen," Plumb explains. "He found Charles *loud* and *obnoxious* and *very American*."

But Plumb got her way. She wasn't a confident cook. It was easier to figure out her wardrobe. A Christian Lacroix dress. Flamboyant, duchesse satin, orange-pink. The dress would look terrible on most women. Plumb knew this. It's exactly why she chose it. Plumb was determined for the evening to be a success. And it was! She found her husband's negative description of his boss perplexing. Charles was thrilling despite the big ears, the shock of red hair. He was funny and playful, talkative. He was charming, generous with his compliments. This man. This conversation. This pulsing pleasure that lived in the base of her throat. She hung on his every word.

Daphne stops eating. She has a vague sense of where this is going. His wife was an artist, Plumb continues. Serious and contemplative. Intimidating. The dining table was round. She sat between Nigel and Charles. When Charles's hand found her leg, it felt like the whole evening had been leading to this point. His hand landed hesitantly at first, a small plane discovering new territory, and waited for her reaction. She didn't move and something crossed over Charles's face, a flash of victory. His fingers made soft circular motions on her thigh, she barely listened to what anyone said. He picked a quiet moment, as they carried plates into the kitchen, to suggest lunch. He offered her his business card. She kept it in her purse, tucked beneath an expired library card. She imagined calling him twenty times before she did. His voice was soft and velvety, and they arranged to meet the following week, but she was too nervous. She canceled at the last moment.

Half a year stretched before she saw him again, at a Christmas party Charles and his wife hosted at their home. That evening reminded her of the parties she used to attend, champagne and cocktails, beautiful dresses, glamor, foreign accents—Italian and Spanish and Russian, although mainly American. The Americans did decadence better than the English, less preoccupied with where the money came from. She loved his home, every inch of it. The driveway, lined with beech trees, the chandeliers, the long staircase, the Christmas tree, as tall as a cathedral, decorated in the prettiest white and gold tinsel.

Charles kissed her on both cheeks. His hand grazed her back. As it dipped lower, she inhaled sharply. Charles told them about his holiday plans. Plumb knew nothing of Vail, she couldn't point to it on a map, but she imagined snow-topped mountains, a perfectly blue sky.

"Excuse us," Charles said, leading Nigel away.

He offered her a brief smile and it felt like a secret present to unwrap later. She was nosy and she went exploring. Up the sweeping staircase. Past bedrooms and long hallways. She paused in the master bedroom. Everything in this room—bed, linen, pillowcases—were covered in gold fabric. She couldn't decide if it was exquisite or vile.

"What are *you* doing in here?"

She spun around unsteadily. Her cheeks flushed with guilt. She imagined what Nigel would say if he learned she was caught snooping. In his boss's bedroom of all places. The mortifying silence in the car ride home.

His voice was soft, teasing. "You don't work for the IRS, do you?"

His eyes were a deep green. They reminded her of long hot summers, tennis courts, freshly mown lawns, the lakes she used to swim in as a child. His hair and beard were golden red, like the best sunsets. Her mind went blank. She mumbled incoherently about the downstairs bathrooms being occupied. He grabbed her hand and pointed her in the right direction.

She took her time. She peed and reapplied makeup. She pressed a damp flannel beneath her armpits. She combed her hair and admired her earrings, small rubies hanging delicately from her earlobes. She found Charles sitting on the bed, hands clasped together.

"You didn't have to wait."

"Women like you are worth it."

What a stupid line, but the heat rushed to her cheeks. He motioned for her to follow. Through a series of doors. Up a small staircase. Sloping ceilings. The room was covered in artwork. His wife's studio, in the attic. Plumb busied herself with studying sketches and oil paintings.

"Your wife is talented," she heard herself say.

It was a reluctant compliment. Plumb was competitive. She knew it was a terrible quality, to dislike another woman for being prettier than her or, in this case, more artistic.

"Recognize this?" he asked, waving something in the air.

She stepped closer. It was a sketch of a tall slim woman in a dress. The Christian Lacroix dress! She recognized the ruffles, she looked like a peacock!

"She drew me?" she asked softly, unable to hide her delight.

He nodded. "She found you fascinating, we both did."

Fascinating. She smiled at this.

"It's my favorite of her sketches."

He took a step closer. She hesitated. She wanted him, but she wanted the dance first. To be flirted with, to be admired. She wanted to tease him with wavering and worries, with a debate over the morals of what they were doing. She wanted to be desired! The anticipation of the orgasm was more interesting than the orgasm itself. She wondered if this was normal. If this was a feminine trait or, simply, hers?

Her lips dry, she murmured, "They'll be looking for you."

"Not up here."

He was right, nobody would stumble up here. Had he concocted this plan earlier? It didn't matter really, did it? She took a step closer. He tasted of scotch. His mouth was soft and inquisitive. Her dress gave little resistance, crumbling to the floor. She wore a black bra beneath. Lacy knickers and dark stockings. The room was drafty, but their bodies were warm. She pulled off his jacket, undid his buttons. He lifted her up, pressing her against the wall. She felt one of the sketches in the small of her back. She heard it flutter, falling to the ground. This isn't me, she kept telling herself. They moved to the small desk, the one his wife worked on. He entered her from behind, his legs slapping noisily into the backs of hers. She noticed it then, the sketch of herself—the peacock dress, all those ruffles—and she couldn't take her eyes off it. It was better than sex in front of a mirror (she'd done that plenty). She was fucking the most beautiful version of herself.

"How long did the affair last?" Daphne asks quietly.

"About six months."

"Did you love him?"

Plumb dabs her eyes carefully, even though she isn't crying.

"I did, but he didn't love me. It was just sex for him."

Daphne's face softens. "That must have been tough."

"I went too far," Plumb admits, glancing away, embarrassed. "I shouldn't have told you all of that. Especially the rude parts."

The rude parts. Daphne smiles, how old-fashioned, how innocent.

"I love the honesty," Daphne reassures her.

"It felt like time to come clean. Now that Nigel has passed."

"Have you told Henry and Mimi yet?"

"Not yet," Plumb shakes her head. "I will, I'm just working up to
it. You know how Henry can be. But I wanted to tell you first . . .
and I know you'll go straight to Dominic. I can tell, you're one of
those couples who share everything."

Daphne almost laughs, if Plumb only knew. Dominic has kept so
much from Daphne. And she's tried to do the same with him, hoping
he's kept his promise not to read her Substack. But the way he looks
at her sometimes, she swears he knows about that incident with the
neighbor upstairs, and the fun she had in Mexico City.

"I won't go *straight* to Dominic," she responds, sitting taller in her
chair. In fact, she likes the idea of keeping this to herself for a minute,
processing it without him. "Especially since it's important to you to
tell Mimi and Henry first." She pauses. "I get that, I don't blame
you."

"Thanks," Plumb whispers, clasping her hand over Daphne's.

Daphne feels emboldened to admit something.

"It always felt," Daphne admits quietly, "like you and dad strug-
gled to love me."

Plumb inspects her face, surprised.

"It's not that I didn't love you, Daphne. I was just tougher on
you."

"But why?"

"All the guilt and the shame, I suppose."

Softly, Daphne asks: "What do you mean?"

"Nigel suspected but it took ten years before we finally had *that*
conversation."

Daphne freezes.

"What conversation?" she asks slowly.

Her mother looks up at her, startled.

"Didn't I say? Charles got me pregnant."

Confessions of a Highly Emotional Cook:

Who's-your-Daddy lamb meatballs

It's taken me a while to process this, and to share it here. I learned recently that my dad, who passed away recently, wasn't my biological father. I've been given an email address for someone who lives in the US who is my actual father. This man does not know I exist, and that makes me feel small and insignificant. Naturally, the feelings around my husband's affair are resurfacing. The unsteadiness, the sensation of being hit sideways, is familiar. I am trying to sit with these emotions rather than leap into action. The action being: what to do with the email address? I don't know yet if I will email him, and I am fine with not knowing. I am listening to what I *need* in this present moment (lots of pork soup dumplings, it transpires). And what I don't need in this moment. Mainly, I don't need another eruption in my life. Equally, I can't handle being the eruption in someone else's life (especially since he doesn't even know I exist). And I worry about giving another man in the world the ability to disappoint me. Is it obvious that I am reeling?

Let me be clear: I am reeling.

I am trying to focus on taking care of myself. Aforementioned pork soup dumplings. Long runs in the park. Each time I place my forehead on the yoga mat I feel a flicker of peace. I wish I could bottle up that feeling of peace and carry it with me everywhere.

I am making meatballs today. In dark times, I can tell you with absolute confidence, meatballs are your friend. I love a meal where the substitutions are effortless. Once you have the basics down, you can play around with the herbs, try other ground meats. Side note: some people stick to the ingredients list in recipes religiously. I urge you <u>not</u> to be that person. Rootle around in your cupboards and throw in whatever herbs you fancy for this meatball mix—except for dill, that really won't work—because this is when cooking is its most enjoyable, when you permit yourself to be creative and use flair and imagination and whatever is in your pantry to create a dish that is truly yours.

WHO'S-YOUR-DADDY LAZY MEATBALLS

Feeds: 2 (with plenty of leftovers)

Ingredients:
Meatballs:
- 500 grams of ground meat. (Note: you can use beef, lamb or pork. I recommend a mix and that your mix includes pork since it makes the meatballs nice and juicy as they cook in the oven. My preference is 250 grams of minced pork and 250 grams of minced lamb.)
- 1 finely chopped onion

- 1 egg
- 1 clove of garlic, minced
- 1 teaspoon of each of the following: parsley, oregano, sage, and red pepper flakes (note: these herbs are super reliable for cooking with, they will always be in your life, and they will never lie to you)
- A generous sprinkle of salt and pepper
- ½ cup of bread crumbs (Note: I bake 4 slices of whole wheat bread in the oven for 15 minutes and then grind it in my food processor to make half a cup. And whole wheat because it feels a touch healthier, but you don't need to.)
- 3 to 4 tablespoons of grated Parmesan

Yoghurt sauce:
- 250 grams of plain yoghurt
- 1 teaspoon of ground harissa
- 1 teaspoon of ground cumin
- 1 garlic clove, finely minced
- The zest and juice of 1 lemon

Couscous:
- 1 packet of couscous—figure out how much you need and what to do based on the instructions on the packet. I know this isn't very specific but, before you post an angry comment, remember, these are "lazy" meatballs.
- The zest of 1 lemon

Garnish:
- 1 bunch of fresh parsley, washed and chopped
- As much grated Parmesan as you need, babe (lots if your childhood, too, was laced in deceit)

Method:

1. Heat the oven to 200 degrees Celsius/400 degrees Fahrenheit.

2. Combine the onion, garlic, breadcrumbs, egg, cheese, herbs, and salt and pepper in a large bowl and mix it up. Your hands are going to get really sticky at this point. Do NOT rinse them clean under the tap (in the same way that you can't just rinse off your family issues either).

3. Add the ground meat and mix some more. And then take some of the mixture and shape it into a meatball, going as large or as small as you like. I'm going BIG tonight to match my feelings—two inches in diameter (but keep in mind the bigger they are, the longer they'll need in the oven). Now if you had a perfect and happy childhood in which you consistently felt the presence of love and affection and truth from your parent(s), then I will not judge you for making your meatballs smaller.

4. Place some foil on a baking sheet. Coat it with a little bit of olive oil so the meatballs don't stick to the foil. Line the meatballs on the foil and place in the oven.

5. Wash your hands. Dry them. Consider the email address your mum gave you, which is folded into fours and sitting in your back pocket.

6. Wait. Like I said, how long will depend on the size of your meatballs. My two-inch ones took roughly 25 minutes. If yours are one-and-a-half inches in diameter, it should take 20 minutes. This part is hard. The waiting, I mean. Imagine waiting twenty-nine years to find out you had a daughter?

7. While they're cooking, prepare the couscous and picture a man in his sixties who has no idea you exist. Even though he created you. Once the couscous is ready, add the lemon zest. Cover until you are ready to serve.

8. Combine the ingredients from the yoghurt section into a bowl. Try not to dip your finger in the yoghurt every thirty seconds as you wait for the meatballs to cook (confession: I did not succeed here. In better news, the yoghurt sauce is delicious).

9. Once the meatballs are ready, spoon the couscous onto each plate, followed by the meatballs and top with yoghurt sauce. Garnish with fresh parsley and parmesan. Sit down for dinner with your husband. When he asks you why you're quiet, shrug and say you're tired. Which you are. You are totally exhausted from all the drama. But these meatballs help. Savor them. You deserve this.

Hang in there and I promise that I will do the same.

Yours,
    The Highly Emotional Cook

—

DAPHNE thinks about him. Too much. Eventually, she decides to get in touch. The problem is she writes the email after a wine-tasting event with the girls. It's an indulgent evening, they drink every grape imaginable, and on her way home, head spinning in the back of a cab, she hits send. The next morning, each dramatic, cringe-worthy line floats back to her. *Do you remember Plumb Hardwick? You two had a connection for a while, the end result being: me.* Elsewhere, she sounds vaguely threatening, like she might mail him a decapitated rodent if he doesn't respond. *I'll admit, there are a LOT of strange types out there on the internet after money. I just wanted to say: "Hi, I exist."* At least, for now. And what about her sign-off? *The most important thing to know about me is . . . I give great hugs.* He's probably looking into restraining orders. And now she *really* can't tell Dominic. She's much too mortified to share it with him.

—

DAPHNE is glancing through the comments on her Substack when one catches her eye.

Hello! I'm really loving your Substack. I'd love to set up a time to chat, because I think there's a book here. Elaine Hetherington at the Crombie-Whyte Literary Agency (you can reach me on: 0207-918-4243)

—

DOMINIC's birthday falls on the first week of warm weather this year. They're at the mixed bathing pond at Hampstead Heath. It's filled with other bathers, swimming gracefully. The water looks deliciously cool. Holding hands, they pause at the jumping-off point.

"Ladies first," Dominic says, gesturing toward her.

Daphne's in a ruby-red halter-neck swimsuit. Deep V-shaped plunge. Enormous sunglasses. Wide-brimmed sun hat. She looks relaxed, fabulous. She plugs her nose, takes a deep breath and drops in. He watches her body descend, head vanishing last. Her sun hat is left behind, bobbing gently on the water. He laughs and dives in after her. The water is fiercely cold. He rises quickly and exhales.

"Incredible!" Daphne exclaims happily as she retrieves her hat. "Swimming in the same water as the ducks."

"I'm steering clear of those ducks," he admits as he treads water, eliciting a light laugh. "But I'm so glad you planned this day."

She smiles indulgently, and blows him a kiss. "My pleasure, birthday boy."

Dominic mentioned wanting to swim here a while ago. Daphne sprang into action; she corralled his friends, telling them what to wear and bring. She booked a table at a local pub for later. The others should be arriving soon.

"I'm glad I get you to myself for a bit," he admits, watching her swim gracefully.

Daphne is an elegant swimmer. Calm and serene in the water. After lunch with her mum, Daphne was acting low for a while, withdrawing again. Whenever he asked, she would shrug him off. She'd blame tiredness. Whatever was pulling her down, she's set herself free.

"Me too . . . because actually . . . I have some news," she admits with a smile.

She looks nervous, happy too. Her smile is so big it eclipses her face. Reflexively, he wonders if she might be pregnant.

"Is it something exciting?"

Her eyes light up. "Very!"

"Something we'd both be excited about?"

She considers this for a second. "I would hope so!"

He laughs. "I'm dying of suspense over here! What?"

She swims toward him, her eyes as wide as saucers.

"I spoke to a literary agent yesterday."

His mouth drops open. He's momentarily stunned.

"A literary agent?" he repeats. "Who?"

"Elaine. She thinks my Substack could be turned into a recipe book. She even has a publisher in mind."

He's aware he should be pleased for her.

"Wow," he manages to say. "Do you . . . think you'll do it?"

"It'd be silly not to, right?"

He feels a pang. A published book was *his* dream. While he's barely thought about it in months, it's painful to hear that Daphne's achieving his aspirations.

The pond is getting crowded. Beyond Daphne, Dominic watches a young couple swimming in sync, talking about something that amuses them, laughing loudly. It's not just the couple behind Daphne. Everyone looks content, floating and swimming, at peace with nature.

"That's great," he says in a tone that feels obviously forced.

He floats on his back. The sky is big and blue, cloudless. What a perfect day . . . almost.

"Thanks," she says slowly. "I had been feeling nervous to tell you, truthfully."

He swallows, wondering what to say. *Snap out of it,* he tells himself irritably. They only recently got on steady footing again after his enormous fuck up; he needs to do better.

"Why, Daph?" he asks innocently, glancing over. "It's great! You deserve it." Straightening up, he swims toward her. He leans in and kisses her just as she breaks into a sunny smile. "I think I just kissed a tooth," he admits.

"I think you did!" She laughs.

"I'm so proud of you," he says cheerily, trying to sound genuine. "So how will they handle your anonymous identity?"

Her smile vanishes. She bites her lip.

"The thing is . . ." She pauses. "Elaine told me I'd need to reveal who I am at publication. She said publishers generally only want to work with authors who can commit to promoting their work. Podcast interviews, readings in bookstores, that kind of thing . . . hopefully."

Dominic stares at her. "Well then, it's impossible, isn't it?"

Daphne's forehead creases in surprise. "Is it?" she asks slowly.

Wow, he thinks. *She wants to publish under her real name, to air their dirty laundry. It doesn't take a genius to understand how much that would backfire. Not for her.*

"We agreed," he reminds her in a careful tone, "that we wouldn't tell anyone . . . it's only worked because of that. Right?"

"What's only worked because of that?"

He looks at her impatiently. "The Freedom Clause . . . your newsletter . . . it's worked because it's anonymous. Because of the rules that we both agreed to."

"I know the rules . . . but a *published* book, I mean"—her eyes widen emphatically—"this changes everything, right? It's a dream."

It's his *dream,* he thinks angrily.

"It . . . no, it doesn't work, not for me."

Her face sets angrily. "It doesn't work for *you*? Even though *you* went off the rails in a major way when you had an affair? But the moment I have a big opportunity ahead of me, you're all about adhering to the rules?"

"I made a mistake and I learned from it," he says with conviction, "and now we're back on track with our marriage, our lives, because we're carefully, *assiduously,* sticking to the boundaries of the Freedom Clause."

Maybe he's overplaying it, he thinks, wincing. He sounded a little pompous there.

"Un-fucking-believable," she mutters, refusing to look at him. "I know what this is *really* about. It's not my fault you've done things you're ashamed about."

"Do you really want everyone knowing our personal business?"

She throws him a haughty look. "What are you so afraid of?"

"Your posts are about me! Our marriage! Our issues!"

"Not all of them! How would you even . . ." She pauses, incredulous. "You've read them, haven't you?"

"Fine," he snaps. "Yes, I read them."

"After I told you not to?" she looks horrified. "And you promised?"

"I was drunk!" he protests weakly.

She nods. "Sure, sure, blame alcohol! Heaven forbid that you actually take *ownership* over a mistake."

"How was I supposed to ignore it?" he responds angrily. "Especially after Lucinda told us what a viral sensation you are?"

"Lucinda?" Her eyes are flashing. "You really want to bring *her* up right now?"

Of course he doesn't want to bring her up.

"This has *nothing* to do with her."

Daphne throws her head back, laughs bitterly. "This has *everything* to do with her. Because guess what? The reason you don't want me to get a book deal is because *you* don't want everyone knowing what you did. The affair! And so you expect me to miss out on the opportunity of a lifetime to cover up your mistakes."

"God, you love to bring up my affair, don't you? Daphne *loves* to play the victim!"

"The victim?" she repeats sharply.

He shakes his head apologetically. "No, no, actually, that was wrong." He pauses, grinning cruelly. "The *martyr,* that's what you are. You'd hate for me to actually be as perfect as you. Your whole identity is centered around being better than your husband."

He knows he's stooping low. His mouth is motoring off, he can barely keep up.

Daphne laughs. "That's pretty easy for me given you fuck up all the time."

"It's called being *human,* Daphne. Nobody likes a perfectionist."

"Well, how about we also call you a hypocrite, then." She glowers at him. "You keep harping on about these rules, but you perpetually break them."

"Not true!"

"*We only do this one night a year.* Broken!" she says, ticking them off on her hand. "*A different person each year to avoid affairs.* Obviously . . . broken! *No questions asked (we don't discuss what happens with each other and we can't seek out the details around each other's sexual encounters).* Broken, twice! On New Year's Eve when you told me you hadn't done it yet, *and* by reading my Substack."

Shit, she's right. He doesn't have a leg to stand on.

"Honestly? It's gone too far already with the Substack."

"Has it?" she smirks at him. "You have a problem with my fifty thousand subscribers? What a shock! I would *never* have guessed your fragile ego couldn't handle that. Is it because I'm the one with the agent and the potential book deal? Is it because I'm the *real* writer?" She clutches both hands to her heart. "Poor Dominic, how does that make him *feel*?"

His mouth twists unpleasantly.

"I don't even recognize you. The Daphne I fell in love with was approachable, down to earth. But now? That ego of yours is so inflated from its success you're forgetting who you are, and who we are as a couple."

His voice is a bellow and it reverberates across the pond. It sounds mean and threatening. The other bathers glance in their direction, their concerned gazes linger on Daphne.

"You know I only started that Substack because I couldn't tell my friends anything about the Freedom Clause . . . one of *your* rules, by the way. And now all I'm doing is asking you to step up and support me, for once, the way I supported you when you suggested it in the first place."

"Yeah, you'll never let me forget that, will you?" he snaps. "But admit it, it's hard for you to keep using that line when it's clear you've had more fun than I have."

Silence. He looks away in frustration and catches sight of them. Mark and Tabitha, holding hands, walking in lock step with Simon. They're headed toward the pond, towels thrown casually over their shoulders, pointing in his direction. Aparna and Poppy are right behind them. They're all waving, and he tries to wave back cheerily, which feels absurd.

Daphne's face is stony. "That's your worry? That I've had more *fun* than you? Grow up, Dominic. Grow the fuck up."

She swims away, arms thrashing angrily. Pulling herself onto the raised platform, she heaves herself up just as their friends arrive.

"Daph! What's up?" Aparna asks, high-fiving her.

Daphne pretends to busy herself with drying off. She grabs her towel and rubs herself down. Straightening up, she offers them a determined grin.

"I'm running over to the pub. Setting up the lunch table for our birthday boy. Enjoy swimming."

She slips her sandals on, and walks away without a backward glance.

"Daphne never stops, does she?" Simon says, catching his eye. "Gets us all down here for a swim and she's already running off to figure out the next surprise."

The others agree:

"She's the best!"

"Really is."

All eyes are on him: the birthday boy.

With a forced smile, Dominic hears himself agree.

"Yeah, Daphne's . . . the best!"

———

HILARY is on maternity leave, so now Daphne's working directly for Steve. She's beginning to understand why everyone calls him dickhead Steve. He's intimidating. Aggressive. Competitive. He barks at the team during meetings. Daphne slips low in her seat, hoping he won't call on her. Today he's talking about an upcoming conference in Las Vegas. He announces Daphne will be coming. Her mouth forms a perfect O-shape of surprise. Heads swivel. But she's so new! This must be a mistake.

"Don't others on the team deserve to go more?" she asks Steve later, trotting to keep up with him.

Steve shrugs insouciantly. "It's your turn, tadpole."

She returns to her desk in low spirits. She doesn't want to spend an entire week with dickhead Steve, she thinks, biting into her sandwich. There are considerable upsides to the trip, however, like visiting the US for the first time, and having space from Dominic.

They've been weird around each other since the argument. Their awful insults hang in the air, taking up space.

The other benefit of this trip is it will take her mind off Charles. She's been checking her inbox continually. It hurts, both the fact he didn't reply, and that she even expected him to . . . she should have known better. The only blessing is that she didn't tell anyone. At least she can move on from Charles without anyone knowing, without reminders.

—

THEIR argument on Hampstead Heath hangs over him. It's immature, but he hasn't apologized yet. Daphne is polite around him, noticeably frosty too. He wishes he could unsay the martyr part, it was downright mean. He's had a lot of time to consider his reaction to her news, as well as why he reacted that way, and he knows that Daphne is right. The reason he doesn't want her book to come out has absolutely nothing to do with the rules, and everything to do with his own ego, his own selfishness.

Tonight, he is home alone. Daphne is working late in the office, getting ahead of her assignments before her big trip. He takes photos of his golf clubs, and places them on Facebook Marketplace. He gets some interest immediately. He's filling a tote bag with old A-level study books, ones he plans to donate to the local library, when she walks in.

"Oh! You're back!"

Daphne crashes on the bed. She looks tired and stressed, and not exactly enthused by the messy state of their bedroom right now.

"What's going on?" she asks quietly, rubbing her forehead. "I need to pack for Vegas tonight."

"I thought I'd clear out some of my crap." He points to his golf clubs that have occupied space in the corner of their bedroom for years, even though he never uses them. He gestures to the bookcase, its newly emptied shelves. "Sports stuff. Books I don't need. I want to make some room."

Daphne sinks deeper into their bed, yawning.

"What brought this on?" she asks with a frown.

He shrugs. "I figure we'll need more space soon. Hear me out, but how about . . . a table in that corner where the golf clubs are? It can be a quiet spot for your writing and editing . . . and some extra space on our shelves, you know, for the day you get published."

Daphne's face stills. "You mean . . . this is all for me?"

He nods his head, takes a seat beside her. "And I'll admit I'm very scared about how people will react when your book comes out. But that shouldn't be a reason to stop you from getting published. You deserve it, regardless of the regrettable things I did."

She stares at him for a long time. "Wow," she says finally.

"And . . ." he drops his head, looks at his hands. "You were right, I was very jealous of you. And I hate that I felt that way. I can only be honest about how I felt, and move on from it."

He glances up at her, their eyes meet. *Thank you,* she mouths at him.

His entire body exhales in relief. He hates it when she's mad at him, there is nothing worse.

"I've missed you, crumb cake," he admits in a small voice.

He buries his head in her lap, and she hugs him, kissing his forehead, his cheeks, his eyelids. And she murmurs over and over, again and again, thank you thank you thank you.

—

THE heat hits her, heavy and dry. The sky, it's the clearest blue she's ever seen, dotted with the tops of palm trees. Her room at the Wynn Las Vegas is enormous. She unpacks. She walks past casinos and swimming pools, the fountain at the Bellagio. She checks her email in case Steve wants to meet. Nothing. She goes for a swim. It gets dark early. In her room, she slips into a white robe made of thick cotton. She orders room service and sleeps.

She wakes at seven, her limbs deliciously heavy. Still in bed, she clicks a button. The blinds open automatically, sunlight filtering in. She checks her phone and bolts upright, gasping. A whole hour has passed since Steve emailed asking for help at the booth. She jumps into the shower. The queue for cabs is too long. She runs to the Sands Expo and Convention Center. She arrives by seven forty-five, breathless. It takes another ten minutes to locate him. By now she is disheveled. The sight of the booth assembled, banner stands up, marketing materials fanned neatly on the table undoes her. Steve taps his watch.

"I need to head out. Stay here all day. If anyone seems like a good prospect, call me."

She nods unhappily, understanding she's failed an important test. She stays by the booth all day, hesitating even to use the bathroom. People stop by occasionally. They ask questions. But for the most part, she is alone. Steve's instructions ring in her ears, although it is hard to assess whether these are "good" prospects or only "average." The air-conditioning is brutal, intense. She wishes she could step outside, bask in the heat. Moreover, she wants to eat. Her stomach growls, it makes obscene sounds. It's almost four. She hasn't eaten all day, save for the banana she picked up in the lobby this morning.

At last, Steve saunters toward her, hands in pockets.

"I need you to join me this evening," he says simply.

She raises an eyebrow. "Where?"

"Just tell me you like steak."

—

DAPHNE is in Vegas. His mind doesn't even want to think about it, but he has too much time on his hands, and imagining Daphne having fun is easy. It's summer, and work is slowing down, and there's only so many consecutive nights he can go drinking with Mark and Simon.

He stays up late. He watches a lot of porn. He thinks about the Freedom Clause. He hasn't done it this year, not even close. He doesn't even know *how* he'd do it without help, which leads him to download Tinder. If Daphne can be in Vegas, he can try out one measly Tinder date. He misses her. He stares longingly at the empty shelves he cleared. The space in the corner for her writing desk. He knows it was the right thing to do, agreeing to her book deal, but it terrifies him all the same. He feels he's earned the chance to let off some steam, so maybe this is why he swipes. And swipes and swipes and swipes. He sends messages, making it clear what he's looking for, and he waits for a response.

—

IN the evenings, they take dinner meetings in dark-green bars with paneled ceilings. Dusky lighting. Cocktail lists as long as her arm. Michelin restaurants and private dining rooms. Steve is a perfectionist. He sends a martini back one evening because it's too dirty. The following evening it's not dirty enough. He favors superlatives. The best cuts of meat. The most expensive wine. His prospects run the gamut. Heavyset men with silver-white hair. Handsome men, young and trim. Bright-eyed, soft-voiced women dripping in jewels. These prospects run luxury travel companies. They own high-end restaurants. They are hoteliers and heads of advertising. They will purchase ad spend in the magazine if Steve can persuade them, and Steve is very persuasive.

Daphne finds it difficult to relax in Steve's company. She watches all his energy conspiring to close a deal. He speaks too quickly. He stares intently. He has intense blue eyes that never seem to rest, a small pointed nose, thin lips, a prominent chin. He tries to mask his intensity and convey an easygoing manner—he smiles often, nods encouragingly, filling everyone's glasses while barely touching his own—but beneath the table, his foot taps quickly, nervously, against the slate-tiled floor.

—

THE bar Dominic chooses has a generic Slug-&-Lettuce vibe. Not that it matters; one drink and they'll go to hers. Simple, transactional. He's early, but so is she. Sitting on a high stool, back to him, nursing a drink. She turns and smiles. Dark hair, poker straight, glossy. They kiss on the cheek. He takes a seat, orders a beer.

"What are you drinking?" he asks.

"Espresso martini."

He rests his arm on the bar. She's wearing a denim jacket, collar turned up, cute dress beneath. She has almond shaped eyes, an easy smile.

"So, what do you do?"

Mae's a money manager at an investment firm. Thirty-seven, divorced, disinterested in romantic relationships or children. She has a busy life, he learns, and she prefers sex without commitment. Finally! This is the woman he's been looking for since he first suggested the Freedom Clause. Somewhere along the way, he stopped believing she existed. But maybe a few do. She's a unicorn, he thinks, gazing dreamily. He finishes his beer and orders another.

"You seem very content with your life," he observes.

She nods, smiles to herself. "Because I am."

"But what about at weddings? Do you feel lonely?"

She shakes her head. "Weddings are great."

"Huh." He pauses, slightly in awe. He can't imagine being single and happy. Surely there would be constant reminders that you're alone? How would you not worry it's a reflection of your personality? Or that you're fundamentally unlovable? Or is it just his mind that would go there? He perseveres: "But you must miss some aspects of your marriage?"

She laughs. "We argued all the time. I honestly don't miss it at all."

"Really?"

"I love the freedom of my life. I love waking up alone on a Saturday morning and *doing* whatever I like, *going* wherever I like."

Dominic understands the concept: the ability to selfishly choose whatever you want. But he's a people person. Waking up alone on Saturday gives him no pleasure. He gets nervous as the weekend approaches if he *doesn't* have plans. He'll always meet Mark and Simon for drinks, whenever they suggest it. And when Daphne is home, he attaches himself to her like a puppy. He'll watch her cook. He'll watch her clean. It's pathetic, but he can't stop himself.

He's hungry to find the flaw in Mae's theory.

"But if you woke up alone on a Saturday morning and wanted to *see* people," he begins, "and everyone you liked seeing just happened to be busy . . . what would you do then?"

Mae shrugs. "I play tennis on Saturday mornings."

"But what if tennis was canceled?"

Mae stares at him strangely. "Why would tennis be canceled?"

He shrugs. "There was a nearby explosion. Police surround the courts, refusing people entry."

"Jesus." Mae frowns. "This turned bleak quickly."

He opens his mouth, he is struggling here. "I guess what I'm trying to get at is . . . don't you miss being loved when you're single?"

She hits his arm playfully and laughs. "I have a lot of love in my life!"

"You do?"

She stops laughing. "Wait, are you suggesting single people don't experience love?"

"They do," he explains, "but love from a friend or family member . . . that's not the same as romantic love. It's not as . . . I don't know, life-affirming."

"You don't actually believe that?"

He nods and her forehead creases in concern.

"How sad for you."

He considers his solitary childhood with his mother. Or how awkward and out of place he felt in Sadie's home. He didn't feel love until he met Daphne. Her love was pure, uncomplicated. It's all that's ever mattered.

"How old are you?" Mae is asking.

"Twenty-nine."

"Clearly you still have a lot to learn."

"About?"

"People, relationships, values."

He disagrees. He grew up too quickly. He learned a lot about people, what they value.

"I think I'm just more cynical than you," he says with a shrug.

She takes a small sip of her martini. "What about random acts of kindness from strangers? You don't find that kind of love life-affirming?"

"That's not love. That's people acting impulsively when they happen to be in a good mood."

She shakes her head and her earrings swing back and forth. Gold hoops studded with diamonds. Expensive. Everything about her is affluent, even her denim jacket. That must be why she's content, he decides. It's easier for rich people to feel good about themselves, they can throw money at their problems.

"You're wrong," Mae says slowly.

"How often have you done that? A random act of kindness?"

"I give a good amount to charity each month."

"Well, that's tax-deductible."

Her face flattens. She reaches for her near-empty drink, takes a final sip, and signals to the bartender. He watches helplessly. Has he blown it? He *feels* like he's blown it.

"For the record, people who bestow random acts of kindness are in love with the world. They want others to feel that way too. It's really quite beautiful, when you consider it."

"I hadn't thought about it like that."

"Well, this was," she begins stiffly, "interesting."

"Please don't leave!" he pleads. "I'm sorry."

"Just because I'm into casual sex," she says, pulling her handbag over her shoulder, "doesn't mean I have no standards."

He gasps. "I never said that!"

"Well, with your attitude, the way you see the world, everyone out for themselves, I just . . . can't imagine you're a good lover."

The bill arrives in a small silver tray. Mae drops a wad of cash in and strides out. He blew it, he thinks as she marches off. He blew it with the unicorn.

—

"I'M heading to a party next," Danny says as dinner ends. "Want to come?"

It's their final night in Vegas. Steve has been nervous, fiddling with the buttons on his blue shirt. He pulled a lot of strings to score this early evening dinner. Daphne senses the success of the trip might depend on tonight. Danny Merino owns a prominent casino and hotel group. Late forties. Sandy hair, deep-set golden-brown eyes. He is tanned. Too good-looking, Daphne thinks. He donates frequently to the arts, charities, local causes. His first wife divorced him. His second wife died in a freak skiing accident. She enjoys his accent, the slowness of his drawl. She's definitely into him; how often does she spend time with attractive multi-millionaires?

"Why not?" Daphne responds with a quick, high-spirited laugh.

They stand by the entrance, waiting for the valet to bring around his car. Danny slides behind the wheel of the black Lincoln Navigator. He wants to talk about England. His aunt married a Brit, he explains. Danny's hand rests on Daphne's arm as he tells them about a trip to Windsor. His aunt told him to wave to the castle in case the Queen was peering out of the window. Daphne smiles. Her parents used to tell her similar things growing up. England feels a long way away. Perched up high in the passenger seat, Daphne glances at the bright lights in the rearview mirror. And the mountains ahead, dark and ominous. It's a different world out here.

The car slows down, turns off the highway. When he invited them to a party, she imagined a sleek penthouse on the Strip. They pull into a gated community. He stops outside a Spanish villa with a circular driveway, terracotta tiled roof.

"My home's in that direction," Danny says, pointing behind him. "Five-minute walk."

It's dark, his gesture meaningless, but she nods regardless. She will sleep with him this evening, she decides. This is exactly what the Freedom Clause was created for.

"Where's the party?" she murmurs.

They are standing inside a gigantic farmhouse. Large fireplace. Beams on the ceilings. There are no people and it feels post-apocalyptic. Danny chuckles. He grabs her hand, leads her through a series of hallways, into an elevator. They step off on a subterranean floor.

"Are you fucking serious?" Steve asks.

A basement club. Speakers hang on the dark walls, vibrating intensely. The staff are dressed in formal attire, they hand out champagne flutes, sparkling water. The room is vast and dark, the floor made of reflective glass. Daphne can see up her skirt. Danny is hugging friends, kissing women on the cheek, introducing Daphne. She chats with them.

"Danny's great," one woman says, offering Daphne an encouraging wink.

Caught off guard, Daphne blushes. "Yeah, he seems to be."

"A real catch," the woman says, excusing herself.

Daphne watches as people dart onto the dance floor. Whitney has come on: "I Wanna Dance with Somebody." Daphne contemplates dancing too, but she reaches for champagne first.

"Danny's a real catch, is he?" A deep voice startles her.

Turning, she finds the voice. He's holding a tray of champagne glasses.

"You look like a penguin," she says, taking in his formal attire.

He flashes her a quick smile. "Penguins have a lot more fun than this, I suspect."

She stares appreciatively. If Danny's good looks are obvious, this man has a subtle appeal. He's intelligently appealing, bookish. Dark glasses magnify his intensely blue eyes. He has a long nose, wide lips. Blond hair, thick eyebrows.

"You bring the average age down," he remarks, nodding toward the dance floor.

For the most part, the crowd is in its forties, early fifties. There are younger guests too, beautiful women with long legs and ample cleavage, sleek hair and toned arms, although they are attached to men twice their age.

"What about those ladies?" she asks, tipping her head in their direction.

He throws her an unkind look. "No offense but you don't seem like them."

"Are you saying I'm not trophy material?"

"Oh, you definitely are." He grins. "But maybe not for this crowd."

She's never been in a position where two men are flirting with her on the same evening. She plans to savor it. She takes a delicate sip of champagne.

"What's your deal?" she asks casually.

"Geologist," he says holding her gaze. "With a lot of school debt. Hence the catering."

"A geologist?"

"We exist." He smiles, more to himself. "I study rock formations. I'm an adorable nerd."

"Adorable, huh?" she repeats archly.

He studies her. He seems okay with the silence that extends between them. It's unnerving, but she doesn't look away, and neither does he.

"Can't you tell?" he whispers at last, raising an eyebrow.

She presses her lips together. She doesn't have a witty response. She doesn't have a non-witty response either. Now it's her turn to stare, a fifteen-second silence that speaks volumes.

"Why Vegas?" she asks at last.

"I'm part of a research team here for a few months."

She nods. "What's your name?"

He offers a friendly wink. "Oh, that's a big step. I'm not sure we're ready yet."

"Fine. I'll just call you The Penguin."

His laugh is rich, deep-throated. "And what are you doing in Vegas, nameless beautiful woman?"

"I'm here on a work trip," she informs him. "I leave tomorrow. Back to England."

"On behalf of the community of Nevada, I wish you a pleasant final evening and safe travels home," he says in a deliberately formal tone. Breaking into a smile, he adds: "And the drugs are in that room in the back left, if that's your thing."

"I'm not sure about that, but I *do* need to pee."

He laughs, pointing out the direction to go in. As she begins to walk away, he calls out:

"I don't think Danny's a real catch. Do you?"

"Sorry," she says, turning and winking, "but I don't think The Penguin's a reliable judge of character."

Theatrically, he pantomimes clutching his chest in pain, upsetting the balance of his tray. Daphne laughs and walks away. In the bathroom, she's still smiling. Danny finds her as she returns, threading his arm in hers as he explains there's a pool party. They pass enormous guest rooms, showers made of Italian marble, a lush garden. Bougainvillea and rhododendrons, pines and ferns. Danny points to the hot tub. Why not? Slipping out of her dress, Daphne eases in in just her bra and knickers. She leans back and stares at the star-dotted sky, small traces of silver in a sea of black. Danny's hand rests on the nape of her neck. It feels good, the way his fingers tap dance against her skin.

"So, what are your fantasies?" Danny asks, wasting no time.

Daphne tells him about the woman in the flat above, the boyfriend who watched.

"You like being with women?"

"Actually"—she pauses—"I think I like being watched."

"Exhibitionism is hot," Danny breathes into her ear.

He is too eager, too straightforward. Would he have said this about any fantasy she'd shared? Three-ways are hot! Bondage is hot! Missionary is hot! A rebellious thought pops into her head: do you *really* want to sleep with *him*? She tries to un-think it.

"This is all I want to do," Danny admits, throwing his head back, laughing. "Let loose, meet cute British girls like you."

It's a compliment, but she feels herself shrinking. Surely, she isn't one of those women who goes off a man the minute he's nice to her? But it's not that. It's that his conversation is too easy and obvious, it's *dumb*. Over dinner they talked about their childhoods, the arts, but the Danny sitting in front of her now is the real Danny. And the real Danny, she notices, is leaning out of the hot tub to snort a quick anxious line of coke. He passes the plate to her. In the spirit of the Freedom Clause, being spontaneous, not planning every second of her life down to a tee, she leans in.

"Go easy," he adds gently as she inhales, "pretty strong ketamine."

"Ketamine?" she exclaims, jerking her head up and laughing. "I thought it was *coke*."

"Okay. That laugh of yours just sent five hundred dollars flying."

She glances down. The plate is empty. "Oh god, I'm so sorry."

Danny winks. "Good thing you're cute."

She swallows. She knows where this is leading. She's just not sure she wants it anymore. It's a relief when she spots Steve, waves him over. Beer in hand, he's the most relaxed she's seen him all week. He grins and jogs over.

"Having fun?" Steve says, removing his shirt and sliding in.

"Sure," she concedes.

She hopes the bubbles hide what Danny is doing beneath the water. His hand is on her upper leg, stroking the skin. Or maybe Steve knows exactly what is happening?

"I think we all need more drinks. Don't go anywhere," Danny says, squeezing the top of her thigh as he leaves the hot tub.

Steve sits quietly, looking out into the dark night.

"Don't move to editorial," he says finally. "You're great in sales."

"But I want to write," she counters pleasantly.

She doesn't need Steve's help figuring out her career. She has it all planned.

"I know, but you're good with people," Steve says holding her gaze. "It's a gift, and it comes naturally to you. You know how to make people happy."

Daphne feels her jaw tighten. Make people *happy*. Why is this an expectation that's always placed on women? She never hears this "compliment" leveled at men.

"Plus, this is where the money is," Steve continues.

"I don't think money motivates me as much as it does you," she answers honestly.

"Right," he says slowly, "but you're good at this. I need you here."

There it is, the real reason: it would suit Steve if she remained in sales. Why do men like Steve think they can cajole women like her into doing what they want? Into thinking their needs are higher? Is their success rate that high—or high *enough* at any rate—to keep doing it? And why does Daphne feel bad that she has to tell him *again* that she doesn't agree? Why *is* Daphne a people pleaser? Where does it come from? Was it her upbringing? Was it that she was encouraged to be cute and adorable from a young age? And while Henry was allowed to do whatever he liked (pretty much), she was encouraged to play quietly with Mimi's Barbies? And can she attribute her people-pleasing gene to the fact that when she showed so much as an ounce of rebellion toward her parents she was admonished, criticized, flattened? Because if Henry had tried to eat more at the wedding banquet, or if Henry had beheaded a Barbie doll, would he really have suffered the same treatment she received? Boys will be boys, as the old saying goes. Except boys grow into men and by then, the damage is done. By then, these men think they can pressure women into doing whatever they want because the world has turned a blind eye toward them for all those years. And, concurrently, they have seen what pressure does to a young girl. Is this why women are trained to be compliant and pretty and persuadable from a young age? To prop up the patriarchy's machinery? And if so . . . god, she's so tired of it. She is so damn tired of being encouraged to please others. Tired of this expectation that women should yield to men. It's exhausting.

"Steve, just stop." She raises a hand up to him. "Because when the next job in editorial opens, I'm going for it. You can't talk me out of it."

"Suit yourself."

He watches her with interest, noting her rising anger. She watches him with tired, angry eyes, knowing he won't be able to help himself. That he will feel the need to impart his wisdom, to mansplain, because this is what men like Steve do to women like Daphne.

"But for tonight . . . maybe you can help me out. The fact he invited us here"—Steve grins wolfishly—"it's a good sign, I think. We have a decent shot."

"At what?" she asks in a monotone.

"We just have to . . . connect with him. You know, in the right way."

"Meaning what, exactly?"

Steve takes a slow sip of beer, watching her.

"Meaning we're all adults here, aren't we?"

It's masterful. He isn't saying anything explicit, yet she feels her entire face tense up as realization dawns on her. Steve watches her with pursed lips, a shrewd expression.

"Has he complimented your hair yet?"

Her voice. When she responds, it doesn't sound like her.

"Why do you ask?" she says tightly.

"Both his ex-wives were redheads."

Ah, *this* is why she's here. It's not because she gets along with people, or that she's good at sales. She's here because she's a type, and she's satisfying a man's needs, his preferences, in the hopes he'll open his wallet. And how strange this feels, because a few years ago, when she didn't feel attractive, when she didn't feel she was anyone's type, Daphne would have loved this attention. But now? She is desired, but she feels like a cheap piece of fish being bartered over at the market. Do men ever yo-yo between these feelings, she wonders? Do they ever feel their worth shoot up and down based on how much they are lusted after by women? She doubts it. The world was built to suit them.

A desperate sinking takes hold of her. She has to get out of here. She steps out, reaches for her dress, pulling it over her head. No towels. She is clothed, soaking wet.

"Where are you going?" Danny asks as he returns.

He's changed into a Speedo, bright pink. He's brought towels and drinks, and more ketamine. He wraps a towel around her hair and rubs it delicately. Is there any part of her that would enjoy sleeping with Danny, she asks herself? While Steve's proposition doesn't sit right, on the other hand . . . because she is in Vegas. Because it is her final night. Because the Freedom Clause gives her free license to act on moments like this. Because—

"You have the wildest hair," Danny remarks.

Something inside her snaps. "I'm out of here."

She reaches for her handbag.

"Hey, my place is only five minutes away."

"Danny, I had a lovely time," she says firmly, "but I really need to leave."

ON her way out, she passes the waiter-geologist-penguin. He's removing party debris, clearing dirty glasses. He doesn't see her. She leans against the doorway. This man, she thinks slowly, is the reason her interest in Danny waned.

"Hey," she calls out before she loses her nerve.

His head shoots up. "Not you again!"

She smiles at this. "You were right."

"What do you mean?"

"Not a catch. At least, not for me."

"Hmm," he studies her. "That's a shame . . . for Danny, anyway."

They stare at each other. She bites her lip. She has to at least try. You'll regret it, she tells herself, if you don't.

"So"—she pauses, glances at her hands—"any chance you want to get out of here?"

HE drives a tinny car with a manual transmission that grinds every time he changes gears. In the elevators at the Wynn, he presses her against the wall, and her back accidentally touches all buttons. They stop at every damn floor. The ride lasts an eternity, his hand tracing the inside of her thigh. They kiss as she fumbles in her handbag for a room key. By the time they reach her room she is breathless, impatient.

"Before we start . . . any preferences?" he asks.

"I'd like you to go down on me."

He smiles, raises an eyebrow. "Well, obviously. What else?"

She wishes every woman could experience this. She wishes every man's top priority was her pleasure. She wishes every man began by slipping his head between her thighs. That every man knew exactly where to press and lick, where to suck and linger. That every man checked in with her this regularly, asking what he should be doing more of, and less of.

His tongue is all over her, followed by his dick. Missionary, doggy, reverse cowgirl. She's groaning. She's murmuring god-awful clichés. Each time is somehow—my god, just there, oh god—better than the previous. She comes loudly. She comes without inhibition. They laugh and they tease, they sleep very little. They order room service. Cheeseburger. Fries. He feeds her and she swears it's the best meal of her life.

In the morning, they take a shower. Her back up against the slate tiled wall. They know each other's bodies by now, how they fit perfectly. All manner of noises escape her lips—compliments, foul words—as he presses her clit. How strange it is to hear these grunts. Loud and ugly and animalistic, and to realize they belong to her.

HE drives her to the airport. He talks about the red rock terrain. How different it is in Maine, where he grew up. Tilting her head back, she studies his profile, his perfect nose, his sleek blond hair, those lovely lips. She pictures saying goodbye to London, the rain and fog, the pre-war homes, the sloping roofs and rust-colored chimneys. *In another world,* she thinks. She imagines the two of them. The weekends. Long hikes in canyons and state parks, kissing, laughing.

But where is Dominic? Guilt appears, peering down at her, and she shakes the fantasy from her mind.

"If I was a romantic," he says, pulling up outside departures, "I might admit I could really fall for someone like you."

"I'd need to know your name first," she says as her heart beats wildly.

"Wilfred," he says, reaching forward, holding her face in both hands, kissing her.

"Daphne."

She walks onto the plane, changed somehow. The grooves in her lips. The sway of her hips. Each strand of hair. "Wilfred," she murmurs before falling asleep.

—

Mimi is over. She's sitting on the floor, legs curled under her, glass of wine in hand. Nick Drake plays in the background, soft and melancholy. They've sunk a few bottles by this point in the evening, and she's telling them about a nightmare photo shoot. For siblings who've rarely spent much time together, they don't seem that way tonight. Daphne looks happy, relaxed. Dominic clears their plates. He stacks the dishwasher. He opens the freezer, pulls out mochi.

"Ooh, my favorite," Daphne coos as he returns. "Thanks, love."

He offers Mimi one too, but she shakes her head. "I'm full. That was delicious, Daph."

"Pleasure," Daphne says, smiling.

"Should I leave you two to catch up?" he asks, not wanting to intrude.

"Stay!" Mimi shouts out.

Daphne pats the space beside her. Turning to Mimi, she says, "I'm glad you were able to come over."

"Me too," Mimi agrees. "I'm sorry it didn't happen sooner after the funeral. My travel schedule has been so busy. But also, I think I had to work through a lot after Dad's death."

"Really?" Daphne asks, looking surprised as she takes a sip of wine.

"Yeah! I'm in therapy actually and of course there's a lot of "let's discuss your childhood" groundwork. As I talked about it, I realized how fucked up our childhood was. How he treated us differently and pitted us against each other."

Daphne's expression changes. "How did he pit you against the rest of us?"

Mimi shrugs. "He'd ask why I couldn't get a nice boyfriend like Dominic. Or why I hadn't done as much modeling as Mum had by my age, that kind of thing."

Daphne's face softens. "I'm sorry, love. I didn't realize."

"But also . . . I was Mum's favorite, Henry was Dad's, and you were just . . . on your own. I sort of saw how difficult it must have been for you."

Daphne bows her head. This must be hard to hear, Dominic thinks. He places his hand on the small of her back and rubs gently.

"I'm really proud of you for going to therapy," Daphne says softly.

"Yeah," Mimi murmurs. "I just have this habit of flinging myself at emotionally unavailable men so we've been exploring that . . . and my daddy issues."

Daphne frowns. "I guess I didn't realize you had issues with him too. I feel bad for not noticing."

"I hadn't either," Mimi concedes. "But Dad was so patronizing, always treated me like an airhead. I keep ending up with these men who treat me the same way."

Daphne shifts uncomfortably. "I think I treated you that way too. I'm sorry."

Mimi shrugs. "I mean I was, for a while there . . . but I want to change! I want to get into charity work. I want to learn Italian. And I'm going to read Tolstoy one day, even if it kills me."

Daphne laughs. "That's great."

Mimi claps her hands together excitedly. "And I'm going to buy a place in London. I need a base. I hate not having that."

Daphne tilts her head to one side. "You're buying a place?"

Mimi's eyes bulge. "With all the money Dad left us? Why not?"

"Oh, that's great," Daphne says, although her voice indicates otherwise.

Mimi picks up on it. "Did he . . . ?"

Daphne shakes her head.

"What a mean fuck."

"What Mimi said," Dominic chimes in, and Mimi winks at him.

"Honestly, it's fine," Daphne says in a casual voice. She changes the topic. "Have you seen Mum lately?"

Mimi shakes her head. "She keeps mentioning we should catch up for lunch . . ."

Daphne's response is emphatic. "You should."

They keep talking, but Dominic stops listening. His mind is on the will. To purposefully leave one child out is a special kind of cruelty. But Daphne seems absolutely okay about it, and he has no idea why.

—

"Daphne!"

She stops typing. She glances up.

Steve is pacing toward her, baring his teeth.

"The Merino team is out."

The white noise of the office stops. Phone calls cease mid-sentence. Fingers pause their tapping against keyboards.

"Is that so?" she asks innocently.

He glares. "They aren't spending anything with us. Not a cent."

Her chest tightens in fear, her fingers tremble, but she won't let him see it. Her smile is small and tight-lipped, dripping in superiority.

"What. A. Shame."

"You blew it," he sneers.

"I have integrity," she says in a low voice. "Better luck next year."

She sees it in his eyes: he misjudged her.

"Go to hell," he says before walking away.

A couple of days later, Daphne receives a call from the editor-in-chief's assistant. Elizabeth would like Daphne to come to her office. Daphne hasn't been on the editorial floor before. The first thing she notices is the energy, it's more relaxed. Elizabeth's door is open, but Daphne knocks anyway, motioning toward her watch: *is now still a good time?* Elizabeth is on the phone, but she nods and beckons her in.

Daphne takes a seat. She studies the books, the white shelving units, the framed photos of family, the selection of plants sitting on the window ledge, until the call wraps up.

Elizabeth extends a hand over the table. "Nice to meet you, Daphne."

Elizabeth has an air of confidence. She's been editor-in-chief for fifteen years. Her gray hair hangs in a long thick plait. She's dressed casually: red jeans, a thigh-length gray cardigan.

"Likewise. Thrilled, actually!"

Elizabeth stares at her in fascination. "So, I hear Steve is furious with you."

Daphne sits back, surprised. "Yes unfortunately, I think he is . . ."

"And that intrigued me."

"Really?"

Elizabeth smiles at this. "Steve and I hate each other. With a passion."

"I see . . ." Daphne says slowly.

"Do you mind if I ask what happened in Vegas?"

Daphne tilts her head to one side. *Careful,* she thinks. *Whatever you say may be repeated.*

"We had a difference of opinion."

"That's disappointingly diplomatic!" Elizabeth laughs to herself. "Tell me about you."

Daphne tells her about her love of writing, her job at the law journal, the job she applied for in editorial that went to someone else, and why she took the sales role. Their allotted thirty minutes together fly by and they keep going. Elizabeth has a lot of questions. When Daphne explains she's scored a book deal for the recipes in her Substack, a detail she has told almost no one, it feels like the most natural thing in the world. Elizabeth inquires which Substack account it is.

"Please don't share this with anyone," Daphne says, before revealing the name.

"I love that newsletter," Elizabeth admits with a slow smile. "I'm the one who told Peggy at the *Times* about it."

Daphne's mouth drops. "No!"

"Peggy and I go way back."

Daphne begins to grin. "Then you're the one I should thank for all my followers. And the book deal."

"Don't thank me, your writing drew everyone in." Elizabeth glances at the clock. "This isn't the reason I called you in today . . . I just wanted to gossip about Steve. But let's just say, in theory, we're seeing a retirement or two approaching at the end of this year, and a couple of positions are likely to open up. . . . Would you, theoretically, be interested?"

Daphne fights the urge to lean forward and kiss her.

Confessions of a Highly Emotional Cook:

A big cocktail, to match that big fucking career move

Apologies for the expletive-ridden title, but I've been offered my dream job. Nope. That doesn't cut it. This job goes beyond my wildest dreams! It combines my love of writing with my love of food, and I get to work with people I've respected and admired for a long time.

The offer has been in the works for a few months, and I just signed my contract today. Maybe I should be hitting the dance floor in glittery heels, shimmying around to Donna Summer. But tonight, my closest friends are coming over to celebrate. They get how BIG this career move is. They view my success as their success, and I love that we celebrate each other this way. These are exactly the type of friends every woman needs.

Now, everyone has a favorite cocktail order, the one that makes them feel like an absolute baller. This is mine. I like to think of it as the love child of a French 75 and a Kir Royale, and I'll be upfront right now: It's not for everyone.

A BIG COCKTAIL, TO MATCH
THAT BIG FUCKING CAREER MOVE

Makes: One cocktail (but you're not stopping there)

Ingredients:
- 3 ounces chilled champagne
- 1 ounce gin

- 1 ounce of liqueur—either Crème de Cassis (blackcurrant) or Chambord (raspberry), depending on which you prefer
- A dash of simple syrup
- Ice

Method:

1. Before doing anything fun with a cocktail shaker, you'll need simple syrup. See longer, more precise recipe for simple syrup <u>here</u>, but in a nutshell for the woman who just got her raise/ promotion/big-ticket move to success and is in a hurry to celebrate: combine a little sugar and water in a small saucepan over a low heat, whisking it until the sugar disappears. Remove the pot from the heat. Let it cool.
2. Fill a cocktail shaker with ice. Add the gin, liqueur, and simple syrup; fasten it and shake. Now would be a good time to turn up the music and sing at the top of your lungs as you shake, shake, shake that drink.
3. Strain into a cocktail glass and top with champagne. If in doubt, add more champagne.
4. Repeat steps 2 and 3 as more friends arrive. Do not consider how you will feel tomorrow. Tonight is all about your success.
5. Wait, was it too syrupy? Too much gin? Too little champagne? Then switch it up and try again, and again, and again, until you get the combinations just right. The same way you have persevered in your career. And guess what? You're going to continue to persevere because that's what you do, you don't give up, even when it's tough. Here's to you, congrats!

Yours,
The Highly Emotional Cook

YEAR
FIVE

Dear Daphne,

Thanks for your message. It must have taken a lot of
courage to hit send. I'm sorry for the delay, the reason
being that your email went straight into my junk folder
where it's been sitting for the better part of a year.

I do remember Nigel and Plumb Hardwick. I remember those three years in England vividly, not always for
good reasons. One thing for sure: not a strand of red hair
between them. And neither seemed like they'd give an
especially good hug! Now, you mentioned a paternity
test. I'm not going to insist on it, but happy to do it if you
prefer.

A little about me: I am retired, and I have too much
time on my hands for someone who doesn't enjoy gar-
dening. I live in Connecticut and I have two children
from my first marriage: Stella, a musician in Brooklyn,
and Eric, a programmer in Silicon Valley. This may seem
sudden to you, and it feels sudden to me too, but my wife
and I have a trip planned to Europe this spring. We'll be
in London for a few days, before flying onto Italy. I don't
want to place any pressure on you to see me. It's something for us both to consider for now.

I have to run, but let's keep this correspondence going.

And nobody calls me Charles these days, so you shouldn't either.

Chuck

—

SUNDAY morning. Dominic wakes slowly and stretches like a cat, yawning. The front door slams. Daphne is on a run, he thinks, drifting off. The next time he's woken up, it's by something vibrating. His eyes flutter open. He hears Daphne humming in the shower. Disoriented, he fans his fingers and slips them beneath the pillows. Daphne's phone is the culprit. A message lights up her screen. It's from someone called Chuck. It says, simply: *I can't wait to see you.* He hears the shower being turned off. Daphne stops humming. He slides the phone back under her pillow. His heart pounds wildly.

—

THEY share more information. They get comfortable, or as comfortable as two people can get when they haven't met yet. Daphne worries she's growing too invested in Chuck too quickly. She wants to be sure there is no deception on his side, and that his wife knows. His reply comes quickly:

Amy is a therapist. Her intuition is off the charts! I can't hide a tea towel from her, let alone a daughter in England.

Daphne laughs. She finds him funny, but what if he's better on email than in person? She's tempted to talk to Dominic, but he'll wonder why she didn't tell him sooner and it's a valid question. The truth is, she wasn't sure Chuck would ever reply. And if he wasn't going to reply, then what was the point in telling people about him?

And what's her reason now? She hesitates to tell Dominic because maybe she'll meet Chuck and not like him and want to bury the entire experience, pretend it never happened? She'll share it with him *after* she's met Chuck, if she decides she wants him to remain in her life. The stakes are too high. She needs to keep this to herself just a little while longer.

—

"CAREFUL, it's hot," she says as she passes him the spoon.

Lentil soup with streaky bacon. Dominic takes a sip.

"Bit more paprika."

He enjoys testing her recipes, it's a small window into the world of her Substack success. He respects Daphne not wanting him to read her posts, and outside of that one mishap a couple of years ago he's diligently kept away. No small feat given his mind is racing, almost perpetually, with fears over Chuck. Does she make subtle allusions to him in her writing?

"I think my period's coming," Daphne says, pulling an annoyed face. "Keep stirring."

He nods, but as soon as the bathroom door closes, he pounces on her phone and scans the most recent thread.

CHUCK: *I was thinking we should start with lunch. My treat.*

DAPHNE: *Great, do you want to pick where?*

CHUCK: *I have some ideas . . .*

DAPHNE: *Which hotel are you staying at?*

CHUCK: *The Dorchester. My wife won't join us, obviously.*

DAPHNE: *How is she feeling about all this?*

CHUCK: *She's been great, very supportive. We are very open. You haven't told your husband?*

DAPHNE: *No. I can explain more on that in person.*

CHUCK: *I've thought about you a lot since our last conversation. I'm looking*

*forward to seeing you. I don't want to place any pressure on you, but
equally I'll admit I want this to go well.*
DAPHNE: *I agree completely. It's all I can think about.*

He puts her phone back, feeling sick to the stomach. He tries to
find a simple, innocent reason for these messages, but there isn't one.
It can't be the Freedom Clause either. She's interacting too frequently
with this man, far beyond what's required for one night of sex.
Which leads him back to his biggest fear.

It's an affair, and as he realizes this, he trembles a little with rage,
and indignation. How dare she! After everything they went through,
after all his groveling, after all those discussions about the importance of trust. How could she turn around and do the same thing to
him? Is she punishing him or is she in love with this guy? He sways
between anger and hurt, crippling jealousy and stunned surprise. He
never thought he'd consider Daphne, of all people, a hypocrite.

The loo flushes. She emerges. He watches her padding round the
flat in navy sweatpants, a gray tank top, open-toed flannel slippers.
What does she wear for *him*?

THE bank Dominic works at is holding their annual charity day. Ce-
lebrities visit the Canary Wharf office and make trades with clients.
The commission the bank makes on the trades is donated to charity,
and everyone is happy. At least, they're supposed to be, but they
haven't confirmed a single celebrity this year. Sasha, head of events,
informs the tightly packed conference room of the latest bad news.

"Zoe Ball's agent said no," Sasha explains. "She has another commitment."

Murmurs and disappointed sighs. Crossed arms and furrowed
brows.

"Who else turned us down?" someone calls out.

Sasha nods, clears her throat. "Phillip Schofield, Les Dennis, Paul Gascoigne. We got a firm no from all the cast of *The Only Way Is Essex*."

Disappointed sighs filter through the conference room. Dominic stifles a yawn. He knows he should care, that he is *paid* to care, but his interest is waning fast. At the ad agency, he was motivated by the big salary, bonuses, business-class travel. Looking after Oscar and Cody messed with his head because he'd been offered none of those sweeteners and yet it was hands down his favorite job. And where, he ponders, does that leave him now?

"We've tried everyone," Sasha says hopelessly.

Dominic leans back in his chair.

"What about a model?" he asks slowly.

"You know models, do you?" Sasha responds in disbelief.

Dubious laughter from the corner of the room. It only makes him more determined.

"Mimi Hardwick," he adds, glancing at his phone, wondering if he can pull this off.

MIMI saves the day. She brings all her model friends. Tall and leggy, cool and disinterested. The trading floor becomes a catwalk, owned by women with limited knowledge of the Dow and FTSE 100 Index, but they've perfected the art of moving effortlessly, and it's all that matters. They flirt. They make trades. They pose for the press. Photos pop up on celebrity gossip columns. The day is a huge hit and everyone knows it's thanks to him. A bottle of champagne is pressed into his hands.

"You're our super star," Mary says, beaming proudly. His manager glances at Mimi, shrugging on her cream coat. "You should take your sister-in-law out for a thank-you drink."

Mimi's head shoots up. "I agree," she says, grinning.

Dominic pulls a face. "Canary Wharf doesn't seem like your scene. Way too corporate."

"God no," Mimi looks horrified. "We're getting out of here."

———

MIMI calls an Uber and, when it arrives, she removes her heels in the back seat. She presses into her feet, wincing slightly. Daphne does this at the end of a night too.

"I thought you'd be used to heels in your profession."

"Not all heels were created equal. These are little horrors. Let's swing by my place first so I can change."

He nods, hardly in a position to say no. They pull up to a white-washed crescent in Notting Hill. He was expecting a fabulous place, but not *this* fabulous: dark floorboards, high ceilings, enormous windows that must flood each room with natural light in the mornings. Daphne would die over the kitchen.

He opens the fridge, looking for water. Mimi reaches past him for some plastic containers. She turns the oven on.

"I thought we were stopping by for a shoe change?"

She yawns emphatically. "Mind if we stay in? I'm beat."

He wasn't expecting this. He pauses, uncertain of himself.

"Sure." He shrugs and gestures to the bottle he's carrying. "We can drink this."

He places it in the fridge to chill. Mimi walks away, returning in stonewash jeans, an oversized navy shirt. She scoops chicken and vegetables into casserole dishes.

"When did you start cooking?" he asks, unable to hide his surprise.

"Ha, I'm not Daphne!" she offers him a withering look. "I have an Israeli housekeeper."

She makes them each an Aperol Spritz, an unusual choice for February. Grabbing her keys and cigarettes from the kitchen table, she gestures for him to follow. They take the staircase up to a small private rooftop with no plants or furniture; it's barren save for a few cigarette stubs.

Dominic leans over the edge of the railing and watches a red bus rumble along the road. The breeze picks up and he shivers, wishing he'd worn his coat. Mimi lights up and extends the pack his way. He shakes his head. They stand side by side and stare at the flat, sloping rooftops, the rows of chimneys, miniature gardens, brightly painted fronts of houses. Mimi is the spitting image of her mother, he thinks, watching her. God, he hopes she turns out better. Mimi has always been slight, waiflike. Tonight, perched against the railing, she looks daintier, like the breeze might pick her up and whisk her out of sight. There's also something terribly lonely about her. She travels often. Does she have friends, besides those models she brought today?

"So." She smiles at him. "Daphne has a book coming out."

He returns the smile. "She told you."

"Last week." She nods. "It's impressive. I flipped through a few of her entries quickly . . . mainly to make sure there isn't anything incriminating on sisters in there. . . . Seems *you* didn't get off so lightly."

He throws her an anguished look. "Keep saying stuff like that and maybe I *will* bum a cigarette."

She laughs lightly. "You seem fine about it. Mum and Henry aren't so thrilled though. Both of them are pretty vocal about the fact they have, and I quote, no desire to read it. But I think they will." Mimi pauses, offering him a sidelong glance. "They won't be able to resist."

It's beginning to happen. People are reading Daphne's work. They know what he did. They have opinions about him, and not good ones, he thinks uneasily.

"How's your mum doing?" he asks, eager to change the subject.

"She's okay." Mimi shrugs. "Henry and I are taking her out to dinner next week, actually. It seems like news of Daphne's book kind of unnerved her."

"Well, I'm glad you're supporting her," he says. "You know, you could make it nice up here." He places his drink down, spreads his arms wide. "Paint the walls a bright color. Grow some plants here. A little herb garden there. You could hang fairy lights. Daphne and I would help."

He wonders how Daphne would feel about him assigning her this task given her limited spare time. He suspects "super stoked" is not the answer? She's busy with her editorial job, preparing her upcoming book launch. But *he* has free time—too much, one could argue.

"I'd love that, thanks," she responds. Something passes over Mimi's face, a flash of incredulity. "I'll admit I didn't get you and Daphne for a while there. You two always seemed so different . . . what attracted you to her?"

It's his turn to look incredulous. "At university you mean?" he asks softly.

Mimi takes another drag of her cigarette. "She's figured out her style recently. God, I love how buzzing and confident she is. But back then . . . those *cardigans* she'd wear."

He closes his eyes, casts his mind back. She was Daphne. Funny, intelligent, self-aware. She had so much joy for life, and it rubbed off on him too. She had appreciation for everything in her life. The freedom of being a student. The opportunity to learn. The time to invest in friends. She loved everything about Bristol, even the bad cafeteria food, or the terrible lecturer that sent them all to sleep. Her eyes sparkled with joy, and he loved her for it. It was infectious, being around her, happiness always within reach.

She was buzzing back then too. Not with sexual confidence, not exactly, but there was a rebellious streak. She was direct and inquisitive, she had a total disdain for boundaries, formalities. The thing about Daphne is, once she trusts someone, she's an open book. She is fearless, brutally honest, and it encourages the same in others. It feels important to remind himself of this quality now. Honesty has not been easy to come by for either of them recently, but they'll find their way back, somehow. He's sure of it.

"We've always had this connection," he says simply. "There's no one I'd rather be with."

"She's so willing . . ." Mimi pauses, struggling for the words. "To fade into the background. How can you not see her as average when she sees herself this way?"

"Daphne," he says, lowering his voice defensively, "is exceptional."

Mimi drains the last of her drink and steps inside. He follows. The kitchen smells heavenly, and his stomach wakes up.

"Do the honors, will you?" she asks, passing him two flutes.

Mimi barely touches dinner. She moves food around her plate. She reminds him of Oscar and Cody, when they were tired or upset or inexplicably obstinate. But she drinks plenty, small and eager sips of champagne, replenishing their glasses often. They are stuffed—at least *he* is—when they move into the living room. Mimi sits cross-legged on the floor, credit card resting between her slender fingers.

"I think it might snow tonight."

He groans. "Please don't tell me that's what you kids call it these days."

"What do you call it, Grandpa . . . blow?"

Truthfully, he was never into it. Mimi cuts lines with practiced ease. She's insatiable, her supply limitless. They do this for a while. An hour passes. Or maybe only ten minutes. Until Mimi leans forward, a wide smile on her face, and presses her lips to his.

"What the fuck?" he mutters, twisting away in shock.

Mimi looks injured, unused to rejection. She wipes her mouth with the back of her hand.

"Huh, I guess I thought . . ." She hugs her knees up to her face.

"You two have some sort of arrangement though, right? I read about it on her Substack."

"Friends and family are off limits," he says sternly.

"But affairs aren't?" she says archly.

He lets out a low whistle. "Ouch."

Mimi starts telling him a story, about one night, years ago, when she ran into Daphne outside a hotel with an older man. They were both disheveled, his arm drawn protectively around Daphne.

"I thought she was having an affair until I read her Substack." Mimi offers him a long disapproving stare. "It's certainly an odd arrangement."

"Mimi," he says as kindly as he can. "I really don't want to discuss the Freedom Clause with you."

"But you two are good?" Mimi asks quietly.

"Yes." He closes his eyes, focuses on his breathing. "No? I don't know!"

"What do you mean?"

He pulls a face. "I saw her phone. She's been texting someone called Chuck."

"So?" Mimi shrugs indifferently. "It's probably just her one-night-off person this year."

"It's different. I think it's revenge, for what I put her through."

"How do you know? What's she saying?"

"I can just tell. It's all very underhand and devious. They talk about whether his wife knows. And there's a lot of I-can't-wait-to-see-you talk between them."

"Oh god, that sounds bad."

"Doesn't it."

"You know . . . I'd never cheat on you," Mimi says quietly, "if you were my husband."

"In one of her texts to him," he explains, his voice wretched, "she wrote: '*It's all I can think about.*' I keep thinking about that message over and . . ." he stops, unable to continue.

Mimi moves closer, her small hand grazes his lower back. He is miserable, but it is lovely for his pain to be acknowledged, validated, for him to be comforted.

"Daphne does seem different these days." Mimi leans in closer, her voice conspiratorial. "More confident and self-assured. Do you think it's him?"

"She's still Daphne at her core," he mumbles through a blur of tears.

"How would you describe me?"

Her face is close. He sees details, hidden before. Hints of freckles beneath her fading foundation. A stray eyelash peeling away from her eye. A chalky trail of white dusting her left nostril.

"You're the type of woman who will never, in her life, wear a cardigan."

She laughs softly. Her dainty mouth lands on his and, this time, he does not twist away. He doesn't do anything except allow Mimi to explore his mouth. He thinks about Daphne's betrayal. She wants to hurt him, the way he hurt her, and maybe she is justified? Maybe they didn't deal with their issues properly. Should they have done couples therapy? Should they have talked to a trained professional about all the hurt and bitterness she was feeling? Maybe . . . as Mimi pulls his clothes off, he is in the room with her, and absolutely not there. *It's all I can think about.* Who is Chuck, and what does he look like? And how is he in bed? Mimi lifts her dress over her head. She has a slim boyish frame, as tiny as a postage stamp, her breasts high and pert. Mimi is kneeling, peeling off his clothes. He runs a hand through her short blond hair. The fact he is hard right now seems miraculous. Mimi's technique is painful, her teeth everywhere. He feels raw and dry, exposed. Another terribly painful minute passes.

She's categorically terrible at blow jobs. What is she doing? More-over, what is *he* doing?

"Stop!" he cries, backing away.

"Why?"

"I can't . . . this is wrong," he says, pulling his clothes on franti-cally.

"But . . . she's having an affair," Mimi protests, reaching for his ankle.

He hops over her hand, and beelines for the door. Fuck! Where are his shoes? He scans the floor, searching beneath cupboards, under the shoe rack. His mind races and already, he is dreading wak-ing up in the morning. To the realization that he went there, that he did *this*.

"It's all going to work out," Mimi calls out, just as he locates his shoes, under the kitchen table. "Everything's going to be fine, okay?"

Pulling each shoe on, hopping toward the front door, he adds giv-ing advice to the list of things Mimi is terrible at.

—

DAPHNE's never been to The Ivy before. She arrives early, she's shown to a table in the corner. Daphne unfolds and refolds her napkin. She gulps down water. She wipes her hands against her knees. A holler makes her head shoot up. At first, all she sees is shopping bags. Lib-erty. Fortnum & Mason. Selfridges. Striding toward her, he raises the bags high in the sky like a gold medal. He's grinning, moving fast, and Daphne stands up. She grips the table. In the long mirror opposite, she sees herself. She looks scared, a woman about to offer testimony in a high-profile court case. She *is* worried over this next part: will it be awkward?

"Daphne! Look at you!"

He's hugging her. Not all the shopping bags make it. She hears them crash to the ground. But the hug isn't awkward, not at all. Daphne knows how to give a good hug, a proper grip that's warm and comforting, that says: *this is exactly where I want to be, right here, right now.* So does Chuck. His nostrils are deep in her hair. He's not letting go. The hug continues indefinitely.

Released, Daphne sinks wordlessly into the green-velvet seat. She studies him. There is so much hair, bright red hair that refuses to be flattened. He orders coffee. He pours in sugar, stirring constantly, licking his lips. He has a great deal of energy. Lots of opinions, expressed quickly, wild hand gestures. His smile is disarming. She watches carefully, taking it all in, focusing on his conversation too. She wants to be—a dreadful term, but still—*present.*

Chuck orders a martini. Daphne asks for a gin and tonic.

"Haven't been here in eight years," Chuck says, tapping the menu happily. "They still have the calves' liver."

She smiles. "Bit of an acquired taste, that one."

"I've missed London," Chuck admits, looking wistful.

He sits back, and a button on his shirt pops open. The glimpse of pale stomach seems oddly intimate. Daphne considers pointing it out, but she doesn't want to embarrass him.

"And you." He waves a hand in her direction. "I want to know everything, but let's order. And don't hold back. We'll stuff ourselves. They'll have to roll us out of here."

Daphne stares longingly. She tries to picture her mother saying this. Impossible!

"What is it?"

She doesn't know what to say. "Your button's undone."

He glances down, chuckles. "Need the next size up. At least now I have an excuse for all this shopping."

He talks to the menu. He treats it like a dear companion.

"Ready?" the waiter asks, bringing their drinks.

Chuck shakes his head. "Don't rush us, please. It's the most important decision of our day."

Hours later, Daphne yawns. The restaurant is almost empty. Chuck is studying the menu, oscillating between the chocolate fondant and the crème brûlée.

"Maybe we should get the truffles too?" he contemplates.

"The truffles?" she repeats, feigning shock. "I didn't think they were in the running."

He laughs and snaps the menu shut.

"I like you, thank god!" he admits, grinning. "What else do you want to know?"

"Well," she tilts her head to one side. "What was it like, meeting Plumb?"

He was in a bad spot. Moving to England was a mistake, one he was contractually locked into for three years. The weather, nineteen consecutive days of rain. He missed the Red Sox, beers on the porch, summers in the Cape, inviting his neighbors over to grill. That said, Massachusetts didn't have a Plumb Hardwick. Flawless skin, intense blue eyes, immaculate lips. Chuck considered himself a good read on people—you had to be in sales—and Nigel and Plumb were wildly mismatched. Not that he and Christina were perfect. Seven unhappy years of marriage would follow (two children, endless arguments, couples therapy) before they agreed to separate. But he knew Plumb's type: self-absorbed, sulky. He wasn't sure why he asked her to lunch, except she seemed bored, frisky. He arrived early, ordered a diet coke, buttered his warm bread and ate it slowly. He ate the entire bread basket before his assistant called the restaurant and said his lunch date couldn't make it . . . she was tied up. He didn't see her again until the holiday party. She was vain and careless, and the affair lasted only a few months. It was a relief when she called it off. He didn't think about her again, not until Daphne's email sailed in.

Holding her gaze, he says, "I'm sorry, I was terrible to my first wife. Amy calls me Chuck 2.0. I want you to know I'm a better husband this time around."

Chuck stares morosely at the abundance of untouched desserts in front of them.

"I have something I should probably share with you," she begins, taking a deep breath. "I have this Substack account about food and my personal life, all the big things happening to me . . . including that I have a new dad, apparently."

He nods his head slowly. "Okay."

"And I kept it anonymous for a few years, but the thing is . . . it has a decent following, decent enough that I got a book deal from it. And now . . . I've a cookbook coming out this summer, and I'll no longer be anonymous. I've started telling people and not everyone is"—she shrugs to herself—"that happy about it. You can include Plumb in that category."

She braces herself, waiting for his judgment. Dominic wasn't supportive initially. Most of her family hasn't been either. Maybe Chuck will feel the same? She feels nervous.

"I look forward to reading it. You must be an excellent cook."

A big smile eclipses her face. "I am."

He stares at her closely. "You know something I've learned? It's that not everyone is going to be happy for you when you're successful. But often . . . that's more a reflection on them, whatever's going on in their lives, and not yours. And you might just be better off . . . learning they're not in your corner. Make sense?"

Is this what it's like, she thinks? To have a parental figure who shares advice in an honest and kind way? How long has she waited for this? It feels like a very long time, she thinks, as he smiles warmly at her.

"Congratulations," he says, raising his martini glass. "I'm really proud of you, honey."

This bit gets her. Her eyes fill with tears. It's not just that he's proud of her, it's that she can't recall a time she was ever called "honey" by a family member. Chuck smiles, offers her a handkerchief.

"Now you're going to set me off."

Out of the corner of her eye, she sees the waiter approaching. He pauses, not wanting to interrupt this tender moment between father and daughter. And it's obvious that that's what they are. They look so alike. They look like they've known each other forever.

In a strange way, it feels like they have.

DAPHNE wakes up with a splitting headache, a parched mouth. She slides clumsily out of bed. Each step is an effort, a small victory against The Hangover. She tries to recall the day before. They stumbled out of The Ivy and ducked into a hotel bar. But wait! There were *two* hotel bars. They were in high spirits, debating if it was ever acceptable to order a piña colada outside of a beach vacation (a flat *no*). There was a lively discussion about the hierarchy of nuts. Cashews versus pine nuts. And then Amy appeared and insisted they drink water.

Daphne moves slowly through the kitchen. Each sound ricochets through her. She opens her ride sharing app. She booked a car from Beauchamp Place last night. What was she doing *there*? Not another meal surely? But memories of fried okra, vine leaves, and kibbeh surface hazily. She stares vacantly into space, clutching her coffee until Dominic appears.

"How was your 'me time'?" he asks unsteadily, leaning into the doorway.

Oh yes, that's what she told him. She spoke in vague terms about browsing bookstores, a gallery or two. But look at the state of her! Her hair is a wild mess, her complexion sickly pale. Dominic is waiting. She licks her lips, clears her throat.

"So, I had plans I didn't tell you about."

"I figured." He looks impossibly sad. "You staggered in a little before ten, beelined straight for bed. Three minutes later you were passed out, on top of the duvet. Snoring heavily."

She groans to herself. "I'm sorry."

And she is. It's not right to keep secrets from him (unless the secret is a surprise birthday party, which she's done before). So why did she not tell him about Chuck?

"Are you trying to punish me? For Lucinda?" he's asking.

"No!" She pauses, genuinely flummoxed. "What do you mean?"

"I know, Daph," he says, sinking unsteadily to the ground. "I know something's going on. Just tell me, please."

He's worrying her now. She crouches beside him, takes his hands in hers, and tells him everything. She tells him about lunch with her mother. She tells him about the dinner party and the Christian Lacroix dress and the Christmas party and the affair that ended when Plumb learned she was pregnant. She tells him about her email to Chuck last year, and his recent reply. She tells him about the shopping bags and the food and the two hotel bars and the debate over piña coladas and nuts and at a certain point, she notices his face has changed. Dominic no longer looks impossibly sad. He looks like he might vomit.

"You mean . . . Chuck's your dad?" he asks shakily.

—

THIS is bad. Beyond bad, it's terrible. But nothing *really* happened. It was just a quick kiss, right? Okay, Mimi's lips were on his dick for a while there, but he didn't come. It wasn't even pleasurable so it definitely doesn't count. The coke is to blame! The alcohol too. He would never have slept with her if he was sober. Anyway, he *didn't* sleep with her. He walked away! Even though he thought Daphne was having an affair, which she definitely isn't.

It's a mess. What a horrible mess.

—

"I met him," she continues, "and we clicked . . . and I just finally felt like I belonged."

She thought he'd be hurt that she kept this secret. Dominic's face crumples and his eyes well up. She pulls him in, hugging him tightly. He gets it, she thinks smiling into his chest.

"I'm so happy for you," he weeps into her neck.

"Oh, sweetie. Thank you," she whispers as his tears drench her.

She's lucky, she thinks, to have a husband so caring, so ferociously dedicated to her happiness. She's filled with profound gratitude and an enormous sense of relief. Dominic doesn't mind that she kept it from him. He understands her and he supports her, completely.

—

DOMINIC sits in a gray cubicle. Surrounded by identical cubicles. He opens emails. He taps out replies. He attends the conference calls and meetings his colleagues place on his calendar. He doesn't get the sense these conference calls and meetings achieve anything significant. He appears to work, but he's doing very little. He is going nowhere, in fact.

Originally, when he accepted this job, he liked the fact he could clock in and out. But now, all this clocking about places seems incredibly *pointless*. He pulls up to the site he's been staring at for the past few weeks. He studies the questions: why would he like to enroll in this program and earn a postgraduate certificate in education (PGCE)? Which age group would he like to teach? Why does he think he'd make a good teacher? He spends considerable time on each question.

Oscar and Cody. He finds it painful thinking about them. He misses their tight-knit school community, parent-teacher events, school plays, sports days and nature walks, the football teams he coached. Overnight, it all disappeared. And with it, his sense of purpose. But recently, he's wondered if there's a way back. There are other schools, there are other communities. He could be a teacher. It's simple and clear, obvious. He feels stupid for not realizing it sooner. He clicks through each question. Once his application is complete, he sits back and closes his eyes. *Please let this work.*

—

PUBLICATION day is coming up, and at last, they are telling friends. What a relief it's been to share her news, especially with Aparna. *I just knew something was off,* Aparna had responded. Her publicist discusses how they will promote the book. She breaks it down by region: local readings, interviews with smaller press outlets, a few podcast interviews. Germany has expressed interest in potentially buying the rights too. Her publicist wants Daphne's expectations to be measured, realistic. Daphne nods, she gets that. It's just a cookbook, but she remains nervous for her identity to be revealed. What if people hate her?

She does a lot of tidying and meal planning. One evening, she makes pasta. The next, chicken. Dominic notices her anxiety. He sets the table and opens wine. He scrubs the frying pan clean. And while all this cooking and cleaning and tidying cases her anxiety, she imagines the rest of her life rolling out this way. A series of evenings. She cooks. They have pasta or they have chicken. Dominic sets the table. He scrubs the frying pan clean. They watch a film or they watch TV. There is nothing wrong with predictability. Inertia is normal, inevitable. A thought wriggles in: *how might the book change things?* She pushes it away. This is a happy marriage, she tells herself.

—

THE kitchen doors open, saloon style, and the heavy scent of seared sirloin wafts toward him. Publication day is one week away, and they're telling Dominic's friends over lunch. Daphne's diligently worked through her entire list of people she needs to notify already, but Dominic hasn't told a soul yet. Not even the twins. Daphne nudges him in the ribs. He jumps nervously in response and makes a pretense of tapping his glass with a spoon.

"Daphne and I have something to share."

"Oh?" Mark's eyes light up. "Is it the pattering of little feet perhaps?"

Dominic feels the excitement radiating off Mark and Tabitha. They got married last year, Tabitha's in her second trimester now. She looks radiant, like an advertisement for giving parenthood a try. Dominic feels a small stir of jealousy. He used to find Tabitha precious, but look at them now: they're in sync, a unit. They've been hinting about Dominic and Daphne hopping on the baby-making train too. He always expected he and Daphne would take that step eventually, and his experiences with Oscar and Cody make him certain he'd be a good father, but Daphne still hasn't come around to the idea. He can't help but wonder if the Freedom Clause is part of the reason.

"No, not that. Not . . . yet," he says, watching Tabitha rub her stomach. "Daphne's got a book coming out."

"A book?" Mark repeats, glancing from Dominic to Daphne.

"What?" Tabitha asks in confusion.

Daphne leans back, pulling her hair into a high ponytail. She nods confidently. She's familiar with this conversation by now, the questions she'll be asked, and how to respond.

"It's a cookbook. With personal stories attached to each recipe."

"That's great," Mark says, raising his glass. "Even though, I must admit . . ." He pauses, looking at Dominic. "I thought *you* were meant to be the great literary talent."

Dominic wraps his arm around Daphne and pulls her in for a clumsy kiss, trying to do his best performance of support.

"I don't have the chops for it." Dominic laughs thinly. "But I'm glad she does."

"To me," Daphne says as they clink glasses, her laughter high-spirited.

He envies her, even as he's grown accustomed to her success. At university, they were enrolled in the same writing seminars. Dominic slaved over his short stories until the early hours, and he spoke often of his dream of being a writer. He assumed he'd succeed because he was driven and ambitious. Daphne was a good writer too, of course, but she'd always seemed content to nurture him, and to support his talent. That's why they made a great couple! But now Daphne has the book deal and she's the one taking a brief book tour around England while he is left . . . floundering.

"Lovely," Tabitha says. "When's it out?"

"Next week."

"And how come we're only just finding out?"

"We're actually not supposed to be telling anyone"—Daphne glances around the restaurant, her voice dropping to a whisper—"because the book is based off an anonymous Substack newsletter I've been writing. Next week, as part of the PR campaign, I'll be revealing who I am. We wanted you to find out from us first."

"When you say personal stories . . ." Mark begins uncertainly.

Dominic has been dreading this question. He doesn't want people reading about his wife's sex life, or his infidelity. Their food arrives and they stop talking, moving glasses to accommodate each hot dish that's placed on the small table.

"Some of them . . . touch on our relationship," Dominic admits as the waiter walks away.

"Like what?" Tabitha asks, eyes narrowing.

Daphne nods at him, indicating she'll take this one.

"A few years ago, Dominic suggested we open up our marriage."

"Like swingers?" Mark snorts. "Oh, well done, you two. You almost had us there!"

"It's not a joke," Dominic insists, draining his wine.

"Seriously?"

"It's not as . . . wild as it sounds, okay?" he begins, certain he's lost them already. "We have one night off a year when we . . . you know, pretend to be single."

"What kind of marriage is that?" Tabitha asks in an outraged tone.

Tabitha sits up straight, crosses her arms over her chest, and glares.

"Our marriage," Daphne says with a simple shrug of her shoulders. "We decided to expand our sexual experiences, within the confines of a supportive partnership built on trust."

Daphne is so much better at this than him, he thinks.

"But I did some things that really . . . broke that trust. Truly regrettable things," he says, his mind flying to Mimi, "and that's explored in the book too."

Beneath the table, Daphne's hand lands on his leg. She strokes his knee in a comforting, nonsexual manner. She offers him a reassuring smile. He places his hand on her shoulder, leans toward her. Tabitha follows the movement, scowling.

"We got through it," Daphne adds. "We're completely past that now."

"Right," he says, blushing.

Tabitha's face resembles a cucumber that's spent too long in the pickle jar. She looks sour, her features pinched together tightly.

"I don't know how you two do it," Tabitha says, in a voice that suggests she holds no admiration for Daphne.

"Is there a launch party? Can we come?" Mark asks.

"Sure." Daphne smiles brightly, her body relaxes. "There's one event in London."

"An erotic cookbook," Mark says, clapping his hands together. "How fun!"

—

SATURDAY morning. Daphne wakes up to an empty bed, the noise of coffee beans in the grinder. She drifts off again. The next time she opens her eyes, Dominic is standing in front of her. He is freshly showered, wearing jeans and a navy sweater.

"Morning, crumb cake." He beams at her.

She smiles sleepily. "Coffee?"

He nods, points to her bedside table. "Did you sleep okay?"

She had strange and fitful dreams about book readings, angry customers shouting about how she ruined a perfectly good cut of beef in her recipe.

"Just okay," she admits, reaching for her coffee.

"I've been thinking about Mark and Tabitha, how they just assumed our news was that we're having a kid. And I don't know." He shrugs happily. "I just think we should go for it."

She gulps down her coffee. "What, now?"

He shrugs calmly. "I know you have this book coming out soon, but the timing's never going to be ideal. And we're both thirty."

"But . . . our lives are full right now."

He smiles breezily. "Our lives would be even *fuller* with a baby. It'd bring us closer."

"Fuller is exactly what I'm afraid of." She shakes her head. "Is this connected to teaching, somehow?"

She supports his decision to do a PGCE, and she's delighted he's been accepted into the program at University College London. They whooped, they danced around the kitchen together when he got the news. He's so earnest in his excitement she's certain this is his calling. Finally, it seems like they're both set in their chosen careers, on a path to sustained happiness . . . but here he is disturbing the balance again.

"Maybe, I don't know. It just feels like the natural next step," Dominic says, rubbing his jaw.

Her molars clench together in irritation. "I've told you I wasn't sure that motherhood was for me . . . for years now."

"But you'd make a great mum . . . the best!"

She nods her head, he's right about that. She knows she'd be a good parent, but that doesn't mean she necessarily *wants* that. God, the work alone it would entail. Daphne already does considerably more than Dominic. She stays on top of the cooking and cleaning, the tidying and laundry. She's the first to notice if they're running low on loo roll or washing-up liquid. And what about all those impromptu tasks? Like opening the bedroom blinds and seeing white poop splashed all over the balcony railing. Those damn pigeons! Whenever the bird poop disappears, it's because Daphne's taken the time to wipe the railing down with a damp cloth. Maybe it doesn't bother Dominic as much or maybe he just finds it easier to wait for Daphne to do it? But throw a child into the mix and where exactly does this leave Daphne? Just how much more work would fall on her? When would she have time to do anything she loves?

"We don't need this," she insists, eyes blazing. "You're just starting the teaching program and I have these amazing opportunities. I'm finally doing everything I love. I don't want to give that up."

In the past, these conversations felt theoretical. *One day, would you be open to . . .* but today's crackles with an intensity that was previously missing.

"But we talked about doing this," he says insistently.

Daphne blinks in confusion. "When?"

"We said we'd do the Freedom Clause for five years and then start a family."

"No, that's what *you* said. Did you ever hear me agree? In case it wasn't obvious, let me be clear now: I don't want children." Watching his shoulders sag, her voice softens. "But I know you do. Maybe when you start teaching, when you're getting to work with kids every day . . . could that be enough?"

His face flattens. "I don't think so."

"Where does that leave us?"

Dominic shakes his head, and stares at her sadly.

"I honestly don't know."

———

Most of Daphne's interviews are with local newspapers. But her publicist has secured one big interview with a daytime talk show, which is a huge deal. Fifteen minutes until airtime. Dominic makes coffee, a bacon sandwich. He settles on the sofa and finds the channel. Tilly, the anchor, is tall and striking. She has white-blond hair, cartoonishly large lips. It's surreal to watch her introduce Daphne, and even stranger to see his wife walk onstage to rapturous applause. He leans forward, suddenly breathless.

Daphne doesn't even look like Daphne. She's a Hollywood starlet. Big smoky eyes. Sleek and glossy hair. Her jacket is bright red, the color of ripened heirloom tomatoes. Beneath it, fitted jeans and dark ankle boots. She looks bold, uber-confident.

He takes photos on his phone as Daphne and Tilly shake hands. Tilly sits in her throne-like chair and motions for Daphne to take the sofa opposite. Daphne's posture is straight, her hands clasped in her lap. Only a small tremor in her voice betrays her nerves. Dominic feels a swell of pride as Daphne explains she set up her newsletter five years ago as an outlet to express her feelings during a big change in her life. She expected only a handful of followers, she adds.

"You got more than a handful," Tilly says.

The audience laughs and Daphne's eyes widen in surprise. She visibly relaxes.

"Now I've got to ask," Tilly continues mischievously, "about that infamous salad."

Tilly gives Daphne credit for addressing how ugly and awkward those "moments between the sheets" can be. Dominic smiles, it's morning TV after all, and he wonders how much they'll dance around the topic of sex without actually saying it.

"Can we just applaud this woman," Tilly says, addressing the audience, "for taking a courageous step in describing how bad it can be? Like really, *really* bad."

The applause is thunderous. Dominic doesn't know how to feel about all those strangers in the audience applauding his wife for writing about having sex with someone else.

"For the longest time," Daphne begins, smiling at Tilly, "I let the act of . . . you know . . ."

"Oh, we know, sweetie," Tilly responds in her signature honeyed voice.

"I'm not sure what exactly I can say on here . . ."

Tilly jumps in. "Let's call it salad time."

Daphne cracks up. "Okay, so I allowed *salad time* to revolve around male satisfaction. Because in the movies I never saw scenes of men doing anything to help a woman enjoy the salad in a way that's . . . unique to women. It seemed like they both enjoyed the salad in the same way, and they both finished enjoying the salad at exactly the same time, right?"

"Miraculous, isn't it?" Tilly says dryly.

"Right, so when I started having . . . *salad time*, and I didn't enjoy it, I felt like a freak because the man was enjoying the salad. Why couldn't I? I genuinely thought I wasn't a *salad* person."

"Maybe it wasn't the right dressing?"

Are they talking about *his* dressing, Dominic wonders, scowling. Meanwhile, a playful smiles stretches across Daphne's face.

"Exactly! I needed to figure out what worked for me and, once I had *that* figured out, I needed to be more assertive about getting the dressing I wanted."

"We're going to learn how to make that salad right after this short break."

Dominic stops holding his breath. He checks his phone and sees the texts streaming in. The twins. Aparna. Simon. Mark. Poppy. Even Mimi: *I just saw Daphne on TV!! She did great. Looked stunning too.* He replies with a thumbs up emoji to each. The commercials end and Tilly and Daphne are standing in the studio kitchen. Daphne is looking calm and industrious, rinsing kale leaves. She's asking Tilly to hand her the chopping board. Tilly is playing up how useless she is in the kitchen, generating laughter from the audience.

Peering at the ingredients, Tilly asks: "So this salad represents you learning to be more assertive in life?"

Daphne nods her head emphatically. "Exactly. From a young age, women are taught to be sweet and polite and pleasant but those "skills" don't help us later in life. When we need to negotiate a pay raise or point out to the man we're in a salad bowl with that he's being incredibly selfish."

More laughter. Even Dominic smiles. Another text flashes up: *Hey, are we okay? I would still love your help with my house btw.* He pauses, but clearly he and Mimi have agreed, without explicitly saying so, that they'll move on from whatever weirdness happened. *Sure thing, I'm around if you need a hand.*

"Let's talk about your newsletter too," Tilly is saying. "Why did you call it *Confessions of a Highly Emotional Cook*?"

Daphne is slicing open an avocado. She pauses, hand resting on the knife. "I was always the emotional one in my family. I still cry very easily, but I don't get embarrassed about it so much these days. The title felt honest."

Tilly nods. "And in your newsletter, you talk about some tough things. Not feeling confident in yourself. Learning your dad wasn't your biological father. Learning about your husband's affair."

"Right," Daphne responds, as she makes the dressing. "The way I decompress is by cooking. I started the account as a way to process one tough thing, but over time it became this place for me to share all sorts of tough moments. Maybe that's why people connected with it. They might be going through something completely different, but the emotions are the same: hurt, anger, confusion. The feeling of helplessness. But making these recipes always gave me joy."

"Cooking is your therapy?" Tilly observes.

Daphne smiles. "A little like that. Try this." She passes the dressing to Tilly. "How is it?"

"Now that," Tilly says, taking a small sip, "is the *right* dressing." She points at Daphne. "I think she's on to something: cooking as a therapy, and now cooking can be our therapy too . . . because Daphne has a book out." Tilly holds up a copy. "You'd better run to the bookstore and buy your copy of *The Highly Emotional Cookbook*. It's out today and it's brilliant."

Dominic stares in disbelief. He had been anxious about this interview for weeks. He was certain they'd discuss his infidelity and the Freedom Clause, but they breezed right over it. It barely mattered. Or rather, *he* barely mattered. He sits back in outrage. This is much worse than he expected. It's like he doesn't exist.

—

Some of our readers are intimidated by fish, what's a good starter recipe? What's your favorite recipe from the cookbook? How do you stop your gravy from getting lumpy? What's your advice for getting the best consistency in a crème brûlée? Where do you see the interplay between emotions and cooking? Is your husband a good cook? Is your husband in touch with his emotions? Do you see a therapist? Do you think your marriage would benefit from seeing a therapist? What's your relationship like with food? Is it healthy? What's helped boost your confidence? Do you keep in touch with the man who came on your hair? If you saw him today, what would you tell him? In which ways has his advice been helpful? What advice would you give to women looking for a

more fulfilling sex life? Have you had any more sexual experiences with
women? Would you like to? How often do you and your husband have sex?
And is it fulfilling? What do you mean, that's too personal?

AFTER one reading, a bald man sidles up to the signing table. He says
he very much enjoyed her salad recipe and he would like to come all
over her. The hot crowded bookstore feels even hotter and more
crowded in that moment. Daphne blinks at him in stupefied silence.

"And who am I signing this to?" she asks stiffly, pen in hand.

—

DAPHNE is on book tour. Bath. Bristol. Birmingham. Leeds. Manchester. She tells him about the questions she receives from the audience, so many questions! And each week, her cookbook nudges a
little higher in nonfiction lists. Dominic receives messages of support
from friends and colleagues. They're excited for Daphne. They don't
seem to be judging him, not the way he presumed they would. He
knows many of them haven't read the book yet. And those who
have? Sure, they've expressed surprise that he had an affair, surprise
too that he and Daphne decided to open up their marriage once a
year, but they seem to respect that it's working for them, and moreover if Daphne has forgiven him, they reassure him it's not their
place to judge. He must be proud of Daphne. He nods in agreement
(because what else is he meant to do?) but in truth, he feels lousy and
miserable, left behind. Her success has nothing to do with him, or
their marriage. Daphne is the star and he's the dust, left behind as she
shoots across the sky. He's been abandoned by the one person he
never expected to do that.

He knows a lot of this is in his head. He knows that if he talks to
Daphne she'll be compassionate and kind, grounding him back in
reality. But when he calls her she's running to catch a train. She

promises to call later. He sighs, and hangs up. He goes to the hardware store to pick up a few items. He takes the District Line to Notting Hill, clutching his heavy tool box in his lap. He spends hours in Mimi's flat, doing jobs that she should have completed the week she moved in. Mimi keeps asking if he needs to be anywhere, but truthfully, he doesn't. He shows her how to hang up artwork on her walls, a curtain rod in her guest bedroom. He installs shelving units at the back of a large impractical closet. When he admits he's starving and asks what they can eat, she shrugs. He finds eggs on a shelf in the fridge and teaches her how to cook an omelet. She is clueless in so many regards that it becomes a running joke.

He glances at his phone. Still no word from Daphne. He texts her: *Did you make the train okay?* She replies two hours later. *All good, just doing a quick podcast interview. I'll call you tomorrow!* His heart sinks. He wants to hear her voice. He wants to tell her about the curtain rod and the fact her younger sister doesn't know how to make an omelet.

But Daphne is busy.

—

DAPHNE is sitting in a noodle shop. She is reading. She turns the pages slowly, yawning. She glances up, signals for the check. The food wasn't good, but she's too tired to care. She should call Dominic, but she just had a long conversation with Chuck and Amy right before dinner, and she doesn't have the energy to do it all over again. What she *really* wants to do is crash into bed and sleep for nine hours. She knows she's been distracted recently. She can tell Dominic's feeling neglected. She picks up on it in his voice, in the punctuation in his messages. She'll make up for it when she returns home in a few days. But he should let her have this moment to shine. Is that a big ask? No, for how many women over how many generations have done exactly this, sacrificing their own needs for the needs of their husbands, waiting patiently and supportively from the sidelines? Dominic can do this for her, she thinks.

She turns another page. She reads on.

—

"WHAT are you doing tonight?" he asks as he packs up tools.

Mimi shrugs. "It's my birthday, actually."

"What?" He stares at her in surprise. "Are you going out?"

Mimi shrugs casually. "Honestly? I've done the whole wild club scene, bottle service, sparklers on everything. I just don't know if I'm in the mood. I don't even think anyone's in town this weekend."

He doesn't buy it, he thinks, watching her dig her hands into her front pockets and bite her lip. The thing about Mimi is, deep down, she desperately needs to be loved. Just like him. Also, nobody should be alone on their birthday, which is why he says yes when she asks if he wants to stay and order takeout. Yes if he wants to split a bottle of wine. And when she invites him to stay over, he says yes to that too.

He's hated sleeping alone in his Putney flat. Besides, Daphne clearly doesn't need him. She's preoccupied with her success, and it's easy to lose himself in Mimi. Afterwards, during a long soak in the tub, they agree this was a bad idea. They agree they only did it because they are lonely, but he sleeps over all the same.

When he wakes up in the morning, he's spooning Mimi. There is no awkwardness. They are both adults here. He makes her another omelet. They take their mugs of coffee onto the rooftop, and discuss how to spruce it up. As he leaves Mimi's place, Daphne texts him. She is about to do an interview with a local radio station. She will call him later that day, she promises.

—

"ALL your hard work's paying off," Daphne tells Ash with a reassuring smile.

They're walking arm-in-arm through Victoria Park. Beneath the shadows of poplar, beech, and maple trees. It's opening night for the musical comedy he wrote and directed. It's showing in a small theater in Hackney. The stage imagines a world in which Prince William comes out and dates a series of high-profile men. The backlash is swift and fierce, the tabloids clamoring for Harry and Meghan's return to English soil, desperate to promote a royal (and, importantly, heterosexual) marriage that remains intact. Beneath the ridicule and sarcasm, the singing and dancing, the gentle fun poked at contemporary celebrity culture, the musical asks: has society truly accepted gay culture yet? Earlier in the evening, Daphne joined the standing ovation in the warm hot theater, her arms prickling with goosebumps. And now, they're headed to the afterparty.

"It's bonkers," Ash admits, leaning into her. "I've never experienced this: my-world-is-complete feeling until now. It's a headfuck, if I'm honest."

He wants to take the musical to Edinburgh Festival Fringe next, *if* he can secure interest. He will, Daphne reassures him. Ash smiles as he talks about another actor in his musical, Dennis, his voice turning soft like honey. It's early days, Ash explains, but this relationship feels different. They speak openly about their feelings, and about what the future looks like. It's easy and natural compared to the headiness of past relationships.

"Easy and natural is good!"

He stares at her. He looks absolutely petrified. "No! I'm terrified."

"Of what?"

He clicks his fingers together. "That it'll all get taken away."

ASH is the star of the evening, the extrovert. He dances in the center of the room, surrounded by friends. Dennis leans against the window, rolling joints, watching quietly. He has green-brown eyes, a close-cut beard, a big Afro, and a slow, shy smile that's impossible not to find endearing. She likes a lot of things about him, but what she likes most is his no-holds-barred affection for Ash. Occasionally, Dennis pulls Ash in for a lingering kiss, and it's met with applause. Daphne smiles, she sips slowly from her beer. The room is warm with the heat of people dancing. The flat feels loud and cramped, or maybe it's Daphne? She feels quieter tonight, contemplative. She blames the book tour. Or maybe it's Dominic. He's been acting strange around her. God, she hopes he's not punishing her for being away for so long. She goes into the narrow kitchen to grab another beer.

Turning, she bumps straight into him. "Whoops, sorry!"

His smile reels her in.

"You're Daphne, right?"

She takes a small sip of beer, nods dumbly. He explains his name is Jaden. He's friends with Dennis.

"And what do you do?"

It doesn't matter how he answers, if he's something deeply boring like an accountant. Tall; her eyes barely skim his collar bone. Long lashes, unfathomably deep eyes. Oh, Jaden, she thinks, you are indiscriminately sexy. She needn't have worried that he was secretly boring. He's a photographer.

Her cheeks and neck are flushed, hot from the warmth of the flat, or from her desire. The kitchen is cramped, and she's acutely aware of his proximity to her as he explains that he lives in London Fields, that his parents are from Trinidad.

"What about you?" he asks, handing her a glass of water.

She tells him about her job at the magazine, the book she just released.

"A food writer," he says, flashing her a dimpled smile.

He tells her in a low soft voice about the food his grandmother used to make, how the smells from her kitchen made the neighborhood envious. Salted fish blended with tomatoes, onions, and hot peppers. Crab mixed with okra pods, pimento peppers, thyme, and coconut milk. She could listen to him all night. They stand close, talking softly, almost touching, but not quite. His hand brushes against her shoulder. She wants to kiss him, she thinks, and she acts on it. Their kiss is slow and exploratory. She's relaxing into it when he breaks off.

"Girlfriend," he explains, shaking his head unhappily.

Stepping back, she knocks her head against a cupboard.

"Ow!" she moans softly.

She expects to feel embarrassed on two counts: his rejection and her extreme clumsiness. Instead, she's indignant. Why give her so much of his attention if he has a girlfriend? Really?

"I didn't see that coming," she admits.

He smiles sheepishly. "I like talking to you."

An hour later, she's sitting cross-legged in Ash's apartment in Dalston. She loves this place, it's *so* Ash. Decorated with treasured items extracted from the hidden depths of flea markets: a jewel-blue Persian rug, a retro coffee table, vintage art prints, porcelain jugs and vases.

"He was *hot* and he seemed *into* me," she's saying about Jaden. "Why are you *grinning*?"

Ash laughs at her from the sofa, he's sprawled on it with Dennis. They look like they've been together for years rather than ten weeks.

"I just keep thinking about when you and I first met."

She frowns. "What does *that* have to do with anything?"

Ash paints the scene, in a low and dramatic voice that proves he's an actor. It was a Monday night, the hotel bar was quiet. A girl sidled in and took a seat at the bar. She looked quiet and studious. She studied the cocktail menu. She waited and sighed and waited some more. Ash was new to his job. This was his first shift without his manager. He made an outrageous mistake, offering a drink to the wrong customer. It was too awkward. He should have left the drink with Daphne and made another for the woman who was supposed to receive it.

"But I took it away from her," Ash admits, looking shamefaced.

"You didn't!" Dennis laughs softly.

Ash offered the crestfallen girl a drink as a peace offering. As they chatted he realized she wasn't quiet and studious at all. She held nothing back, baring her entire soul. When she told him about an arrangement with her husband—the Freedom Clause—the girl looked wide-eyed and scared, utterly clueless.

"You shuddered at the thought of hitting on a man . . . convinced he'd reject you."

Daphne sighs regretfully. "And now someone *has* rejected me."

"Right," Ash concedes, "but you don't actually care about the rejection, you're just irritated that Jaden wasted your time, that he didn't reveal the girlfriend sooner. My point? The Daphne I met five years ago would have gone down in flames from this rejection. Now? You don't give a fuck! And you know what that means?"

"What?" she asks, genuinely uncertain.

He breaks into a wide smile. "You're unstoppable."

—

DAPHNE is home again. Order has been restored. He feels steadier. They're having friends over for dinner tonight. Aparna, Poppy, Mark, Tabitha, Simon. Daphne's making pork chops with roasted potatoes, fennel and red cabbage. She hums happily. She tells him about all the bookstores she visited, the interesting people she met. She's glowing. Dominic listens and watches carefully. He pulls her in for a hug. He inhales her scent, soaking her up.

"By the way, Mimi sent me pictures of what you did for her."

"What?" His face freezes over.

"It's looking *fab* with artwork on the walls. She needed a hand. Thanks, my love."

Daphne places her arm around his waist, and leans in for a kiss.

"Any time," he manages to say, adding, "I love what you've done with *our* place, by the way, all the plants."

"Hmm," Daphne responds in a teasing tone. "Seems like I'm encouraging you to take even longer showers."

Green fronds hang from the tops of bookcases, and sprigs of eucalyptus, wrapped with twine, hang in the shower. Dominic stands under the stream of water, often until Daphne hammers on the door. He inhales the minty earthy aroma and wonders if eucalyptus, or sheer proximity to his wife, can cleanse his soul.

—

DAPHNE waits beneath the departures board, shivering, tickets in hand. She's nervous they'll miss the train to Yorkshire. She understands it's tough for Dominic to leave his teacher training early, but the next train will take longer, stopping at every hamlet along the way.

Daphne doesn't want to spend a week in Yorkshire with her family. Plumb wants this: a cottage in a bucolic spot for Christmas. Those were her exact words. Daphne only agreed out of guilt, and because Plumb pointed out last year Daphne spent Christmas with Dominic's dad, Sadie, and the twins. Henry, his wife Deborah, and Mimi are coming. Daphne gets the sense they're dreading it too. But the three siblings agreed that Christmas last year was tough on Plumb, her first without Nigel, and they should rally around her. Daphne offered to find the rental, selecting an eighteenth century converted water mill with views that overlook craggy hills.

Dominic arrives twenty minutes late, red-faced, out of breath.

"I'm sorry. It was manic today in class."

As predicted, the following train stops at every tiny town, doubling the travel time. Without reserved seats, they are forced to stand the whole way. By the time they arrive, the best rooms are claimed. All that's left is the drafty room with twin beds and Mother Goose wallpaper. The adjoining bathroom is dated, a little creepy, with mirrors on every wall. Why would I want to watch myself pee, she thinks, sitting on the loo. They push the beds together and try to make the best of it, but Daphne can't shake the feeling she's sleeping in the nursery.

They order Indian the first night and play Monopoly. One by one, the players peel off until it's Henry versus Dominic. Plumb is soaking in the bath tub. Henry's wife is reading in bed. Mimi and Daphne stand in the kitchen, catching up.

"What's up with you? Any fun dates?" Daphne asks, grinning at her.

Mimi offers her a strange look. She seems unusually light on news.

"Not really," Mimi says, shrugging uncomfortably.

"That's okay . . . sometimes it's best just to focus on you, you know?"

Daphne decides to drop the topic. She doesn't want to be *that* person, putting pressure on a single woman to have dating-life updates.

"Oh, Daphne," Mimi whispers, giving her an unexpected hug, "you're too good for us."

—

DOMINIC's been dreading this trip for weeks. Missing the train felt like a subconscious attempt to sabotage plans, but here they are. The water mill is beautiful. Even if the room they share is a bit of a dump. Mimi seems to be avoiding him, which suits him just fine.

Today, everyone is on their own schedule. Henry's wife, Debbie, is pregnant. Plumb and Mimi want to take them shopping for baby clothes. Dominic and Daphne borrow the car and drive to Whitby. They stop in a tea shop, they share a scone. When Daphne gets jam on her nose, Dominic licks it off, grinning at her.

"Shall we head for a walk?" Daphne suggests.

He nods his head happily. They stroll along the beach, holding hands. The sea is gray, choppy. He notices the sky darkening, and it begins to rain. They open the umbrella until the wind turns it inside out, and now it's a heavy sideways rain, impossible to avoid. They dash back to the car, laughing. On the drive home, they listen to an old station playing sixties classics. Daphne hums along, her hand resting on his.

"Things are good, aren't they?" he asks her as he drives.

"Of course they are!" she exclaims. "Why wouldn't they be?"

She turns the volume up, and they sing loudly all the way home.

"I should probably get through some more reading," Dominic says as they pull up to the water mill. "What are you going to do?"

Daphne glances at her watch. "I might go for another walk."

"Out there?" he asks, pointing to the dark clouds, wincing. "You sure?"

Daphne grins. "Don't worry! I'll be fine."

"Be careful," he says, kissing her nose. "You organized a great trip, by the way. Don't know why I was dreading it."

"I don't know why either," Daphne says, raising an eyebrow. "You know all the family loves you. You're their favorite."

———

IT's beautiful here. Each morning she throws on her dark green anorak and Wellington boots. She leaves Dominic at home, studying reading materials he's been assigned over Christmas break. She's thrilled to see him so absorbed in his coursework. She's pleased that everyone is doing their own thing. There are no arguments, there is no pressure to collectively have fun. She was expecting Henry to give her a hard time over her cookbook, the way he did when she first told him about it, but maybe the prospect of fatherhood is softening him. In fact, the other night he took her to one side and said how hard it must be, learning Nigel wasn't her real dad, and he hopes she knows she's still "very much a part of this family." Those were his exact words. He looked hot and bothered, and incredibly relieved when she hugged him and said thanks.

The week passes easily. Plumb and Henry and Debbie spend a lot of time shopping and sitting around in teashops. Mimi lies on the sofa, clutching a hot water bottle and complaining dramatically about period pains. Daphne rambles through hills and dales, along rivers and gorges. She finds it relaxing, having this time alone. She considers all the dishes she wants to make on Christmas Day, what she needs to buy in advance.

On Christmas morning, Daphne wakes early. She wants full run of the kitchen before they descend on her. Dominic's snores are soft, melodic. It's dark as she slips out of bed. The floorboards are cold against her feet. She pulls on her terry-cloth dressing gown. She pulls her hair back into a messy high bun. The sky looks coated in tar, still and intensely dark.

Daphne works quietly on meal prep. She peels potatoes. She chops red cabbage. She peels parsnips. And of course, the turkey, placed on a bed of shaved fennel and shallots that will caramelize in the oven, stuffed with lemons and herbs. With meal prep done, she turns to breakfast. It's her tradition to start Christmas Day with bacon sandwiches. She takes the bacon from the fridge. She prepares the griddle. She hears footsteps on the landing, sounds of her family waking up. Daphne sets the table. She stands back and admires her hard work. Henry and Debbie emerge first, their faces lighting up at the spread. They wish Daphne a Merry Christmas and sit down to eat. They pass around the ketchup. The salt and fat of this meal hits her perfectly. Daphne licks her lips. She washes it down with coffee.

Henry turns on the radio. They hum along to Christmas songs. Daphne feels happy and relaxed. She's excited to call Chuck later, and wish him and Amy happy holidays. Time to shower. She takes the stairs two at a time. The bedroom door is open. The room is empty. Dominic's not in their bathroom either. Where is he, she wonders, staring at the Mother Goose wallpaper. Her body is sticky, her armpits stink. She hops into the shower, she washes her hair and face. She brushes her teeth, gargles. She sets out the clothes she'll wear: a plaid dress, thick black tights. She sits on the bed, in her towel, engrossed in texts from Ash and Aparna. She doesn't register a door opening in the distance, heavy footsteps on the landing.

Dominic appears.

"Hey, I thought you were cooking," he says quickly.

She glances up from her phone. "Came up to shower. Merry Christmas!"

He looks uneasy, rattled. "Merry Christmas."

"Where've you been?" she asks.

"Oh, you know . . . around."

His gaze is shifty, nervous. He takes a step toward her, changes his mind. He turns on his heel and enters the bathroom. She stands in the doorway, watching him brush his teeth.

"There are bacon sarnies downstairs," she volunteers, studying his reflection in the many mirrors of the dated bathroom.

"Great," he says, smiling at her.

But his smile is tight and forced. There's a strange mark on his face, beneath his mouth, a reddish stain.

She frowns. "Did you have one already?"

He spits toothpaste into the sink. "Have what already?"

"A bacon sarnie. There's ketchup on your face," she says, pointing at the small smudges of red. It almost looks like blood. "Dom?"

Her frown deepens, and she takes a step closer.

"Leave it," he says, turning away, but the mirrors are everywhere.

His reflection looms in every direction, magnifying his frightened eyes.

Her heart pounds. "What's on your face?"

He's silent. His expression gives it away, drowning in guilt. Watching him, her mind whirs. It's a simple process of elimination. There are only so many rooms. There are only so many activities he could indulge in. Mimi curled up on the sofa, sighing about period pains. Blood. And there it is, blindingly obvious.

Dominic stands still, clutching a towel helplessly. He looks desperately afraid, and he should be. Daphne is seeing at last what she's chosen to ignore for so long. She's seeing Dominic for who he is.

Confessions of a Highly Emotional Cook:

Life is messy and so is this chocolate lava cake

New Year's Eve. The final day of this very strange year. I hope you have fun plans tonight, and fun can include a bath, a book, and an early night if that's your jam. I'm choosing this recipe because my life feels a lot like chocolate lava cake right now. From the outside, to the average onlooker, my life might look normal, appetizing even, but the moment you prod my exterior and ask how I "really" am, I promise you a gooey mess will gush out.

I am in no position to preach about the beauty of a messy interior. I am not good with mess. I do not like mess. I have no time for it in my life. I like control and order, I pride myself on my meticulous planning. But sometimes, life hits you sideways and you have to roll with the punches, and embrace the mess. This is what I am trying to do now, with heavy emphasis on trying. I am attempting to persuade myself that what is happening is good. That life is serving me a lesson, reminding me there is some beauty in the wild, the rocky, the unpredictable, that you don't want to become complacent, you don't want to operate on autopilot, because it means you're not appreciating what it means to be here. And that you needed this moment. It's a wake-up call. It's a challenge, and you're going to absolutely hate it, until it gets better. But it will get better. I have to trust in that.

I will stop talking in riddles now. What a relief, I hear you say. My Christmas was tough. I discovered my husband had cheated on me. Again. He cheated on me with someone I know. Someone I was getting closer to. I am feeling all the feels right now (betrayal, hurt, sadness, despair) but what is genuinely strange is that my busy mind seems very focused on my age. I am thirty. Next month, I turn thirty-one.

Why does it matter that I am thirty? Why does the breakdown of a marriage at thirty feel extra shameful? I think because many of us subscribe to this notion (thank you, societal pressure) that by the age of thirty, our lives should be "sorted." Women especially feel this pressure intensely, much more than men, which is deeply unfair. But do you want to know what sounds like a terrible idea? Remaining unhappy for the sake of appearance. For me, being thirty and "sorted" does not mean staying in a relationship where I've chosen to look the other way. It does not mean continuing to pretend to myself that we're compatible even though we have wildly different views on topics like parenting. It does not mean allowing myself to continue this way, in a state of inertia, reluctant to think too much about the future, tolerating all those "not good enough" moments.

When women are pressured to conform, and we are, I have no doubt about it, it gets in the way of us doing what's truly right for us. And what's right for us can look and feel and be messy. I hate the mess of my life right now, but it's the only path forward. Maybe you are in a similar position. Are you staying in a "just okay" relationship because it feels neater, easier? Are you delaying breaking up with him because you don't know where you'll live, or you can't bear the thought of hurting him, or you feel like you should stay given you've invested all this time in the relationship, years of building blocks? And starting over would mean kicking those blocks down, and being left with nothing. And nothing looks intensely scary to you. Whereas hiding in the neatness, the tidiness, the supposed order of your relationship feels safer. I implore you, please don't choose neat and tidy and safe over messy. Messy is honest. Messy is authentic. Messy is real.

I never want to present myself as something I am not. So happy New Year's Eve, dear readers. Let's make next year a good one. And let's embrace the messiness of our lives.

LIFE IS MESSY
AND SO IS THIS CHOCOLATE LAVA CAKE

Feeds: 4

Ingredients:
- 170 grams of dark chocolate
- 6 tablespoons of unsalted butter
- 56 grams of all-purpose flour
- 85 grams of caster sugar

- 2 eggs
- 2 egg yolks
- 1 teaspoon of vanilla extract
- The grated zest of 2 oranges
- ¼ teaspoon of salt
- Vanilla ice cream (for serving)

Method:

1. Spray 4 ramekins with cooking spray. There is no correct way to spray these ramekins, there is only *your* way. Please trust that yours is the best way.

2. Heat the oven to 220 degrees Celsius/425 Fahrenheit. Press your cold fingers giddily to the oven and remind yourself there is heat and warmth in the world, and it will come from unlikely places. It is hard to remember this sometimes, especially in the dead of winter. Let this be enough for now.

3. Place the chocolate and butter in a bowl. Now, you can either place the bowl over a boiling saucepan and watch the chocolate and butter melt slowly thoroughly or place the bowl in the microwave for a faster outcome (I choose the latter, in ten-second increments). Note: some people believe the first way is the only way. We do not like these people. My god, these people have a rigid way of thinking, which means they are highly likely to find themselves trapped in unhappy, deeply unhealthy relationships. They will not do anything about this trap because they frown on the "shortcut" of divorce, even as they medicate themselves to sleep each night because misery is a bitch of a nocturnal stimulant. Choose the way that works for you, dear reader, and listen out for the ping of your microwave!

4. Place the orange zest, sugar, salt, eggs, yolks, and vanilla extract into a separate bowl and whisk it all together until it's

very thick. Now, whisk in the flour until the mixture is smooth. Combine with the chocolate mixture.

5. Stare at the bowl filled with all that chocolate goodness. Contemplate having some. You are going to hesitate because you know there is raw egg in that mixture, but for the love of God dip your finger in there and TASTE IT.

6. Pour the mixture into your four ramekins. Place the ramekins on a baking tray and cook in the oven for 12 to 14 minutes. It will cook faster if you have a convection oven.

7. Pull out, and immediately place the ramekins upside down on a plate. If you hesitate, the mixture inside will continue to cook and we do not want that. We're in encouraging-the-messiness-of-life mode, remember! Remove the ramekins and serve immediately with vanilla ice cream.

8. Enjoy prodding the exterior with your spoon and watching the chocolate liquid gush out. Luxuriate in how messy it is. Admire how imperfect your plate looks. This is your life, dear friend. Expose it. Welcome it. Live it without fear of what anyone else thinks.

Yours,
Daphne

Epilogue

New Year's Day. He sits in the silence of the flat. Each time he moves, the floorboards creak and it sounds a lot like his own loneliness. He hasn't seen Daphne since Christmas Day. She dropped him at the train station after a surreal drive. Daphne, calm behind the wheel, turning the indicator, glancing in the rearview mirror, while he sat beside her in a complete state of panic. He heard himself speak but his words were utterly futile. She didn't say goodbye, or when she would return, and she's ignored his texts. He jumps up as he hears keys in the door. Daphne is wearing high-waisted denim jeans, a red chunky knit sweater. Her face is free of makeup. Her hair is plaited. She nods at him as she removes her coat. She thrusts her hands deep in her denim pockets. She takes the furthest end of the sofa, perching on the armrest.

"Tea?" he asks unsteadily.

Her gaze is alert, uncompromising. "Sure."

He nods, pleased to have a purpose. While he makes tea, Daphne heads into their bedroom. She returns with two totes filled with underwear and clothes, toiletries. She places them in the center of the living room. They serve as the focal point, a reminder that this time together is fleeting, every word critical.

"Where are you staying?" he asks, passing her a mug.

She clasps it with both hands. "With Ash."

Of course. Ash will encourage Daphne's newly single status. He'll want to celebrate, take her dancing and Daphne will wonder why she didn't leave her marriage sooner. Dominic stops this thought. It's not fair to blame Ash. Not when he fucked up so tremendously.

"Well, Happy New Year," he says with a sigh, watching her sip her tea.

She meets his gaze, and nods firmly. "Can you believe five years ago today we agreed to it?" Daphne asks, glancing around the room as though in disbelief. "I hated it then, but I'll admit . . . I'm grateful for it now."

His heart sinks. Just as he knows Daphne is vastly more confident and self-assured than she was five years ago, he understands that the person she has grown into cannot take him back. It would go against every grain of confidence and self-esteem she has steadily built within herself. If he is honest with himself, the Daphne sitting across from him today scares him. The sex is better with this Daphne, she is confident and bold, empowered, not afraid to say exactly what she needs, but he misses the woman he married; she permitted his voice, his needs, to be the loudest in their relationship. So loud, in fact, that oftentimes he didn't hear her voice, or maybe he should have tried harder. He understands too that over the past five years, Daphne's voice has grown louder, throwing the balance of their relationship off course. To find that balance again would have required some radical change in him, being as selfless and supportive of her perhaps as she has been of him. He still wants to be the most important voice, and that's the problem. He says none of this.

"The Freedom Clause has been good for you," he concedes.

She nods in agreement. "I wouldn't have come this far without it."

It is time to apologize. Moreover, it's time to take responsibility for his actions. And, if it comes to it, he will beg and plead and cause a scene. He's not above doing any of these things.

"I did a terrible thing," he admits, bowing his head.

"Things. Plural."

Her face is placid, unmoved. She places her mug on the coffee table and stands up, slinging a tote over each shoulder. He glances up at her in panic. She's leaving already? She leans in and hugs him, it's an awkward hug. The bags slide down her shoulders, knocking into his arms. The hug is fleeting and perfunctory. On her part, at least.

"Please, Daph," he cries out in anguish. "Don't go."

Daphne is an empath, her emotions never far from the surface. But today, their roles are reversed. She is shuttered, her face stiff and somber. There is no kindness in her eyes, only a hint of impatience. He makes strange noises, sobbing, what sounds like the caw of a seagull, as he follows her down the hallway, as she opens the door. Dry-eyed, she stands on the top step in the hallway and surveys him.

"Do you remember that research study that came out a few years ago?" she begins to ask, hunching up her shoulders to keep the totes from slipping. "It showed women were significantly less happy than men most of their lives, but at the age of eighty-five a funny thing happened. The trend reversed. Women's happiness jumped much higher than men's."

He shakes his head uncertainly. "I don't think I read that one."

"Psychologists think it's because widowed women are happier than widowed men. Isn't that a fascinating peek into the institution of marriage? How men fare better? I've thought about it a lot, and I don't want to wait until I'm eighty-five. I want to be happy now."

Daphne is on the top step, and then she is gone.

—

It is a struggle for Daphne to walk through Hackney in the blistering cold. It is a struggle to spend eight hours in the office, to write and work and attend meetings and concentrate. The articles she writes are dreadful, some barely make sense. By the end of January, she has no choice but to knock on Elizabeth's door, weep into her box of tissues, and admit she is finding this hard. Elizabeth thanks her for being honest. She suggests some time off and Daphne weeps again, this time in gratitude. Ash does the rest. He makes her dark cocktails that taste faintly medicinal. He tucks her into bed. He invites Aparna and Poppy over. It is a relief to be surrounded by people whose love for her is simple, uncomplicated.

Ash finds a van rental company. They drive to Putney while Dominic is in school. They load up her belongings, placing most of it in storage. Daphne is low and sad, but mainly she is angry, at Dominic and Mimi, and at herself. She should have seen this coming. She should have ended it sooner. Right after Lucinda. Ash tells her to be kinder to herself, to practice compassion. But what does compassion look like? She takes long baths. She makes tea. She posts to her Substack. She listens to podcasts. She ignores the calls that come in from Dominic and Mimi.

Daphne wants to talk to someone who understands what it is like to be married. And who understands too what it is like to find themselves *not* married. She calls Chuck, and as soon as she hears his warm voice she begins to cry. Within the hour, he's booked her a flight.

Chuck's waiting at the airport. He's in a gray featherdown coat. Soft and shiny, billowing, it's like hugging a sleeping bag. The cold air, as they exit, hits her and Chuck stares at her pea coat in alarm.

"We need to get you something warmer. February here's no joke."

Amy's in the car. She beeps, flashes her lights. Daphne tries to place her bag in the trunk but Chuck won't allow it, confessing he has a very specific routine.

"Don't get between Chuck and his luggage configurations," Amy jokes.

Daphne didn't sleep on the plane but she does now, curled up against the window. She wakes as they enter a circular driveway, her neck stiff, her shoulder aching.

Their Connecticut home is pleasant, suburban, lots of land. The sloping garden has cedars, a large oak tree. The pool is covered in bright blue tarpaulin. Daphne pictures summers here—barbeques and pool parties, fireworks on July Fourth—and feels something pushing past the numbness and pain, it's a desire to return. The rooms are spacious, contemporary. Cream walls. Abstract art. A dining table, long and made of glass, that could easily fit twenty. She accepts their coffee. Hazelnut, it reminds her of their conversation about the hierarchy of nuts, and she smiles to herself.

"Thanks for booking my flight," Daphne says. "I can pay you back."

Chuck pulls a dismissive face. "My treat, honey."

Amy gives her a tight hug. In her firm clasp, Daphne feels like Amy could protect her from anything.

"Breakups are tough," Amy whispers. "You're going to go easy on yourself, aren't you?"

She should listen to Amy. The therapist, after all.

"Am I your latest client?"

"Please," Amy responds, her tone deadpan. "You can't afford me."

—

THE weekend arrives, long and flat, miserable. Dominic surprises himself when he picks up the phone. It's the strangest conversation of his life. He barely speaks. He gulps and cries silently, but Sadie understands what he needs. She texts him the train schedule. She waits at the station and, upon seeing her, he collapses into her arms. He would stay like this forever if he could, he just wants to be held. They stand on the platform for a long time, clinging to each other, and he wonders if Sadie's support has always been here. All he had to do was ask? His dad is waiting in the car, Sadie explains finally, taking a step back. Dominic steels himself; how will he be able to talk to his father about this?

"We're glad you called," his dad says as he slides in.

Sprout wags his tail and licks his face, and Dominic finds himself smiling. They avoid the topic all afternoon. They watch football. But that evening, Sadie runs out to do errands. His dad pours them both a drink. They sit by the log fire, the flames mesmerizing. Maybe it's easier to talk about the hard stuff when they don't have to look at each other.

"Leaving your mother was the hardest thing I ever did," his dad admits.

Dominic nods and wonders if Sadie's errands were a ruse.

"It felt like you left us without a backward glance."

Their eyes meet. "I'm sorry, Dom. But your mother, I had to do that. Even without Sadie in my life, I had to leave her. I hope you understand that."

"I didn't leave Daphne," Dominic croaks. "She left me."

"It'll be hard for her too."

"She's doing fine," he says a little sourly, gulping his drink.

The amber liquid roars in his mouth. He feels light-headed.

"She's not. Something died in your relationship. You're both grieving the end of it."

—

STELLA will be here soon. The musician, she lives in Greenpoint. She takes the train up. Daphne is nervous. She pictures a serious woman with a stern expression. Someone who dedicated her entire life to classical music. What will Stella make of Daphne? Stella lets herself in. She's on the phone, biting her lip, her voice cold and irritable as she kicks her shoes and socks off. She turns on her heel and marches away, barefoot. But Daphne catches glimpses of her half sister. Pale skin. Long flowing hair. A tattoo of a flock of birds running down her left arm. A few minutes later, Stella appears in the kitchen, her voice fragile.

"Our band's breaking up," Stella explains, suddenly tearful. "It's a shit show."

Stella begins to cry softly. Amy hugs her from behind.

"Oh, honey," Chuck exclaims.

"I'm sorry," Daphne murmurs helplessly.

"How was your flight?" Stella sniffles, glancing at her. "Did you get in on Friday?"

Daphne nods uncertainly. Jet-lagged, she barely remembers what day it is. Stella is fascinating to watch. Within a few minutes, she's recovered. Her tears are forgotten and she's asking if Daphne's been to the US before. They talk about Vegas.

"Pretty cool to have a new sibling, right?" Stella says, pushing her hair back from her face.

Her hair springs back, red and thick and wiry, just like Daphne's.

"It is," Daphne murmurs.

Stella must be having the same thought.

"Hey, we kind of look like sisters, don't we?"

Stella's face is pale, ethereal. She has the same wide hips, thick calves.

Daphne nods. They kind of do.

STELLA is irritable, fractious. Chuck seems to madden her. Overly protective, he treats her like a child. Daphne thinks he cares deeply, his protective nature comes from a good place. They are fun to watch. Chuck is patient, Stella's complaints bounce off him easily. Stella doesn't hold her grudges long, she knows when she's being unfair or irritable.

"Sorry, Dad," Stella says before going to bed, "for being so snappy."

"It's okay, my little croc," he says, kissing her forehead.

Daphne is moved by the depth of their affection. When she pictures her own childhood with this man, she is filled with a gentle yearning for what could have been.

—

THE classroom is healing. Dominic loses himself in literature. *Middlemarch*. *The Taming of the Shrew*. *The Bluest Eye*. He's shadowing Julian, a teacher in his late fifties with a gentle voice, gray hair, a sloping walk. Julian has the respect of the classroom. He understands his students, when they are too tired to focus, when to push harder. Dominic learns from him and he's excited to put it into practice. He wonders where he'll be placed once the year ends—probably not in this school. He tries not to worry about it. For now, he assists. He sits at the back of the classroom and takes notes. He passes out exam papers. He stays behind and helps the students who need more attention. He doesn't have to. Julian tells him he's welcome to leave as soon as the day is over. Dominic is tempted to respond: and go where? Outside of school, he books a session with a therapist on a whim. They explore his childhood, his relationship with his parents. They explore why he cheated on Daphne and why he wants children desperately and why he clings to the belief that Daphne is the right partner for him even though she doesn't want to be a mother. These are big questions and he finds himself taking long walks through the city, across parks, along the river, combing through their conversations. He considers the next chapter. He needs a new flat, one where there aren't memories of Daphne in every closet and doorway. For someone who was always desperate to avoid his own company, he finds himself adjusting to the empty space that stretches in front of him, and not being afraid. Or at least, less afraid than he expected to be. He takes his life one day at a time. On certain days, he takes his life one hour at a time. He permits his heart to hurt. He permits his pain to show. He exists.

—

ACCORDING to the news, there's a nor'easter coming.

"Good thing we have enough food to last at least two months," Amy remarks drily.

You have an actual following! Stella says, flipping through Daphne's cookbook. "Dad, why didn't you tell me about this?"

Chuck catches Daphne's eye and winks. "I thought Daphne might want to tell you *herself*."

Stella scrolls through Daphne's Instagram. She asks why Daphne isn't posting videos. And why isn't she on TikTok?

"I'm not sure how to . . ."

Daphne's voice trails off. She admits self-promotion isn't her strong point.

Stella's eyes light up. "I could film you. While you're here."

They start with an easy one: banana bread. As she cooks, Daphne tries to forget she is being filmed. Instead, she talks to Stella about the strangeness of being in a new country with a different vocabulary ("What's a nor'easter?"). She wants to be happy around her new family, but she doesn't always feel like smiling. When they ask how she's doing, her instinct is to be polite, but she doesn't want to sugarcoat her feelings.

"I'm a little exhausted by it," Daphne admits, glancing at the camera, "are you?"

Stella nods, and her phone moves up and down. "Shit. Sorry, Daph."

"That's my sister, Stella," Daphne says with a smile. "Isn't she adorable?"

And the internet agrees. Stella is adorable.

ON Thursday, Chuck drops Stella and Daphne in Brooklyn. Daphne watches a group of women crossing the street. Their arms are threaded together, and they are laughing. That will be her again, Daphne tells herself, she will be carefree and happy.

"That's the bar I work in," Stella explains, pointing.

Peering out of the car window, she gazes at the faded black windows, the neon sign that announces half-price cocktails Mondays through Thursdays. Stella's building has a faded blue façade. Daphne stares at the fire escape, thinking: *it's just like in the movies.* They walk up six flights of stairs. The apartment is narrow and dark, and it smells of popcorn. It has a strange layout, a series of interconnecting rooms, and there's little-to-no privacy from one bedroom to the next. Daphne sleeps in Stella's roommate's bedroom—she is visiting her boyfriend in Boston—on a mattress on the floor. At night, she props the window open with a small book because the heat from the pipes is on, always, there is no way to shut it off, and it is brutally hot in this building despite being winter. By morning, she is freezing. Daphne enjoys pretending to be Stella's roommate and running to the bodega for almond milk and swinging by the liquor store for wine. Most of all, she enjoys getting to know her sister. They take chilly walks together. Stella points out the bar her band used to play in. She talks about her failed relationships, her attraction to men who are emotionally distant, complicated. Stella's been reading old entries from Daphne's Substack. She has specific questions about Dominic and the Freedom Clause. Stella has a tendency to reference posts Daphne wrote years earlier. It startles Daphne, jolting her into a reminder of who she was. Answering Stella's questions, she feels like she's telling the story of her life to someone who already knows the punchline. When she admits this, Stella goes very quiet. She walks into her bedroom and closes the door. The next sound Daphne hears is the strum of Stella's guitar.

They go to Stella's favorite noodle bar. They sit on high stools by the front window, knees nudged up against the ledge they eat off. Each time the door opens, cold air blasts over them. Daphne shivers into her coat. They slurp on noodles and share a bottle of screw-top wine.

"Stay," Stella says as they leave.

Stella is wearing her tipsy smile, and Daphne loves that she's grown to recognize this.

"I wish I could," she says honestly, threading her arm through Stella's.

"But you'll be back?"

This summer. It's an anchor they both cling to. She hears Stella's soft sigh of relief as she nods. Daphne is grateful for this experience. She is grateful for all of it. The distraction of another city, a new person in her life, it's the greatest gift she could ask for.

—

He watches Daphne's Instagram. She's started to post videos. It's painful to see her and know this is the closest he can get. She's talking about her American family. That explains the big kitchen in the background, then. Her "No Frills Banana Bread" is getting a lot of likes. He decides to make it himself. The twins are coming to visit this weekend, and it'll be nice to offer them something to eat as soon as they arrive.

He takes the short walk to Tesco. He picks up bananas and flour, butter and eggs. At home, he watches the video again. Daphne is explaining it's best to use blackened bananas. He looks at his: green-yellow. He isn't a baker and he muddles through each step. He places the baking tin in the oven and sets a timer on his phone. After twenty-five minutes, the flat fills with a delicious scent. The scent is healing, and it intensifies. It makes him smile.

For now, at least, it feels like Daphne is home.

—

IT's been a busy six months since she returned from the US. She never expected to be sitting *here*. In these offices in west London discussing *her* career.

"We'd play up the fact you're single and in your thirties," Quincy is saying in a deep, authoritative voice. "We're thinking *Sex and the City* meets the *Jamie's Quick & Easy Food*."

Daphne takes a small sip from her bottled water. She screws the lid back on, frowns.

"What do you mean by play up?"

Quincy is in his early forties. Sandy-haired, full beard. Successful, he works for a UK cable network. He explains he works on scripted reality TV with a focus on romance and dating. She can tell Quincy is used to commanding a room.

Daphne was excited when her agent, Elaine, called and explained there was interest from a TV network in producing a cooking show with her. But this isn't how she imagined it would go. A quick glance at Elaine, visibly grimacing, confirms this isn't what *she* was thinking either.

"First episode," Quincy begins, spreading his hands out, casting his vision. "It's morning. We see you waking up. Tiptoeing out of bed. But it's not *your* bed. You're slipping into heels, your hair's a mess, running out the door before the stranger next to you wakes up. We follow you doing the walk of shame home. Maybe," Quincy shrugs, "you stop by a food market, pick up some fresh ingredients, have a fun and flirty conversation with the man who sells vegetables. See? We're showing you as sexy but also down to earth. And then, bam! We're in your kitchen, and you're telling the camera about your favorite breakfast to make when you're hungover and you stink of sex."

Daphne struggles to find the words. "That sounds a bit . . . cheap."

Quincy nods. "You're right, it won't cost much to produce."

"So it's a dating show?" she asks with narrowed eyes.

"Exactly!" Quincy replies, nodding eagerly. "We'll watch you dating and cooking. It's a nod to your newsletter! Fun and sexy, it's a *vibe*."

"I'd like the vibe to *not*"—Daphne pauses—"be about dating. It's just not where my head's at. That was never really what the Substack was about for me."

"Hear me out," Quincy continues, undeterred. "We show you on a bad date. The conversation is awkward. The food is tasteless. There's no chemistry. Next scene! In your kitchen making a better meal. And guess what else is better in this scene? The strapping man in the background."

She stares silently, unsure of how to even respond. What he wants, she realizes, is a show with the woman who was writing posts about her sex life a few years ago. But she's come a long way since then, and a long way since the start of this year. She's moved into a new flat: a sunny one-bed in Finsbury Park, close to Aparna and Poppy, with a big sun-filled kitchen. She recently got promoted to editor at the magazine.

Daphne shakes her head. "I don't want a dating show."

"What Daphne means," Elaine says, jumping in, "is she wants to focus on cooking, and not on her sex or dating life. Something more in line with her second cookbook, the one we just finalized a deal for."

Elaine smiles and gestures to her. Daphne begins eagerly:

"Yes! This book is going to be more mature, no mention of men. I'm exploring self-acceptance: being alone in a society that values romantic relationships, each meal designed to produce one serving. I actually outlined some ideas of how it could work for the show already." She looks back at Elaine, who nods, encouraging her to keep going. "The tone of each episode, and each recipe, would focus on challenging the stigma around being a single woman in your thirties. Or a single woman at any age, to be honest. You can be alone and perfectly content. I know, I know, how shocking! Because we're preconditioned to *not* think this way. We're made to believe that being single on Valentine's Day is a personal failure . . . probably because society is absolutely petrified by the prospect of a generation of women who have no interest in getting married or having children."

Quincy cuts her off. "How would cooking tie into this . . . societal discourse?"

He makes a face as if he's having trouble digesting his lunch. Daphne glances at her watch. They may as well cut their losses now, but she will try one last time.

"Each meal would be a celebration of being single," she says brightly. "Throw a dinner party just for yourself every night of the week if you—"

"Don't get me wrong. I love . . . *love* the empowered woman thing," Quincy says, cutting in, "but we need drama, that's what viewers want."

Daphne smiles. "But my life is free of drama now . . . thank god! The show would be about the joy of dating yourself."

Quincy frowns, licks his lips. "That's like opening a shop that sells frisbees. Getting a lot of customers who like frisbees. And then telling them you no longer plan to sell frisbees. Now you sell . . ." He pauses, and his eyes narrow as he considers this analogy carefully: "Pogo sticks."

Daphne raises an eyebrow. "Is it, though?"

"Just saying," Quincy continues, pointing at her in an accusatory way, "fans might be disappointed. Daphne Hardwick, known for sharing her spicy personal life, sits around saying how happy she is being single. What a yawn fest! But divorce, on the other hand . . . divorce is interesting. It's a big deal, you know, a big personal failure. What if . . . we weave in your messy divorce? Who keeps the china you were given on your wedding day from your dead grandmother? Your lawyer screaming at his lawyer, that type of thing?"

"My divorce wasn't messy, though," Daphne answers slowly. And she means that. They finalized the divorce a few weeks ago. She was dreading the process, but it was all quite fast. Dominic was surprisingly agreeable. He just wants her to be happy, he told her.

Daphne has worked hard to reach this point, and now she wants to be alone.

"That's your opinion, by the way," Daphne says firmly.

"Excuse me?"

"That's your opinion," Daphne repeats. She sits straighter now, pushing her shoulders back. "That divorce is a big personal failure. I happen to think staying in a marriage that *isn't* right for you is a much bigger failure."

Elaine cuts in: "I'm not seeing a path forward here, Quincy."

"Maybe we just aren't the right fit for each other," Daphne concedes with a friendly smile. "If I do a show, it's important to me that it *isn't* about men. I don't want women to be sent the message: you're only as interesting as the man you are with. The opposite is true: women are worth so much more than the men they're married to, the men they're divorcing, the men they're sleeping with."

Quincy falls completely silent. He looks moody, unconvinced.

"No dating?" he asks snippily.

She nods and watches a range of emotions dance over his face.

"What if . . ." he begins, placing his hands in a steeple shape and smiling at her.

Daphne isn't interested in Quincy's suggestion because he's not listening. Quincy is only interested in pushing his own agenda. Daphne understands this. She's seen it before, this exact behavior many times over. Quincy is that type: dogged and determined, used to coaxing women, disregarding their needs in favor of his own. With men like this, each interaction is a power grab, a hierarchy of needs, a question of whose will topple first, but she won't let him do this to her.

". . . what if your female friends are the mess? Constantly getting involved with the wrong men. The first episode could be you helping a friend out. She's sleeping with a married man. She wants him to leave his wife. You know he's never leaving the wife. But you're a good friend. You're baking this cake that looks like a wedding cake but it's a divo—"

"I'm not doing this."

Quincy looks outraged that she's cutting him off. Even though he's done it repeatedly.

"This is a huge network. "We'd put you on the map."

"Thanks, Quincy," she says, standing up. "I wish you all the best."

"That's it? You're leaving?" Quincy sputters. "I thought you were interested in a real opportunity. I don't have time for this crap."

Does he not realize how busy *she* is? It's her lunch hour and, from here, she'll run back to the office. She has a dozen articles to review. She has meetings with the team she manages. On top of her job, she has a second cookbook to write. She wants to test out new recipes. She wants to catch up with Ash and the girls. She wants to talk to Stella in New York, and her dad and Amy. She wants to read. She wants to get her hair done. She wants to go dancing. She wants or-gasms. She wants it all on her terms, and no one else's.

Daphne is composed as she grabs her rain jacket, her handbag, and umbrella, as she walks toward the exit. Hand on the door, she turns, her gaze landing on his hot angry face.

"And neither," Daphne responds pointedly, smiling to herself, "do I."

Acknowledgments

First and foremost, thank you to my talented agent, Jessica Felleman, for seeing potential and making it happen. Thank you for helping me fine-tune the early draft into something much more presentable, and for your wisdom, guidance, and patience at each and every turn. You're a delight to work with, and I so appreciate your passion for, and dedication to, this book and my writing. Thanks also to everyone at the Jennifer Lyons Literary Agency, and to Paula Breen.

Thank you to my editor, Emma Caruso, for your keen editorial eye, enthusiasm, and insights that have made this book undoubtedly sharper and smarter. Thank you for guiding me throughout this process, pushing me harder, and making this process enjoyable, because, truly, you are such fun to work with. Thank you to Whitney Frick for seeing this book as one that belongs at Dial Press. It is beyond my wildest dreams to publish with this imprint and join the talented authors represented here. And many thanks to the whole team at Penguin Random House whose talent, dedication, and hard work has helped make this book what it is today. You are so appreciated: Avideh Bashirrad, Ted Allen, Kathy Jones, Michelle Jasmine, Maria

Braeckel, Corina Diez, Deb Aroff, Donna Cheng, Diane Hobbing, and Katy Nishimoto.

Thank you to my earliest reader, Natasha Zuccolo Rawdon-Rego, for your wild enthusiasm, even when this book was a wobbly ten pages long. Thank you for cheering me on through every chapter, and for being a great friend in every way imaginable.

To Meghan Hemingway, your insights on the early draft were spot on, and your passion for the book kept me smiling. Thank you for calling me a writer well before I considered myself one. It meant the world to me then, and it still does.

To Christian Sjulsen and Jeff Billingham, thank you for being a lifeline in those strange early months of the pandemic as the first draft came together, and again during subsequent redrafts. I am so grateful to you both for your friendship, and your martinis.

To Alison Preece, thanks for your feedback on the first draft, for Mahopac, whiskey sours, and Trail Mix.

To Jared Bloch, thank you for connecting me with Jessica.

To Jami Attenberg, whose #1000WordsofSummer program helped me take this from one chapter I kept "polishing" (okay, procrastinating on) to something that resembled a novel-in-progress and spurred me to keep going.

To the literary journals that have published my short essays and stories, thanks to every editor who chose to publish me; you helped me immeasurably in both the craft of writing and in beginning to feel like an actual writer.

To my friends who have cheered on my writing (read: indulged me) for years, I am so lucky to count on you. I'm looking at you: Kat Blennerhassett, Tobias Carroll, Vivien Cheung, Lindsay Faberij de Jonge, Katherine Grinter, Matt Horner, Ruth Ingram, Olivia Lee, Jane Liddle, Euan Mann, Kristy McKenna, Katie Meitiner, Caroline Nicolay, Sebastien Robcis, Jenny Pistella, Siân Quipp, Sara Stefanini,

Kate Taylor, Francesca Turquet, Sarah Walsh, Emily Zawislak, and many more.

To my parents, thanks for raising us in a home where reading was encouraged. Mum, thanks for being so generous with your time and affection; growing up I swear we were the envy of all our friends (obviously, we still are). Dad, thanks for teaching us from a young age to dream big; it was all within reach if we worked hard.

Thanks to my wildly funny sisters, Jackie and Val, for being exactly as you are, for keeping it real on WhatsApp, and for all things sisterly; and thanks to Al and Rick—I really won the brother-in-law lottery.

Lastly, Sam Arenson. Thank you for risking it all and moving to New York. Thank you for being such fun and making me laugh every day of the week. Thank you for every hard, brutally honest conversation we've ever had (I don't want it any other way). Thank you for so many positives you bring to my life, they are impossible to capture in a few sentences. And now for our next chapter, my love. Take my hand and let's go for a walk, let's walk toward the future, and let's do it all together.

Photo: © Sylvie Rosokoff

HANNAH SLOANE grew up in England. She read history at the University of Bristol. She holds dual citizenship and lives in Brooklyn with her partner, Sam. *The Freedom Clause* is her debut novel.

Instagram: @hannahsloane
hannahsloanewrites.com

ABOUT THE TYPE

This book was set in Bembo, a typeface based on an old-style Roman face that was used for Cardinal Pietro Bembo's tract *De Aetna* in 1495. Bembo was cut by Francesco Griffo (1450–1518) in the early sixteenth century for Italian Renaissance printer and publisher Aldus Manutius (1449–1515). The Lanston Monotype Company of Philadelphia brought the well-proportioned letterforms of Bembo to the United States in the 1930s.

THE
FREEDOM
CLAUSE

HANNAH SLOANE

A Reader's Guide

The seed of the idea for this novel came years ago. I was in London, at a friend's house for dinner. It was getting late when she shared, unexpectedly, that she wished she'd met her husband later, specifically ten years later (they met at university). It would've been fun to date in her twenties, she continued. I glanced at her husband, wondering what *he* had to say about this, but it was a topic they'd discussed already. They both would have preferred more experiences in their twenties. There was no desire to course-correct the past at this stage in their marriage. It wasn't a deep regret. It was a passing thought, spoken wistfully, in the same manner one might murmur: *I wish I'd lived in Paris at some point.*

That evening sat idly in my head for years. My friend's remark fascinated me, mainly because it posed a myriad of other questions. Is there a perfect age to meet your partner? And if you *do* meet your partner sooner than you'd like, is there a way to manufacture experiences with others within the safe confines of your existing relationship? While my friend and her husband considered which defining moments they might have missed out on, I reflected on my twenties too.

As an idealistic teen, I'd had big plans for this decade. I'd nurture my independence and my yet-to-be-defined career, living life on my terms, discovering who I was. And once I'd done *that* (hopefully as the end of my twenties sharpened into focus), the right person would waltz into my life. And while a lot of that *did* happen, there was plenty I didn't anticipate. While it was fun to date, most of my relationships were short-lived, and there was nothing fun about getting my heart broken (often). But most of all, I'd neglected to factor in bad sex, lots of it, or just how long it would take for me to understand sex, to enjoy it, to assert what I needed. Much of my twenties were strange, a mundane slog, a too-steep learning curve, but I was checking the experience box. Would I have felt differently if I'd spent the entirety of that decade cocooned in a forever relationship?

By the time I started seriously considering this idea as a novel, with an actual plot and characters and pacing and tension, I was navigating other questions too. I was thirty-seven. I was in a long-term committed relationship, but rather than happily cocooned, I felt stuck and anxious. I tried to compartmentalize these feelings, ignoring the uneasy twinge in my stomach late at night. Why didn't I just end it, you might ask? Because ending a committed relationship in my mid-to-late-thirties felt like an enormous personal failure. Because the single woman in her forties is not a celebrated figure. Because I was worried about how the breakup would impact him (classic people-pleaser move). Because I didn't want to go against the grain of societal pressure, which dictates that the women we aspire to be in our thirties, the women who are truly accomplished, are married or in relationships headed in this direction. Finally, at a wedding in Italy, as I watched my friend who was clearly, deeply, wonderfully in love exchanging vows with her husband-to-be, I made a vow of my own. I broke up with my boyfriend a week later. I was thirty-seven, and very single, and exactly where I needed to be in life. And I decided to channel my experiences and emotions into this book.

Initially, I was writing *The Freedom Clause* for my younger, less-experienced self. I wanted to rewrite the romanticized, misleading versions of dating, and more specifically sex, that I had seen across countless mediums. For years, women have been informed through movies and books and porn that sex is beautiful and effortless which is simply, and categorically, untrue. In writing Daphne's first sex scene, I set out to write about the kind of sex that leaves you feeling vulnerable and exposed. The kind of sex that serves as a reminder that you are young and insecure and clueless. The kind of sex that leaves you with a distinct sense of loneliness, an overarching concern that there is something wrong with you. It was not difficult to write this scene, as these moments were deeply familiar to me.

But as the book developed, I began to write this novel for my current self too, for the woman looking to define herself beyond romantic relationships and societal expectations. I wanted to reimagine the traditional definitions of a relationship by exploring what happens when a couple tests the waters of freedom. Most of all, I wanted to write about a young woman on a journey of self-assertion, and how finding her own sexual confidence plays out in other areas of her life, particularly as she ignores external pressures and focuses on what she needs. These are the women we must aspire to be, and these women are truly accomplished.

Confessions of a Highly Emotional Cook:

The Stunning Simplicity of Marmalade on Toast

I'm on day fifteen of the publicity tour for my second cookbook. It's been a lot of fun, meeting all the wonderful folks who work in bookstores and also the marvelous people who come out to readings and share my genuine love of food. If you are reading this, and we met, thank you for coming! I so appreciate you! But it's also been a lot of frantic unpacking and repacking, a lot of time spent in transit, on planes and trains (and there was that one missed bus connection), and a lot of washing underwear in the sink of a hotel bathroom. Rinse and repeat. And a girl needs to eat. This usually means picking something up near gate 15 of the departure lounge, the nutritional value of which I would not count on. Bottom line: I miss simple meals. I miss homemade meals. I don't want to see another congealed slice of pizza for a long time, possibly forever. And right now, I'm craving something very specific: homemade marmalade. It's tart and familiar and refreshing. Marmalade on toast: simplicity at its finest.

THE STUNNING SIMPLICITY OF
MARMALADE ON TOAST

Feeds: 1 (with plenty left for future use)

Ingredients:
- 1 pound of oranges and lemons (approximately 1 large orange and 1–2 lemons)
- 2 cups of water
- 1 cup of sugar (optional: add more if you prefer it sweeter)
- ¼ cup of fresh lemon juice
- 1 piece of bread or an English muffin, toasted

Method:
1. Wash the orange, followed by the lemon(s). Dry them thoroughly, until they are as dry as the in-air circulation on your flights.
2. Use a knife to remove the peel and the pith (white part) from the orange and lemon(s). When your friend Ash teases you for making marmalade instead of joining him for a drink ("only elderly women make marmalade in their spare time, you know"), text back reminding him that older women are, for the record, icons in their own right (hello Joni Mitchell, Carole King, Joan Didion, the list goes on).
3. Place the peel and pith in a food processor and pulse. How much you pulse will depend on how chunky you like your marmalade. If you are new to this, I recommend pulsing it until it resembles breadcrumbs (about 10–20 seconds). As a seasoned marmalade aficionado, I go on the chunky side. Place the pulsed peel and pith in a large bowl.
4. Now you want to focus on the inner part of the lemons and oranges. Cut them into segments, removing and discarding

any seeds. Cut each segment into thirds. Drop the chopped lemon and orange segments into the pulsed peel and pith bowl.

5. Add two cups of water. Cover the bowl with clingfilm (or, Saran Wrap, as it's called by our friends in the U.S, which is where I am right now) and leave it for at least 24 hours in your fridge. Speaking of cooler temperatures, I cannot get over how fiercely intense the air conditioning is over here! I live in a country where we roll out a small, highly ineffective plug-in fan for those two to three weeks of the summer when we experience a heat wave (and generally don't sleep well). My toes are both alarmed and impressed by the system over here.

6. Twenty-four hours later (in the comments section, please feel free to share what you did during those twenty-four hours, even if it feels very boring to you. I live for the boring details), place all the contents of the bowl that's been sitting in the fridge into a saucepan and bring to a boil. Once the contents of the saucepan reach boiling point, reduce the heat and simmer for 40 minutes. Over the next 40 minutes, the water will reduce in volume, but should not completely dry out (in fact, if your mixture already resembles a thick paste, you should add a little more water). Side note: As I type this, I am thinking I should take my own advice and add a little more water to *myself* since my skin has *completely* dried out. Just call me prune face.

7. After your initial 40 minutes are up, stir in one cup of sugar. Now, a lot of marmalade recipes recommend a higher amount of sugar. I happen to like my breakfast on the tart side, so I always stick with one cup (it feels healthier too) but who am I to micromanage your preferences? Taste the mixture, and if it is too tart, add another half cup of sugar.

8. Let the mixture simmer for another 40 minutes and stir near

constantly. I know what you are thinking: all this effort for something you spread onto toast? Absolutely. Also, this is the most satisfying part of the recipe. Thanks to the sugar, the mixture should be becoming a lovely dense texture.

9. Once your second 40 minutes are up, add the lemon juice and stir for about 5–10 more minutes. By now the consistency should resemble a risotto when it's thickened and ready to be served.

10. Turn off the heat and place it in sealable mason jar and store in the fridge. Unless you are canning. I am not a canner.

11. The next morning, take your bread or English muffin and toast it. Spread on the marmalade. Bite into it and enjoy the delicious mixture of sweetness and citrus. It tastes like home.

Sending you all the airport love imaginable!
Daphne

Confessions of a Highly Emotional Cook:

Leek, Ham, and Gruyere Breakfast Egg Pots

There comes a time in every woman's life when she needs an impressive-yet-easy weekend breakfast dish. Maybe you are in the early throes of a new relationship and you'd like sustenance from all those orgasms without leaving your flat (good for you), or your little sister is visiting you from the States (*again?!*, I hear you say), or you need to win over a demanding mother-in-law who is staying for the weekend (in which case Sunday evening cannot come soon enough).

Either way, my friend, I've got your back. This recipe is simple and tasty and there is something so right about beginning your weekend morning this way. Also, who doesn't love eating from an adorable little ramekin? Please enjoy with whomever you happen to be with today (clue: I am NOT making this for a mother-in-law).

LEEK, HAM, AND GRUYERE BREAKFAST EGG POTS

Feeds: Two

Ingredients:
- 1 small leek, washed thoroughly, cut lengthways first, and cut again into ¼-inch half moons
- 2 eggs
- 2–3 slices of prosciutto (trimmed into smaller bite-size pieces)
- 30 grams of grated cheese (Gruyere or Comté works well)

- 2 tablespoons of crème fraiche
- 2 teaspoons of Dijon mustard
- Olive oil or butter
- Salt
- Black pepper
- An herb of your choice, for the topping (I recommend fresh rosemary)

Method:

1. Preheat oven to 180 degrees Celsius/350 degrees Fahrenheit.
2. Using olive oil or butter, sauté the leeks (which should be washed and cut, see above) in a small frying pan on the lowest heat until soft and beginning to brown. This will take longer than you think because leeks, like the kindest of sisters and the best of lovers, give you all the time in the world.
3. Once cooked, switch off the heat and spoon the leeks into the base of two ramekins. Add the ham and grated cheese to each ramekin, and season with some black pepper. Glance out of the window, coffee in hand, and take a moment to appreciate the bright blue sky, the scarcity of people, the quiet beauty of a sleepy weekend morning.
4. In a separate dish, mix together the crème fraiche and Dijon mustard and immediately spoon mixture into ramekins over the leeks, ham, and grated cheese. Finally, break an egg on top. Season with salt and pepper. Admire how this is all coming together relatively quickly.
5. Place water in a kettle and turn it on to boil.
6. Place ramekins in a quarter sheet pan. Loosely cover the top of each ramekin with some foil. Place the quarter sheet pan into the oven. Now (this part requires a steady hand) pour the boiling water from the kettle into the quarter sheet pan until

the water reaches up to approximately the first quarter of the ramekin. Close the oven door.

7. The eggs should take 18–25 minutes to cook (it will depend on your oven and the sheet pan you are using. The yolk will have the runny consistency of a poached egg and the whites will be fully cooked). Occupy yourself for those 20-ish minutes in ways that make you smile.

8. Add an herb of your choice on top, if you wish. I recommend fresh rosemary. You may want to serve with some bread.

Yours, truly and happily,
   Daphne

*The Dial Press, an imprint of Random House,
publishes books driven by the heart.*

Follow us on Instagram:
@THEDIALPRESS

Discover other Dial Press books and
sign up for our e-newsletter:

thedialpress.com